CW00539499

# THE BASTARD PRINCE OF VERSAILLES

A novel inspired by true events

BY WILL BASHOR

Library of Congress Control Number: 2023916035

House of Bourbon - Family Tree

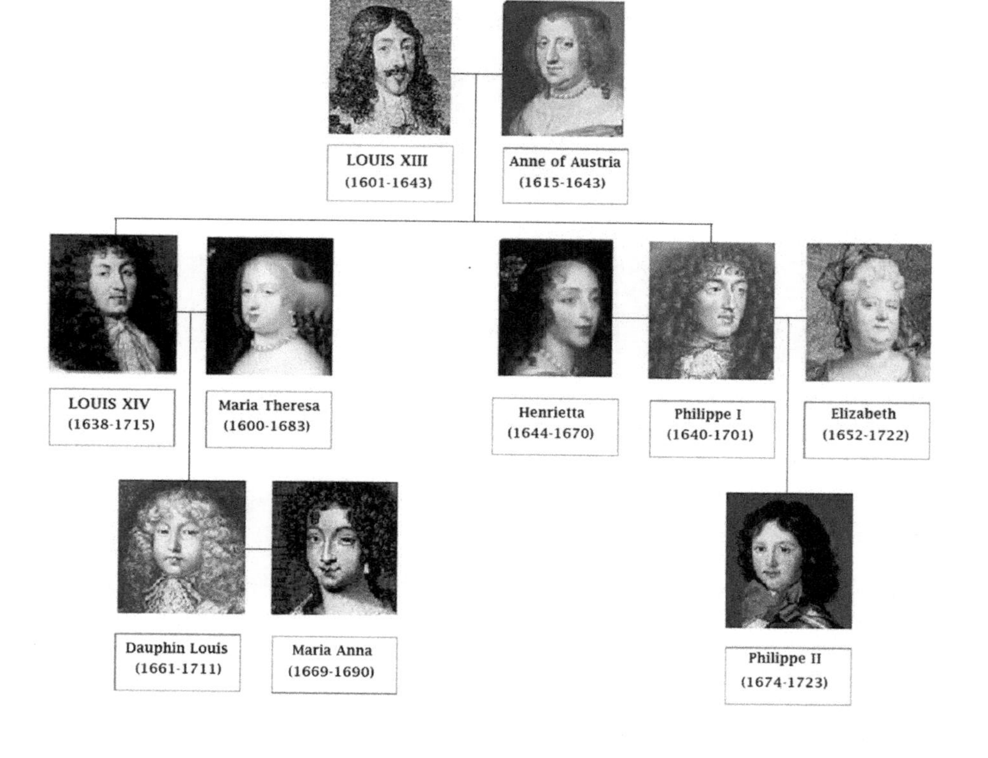

Children of Louis XIV and His Mistress, Louise de La Vallière

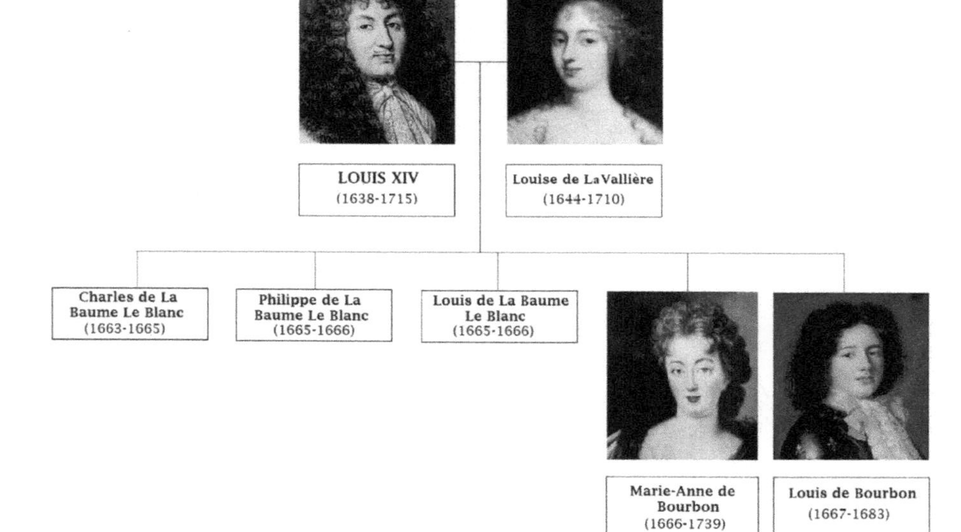

Map of Paris and Surrounding Areas

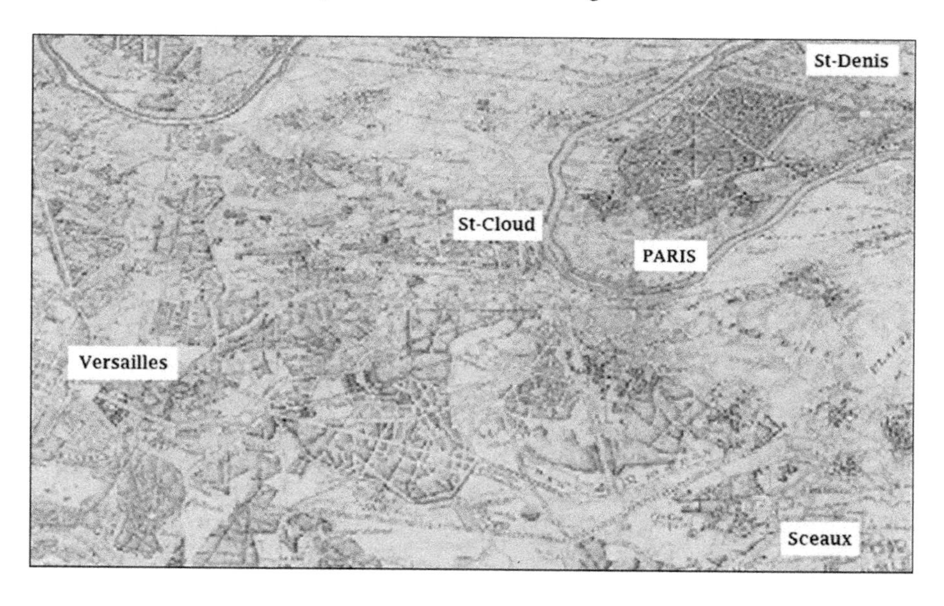

# Table of Contents

# PROLOGUE

## Château of Versailles, October 1682

The gathering of nobles and courtiers in the marble-tiled courtyard gasped when fifteen-year-old Count Louis of Vermandois collapsed after the final blow of the whip, his body dangling from the ladder's frame. King Louis XIV, his expression grim, raised his hand to end the spectacle and motioned for his son's lifeless body to be carried away.

Hours later, in a dungeon cell reeking of rat urine and pipe smoke, Count Louis woke up on a cot with vermin-infested straw prickling his bare stomach. Despite the sounds of vicious dogs growling and drunken jailers cursing in the corridors, his mind wandered back to his idyllic youth, trying to understand how he ever ended up in a dank, dark prison cell.

# PART ONE

# ABANDONED

# CHAPTER ONE

# The Dance of Faeries

*Château of Sceaux*

> In the middle of our life's path, I found myself in
> a dark forest, where the straight way was lost.
>
> — Dante Alighieri, *Inferno*

## Château of Sceaux, January 1674

In a peaceful country château, far from the constant intrigue of infidelity and adultery that tarnished the Palace of Versailles, lived a young prince who, despite all that he'd ever been told, was not a true prince. Even though his father, King Louis XIV, had named him Louis de Bourbon and ennobled him under the titles of Count of Vermandois and Admiral of France, he was still not a true prince. Not yet.

From his chambers on the second floor, seven-year-old Louis gazed out of one of his two large windows encased with leaded panes and carved wood, overlooking an imposing courtyard. The enchanted château and its seven pavilions were linked by ornate galleries with gardens, a basin showered with waterfalls, and a grand canal flanked with trellises of greenery. The view always offered Louis a sense of harmony and serenity.

But today was different. His foxlike, deep brown chestnut eyes were wider than usual as he waited anxiously at the window for the first of the royal coaches to appear. His mother, Duchess de La Vallière, and the king rarely visited but were expected to pay a visit to Sceaux on this twenty-eighth day of January. Even though the king had legitimized him and his sister, Mademoiselle Marie-Anne de Blois, at an early age, recognizing them as his natural children, Louis never understood why they didn't live at Versailles. Still, he dreamt of one day living at the fairy-tale palace and maybe even inheriting the crown. What he was too young to understand, however, was that a decree of legitimization only ensured him a certain number of limited rights.

Louis' foster family, the Colberts, also chose this visit for a special event—his breeching. Like most princes before the age of seven, Louis had grown up in the company of women, and as such, court tradition required him to wear a girl's gown. Until today. Today, the valets in his chambers were meticulously laying out his crisply pressed chemise with ruffles, embroidered breeches, and silk stockings in preparation for his *rite de passage.*

When Madame Colbert entered Louis' room to check on their progress, Louis, after wiping the foggy window with his sleeve, looked up at her with an innocent smile. He knew there was something in his brown eyes that could melt any woman's heart. He'd often admired himself in the mirror and his eyes offered him a sense of solitude. Or was it loneliness? With his parents living at Versailles, and the beautiful and graceful eight-year-old Marie-Anne caring little for her younger brother at Sceaux, he often felt quite alone.

Madame Colbert ran her fingers through Louis' hair. In the window's reflection, he noticed how his hair spilled down his neck like ink on a tilted piece of parchment. The subtle rays of light reflected an indigo blue on his curly locks, contrasting with the moonbeam paleness of his face. He remembered courtiers who'd visited Sceaux and found themselves speechless when searching for words to describe him, often deferring to "pretty" or "lovely."

"Stop wriggling, Count Louis," said Madame Colbert. "Remember, you have royal blood running through your veins."

Still, he thought, Madame Colbert never really treated him any differently than her other three sons. Her youngest, the impetuous Jules-Armand, was only four years older than Louis and, unlike his older brothers, still lived at Sceaux. Jules-Armand often invited Louis to play with him and his friends, but Louis had nothing in common with Jules-Armand. Instead, he preferred playing on his own in his chambers, shying away from the rough-and-tumble diversions in the courtyard. Because Jules-Armand's bedroom was just across the hallway from his, he could sneak into Louis' bedroom at night to play games. Or at least Louis thought they were games.

Although Louis had less space in his room than Jules-Armand, it was well lit with a varnished writing table cluttered with books, toy soldiers, and maps. Today, the room was busier than usual. One of his valets opened the doors of an intricately carved armoire, removed a blue velvet jacket, and laid it out on Louis' poster bed. Madame Colbert picked up a small box from his night table and opened it.

"You could wear your gold medallion today, Count Louis," she said.

Louis turned to her with wide eyes. "But I've never worn it before. Am I allowed?"

"Why not? You *are* the Admiral of France."

Not only would Louis don his military uniform and medallion, but he and his sister, having practiced for weeks, would surprise their father with a dance. Louis had heard stories that the king was an accomplished ballet dancer, and he was worried because he didn't excel in dance like his sister. But he would do his best, knowing that Monsieur Colbert wanted the performance to reflect on his diligence in raising the king's children.

As soon as Louis was dressed and Madame Colbert had finished fussing about his outfit, she left the room and Louis returned to his window.

The château buzzed loudly with excitement, only unnerving Madame Colbert even more. Valets could be heard rushing from chamber to chamber with stiffly pressed clothing for the men, ladies-in-waiting were fervently polishing the furniture and sweeping the marble-tiled floors, and musicians were tuning their stringed instruments in the orangery. Even the kitchen was a discord of gossipy whispers and restrained laughter—until a loud shriek came from the second floor, causing all the servants to stop in their tracks.

"His Majesty, the king! Papa! Papa is here!" cried Louis when he spotted from his window the over-the-top procession of horse-drawn carriages emerging from the wooded landscape. Gilded in 24-carat gold leaf, the royal coaches glistened from afar, even on this overcast morning. The sight of the grand structures of wood and iron with ornate doors and glass windows took Louis' breath away.

The sides of the road leading to the château filled with carriages and onlookers from nearby villages as the king's coach, flanked by musketeers on horseback, led the way. Inside, King Louis XIV sat across from thirteen-year-old Dauphin Louis of France, his eldest son and heir to the throne. Stout with a ruddy complexion, the dauphin gazed blankly into the distance with his head leaning against the window. He had barely finished yawning when he broke the uncomfortable silence.

"This would have been a perfect day for hunting," he said in a whiney tone.

The king swallowed down annoyance at his son's cranky comment. "I chose this day to honor Minister Colbert with a special visit," said the king. "We will hunt tomorrow at Fontainebleau."

The dauphin replied with a slight grunt and returned his gaze to the window. He watched military troops traveling alongside the king's coach on horseback, focusing on their military-blue coats, decorated with gold braids and a silver silk sash tied around the waist.

Queen Maria Theresa's coach, surrounded by her bodyguards, followed closely from behind. Inside, the queen sat opposite the king's former, but still official mistress, Duchess Louise de La Vallière, and his current favorite, Madame Françoise-Athénaïs de Montespan. The air could be cut with a knife. The three women had hardly spoken a word since leaving the gates of Versailles over an hour earlier, only breaking the silence once, when the queen had pulled her cloak up around her neck to protect it from a draft and motioned for the mistresses to change sides with her.

"I am not fond of the cold," she'd said in broken French with her heavy Spanish accent. "I wish to be at my ease."

When Françoise stood to change places, she whispered into Louise's ear, "She's so childish."

Louise ignored her.

Although the king had mistresses, he was still fond of his Spanish wife. She was not as attractive as the king's favorites, however. She had short legs, and she ate so much chocolate and garlic that her teeth were blackened.

As her coach approached the château, onlookers at the gates stretched their necks to get a glimpse of the women. The queen grimaced when her subjects cried out, "Look at them! Look at the three queens!"

When Madame Colbert heard the brouhaha outside, she fidgeted with her husband's scarf until he took her hands.

"Please calm yourself, madame. We've paid attention to everything that would be most agreeable to His Majesty: cleanliness, order, delightful entertainment..."

"But we've invited so few guests to receive the king."

"Rest assured, madame, that I took great care to invite only the most distinguished persons to welcome him today. Trust me, he is most embarrassed to be received in the midst of unknown persons."

She pulled her hands away to add a final twist to her husband's scarf. "I'll have a valet escort Count Louis and Marie-Anne to the salon for their audience with the king."

He nodded and motioned for the doormen to open the doors to the courtyard.

Still in his chambers, Louis' eyes were fixed on the very same courtyard below as he watched the guests take their places according to their rank. There was a flourish of trumpets when the king descended from the royal carriage with his distinctive mane of curls, his *justaucorps à brevet,* a light blue silk jacket worn over a long-sleeve shirt edged with ruffles and ribbons, his knee-length breeches with silk stockings and his signature red, black-buckled high-heeled shoes. Louis could almost hear the château's banners snapping in the icy wind to highlight the stunning arrival, and he couldn't understand why court etiquette prevented him from being there.

When Monsieur Colbert and his wife approached the king, their eyes sparkled as they gazed at the splendor of his father's royal attire. The king greeted them with his engaging air, his shoulders back and his chin high. The dauphin had not yet descended from the coach, but the king proceeded, walking with wide steps to the château's grand entrance. When the dauphin finally appeared, he rubbed his eyes and clumsily stepped down from the coach. The lackeys slammed the door behind him and waved for the driver to move along.

The queen's coach pulled up into the recently vacated spot and the queen stepped out, punctually followed by the king's mistresses. Timidly, but gracefully, a young girl dressed in white presented the queen with a splendid bouquet of flowers. She accepted it with a quick smile but immediately handed it back to Françoise before making her way to the grand hall where everyone had gathered to greet the royal entourage.

Upstairs, Louis' valet entered his chambers. "You are expected to join your sister in the salon, Count Louis."

When they arrived at the upper balustrade, Louis sneaked a peak of the procession below. *Who are all these nobles?* he thought, and he was struck by the overpowering scents of the potted lilacs and lavender that filled the hall on this special occasion. Sharply clad violinists played soothing Baroque melodies directed by Jean-Baptiste Lully, a good friend of the Colberts and a frequent visitor to Sceaux.

The gentlemen bowed and ladies curtsied as they acknowledged the king and queen.

Monsieur Colbert stepped forward. "Your Majesties, permit me to express our hearty gratitude for your visit today."

The king and queen nodded graciously amid the warm applause of the guests and the air was punctuated with an occasional "Vive le Roi! Vive la Reine!"

The king raised his hand, informing the crowd that he would speak. "The Colbert family has been so kind to invite us to admire the apartments," said the king. "Shall we?"

Doormen threw open the doors to an adjoining antechamber and the Colberts motioned for the entourage to begin their tour.

Still on the upper balustrade, Louis' valet became impatient. "S'il vous plaît, monsieur count," he said, and Louis complied.

Madame Colbert tugged on her husband's sleeve and discreetly gestured toward a tall, well-dressed noble with slightly curled blonde hair in the back of the queue.

"The Chevalier de Lorraine was not invited, madame, but he has a habit of irritating the king with his presence," he said.

"We must overlook this slight?"

"Yes, the chevalier has the ear of Monsieur, the king's brother."

"He has more than just his ear, husband."

"Madame, please," he said with a wrinkled brow. "Will you join the children now?"

"Yes, of course."

The king walked ahead of the entourage with no one alongside him, so nothing was hidden from his sight as he wandered from salon to salon, each one as magnificent as the last. Monsieur Colbert soon joined him. As the royal entourage entered each room, the invited guests waiting there bowed or curtsied to show the most reverent respect, but their attention was largely directed toward Duchess de La Vallière's rosy complexion, her blonde curls, and her warm eyes that shined tenderly.

"Her nose is a bit long for such a lean face," whispered a courtier to her companion. "And she has a slight limp."

"I believe it's the result of a childhood riding incident," answered her friend from behind her fan. "Yet she seems to have a sweet disposition."

"But after all the talk, I'm surprised to find her so plain."

When doormen opened the doors to a brightly decorated, elegant salon at the end of the corridor, the king entered, his eyes drawn to the ceiling frescoes. "Le Brun's?" he asked.

"Yes, sire," said Monsieur Colbert. "Madame Colbert's favorite."

In the middle of the salon was Madame Colbert with two small children, who looked like girls from a distance, sitting on a velvet settee next to her. When the king approached them, Madame Colbert prompted them to stand with her. Louis bowed and Marie-Anne curtsied.

The king turned to Louise. "Such angelic, smiling faces, duchess."

Unmoved by the king's comments, she stepped forward and leaned over to kiss them on the forehead, address them as "Monsieur" and "Mademoiselle," but there was no warmth in her tone nor her eyes as she greeted them. They answered her with "Belle Maman."

When Louise ceremoniously stepped back, Louis' smile disappeared, and he noticed Madame Colbert standing frozen with her mouth agape. He wondered if she, too, had noticed his mother's coldness.

Marie-Anne, on the other hand, seemed not to take much notice of her mother. Instead, her eyes twinkled in the presence of her larger-than-life father. He was equally smitten with this beautiful creature, holding out his arms for her and embracing her. He then turned to Louis, eyeing him from head to toe.

"You are growing up so quickly, my son," he said. "How old are you?"

"Seven," he answered, yet disappointed that his own father didn't know his age.

"I would like you to meet Dauphin Louis of France," said the king, motioning for the dauphin to come forward. "Monseigneur, this is your brother, Count Louis of Vermandois."

Louis glanced at the queen, whose face reddened when the dauphin offered him his hand. *Why is the queen not happy that I'm finally meeting my half brother?* he thought. *After all, we are the king's only sons.*

"And monseigneur," said the king, "you must promise to love Count Louis as your brother."

"I promise, Father," said the dauphin as he glared at Louis. "But why is he still dressed like a princess?"

Louis blushed and looked to the floor, and Monsieur Colbert broke the silence. "Count Louis will be breeched today, monseigneur."

Madame Colbert patted Louis on the shoulder. "And he will no longer be under his governess's supervision. Instead, he will be tutored in the manner befitting his rank at court."

Monsieur Colbert turned to the king. "Sire, Count Louis and Mademoiselle de Blois will also celebrate this special occasion with a dance for Your Majesty."

The dauphin gazed at Marie-Anne with admiration.

"Monseigneur," the king said, "this beautiful princess, Mademoiselle Marie-Anne de Blois, is your sister. I ask you to embrace her and keep her dear to your heart."

The dauphin stepped forward and awkwardly kissed her on the cheek.

Finished with the introductions, the king turned to Madame Colbert. "Please remain with the duchess and her children, madame, as we conclude our tour of the château."

The king proceeded toward the door but stopped, turning to Louise with a raised brow. "And, duchess, I hope you will remember to graciously thank Madame Colbert for raising and educating your children with such fine care."

The king and his entourage left the salon, and Madame Colbert offered Louise a seat on the settee. "Madame duchess," she said, "the children would like to recite one of their favorite fables for you."

Louise nodded, and Madame Colbert signaled for Marie-Anne to take her place. Dressed in a magnificent dress of blue taffeta and gold brocade, she faced her mother with her head held high.

"The grasshopper gay sang the summer away,
But found herself poor by the winter's first roar.
Of meat or of bread, not a morsel she had!
So, a begging she went to her neighbor the ant,
For the loan of some wheat which she could eat,
Till the season came round.
'I will pay you,' she saith. 'On an animal's faith,
And I will double the weight if the harvest be great.'"

As Marie-Anne recited her verses, Louis noticed his mother's sweet but distant gaze. *What does she see so mysteriously and so far away?* It was then Louis' turn to recite.

"The ant is a friend, but little given to lend.
'How spent you the summer?'
Saith she, looking with shame at the borrowing dame.
'Night and day to each newcomer I sang, if you please.'
'You sang! I am at ease.
For 'tis plain at a glance, madame, that now you must dance.'"

Madame Colbert twisted her mouth. She too noticed that Louise was staring into the distance as the children finished their recital. She cleared her throat to get Louise's attention.

"Very entertaining, children," said Louise. "Monsieur Fontaine would be gratified. And thank you, Madame Colbert, for such dedication to my children's upbringing."

"They are lovely children," Madame Colbert said as she arranged the lace on Marie-Anne's collar. "And I spared no expense in dressing them today for this special occasion."

"I am overjoyed at seeing them so lovely," said Louise with a forced smile that quickly vanished. "But at the same time, you must understand that I do have my scruples."

"They love their belle maman dearly, duchess."

"And I love them, but that doesn't hold me back. I see them with pleasure, but it will not be difficult for me to leave them in your care."

Tears welled in Madame Colbert's eyes. "Are these feelings not contradictory, duchess? From one mother to another, have you no regrets?"

Louise frowned. "Madame, I will forgive your impertinence but please know that it is only necessary that my children know I cherish them." She glanced at her children and then turned to Madame Colbert, speaking softly so the children could not hear her. "As much as I curse myself for having conceived them. For that, I can only find solace in prayer."

Madame Colbert was lost for words for a moment, then she summoned the doormen to escort the children to their chambers.

"I believe the king awaits us at his table, duchess."

~ ~ ~

Monsieur Colbert, informed about the rise of poisonings in Paris involving aristocrats and noble families, took the utmost care in serving the king. Colbert's household was busy tasting the bread and testing the plates, the silverware, and even the king's toothpicks to guarantee his safety at the dinner table. Once all was deemed fit for the king, servants paraded platters of pheasant, chicken, mutton, ham, boiled eggs, salads, pastries, and fresh and candied fruits in front of the king's table. Monsieur Colbert himself served the king while his valets served the queen, Françoise, Louise, and other courtiers seated at His Majesty's ladies-only table.

Those guests who were not invited to dine on this special occasion were free to partake in the king's *Plats de la Desserts*, a lavish assortment of macarons, honey cakes, and bonbons. After the magnificent meal, His Majesty rose from the table and turned to Monsieur Colbert with that very engaging air so natural to him and said, "Superb, simply superb."

The meal was followed by a spectacular firework display, which entertained the king even more. With the fireworks hardly over, however, valets began escorting the guests to the orangery, where a magnificent theater had been constructed for a selection of Lully's newest airs.

"Never has a night at Sceaux shone so brightly," Madame Colbert told her husband. All the trees were laden with lights and the walkways were bordered with candles. When the king entered, oboes played amid the cries of "Vive le Roi et la Reine," and the violins echoed the audience's cries of joy.

Monsieur Colbert whispered in his wife's ear, "His Majesty has surely never been more pleasantly entertained." Her smile expressed how proud she was of her husband's mindfulness. He had entertained the king from room to room with such pleasurable surprises, and his orders had been carried out with such precision that there was never any confusion.

After the king and his entourage took their seats, Lully set the much-awaited performance in motion. He had himself choreographed Louis and Marie-Anne's dance to fit his music exactly, heeding Monsieur Colbert's advice not to include any complex movements that might confuse the children. When the curtain rose to reveal a stage full of clouds, there was a crash of thunder. The allegorical figure of the Nymph of the Seine stood by the riverbank, and that of Glory floated by wires in the clouds.

Marie-Anne moved to the center of the stage with a modest smile, taking two steps forward and bringing her left foot into place to curtsy. She then bent her knees and, with a delicate twist of the head, acknowledged the audience. That was Louis' sign. He joined his sister with his head held high, scanning the audience from right to left. Then he placed his right foot forward, lifted his left heel, and bowed with his head down.

The king smiled, the duchess wiped tears from her eyes, and the queen smirked as the children began their dance.

The Nymph of the Seine began to sing.
Alas, superb Glory, won't the hero I've been waiting for ever come back?
Will I always languish in such a cruel wait?
"Alas, superb Glory, won't the hero I've been waiting for ever come back?
The birds without song and the flowers without blooms are our fate."

The king's delight was plain to see. Because he was often far from Versailles on his army's campaigns, the Nymph was singing about him. Glory then sang:

"Why murmur so much, Nymph.
You cannot see the hero without me.
See what he does when Glory takes him away?
He makes the Seine the proudest River this day!"

As the audience applauded, Madame Colbert winked at Louis, and she leaned into her husband's ear. "Count Louis is a phantom of his mother."

"But now in breeches, madame."

Madame Colbert had often spoken proudly of her role as Louis' guardian. She had raised the king's second and youngest son, who even called her "Maman Colbert."

The entertainment concluded, Monsieur Colbert took Louis and Marie-Anne's hands and escorted them to greet the king after the crowd's accolades. Louis waited for his father's congratulations, but the king was more fascinated by Marie-Anne. Although still very young, Marie-Anne had already learned the art of seducing and entertaining her male admirers; that is, when she was not throwing tantrums and pouting as if she were a true princess.

The king motioned that the audience was over and bid everyone adieu. As he prepared to take his leave, Louis called out to him, "Papa," causing the courtiers to turn to each other in disbelief. The seven-year-old was not a Prince of the Blood and he had broken court etiquette. Granted, he was the king's natural offspring—but he was still a bastard. When the king did not respond, Louis' chin dropped. His breath was shallow, and he felt weak in the knees. He couldn't understand why his father would ignore him.

The king then took Monsieur Colbert's arm. "Thank you, Monsieur, for an unforgettable visit. Your lovely estate is worthy of your esteemed position at my court."

Monsieur Colbert bowed.

"And you and your wife's loyalty and generosity in raising my two children does not go unnoticed."

As they made their way through the long corridors to the grand hall, Monsieur Colbert broke the silence. "Two matters, sire, if I may." The king nodded.

"I was not informed that the Chevalier de Lorraine would be present," he said.

"Do not fret, Monsieur Colbert," said the king. "I am never shocked by the chevalier's behavior, and his animosity toward me takes many forms."

Monsieur nodded in agreement. "Also, sire, please accept my apologies for the young Count of Vermandois's forthrightness."

The king motioned with a flick of the wrist that the *faux pas* was of no importance.

Monsieur Colbert, looking to see if anyone was within hearing distance, lowered his voice and added, "If I may ask, sire, are we instructed at Versailles to treat the Count of Vermandois at the same rank of the Princes of the Blood?"

"Yes," said the king, "but avoid doing so on more intimate occasions such as the morning ritual of my rising. It would also be wise that the Count of Vermandois is not ranked side-by-side with the Princes of the Blood in the chapel during Mass. Otherwise, or when in doubt, you may treat him as you would the Princes de Conti... at the table, for example."

"Understood, sire," he said. "Your wishes are my command."

"Let us keep this conversation between us," said the king softly when he noticed Madame Colbert approaching with Louis' hand in hers.

"Sire, the Count of Vermandois wishes a word," she said.

Louis looked at the ground. "Your Majesty..."

"Father," said the king.

"Father, I'm sorry if I disrespected His Majesty," said Louis.

"You are unaware of the ways of the court, Count Louis. However, you will have the opportunity to be better informed when you visit the Palace of Versailles—at your mother's request. It will also be the perfect opportunity to secure a new tutor and plan your future."

Louis smiled from ear to ear, finally feeling like a part of the royal family.

"Also, tell your sister, Mademoiselle de Blois," said the king, "that I will personally give you both a tour of the palace gardens and the collection of exotic animals in the menagerie when you visit."

Madame Colbert nudged Louis to bow as the king took his leave. The visitors all gathered in the courtyard to watch the coaches whisk the king and his entourage back to Versailles. The dauphin approached the door of his coach and the king, with a slight frown, invited him with a gracious gesture to enter first. The dauphin did so—with no hesitation.

"Courtiers told me that you are the best mannered royal at court. Now I can see how truthful they are."

The dauphin shrugged and took his seat. As the coach departed, the king nodded majestically at the crowd. The dauphin looked out the back window and, when he caught Louis' eye, he first smiled and then made a wretched face, sticking his tongue out at his half brother. Louis didn't know if he was just teasing or being mean.

The duchess said farewell to her children with a kiss on their foreheads before entering her coach after the queen and Madame de Montespan. As the coach departed, the children waved, but their mother showed no emotion at all, gazing straight ahead of her.

Louis' heart sank, but Madame Colbert took his hand. "Come, child, we'll see if Jules-Armand has any new games to play in his chambers."

To her surprise, Louis recoiled. "No, please, Maman Colbert," he said, shaking his head. "Not tonight. I prefer to play alone."

Overhearing the comment, Monsieur Colbert glanced at Madame Colbert with questioning eyes.

As the remaining courtiers slowly departed, Louis noticed the chevalier in the crowd staring at him. "Maman Colbert, who is that gentleman with the colorful clothing?"

She followed his gaze to the chevalier. "Come now, the night air is not good for you," she said and escorted him into the château.

Once in his chambers, Louis went to his window. The courtyard was empty now. From afar, however, the tall trees of the forest surrounding the château resembled a line of soldiers encircling its foe. Louis had been fascinated by the forests ever since hearing the adventurous tales of Perceval.

When his governess arrived, he begged her to tell him the bedtime story of how Perceval's father and his two brothers had fallen in combat, leaving the young, inexperienced Perceval the family's last hope. Louis had heard it many times before, but his eyes always twinkled whenever he heard about Perceval's mother retreating into the forest with her son.

"Why did Perceval live in the woods?" he asked.

"His mother wanted to keep him from learning about weapons, chivalry, and the ways of men," said his governess.

"But why?"

"Because of the heartbreak and grief that she suffered from the tragic deaths of her husband and her other sons in battle."

"The knights were dressed head to toe in armor of glittering silver and black scales. Whenever the knights moved, ripples of light ran from scale to scale. Even their hands were gauntleted in silver. Struck by their heroic aura, Perceval was so stirred for military fame that he defied his mother, left the forest, and traveled to King Arthur's court."

Louis' toes curled as he heard about Perceval's first encounter with the king's knights.

"What happened then?" asked Louis, even though he knew the answer.

"Perceval trained hard to prove himself a worthy warrior and earned himself a seat with the shimmering knights at the Round Table."

Louis pictured himself at the court of Versailles with the dauphin. The Sun King presented them with medals for their valor at battle.

"Now, sleep well," his governess said, breaking his reverie.

Experiencing a strange, sinking feeling in his stomach, Louis held onto to his governess's hand. She had to tell him his favorite fairy tale, *Sleeping Beauty in the Woods*, too. He wouldn't let go of her hand until the princess had finally woken from her long sleep, only to find the dashing prince kneeling beside her. "Is it you, dear prince?" she said. "You have been long in coming!"

~ ~ ~

The following day, life at the château was far from back to normal. Plans were already being made for the upcoming trip to officially present Louis and Marie-Anne at the court of Versailles. New clothing, befitting the children of the Sun King, needed to be tailored, and lessons in court etiquette needed to be scheduled. In his library, Monsieur Colbert was busy consulting his calendar at his desk when a valet knocked and opened the door.

"Monsieur, Madame Colbert and Count Louis request an audience," he announced.

At first glance, Monsieur Colbert's appearance might have struck fear in the heart of anyone disturbing him. His face was large and round, with a clenched jaw, thick eyebrows, and sullen, red cheeks. He also wore a cap on his head like that of a priest. However, as soon as he nodded with a quick smile, the valet immediately knew to show Madame

Colbert into the musty-smelling chamber. Monsieur Colbert greeted them by pulling up two armchairs for them, but quickly wound the clock on the mantle before taking his own seat.

"It's early morning, madame," he said. "Something must surely be weighing on your mind."

"Husband, I understand that Count Louis will be assigned a male tutor and perhaps residence in Versailles," she said with a furrowed forehead. "Is that true?"

"Yes, possibly." When her demeanor did not change, he continued, "But why are you so preoccupied with the boy's future?"

"Well, you spend most of your days at Versailles!"

"Yes, I do—"

Madame Colbert rose from her chair and, to Monsieur Colbert's surprise, raised her voice. "The morals at court are deplorable! Rouge-cheeked men in high heels! Drunkenness and debauchery in the corridors. "And, sir, lest you forget, Count Louis is but a vulnerable, very vulnerable young boy!"

When Monsieur Colbert noticed Louis' eyes widen at Madame Colbert's outburst, he stood up. "Madame, please," he said. "In front of the child?"

"He will soon learn the ways of the court," she said with a resolute tone.

He politely motioned for her to take her seat again. "I will keep an eye on him. And if it pleases my wife, I will have weekly reports prepared about his well-being."

He motioned for the valet to open the doors, an indication that the audience was over. Madame Colbert rose and took Louis' hand.

"You will speak to Count Louis before he leaves Sceaux?" she said.

"Yes, most certainly, madame."

They left the room, but Madame Colbert quickly returned alone. "One more word, husband."

"Yes, madame," he said with a grin, as if expecting her.

"I've never understood the duchess's infrequent visits to Sceaux and her distant demeanor with her children."

"Madame, she is subjected to a very unpleasant situation at court. She is so distressed that she speaks of nothing but leaving this world and taking up the veil."

"Pray tell why."

Monsieur Colbert slowly stood to accentuate the gravity of the matter. "The ex-mistress is still the *official* mistress and still enamored with the king. However, she is forced to live in rooms adjacent to those of the new favorite, Madame de Montespan."

Madame Colbert's frown wrinkled.

"And the king must pass through the duchess's chambers before visiting Madame de Montespan for certain… affairs."

"*Mon Dieu*," she said, quietly departing.

~ ~ ~

Later that afternoon, Louis was playing with his toy soldiers at his small table when Monsieur Colbert entered his chambers and pulled up a chair.

"Count Louis, Sceaux has been your home since birth, but now we must think about your future. A new mentor will be provided to help you prepare for it, but it is possible you might soon have a new home."

Louis' eyes brightened. "Versailles?" he asked.

"Well, perhaps, but please don't set your heart on it."

"Papa Colbert, why can the dauphin live with my father, the king? And not me?"

Monsieur Colbert took a deep breath. "I'm glad you asked, but you will have many such questions when you arrive at court. For the time being, few courtiers know of your particular situation."

"Particular situation?" asked Louis with his trademark squint.

Monsieur Colbert nodded. "I'm certain your mother will explain everything to you," he said and stood up. "Count Louis, your life is going to be much different than it is here at Sceaux, but there is no need for worry. We all plan to accompany you and your sister to the palace, and I will visit you from time to time whenever you like. With your permission, of course."

"Yes, Papa Colbert, I would like that," Louis said with a warm smile.

"So be it. Come embrace me," he said, motioning Louis into his arms. He then left the room, not letting Louis see his smile disappear and his expression sadden.

CHAPTER TWO

# The Enchanted Palace

*Palace of Versailles*

"From there we came outside and saw the stars."

— Dante Alighieri, *Inferno*

## Château of Sceaux, April 1674

Keeping Count Louis and Marie-Anne preoccupied for the next few months was no easy task. They spoke of nothing but their excursion to Versailles. Marie-Anne inquired incessantly about court fashion, and

Louis was curious about his new mentor's lessons. However, the Colberts were worried about one of Louis' flaws and whether it might cast a doubt on their upbringing skills when he leaves Sceaux. His carelessness.

Often late for his morning lessons, Louis' governess complained to Madame Colbert, "Madame, I'm afraid that this child will not make his way at Versailles. He wastes so much time losing his books or overturning his chambers to find a missing stocking."

"But the child has just turned seven years old," said Madame Colbert. "He's at an age when boys cannot keep an eye on everything—unlike his sister."

"Yet he crawls on his stomach under his bed on the dusty floor, tears his nightshirt, nicks his knees, and bumps his head while looking for lost items. When I ask what happened to them, he tells me a dwarf or a gnome must have come down the fireplace to play tricks on him."

Madame Colbert laughed. However, she was faced with the same dilemma the very next morning when the family had planned a surprise coach ride through the countryside. The château's valets were sent to ready the children.

"What does Papa Colbert want?" Louis asked his valet, rubbing their eyes. "Is it time to come down?"

"Those who are ready will know what Master Colbert wants," said the valet dryly.

Louis could hear his sister and Jules-Armand laughing and rushing down the steps, but Louis couldn't find his left shoe. He ran down the steps and begged Monsieur Colbert to wait on him, but Louis could see in Jules-Armand eyes that he was going to be punished.

In vain and driven to despair, Louis clung to Monsieur's coat, crying, "Please take me! Take me! I will behave!"

Monsieur Colbert looked at Madame Colbert, who shook her head, and then motioned for the valet to lead Louis back up to his chambers. Under arrest in his room, he watched his happy sister and Jules-Armand enter the coach below from his window. He asked himself why everyone was so hard on him. He was neither a thief, nor an insolent, nor a villain, nor a coward. He was as pale as a man condemned to the galleys as he stood in his window.

The governess entered, found his shoe, and placed it at his feet. Her gentleness mingled with the pain of his punishment. He looked silently at his shoes and burst into tears. "I will do better," he said. And I will be respected as much as my brother, the dauphin.

His governess combed his unruly hair with her fingers and said, "Yes, I believe you will."

~ ~ ~

Time flew quickly, so quickly in fact, that Madame Colbert couldn't believe the day had finally arrived to take the children to Versailles. As the family's grand carriage departed and meandered through the château's dense forest, Louis squirmed in his seat, rubbing the sleep from his eyes. Marie-Anne, sitting next to him, fidgeted with the ribbons in her hair. Across from them, Monsieur Colbert, his wife, and Jules-Armand were calmly settled in for the ride on this brisk spring morning. Within minutes, the coach emerged from the forest onto a secluded road before passing through the town of Châtillon-sous-Bagneux.

With a grin, Jules-Armand teasingly kicked Louis. When Madame Colbert noticed red-faced Louis respond by pulling his feet to the side, she nudged her son with a sigh of disapproval.

"Only your best behavior at the palace today, children," she said.

"Yes, Maman Colbert," said Marie-Anne.

Louis frowned. "Is Versailles bigger than Sceaux, Maman Colbert?" he asked.

With a proud smile, she deferred to her husband for an answer.

"It's now the envy of all the kings of Europe," said Monsieur Colbert. "No one could have imagined that your grandfather's small hunting haven could have attained such glory."

Louis' gaze prompted Monsieur Colbert to continue.

"Louis XIII detested his court at Saint-Germain, so he built a small manor in Versailles for his men and his musketeers when hunting. Your father hunted there for the first time when he was about your age. It was known as a mere folly or a château of cards until he began expanding it in 1664. I'll never forget the year, because he had just discovered the splendors of Vaux-le-Comte, the grand château built by Nicolas Fouquet, his finance minister at the time."

Madame Colbert perked up. "Mon Dieu, such a scandal."

"Indeed," Monsieur Colbert continued. "Your father discovered that Fouquet had used the royal treasury to finance his lavish lifestyle. Alas, Fouquet was imprisoned for life at Pignerol."

"Pignerol?" said Louis.

"A secluded fortress prison in the mountains. For reprehensible criminals or anyone who embarrasses the crown."

"Monsieur Colbert was honored to replace the fallen minister," said Madame Colbert.

"And one of my first tasks was to order the contents of Fouquet's château to be confiscated and brought to Versailles."

"Along with Fouquet's gardener, his architect, and his painter," added Madame Colbert. "You will see their magnificent work today, children."

Louis stared out the coach window as it passed through the small town of Châtillon-sous-Bagneux and wound along the banks of the Seine. Tall poplar trees cast their shadows over the coach as it plunged into the well-wooded valley of Versailles.

"I was rather partial to the Louvre in Paris for the royal residence, but the king was resolute in bringing his court to Versailles ... despite the cost," Monsieur Colbert mumbled sadly, staring blankly in front of him. "I once advised His Majesty to watch the royal purse, but he replied it was better to save pennies on unnecessary expenses in order to spend millions...whenever there was a question of His Majesty's glory."

"And, instead of slowing down the expansion, the king ordered new works. The number of gardens and fountains multiplied," said Madame Colbert.

Monsieur Colbert turned to Jules-Armand. "One day, son, you will take over my role as building superintendent."

"And what a relief that will be," sighed Madame Colbert, straightening the pleats in her gown. "But you, my son, will work from dusk to dawn. It seems as if there's just one elaborate feast after another."

"Yes, the king does cherish his magnificent entertainments," Monsieur Colbert said. "In fact, children, the first elaborate feast at Versailles was in honor of your mother, the king's first official mistress. The celebration was called 'Pleasures of the Enchanted Isle' with plays by Molière and spectacular fireworks."

"I remember it well." Madame Colbert giggled. "All the king's courtiers and nobles arrived in Versailles, but there was no room to lodge them."

"Over three thousand guests," he said. "We had to begin work for housing them all at the palace. The king wanted to keep them there permanently."

"But why?" asked Louis.

"The king wanted to keep a close eye on all the devils," said Madame Colbert with a wink.

The coach entered the town of Versailles. Masons and laborers were busily working, shops were open, and women were washing in the open air. Marie-Anne, who had been mostly silent for the entire trip, shrieked when she noticed the palace shimmering in the late morning sunlight. It was almost noon when the carriage finally passed through the gilded gates onto the marble courtyard. Before them, high up on his bronze horse, sat their father, the great Sun King, carved in stone and pointing to the town behind them.

When the horses were pulled to a stop in the courtyard, Monsieur Colbert tapped Louis on the knee.

"Voilà, the spot where your grandfather's hunting retreat first stood," he said, directing Louis' gaze to the opulently tiled courtyard in the Roman style, then to the marble busts on stone pillars between the windows on the brick façade, and finally above to the magnificent chapel with its lofty roof. "We are now at the center of Versailles, the center of France, and some would say the center of Europe."

The palace guards and the nobles in their elaborate carriages with splendid horses added the final touch of elegance. The blaze of color and pomp could overwhelm any visitor.

After Monsieur Colbert's lackeys and footmen assisted the travelers from the coach, the doormen opened the entrance doors, giving way to the vestibule and the staircase of the Grand Monarch. A valet escorted the visitors up the marble steps to the first landing. Louis counted them aloud.

*The Staircase of the Grand Monarch*

"Twenty-two," he cried out at the top, earning him a fillip to the ear from his sister.

On the landing, they passed a bust of the king in white marble, which ornamented a fountain before ascending to the Salon of Diana. This room, paneled in marble and decorated with portraits of Diana and her Nymphs, served as the king's billiard room, and Louis' eyes were as wide as gold coins as he admired the ceiling, representing Diana on a chariot. On the walls, Cyrus was seen striking a wild boar and Alexander striking a lion. Louis also noticed a portrait of Queen Maria Theresa hanging above the fireplace and he was surprised that she looked so much better in the portrait than in person. But he kept such thoughts to himself.

The valet continued through the Salon of Mercury to that of Apollo, the king's crimson and gold throne room, where the ceiling was painted to represent Apollo sitting on his chariot. Here, the visitors found themselves in the presence of the king, who rose to welcome them. After curtseying, Marie-Anne ran into his arms while Louis remained in place after bowing lowly.

"Monsieur Colbert," said the king, "today's hunt has been postponed until the day after tomorrow." He turned to Louis. "Count of Vermandois, you will join us, along with your uncle, Monsieur Philippe, and his wife, Madame Elizabeth."

Louis remained silent, showing no joy at the thought of hunting animals. To him, they were mystical. His governess had read many stories about them and their unbelievable powers: they could fly, see in the night, live underwater, crawl on walls, dangle upside down, and frighten away monsters. Everything he would like to do.

The king continued, "Madame Colbert, please escort the children to the duchess's chambers. Monsieur Colbert and I have state matters to discuss before our garden promenade."

The children's eyes sparkled as they passed from one opulent salon to the next on their way to Louise's chambers. Louis, however, noticed an odor that permeated the air, reminding him of the smell of pee… and more. But again, he thought it better to keep his thoughts to himself.

Ordinarily, the windows in Louise's bedroom would offer a spectacular view of the vibrant gardens below, but the drapes were partially drawn today when the children arrived. A few scant rays of sunlight cast images like a kaleidoscope on the faded Persian rug. The windows were cracked open, and wafts of brisk air clashed with the acrid scent of dying embers in the fireplace.

The valet pulled the drapes open and took his leave with a quick bow, leaving Madame Colbert and the children standing in the middle of the room. Louis looked up at the tarnished chandelier hanging heavily from a lofty but slightly cracked and peeling ceiling. Louis pointed to the faded allegory there and Madame Colbert replied, "Faith, Hope, and Charity."

At one end of the room and mounted on a platform, a purple alcove housed Louise's bed, isolating it like a convent's sanctuary with its canopy of black linen draped down the sides. At the head of her bed, an enclave of stiff, tapestry-covered pillows guarded a small crucifix on a headboard of unadorned silk.

The first impression of his mother's chambers weighed heavily on Louis' heart, although he could not, as such a young boy, understand why. He scanned the paintings in gilded frames that tried to break the monotony of the room's drab, pastel-papered walls. They were stern-looking portraits of kings, scantily clad goddesses, and Venus in the arms of Adonis. The only table in the room was flanked by two small, tufted settees against a wall. In one of the drawers, unbeknownst to Louis, his mother kept the king's gift of luxurious jewels—discreetly and ashamedly, not wishing to insult the queen by wearing them.

The room's forlorn silence was broken by the creaking of the parquet hallway outside. Its dreary grandeur was lost to the subdued chatter of the servants about Louise's arrival from the queen's morning *levée*. It was Louise's duty to attend, even though she had recently been replaced by Françoise, the king's current mistress.

When Louise arrived minutes later, she greeted her children with the usual titles of "Mademoiselle" and "Monsieur" and kissed them on the forehead. She acknowledged Madame Colbert's presence and then reminded the children about sitting for their portrait.

"We shall meet later, after your tour of the palace gardens," she said, motioning to Madame Colbert that the children were dismissed.

"Come children," said Madame Colbert. "His Majesty awaits us on the terrace."

Louis reluctantly left his mother's chambers; he thought he would have had more time to visit her. However, as soon as he was led to the terrace situated just opposite the principal entrance of the palace, his face beamed like a ray of sun at the view of the pools with fountains, all bordered by clusters of nymphs, cupids, and zephyrs.

The king opened his arms to the breath-taking view when his children joined him. "This was nothing but dense woods and pestilent wastelands when your grandfather came here to ride and hunt stag. He slept on a bed of straw in an ancient windmill while his men took shelter in a nearby cabaret."

Marie-Anne looked around. "Where is the mill, Father?"

"It was too uncomfortable, my child," the king said, pointing to the center of the palace. "Here, in its place, he first constructed a small hunting retreat with a garden. When he brought me here for the first time, it was really nothing more than a little pasteboard box."

The king then began his tour down the broad flight of stairs that led to the gardens.

"There are over a thousand orange trees there," he said as he pointed to the orangery. "During the summer, they are kept out of doors and one of them is over two hundred years old." He then continued the stroll downhill to Latona's fountain.

"Here, children," said the king, "is Latona, who sought help to protect her children, Apollo and Diana, from the insults of the peasants of Lycia. She begged Jupiter to avenge her."

"What did Jupiter do, Father?" said Louis.

"He obliged her by turning all the inhabitants of Lycia into frogs and lizards," he said, causing the children to giggle.

Pleased to find the children enjoying the tour, the king personally drove them in an open carriage down a lane bordered by fountains and trees to the Neptune Basin and the *Grandes Eaux*. Here the children gasped at the most striking display of fountains, statues, and ceramic vases. And to their surprise, as precisely planned but reserved for special occasions only, the fountain erupted at three o'clock with an explosion of sprays. Afterwards, he drove them to the palace's famous maze of shrubbery, where he explained how the labyrinth's fountains depicted stories of Aesop's fables.

"Each fountain has a plaque on which a fable is written. It is from these plaques that my son, the dauphin, learned to read," said the king proudly, until he noticed a grimace on Louis' face.

"Count Louis, are you not enjoying yourself?"

"Oh, yes, Father, I am," he said, feeling a pang of jealousy creep over him.

"Shall we visit the menagerie now?"

"Yes, please," he said, and his smile returned because he had heard of the exotic animals from around the world in the king's zoo.

After the tour of the menagerie, the king and his guests bypassed the greenhouse and returned to the palace terrace, where refreshments were served.

"I promise to give you a tour of the Trianon on another day, children," said the king as courtiers slowly arrived at the terrace to enjoy a selection of fruit, ices, and confections. Louis noticed all the newcomers discreetly eyeing the two new faces at Versailles. He didn't mind. This paradise was going to be his home.

The king held up his hand to attract the crowd's attention. "We are now expected in Duchess de La Vallière's chambers." He then turned to speak to Louis and Marie-Anne in private. "Your mother is going to present you to the court. Afterwards, I believe, you will have your first sitting for a portrait with her."

He looked at Louis. "Count Louis, you will have the honor of attending the *coucher* this evening." With that, the king departed, leaving Louis standing with a blank stare. *What is the coucher?* he thought.

When the children arrived at a salon especially arranged for the presentation, an orderly line of curious courtiers had already formed outside the door to enter the room. According to protocol, the ever-frowning queen and the dauphin were first in line, followed by the king's brother, Monsieur Philippe, and his German wife, Madame Elizabeth. After the king's cousin, the Grande Mademoiselle, the Princes of the Blood took their place before the king's favorite, Madame de Montespan, and her children's governess, Madame Scarron.

The remaining nobles and courtiers pressed forward to get in line. When the double doors finally opened, the queue moved slowly inside and were paraded past a tufted, red velvet settee adorned in gold embroidery. In a taffeta robe with silver lace and diamonds, Louise sat upright on the edge, acknowledging everyone gracefully. Louis, sitting next to her, had donned his military jacket as Admiral of France, and Marie-Anne, sitting to her right, shined in a delicate gown with pearls. Louis' gaze was sweet but noble; Marie-Anne's gaze, however, was nonchalant but interrupted with coquettish smiles.

Having already met the children, the queen simply nodded at Louise and exited the room. Holding Monsieur Philippe's arm, the plump and jolly-looking Madame Elizabeth, however, brought the flowing queue to a stop.

"Madame duchess," she said with a thick Prussian accent. "These are children made for a fairy tale. Such a beautiful princess and a such a charming prince."

Louis couldn't help but smile upon seeing his larger-than-life aunt.

"Children," Louise said, "greet Madame Elizabeth, who speaks so kindly of you."

Marie-Anne quickly blew madame a little kiss and Louis bowed. Monsieur Philippe nodded with approval, but noticed the impatient nobles behind him were whispering.

"If only the boy knew," a courtier whispered to her companion. "The title of admiral was only meant to appease the duchess."

Her companion opened her folding fan to hide her face. "Rumor has it that she once fled Versailles and her absence so deeply affected the king that Monsieur Colbert had to persuade her to return to court. The boy's title was but an empty ploy to keep the duchess at court."

The whispers were getting louder, prompting Monsieur Philippe to tug on Elizabeth's arm to leave.

In passing, the remaining courtiers were heard to remark, "such pretty little creatures" or "what lovely children." But more important, having observed the offspring of the king's adulterous relationship with the duchess, their curiosity was finally appeased.

After presenting her children to the court, Louise led Louis and Marie-Anne into an antechamber where the court artist, Pierre Mignard, had already set up his easel with a canvas that had a dark, somber feel to it. The foreground depicted heavy drapery, dark walls, and a vertical stone column, while the background outside the window portrayed an almost wintry scene with stormy skies.

Louise's portrait was nearly complete in the portrait. She was painted, sitting to the right of a table in the center of the room. Two areas to the left of her were left blank, wherein Louis and Marie Anne were to be sketched today and then painted later.

Louise took her seat and resumed her pose with her right arm on the draped table, holding a fading rose in her fingers. Marie-Anne was asked to stand in front of a vase of flowers placed in the middle of the table. Mignard stepped forward to turn her waist towards him and have her lean her left elbow on the table and touch the vase of flowers.

Louis was then asked to sit on a cushion at his mother's feet. He threw himself into such an easy, natural position on his own that

Mignard made no changes. He did ask Louis, however, to hold a compass as if taking measurements on a map of France, Spain, and America. After all, he was the Admiral of France, and the sea was his domain. But, after several hours of posing for Mignard and being told to keep quiet, Louis was yawning and getting fidgety. Why would anyone want to sit for such a long time, he thought, when just outside the antechamber doors was a mythical palace just waiting to be explored.

~ ~ ~

After the sitting, Louise instructed her valet to escort the children to their chambers and to request an audience for her with the king before his dinner, the *grand couvert*, at ten o'clock. Permission was granted.

The king rose from his armchair when Louise entered his chambers. "You have made your decision, madame, without discussing it with me?"

"Yes, sire," she said. "To withdraw and become a nun cost me nothing, yet to speak with His Majesty about it costs me infinitely."

"I have long known of your intentions, madame," he said, tears rolling down his cheeks. "The walls of Versailles have ears."

Louise fell to her knees, weeping. "The tears in your eyes, sire, are they from my decision to leave the court? Or just from the memories of our love?"

The king ignored her questions and his expression turned cold. "Was it me whom you truly loved, madame?"

"Has your new mistress succeeded in creating suspicion about an affair with the Duke de Lauzun? About the paternity of our son?" she asked and then stood up to approach the king. "She has already taken His Majesty's heart from me. Now she takes away his tenderness for his son?"

"It has been impossible, madame, to escape the rumors of your infidelity."

She moved in closer, gazing at him with fixed eyes. "What! I only loved *you*, sire. Did I not show you my affection in every way?"

"No," he said. "I was never able to triumph over your scruples."

"My principles were dearer than my life, but I sacrificed all of them for you."

"No, madame, your sacrifices were not for me, they were for your own ambitions," he said, motioning that she was dismissed.

Louise stood firm. "For my ambitions, sire?" she said, her face reddening. "Yet, you excuse the vile, insatiable greed of the one you now prefer over me!"

"Madame de Montespan secured her position with a real passion."

"More tender than mine?"

"A thousand times more real."

"Ungrateful, heartless man!" cried Louise. "Dishonored in everyone's eyes at Versailles and deprived of your love, I've been stripped of everything."

"Madame!" he said, his voice faltering.

"And now you have the cruelty to tell me that Madame de Montespan knows how to love better than I do! All this time I've withheld my hatred, my resentment, and my jealousy, hiding my pain and my love."

The king raised a warding hand, pushing against the continuous flow of Louise's words. "I beg you, madame, please spare me such scenes. They are as unnecessary as they are distressing."

"I will obey, sire, because my remaining days at Versailles are numbered," she said, wiping the tears from her cheeks. "I will keep an eternal silence. I have nothing more to say."

She curtseyed and left the room. The king's steward entered moments later and had to remind the king twice that it was time to dine with the family.

A crowd had thronged into the antechamber of the king's apartment to attend the supper. Silence fell when the king arrived, and princes and princesses stood to wait for him to be seated before taking their own seats. Servants stationed themselves at the ends of his table to begin the dining service; it was their responsibility to taste any dish before it was served to the king. When the king motioned for a drink, the cupbearer announced, "Drink for the king," and two nobles approached him. One carried a tray with an enameled cup and two decanters; the other poured the wine, tasted it, and then presented the goblet to the king.

When the meal was finished, the king left the room to greet the ladies of the court and then proceeded to his *coucher*. Monsieur Colbert stood waiting just outside the king's door with Louis.

"Do you understand now what is about to happen and what you need to do?" he said.

"Yes, Papa Colbert."

When the king arrived, the princes and nobles took their places and Colbert motioned to the spot where Louis should stand like everyone present, outside the balusters of the bed. Slowly, the visitors took turns undressing the king, one piece of clothing at a time. After the king had donned his nightgown, he went to his bed's alcove to pray. Because it was dark, the alcove was first lit by the king's chamberlain, holding a candlestick. And the ceremony of the candlestick began.

The king's chamberlain asked, "Sire, to whom do you entrust the candlestick?"

"This evening," said the king, "I wish to honor the Count of Vermandois, Admiral of France."

Prompted by the chamberlain, Louis stepped inside the balustrade and held the candle holder throughout the grand coucher. *He'd just entered a sacred place*, he thought.

The king looked up at Louis. "The ceremony of the coucher is one of distinction at Versailles, my son."

The room gradually emptied, leaving only the king's most intimate friends. The ushers then cleared the room, leaving the king alone with his chamberlain. Monsieur Colbert met Louis outside the king's door and escorted the sleepy boy to his chambers. The clock chimed eleven o'clock. It had been a long day for all.

The daily routine at Versailles started every morning at eight o'clock for the king's *petite levée* when the valet who slept at the foot of the king's bed said, "Sire, it is time." The palace doctors then entered the room to examine the king while still in his bed. After his valet opened the curtains and poured a little wine into the king's hands, the chamberlain then entered with holy water, which the king used to make a quick sign of the cross. Within fifteen minutes, the king's family and the Princes of the Blood were invited into the king's chambers.

Louis was escorted into the room by two young princes, who showed him where to take his place behind them. One held his fingers to his lips, reminding Louis not to make a sound.

After receiving the abbé's blessing, the king rose to put on his socks and his morning robe. The valet removed his nightcap, and the barber combed his hair. He did not shave the king this morning because that only took place every other day. Now half-past eight, the *grande levée* began, and the king's first valet of the wardrobe and his gentlemen-in-waiting entered the room.

As court protocol required, Count Louis stood behind his cousins, the Princes of the Blood, during the ceremony. His eyes were still sleepy, but they opened widely when the king proceeded to sit on his *chaise percée* for his bodily needs—in front of all to see. Louis held his hand over his mouth to keep from giggling aloud but when one of the king's valets cast a foreboding frown at him, he straightened up.

The king remained sitting on his chaise while his barber adjusted the morning wig on the king's head. Louis watched closely as the barber added the finishing touches to the wig. Then, the king's ministers, counselors, and marshals entered the room to watch the official dressing ceremony.

Now nine o'clock, a breakfast of vegetable bouillon was served. The king took a few minutes to choose the menus for the rest of the day while the master of the clocks made sure the king's timepiece was correct. Finally, the barber changed the king's wig for more formal affairs.

By now, at least fifty onlookers had gathered in the king's bedroom, including lesser nobles, according to rank. Then, it was time for the king to make his way to the queen's chambers and escort her to Mass. Along the way, palace guards protected the king from the growing crowd of courtiers, many hoping for a glance from the king or even a word. The royal family and princes followed closely behind, including Louis, who, exhausted by endless ceremony, wondered why it was so necessary.

One of the two Princes of the Blood towered over Louis. "I'm your cousin. Well, our fathers are cousins. My name is Louis-Armand de Conti, and this is my brother, François, Prince de la Roche-sur-Yon."

"Monsieur Colbert gave us instructions to escort you this morning," said François, inspecting Louis from head to toe.

"Where are we going now?" asked Louis.

"To join the king at Mass," said Louis-Armand. When he saw a confused look on Louis' face, he added, "Don't worry, we'll guide you. You'll soon learn the ways of the court."

On this day, with Louise and her children expected at Mass, the chapel had hardly ever been so crowded. In fact, several people found it impossible to enter. Men were gathered in the doorways, gratings, and adjoining galleries, because ladies had already filled the places generally reserved for them. Throughout the chapel, there was a dazzling confusion of feathers, embroidered sashes, and swords.

Due to the chatter and movement in the room, Louis thought himself in a theater before the rising of the curtain. When the Swiss Guard's drums rolled, however, an absolute silence fell over the chapel. It was a sign the king was arriving. Louis thought it could be God himself who would fill the chapel with His glory… but it was his father.

The king entered with the priest to his right. In turn, Dauphin Louis, Monsieur Philippe, the Princes of Conti, and Count Louis followed him to the altar. Then the queen, the Princesses of the Blood, Marie-Anne, and the king's courtesans, notably Louise and Françoise joined the procession. Madame Scarron, the governess of Françoise's illegitimate children, was at the end of the queue.

Louis watched the king take his place with the dauphin on the royal tapestry. At that moment, Louis had an empty feeling in his stomach. Although he was one of the king's two sons, he was again socially ranked behind the dauphin and even the Princes of the Blood for the Mass. Feeling isolated, Louis thought back to the chapel at Sceaux and celebrating a more intimate Mass with the Colberts. At Versailles, he also noticed that the center of attention was not the priest's lectern, but where the king was seated. Only in the most solemn of moments did the priest ever draw any attention to himself.

After Mass, Monsieur Colbert approached Louis. "Count Louis, you've had a very busy morning. You must be tired."

"A little, Papa Colbert," he said.

"I'm sorry, but we have been summoned to join the court for an audience with the queen in her chambers," he said. "This is highly irregular but come along. You can rest later."

# CHAPTER THREE

# Adieu!

*King Louis XIV and Louise de La Vallière*

"There is no greater sorrow than to recall
our times of joy in wretchedness."

— Dante Alighieri, *Inferno*

## Palace of Versailles, April 1674

On his way to the queen's chambers, Monsieur Colbert was stopped by the king's secretary. "A message from the king, monsieur," he said, as he handed him the parchment. Monsieur quickly unrolled it and read it to himself.

> *Our cousin, Duchess Louise de La Vallière, has permission to bestow a pension of two thousand écus to her mother, Madame de Saint-Rémi, two thousand livres to her stepsister, Madame de Hautefeuille, and one hundred livres to each of her servants. Any remaining sums are destined to the poor and elderly at the Château la Vallière hospital. As for her current debts of 150,000 livres, Count Louis of Vermandois is authorized to lend her this amount from his annual pension with interest. Her jewels shall be divided between her two children. Written and signed in the hand of King Louis XIV.*

Monsieur Colbert then understood the rumor was true. Louise de La Vallière finally had permission from the king to leave court and take up the veil. It was no surprise to him. Louise had fled to a convent several years earlier. He remembered the Saturday evening when Louise did not appear at the court's masked ball for the king's new favorite, Madame de Montespan.

The following morning, the king discovered his former mistress had taken refuge in the Dames de Sainte-Marie convent in Chaillot. Distressed, he ordered Monsieur Colbert to convince her to return at once. Having a congenial relationship with Louise, his minister succeeded, and the king wept with joy when she arrived back at court.

Today, however, Monsieur Colbert's duties were of a more solemn nature. Taking up the veil symbolized death, and as such, it required that the inheritance of Louise's worldly goods be documented and distributed with the king's approval. Monsieur Colbert carefully folded the parchment and placed it in his vest pocket.

When he entered the queen's chambers, members of the royal family had already fallen into their proper places, according to court protocol, on the right side of the room. Louis, who was placed next to Madame Colbert with Marie-Anne on the left side of the room, marveled at the luxury of the queen's apartment. The sunny chambers where Her Majesty received guests were paneled with white marble on which the winter's rich tapestries were still hanging. Louis thought about his mother's humble chambers, while here the early afternoon sun highlighted the room's intricately designed blue and gold furniture. Gilded cabinets showcased her jewels and the crown diamonds. Today, because the queen was giving a public audience, her purple tufted armchair was placed at the end of the room on an estrade beneath an elegantly draped canopy.

Louis noticed that Madame Elizabeth, with a peculiar glare, couldn't take her eyes off him. Was it his posture? He lifted his shoulders in his light-crimson silk coat and checked the scarf around his neck. Maybe the white ruffles that fell around his hands contrasted with his dirty, little fingernails. Did they betray him? He glanced at the fingernails of the princes in front of him. They weren't so clean. He then looked at Madame Elizabeth again, who was no longer staring at him, but she was frowning and holding her belly.

Madame Elizabeth's stomach never failed to growl when she was hungry and tired. She had been waiting for almost half an hour for the peculiar gathering. She stood amid the most bizarre group of nobles to gather in the queen's chambers, and she wondered why they were all whispering. Was it about the presence of the former mistress's children or the absence of the mistress herself? Or were they whispering about the king's current mistress, Madame de Montespan, who stood tirelessly tapping her foot in her gown cluttered with jewels. It was a free-flowing gown—obviously to hide another pregnancy. Oh, who knew, she thought. They may have been whispering about the noise erupting from her stomach. It longed not for French cuisine, but for the hearty delights of her German homeland. Homesick, she could almost smell the robust scent of cooked cabbage and sausages.

Standing to Madame Elizabeth's right, Monsieur Philippe, simply known as Monsieur at court, leaned in. "My brother told me the duchess is saying farewell to the queen. She's going to enter a convent."

Madame Elizabeth grimaced, still holding her stomach. "What will happen to the children?" she said.

Madame de Montespan, overhearing them, said, "The king cherishes Mademoiselle de Blois. He told me she will reside at the Colbert's residence in Paris and attend court."

"And the boy?" asked Madame Elizabeth, her gaze again fixed on Louis.

"You didn't hear this from me," said Madame de Montespan, "but some say the Duke de Lauzun is the child's real father—not the king. So, it is doubtful he will attend court but for special occasions."

Their eyes were all turned to the children. Louis and his sister held Madame Colbert's hands, avoiding the gaze of the queen sitting in front of them. Wearing a dark blue velvet ceremonial dress with gold brocade plaits and ermine skin appliqués, Her Majesty was flanked by the king and the dauphin. When footsteps were heard in the hallway, the room buzzed with anticipation.

Elizabeth noticed the king's desperation as he tried to hold back his tears. She also spotted the dauphin's grimace. Was he scowling at Count Louis? More curious, however, were Monsieur and the chevalier's strange looks. Why were they so interested in the boy?

"Perhaps we should take the young lad in, Monsieur Philippe," said the chevalier with an ornery grin.

Madame Elizabeth cocked her eyebrow. "Have you no shame? Everyone can see how you are gawking at the boy." When Monsieur shushed her, she lowered her voice. "No matter, I will never recognize a royal bastard. Let alone keep one at Saint-Cloud."

Despite her harsh words, Madame Elizabeth still could not help but focus on Louis' sweet features and curly locks. They reminded her of his mother, who had always treated her with the utmost respect and sincerity. Louis' almond-shaped eyes only made his face even more angelic, almost effeminate. *But still*, she reminded herself, *he is but a bastard at the grandest court of Europe.*

"Does he know what's happening?" said Madame Elizabeth.

Madame de Montespan shrugged her shoulders and, as the room quieted, whispered, "I don't think so."

The room became silent. The pale Duchess de La Vallière had just entered the chambers. Somberly dressed in dark blue silk, she walked solemnly to the queen's dais and curtsied low and reverently. "My crimes were public, Your Majesty," she said. "And my repentance must be public, too."

The duchess then flung herself at the queen's feet. "I've come, Madame, begging your forgiveness for all the pain I have caused Her Majesty." She pressed her palms together. "Please do not deny me your generosity. Within hours I will be forever secluded with the Carmelites."

The room gasped softly, and to everyone's surprise, the noble queen took the duchess's arm to raise her up and embrace her.

"Duchess," said the queen. "I have no ill feelings toward you. If you have done me any wrong, you have certainly made amends with your kindness and good works."

"At this moment, I am truly reconciled with virtue," said Louise, pressing her lips against the queen's hand and then holding it to her heart.

Madame Elizabeth couldn't help but notice that Madame de Montespan was fidgeting incessantly, surely affected by such an emotional spectacle. As the king's current mistress, Madame de Montespan was no doubt worried about the queen's behavior. She was publicly acknowledging Louise's adulterous transgressions with the king. Must she, the new mistress, now feel guilty too? After all, being a married woman, she was a double adulteress in the presence of the most honorable queen of France.

Louise took her leave from the queen. "Adieu, Madame," she said with a solemn curtsey and walked past her children without a word. Louis experienced that strange, sinking feeling in his stomach. A feeling he could not describe.

When the queen raised her hand to let everyone know the audience was dismissed, Madame de Montespan hurried out, catching up with the king's ex-mistress.

"Duchess, may I walk with you?" she asked.

Louise nodded and Madame de Montespan took her arm. "Are you not aware, duchess, of the privations and the discomforts you will suffer in a Carmelite convent? Even your shoes that allow you to walk without a limp will be forbidden."

"If I shall suffer in the convent," Louise said, "I will only have to remember the misery I've suffered here to ease my pain."

Madame de Montespan frowned. "And your dear children, duchess, can you leave them so?

"God will look over all those who I love," said Louise calmly. "As for my own family, Madame, I can only rely on my prayers to the Almighty in Heaven."

Madame Montespan may have wished that Louise was no longer at court, but the ex-mistress's departure pained her. She could no longer use Louise's presence as a screen for her love affair with the king. Moreover, the very austere Carmelite order might unreasonably be regarded as a reflection upon her own indiscretions.

When Louise returned to her chambers, she consoled her ladies-in-waiting and then sat at her desk to write a letter to a dear friend at court, Maréchal de Bellefonds. She had asked for his counsel about joining a religious order in the past, and she wanted to explain her final decision.

> *At last, Maréchal de Bellefonds, I can leave this world behind. I do so without regret, but not without pain. My weakness has kept me here for a long time with a thousand sorrows. Without any taste for it, I can readily give up riches and grandeur amid such infinite vexations. Everyone is leaving Versailles for Franche-Comté to visit the king's troops. I am leaving too, but only to take the safer road to Heaven. God will look over me as I make my journey in the convent, as I must, to be forgiven for my sins.*

After she sealed her letter, she made her way to the chambers where the children were sleeping. When she approached Marie-Anne's bed, she carefully drew the curtain aside to find her daughter sleeping peacefully.

"My daughter, you will awaken tomorrow," she tearfully whispered, "and you will ask in vain for your mother. But she will be in a safer place, sheltered from all the dangers that surround your youth. Oh, my daughter, if you only knew how I've suffered in this palace, you would know what to fear. Adieu, my child."

She wiped the tears from her eyes as she entered the adjoining apartment where Louis was sleeping.

"You, too, my son. The grief for leaving you is not any less painful, but you will someday understand that it is genuine. Fare thee well, my dear Louis, and may you be happier than your mother."

Louise shut the door behind her and returned to her chambers, where she gathered faithful servants around her. She asked them to forgive any unintentional offence she might have given them. She also informed them about the pensions they would receive once she was gone. She then gave her most trusted confidante her wishes for the remainder of her estate to be divided among the poor. Her children's welfare was already secured. Louis and Marie-Anne had a generous annual pension of 80,000 livres per year. The king had also just allotted 30,000 livres to set up their new households, providing them with silver dinnerware, horses, carriages, and other furnishings.

The next morning, the king was visibly emotional in the chapel. He knew that Louise was attending Mass with him for the last time. After the service, his eyes were red as he and Madame de Montespan watched Louise from his window arriving in the courtyard below. Madame Colbert followed closely behind, with Louis and Marie-Anne by her side.

In the mid-morning fog, an inconspicuous carriage stood ready for the journey to the Carmelite convent in the Faubourg Saint-Jacques, the final refuge in Paris where Louise would renounce her shameful world and take up the veil. Courtiers slowly gathered to show their respect and bid her adieu. Some, who knew the piety of the duchess, wiped tears from their eyes. Others, perhaps relieved that she was leaving, calmly chit-chatted among themselves.

Madame Elizabeth and Madame Scarron, according to the king's instructions, joined Louise and her children in the coach to escort them to the convent and then back to Versailles. A second coach followed with Louise's mother and sister-in-law. In Louise's coach, all was quiet. Madame Elizabeth and Madame Scarron looked out the windows to avoid

Louise's blank stare. Marie-Anne seemed unaffected by the day's events, but Louis' head was bowed and his shoulders slumped. He was motionless except for an occasional squint of the eyes.

Louis was too young to understand that his mother was now seeking a pious life after having lived a sinful one for the past twelve years as the king's mistress. He didn't grasp her need to atone for her past. That she wanted to die an ever-living death of endless agony. That she wanted to die to the world, to the court, to the noble societies in sumptuous palaces, to everything that once enchanted her.

The morning fog was slow in lifting as the coach pulled up to the massive gate of the convent, an edifice as colorless as Louise's cloak. Madame Elizabeth looked at the austere structure with all its openings—except for the main door—walled up, including ground-floor windows, first-floor windows, attic skylights, and the cellar vents. It was in this austere dwelling that Louise chose to sacrifice her beauty, her youth, her fortune, her children, and the only man she had ever loved.

When the prioress came to receive her at the massive gate, Louise turned to her children and kissed them on the forehead. To her onlookers, she said, "Thanks be to Heaven. I am now delivered from all the cares which only such fortune can cause. I am now at peace."

Louise entered the gate, carrying nothing with her from the magnificent palace she had just abandoned. Her mother and sister wept. Marie-Anne was impervious, but Louis, who was left standing next to Elizabeth, could only murmur, "belle maman," as tears rolled down his cheeks and a strange, sinking feeling overcame his soul.

The crowd that had gathered outside slowly dispersed. Louise's family invited Marie-Anne to join them in their coach to Versailles. Françoise escorted her, while Madame Elizabeth stood silent, somewhat numbed by what had just taken place, with Louis standing next to her. To her astonishment, a sense of wondrous dread took hold of her body when the little stranger put his hand in hers. As hard as she tried, she could not for the world pull her hand away. She, too, knew the pain of being neglected. She remembered scenes of her own father separating her from court when he divorced her mother. More painful, she remembered the thirteen illegitimate children that he had fathered and kept close to him.

She took a deep breath. It was decided.

"Madame Scarron," said Elizabeth. "Please inform the king that Count Louis will join Monsieur and me at Saint-Cloud."

Madame Scarron paused before entering her coach. "The king will be relieved to hear this," she said.

# CHAPTER FOUR

# The Iniquitous Château

*Château of Saint-Cloud*

> "My thoughts were full of other things
> When I wandered off the path."
>
> — Dante Alighieri, *Inferno*

## April 21, 1674

The Château of Saint-Cloud sat upon a wooded hill that overlooked the Seine River. Louis couldn't believe his eyes when he entered the main gallery. He was overwhelmed by the menagerie of sculptured, nude Greek soldiers of exquisite marble and portraits of scantily draped Greek gods and goddesses. Unlike Versailles, the décor was less stately and more ornate.

"May I go to my chambers, Madame Elizabeth?" he said softly. The past few days had been stressful. Although his mother had not been around when growing up, he still had trouble grasping the fact that his mother had just deserted him—for good.

"You're no longer at Versailles, Count Louis!" said Madame in her gruffest German accent. "I rule this palace. Here you will address me as Aunt Liselotte. Come, you look hungry. We'll find some sauerkraut and beer in the kitchens."

On the way, Elizabeth informed her lady-in-waiting to prepare Louis' chambers and to instruct a valet to fetch his belongings from Versailles. Once sitting at a table in the busy kitchen, Louis was taken aback by his aunt's informality with the cooks and servants. He tried to hide a grin when she belched out loud after drinking a cup of ale.

"You are not from France, Aunt Liselotte," said Louis. "Why do you live here?"

"Pure obedience and against my will," she said. "If my father in Germany had only loved me as much as I loved him, he would never have sent me to this dangerous country."

"Dangerous?" said Louis.

"Courtiers here believe themselves witty when they are deceitful," she said. "I don't participate in such folly. Why should I torment myself with such theatrical farces at court? I leave that to Monsieur Molière."

"Don't you like living here?" asked Louis, surprised at hearing her complain.

"*Junger* Louis, I had no choice. I was obliged to marry Monsieur. You'll soon learn he's a very peculiar man," she said and rubbed her big belly. "But he did give me a gift."

Louis thought she might have been pregnant, but he wasn't sure because she was so big.

"You'll soon have a cousin," she said. "I just hope he looks more like his father than me."

Louis frowned. "Why, Aunt Liselotte?"

"There are two types of German women at court, the beautiful and women like me. Undeniably, I was born ugly." She laughed. "Look, my eyes are small, my lips are long and flat, and my nose is so short because it is hidden by my big fat cheeks."

When Louis giggled, she stood up. "And my stature is short and stout. With such legs and thighs, I could've been a boy. When I was younger, I loved swords and guns much more than dolls and other toys. I wanted to be a boy, but that almost cost me my life."

Louis' eyes begged her to tell more.

"Well, I heard that my friend, Marie Germain, became a boy by jumping off things," she said. "I took so many frightening jumps that it was a miracle I never broke my neck."

Her belly shook so much with laughter that she had to sit back down.

"Yes, I was very lively in my youth. People called me *Rauschenplatten-Knect*."

"Rau—shen—platen—nekt," repeated Louis, his forehead wrinkled.

"A lad rattling plates," she said, laughing. "I was as noisy as a kitchen lad rattling the plates."

The cook brought two plates of steaming sauerkraut and sizzling sausages. Louis was not too keen on the sauerkraut, but he devoured his sausage. Elizabeth offered him a sip of her ale, bursting into laughter when he tasted it and stuck out his tongue.

"Come, let's show you to your accommodations," she said, scooting her chair back to get up. On the way to his new chambers, Elizabeth introduced Louis to several courtiers in the galleries. Gentlemen bowed and ladies curtseyed, all the while eyeing his charming smile. Many commented that he had his mother's dainty features. When Elizabeth and Louis happened upon a clutter of mignons in one of the galleries, Elizabeth took hold of Louis' hand.

"*Junger* Louis, these are the Italian chevaliers," she said in a tense tone. "Ignore them."

The young men stopped conversing upon seeing the newcomer. Elizabeth whispered, "And you'll soon learn why they are called Italian."

Louis had never seen young men dressed so frivolously. The sleeves of their shiny, short satin jackets were open from the shoulder to the laced cuffs at the wrist, showing the billowy sleeves of their silk shirts. Their short breeches were elaborately tied with bands of ribbon above the knee, and their red-heeled boots were topped with ruffles or lace garters.

When Elizabeth caught the minions gawking at Louis, she barked, "Pathetic dolts!" and the mignons vanished from the salon.

As she escorted Louis down the long corridors, she passed an enormous wind. He looked up at her in disbelief.

"This is not Versailles, *mein lieber* Louis," she bellowed.

They both chuckled, and Louis knew they were off to a great start.

For the next few days, Elizabeth kept him busy settling in, meeting her husband's bizarre followers, and learning the few rules of court etiquette. It wasn't Sceaux. And it certainly wasn't Versailles.

~ ~ ~

At the end of his first week at Saint-Cloud, Louis was summoned to Elizabeth's chambers. Or was it her library? He looked about the room, noticing the heavy armoires filled with books and the walls cluttered with portraits of German rulers in broad billed black hats and fur cloaks. The room was void of color and unlike most chambers at Saint-Cloud, the room was absent of vases of flowers. Near the windows was a small sitting area, where Elizabeth's dogs were napping.

In the center of the room, Elizabeth was sitting behind a desk cluttered with quills, parchment paper, and ink bottles; across from her sat a venerable old man in an armchair. Louis eyed his white, frizzy hair, and his forehead, marked with freckles. The man was running one hand through his bushy beard and tracing a line on Elizabeth's palm with the other.

"Well, sir, I hope it will be a prince," said Elizabeth.

"Madame," he said, "if so, this male child will live a long life, encountering circumstances beyond the comprehension of normal souls. He may be prone to ill manners and pleasure seeking. But he will be well-esteemed."

"Sounds just like his father," she said with a sigh. Then smiling, she added, "This is my nephew, Count Louis of Vermandois."

Louis approached them and the old man glanced at him. "When was the lad born?"

Elizabeth looked to Louis for an answer.

"The second day of October," he said. "1667."

The old man's nostrils grew larger as he took a deep breath. "The Sun in Libra. Hmm. Honest, balanced, a connoisseur of luxury…so much so that he longs to be part of the art or at least part of the spectacle."

When Elizabeth found Louis gazing out the window, she said, "Listen up, *junger* Louis."

He jolted to attention, and the old man continued. "Emotions can be undeveloped, making it difficult to express them in a mature way. Mercury in Virgo can make one curious, but books will satisfy any lack of imagination."

Elizabeth caught Louis' eye and proudly pointed out her armoires of books near the entrance.

"Venus in Virgo—loyal but cold in relationships," said the old man sternly. "Mars in Leo—a leader with a sense of entitlement. Saturn in Capricorn—determined to succeed, but it could cloud one's decisions and ideals."

The old man shook his head and looked at Elizabeth. "Mercury in Virgo—being determined to reach unattainable goals can cause self-doubt. This can lead one down a dangerous path." He then glared at Louis. "Take heed, young man. Take heed."

Louis' back straightened.

The old man got up from his seat and snatched a small velvet bag from the table. He wiggled it so that the jingle of gold coins could be heard.

"Sir?" said Elizabeth, raising her eyebrows.

"I do not wish to continue, Madame," he said. "Good day."

Elizabeth nodded. "Good day, kind sir."

Once he had left the room, she stood up and noticed a surprised look on Louis' face. "Don't mind the old fortune teller, Louis," she said. "He can be rather theatrical at times."

She walked to her collection of books. "You're welcome to come read with me whenever you want. I'll ask Abbé Choisy to choose something for you. Perhaps tomorrow?"

Louis squinted at some of the books' titles. "But now," she said, "we must prepare for the hunt. His Majesty expects us at Versailles."

"I would like to see my father, but do I have to go hunting, Aunt Liselotte?" he said, his face turning pale.

"Louis, it is an important part of court life. You should be proud you've been invited. Permission to join the royal hunt is an important step in earning the king's favor."

Louis begrudgingly conceded her point. "I'll do my best."

"Good. Let's find you some riding clothes."

~ ~ ~

The marble courtyard at Versailles was already crowded when Elizabeth and Louis arrived later in the afternoon. Lines of coaches of anxious couriers gathered to follow the royal hunt. Guards, servants, dog-keepers, and musicians scurried about the courtyard. Cooks loaded their coaches with freshly baked bread and smoked meats, the king's favorites when hunting. Then, a stable boy with corn-silk blonde hair arrived from Sceaux with Louis' mount.

"Where is your mount, Aunt Liselotte?" Louis said, standing upright in his newly fitted riding jacket and hat with plumes.

"I join the king at least three times a week to hunt, but the doctors persuaded me not to ride while I'm with child."

"But you're still dressed for hunting," he said, gazing at her dark, frock-like coat padded like a man's doublet, her gray scarf, and her straw hat covered with feathers, he knew why she was fanning herself like a shy girl waiting to meet the king at court.

"You'll see, Louis, that I love nature. I prefer the warm wind against my face to the rouge that the gossiping ladies at court wear."

Louis admired her upright posture—like that of an Amazonian in his favorite adventure books. He wished that she was riding with him. He had only ridden a few times with Jules-Armand at Sceaux and once settled in his saddle, he trembled a bit, but he was put at ease when Elizabeth instructed her stable boy to ride closely behind him. Louis noticed how comfortable the boy was on his mount. He wore a sun-faded violet justaucorps, short breeches, and shoes with long toes. For some reason, Louis envied the boy's straw-like hair and his sun-drenched skin. He looked at his own arms. No, they were as white as milk curds.

Part of Louis was thrilled, though, knowing he would follow the king immediately after the dauphin and the captain of the guards. The king arrived in his red velvet jacket with brocades and knee-length boots on a white mount. With the white plumes of his broad-brimmed gray hat floating in the warm afternoon breeze, the king acknowledged Louis with a proud nod and then turned to Elizabeth.

"You will be missed today, sister," he said.

Elizabeth took in a deep breath of fresh air and rubbed her belly. "It won't be too long, sire, until we hunt together again." And she returned to her coach.

"The horn, captain!" said the king, and the fanfare immediately filled the late morning air. The dogs howled, pulling their masters by their leashes to a swift run. The horses quickly picked up the pace. Everyone else followed behind in coaches or on horseback.

Louis' heart was throbbing as the hunters slowed to enter the forest, with its ancient oak trees as lofty as the nave of a medieval cathedral. As he made his way around the rotting wood of crumbling logs, he could hear the trees creak and groan as they swayed.

He tried to keep pace with the riders in front of him, but just as he lifted himself up from the saddle to rearrange his riding pants that were too big, a rabbit bolted in a clearing. When his horse jolted to follow the others in pursuit, Louis fell to the ground face first with his nose in a patch of wet grass that smelled and tasted of moldy moss. The stable boy called out for the captain to stop the runaway horse.

Dazed, Louis moaned as the stable boy helped him to his feet. But only his pride was injured, especially when Elizabeth arrived with the king and the dauphin.

"I was hunting wolves when I was his age," said the dauphin snootily as the king dismounted.

"But monseigneur," said Elizabeth to the dauphin, "Louis has no experience in riding."

"That was quite a fall, Madame. Shall I summon the doctor?" said the king.

"No, sire, he is fine," she said. "I've fallen twenty-four or twenty-five times and it never frightened me."

The king tipped his hat and Elizabeth motioned for the stable boy to take the reins of Louis' horse. "You can return to Sceaux," she told him.

Louis caught the stable boy's eyes. He appeared to be about his own age, and for some reason Louis felt embarrassed that the boy could handle the horses so skillfully. When he nodded to express his thanks, the boy didn't react.

"Come, *junger* Louis," Elizabeth said, "we'll return to the palace in the coach and wait for the hunting party there."

Once inside the palace, Elizabeth ordered her valet to retrieve their clothing. Louis was surprised.

"Oh, I made sure we had extra outfits," she said. "I sweat so much I need to change two or three times after the hunt."

They went to the chambers reserved for them at Versailles and as soon as they had changed, they made their way to the Salon of Mars, used as a ballroom, to await the hunting party. Louis couldn't tell whether Elizabeth had changed or not; she looked the same. But he wasn't happy with the breeches she had brought for him. They were too saggy and loose-fitting, and he felt out of place in the salon with green velvet curtains and furniture bordered with gold. He paused to pull up his breeches.

"Come along, *junger* Louis," she said. "Monsieur and the Chevalier de Lorraine have already found the refreshments being served."

They walked to an intricately carved table with silver baskets of flowers, silver candlesticks, and silver punch bowls. Louis was confused. His uncle, hanging on to the chevalier's arm, wore makeup, a magnificent gown, high heels, and a powdered wig with ribbons. His dazzling rings and bracelets were as remarkable as the pungent odor of his perfume. All the while, his aunt Elizabeth looked more like a valet de chambre in a gown. *Monsieur is more Madame and Madame is more Monsieur*, he thought.

"You and my nephew have returned early," said Monsieur, after checking his appearance in the mirror above the table.

"Yes, husband," Elizabeth replied. "*Junger* Louis had a slight mishap."

"That's one reason why I did not join you today," he said to Louis with a wink.

"Louis," said Elizabeth. "Monsieur neither loves horses nor hunting. He only takes pleasure in playing cards in the salons, in court gossip, and in masquerade balls."

"And battle," said the chevalier, leaning in to straighten Louis' collar. "Well, this is still quite a small lad for hunting… but nothing a little physical exercise and riding lessons couldn't correct."

Louis had never seen the chevalier up so close. He looked much younger and much more handsome than his uncle. From the looks of his admirers in the room, he was certainly the most attractive noble at court.

Elizabeth pulled Louis to her side and away from the chevalier. "I'm sure, Monsieur Chevalier, that *junger* Louis will master the hunt by autumn." She turned to her husband. "And I see you're ready for this evening's festivities."

"Yes, he is," the chevalier said. "Will you not join us tonight for the ball and supper, Madame?"

"Not tonight. We must return to Saint-Cloud and have the doctor examine Louis."

"But the king?" he said.

"His Majesty will understand."

Madame de Montespan then entered the salon and approached Elizabeth with a slight curtsey. "Your Highness, I'm on my way to see the portrait of Duchess de La Vallière and her children. I hear it has just been unveiled by Mignard. Have you had the opportunity to see it?"

"Not yet, Françoise. May we join you?" she asked.

"But of course. I would be delighted," she said. "Gentlemen, will you please excuse us?"

"No, I believe we will join you," said Monsieur. "With your permission, naturally."

Françoise nodded with a smile and Elizabeth took Louis' hand.

When the newcomers entered the gallery and approached the painting, Françoise said, "It's a rather gracious scene, but somewhat too melancholic for my taste."

"Yes," said Elizabeth. "Like that of an autumn afternoon."

"It is difficult to detect the duchess's demeanor too," said Françoise. "Shouldn't she have looked more saddened at leaving her children behind?"

Elizabeth looked at Louis. "I'm certain she was distraught, Françoise," said Elizabeth. "But she's now at peace, far from the prying eyes of the court."

"And far from any witnesses to her indiscretions," said the chevalier slyly.

"Sir!" said Elizabeth. "Must you? In front of the child?"

Elizabeth fixated on Louise's gaze in the portrait. It was not fixed on the artist but was aimed higher and to his right. *Perhaps,* she thought, *Louise feared that viewers would look into her eyes for an answer to so many questions.*

"Why did she choose a white silk gown for the sitting?" mused Françoise. "It's more befitting a bride."

"Well, it's elegant but not too luxurious," said Elizabeth. "Perhaps most suitable for a woman about to leave her world behind to take up a nun's attire."

Françoise stepped forward for a closer look at the gown. "But look at the gold braids on her shoulders and the cuffs. Not really befitting a bride of Christ."

Elizabeth didn't reply. *Well, why not,* she thought. *Louise was the royal mistress of Louis XIV, the king chosen by God to rule France.*

Elizabeth then looked at the ruby earring with an oblong pearl that adorned Louise's left ear. The matching earring dangled from her right hand, as if she were removing any signs of her former sumptuous life—one jewel at a time. More telling, however, was the red rose also in her right hand. The flower had just begun to wither, and the fallen petals marked the end of a blossoming love affair with the King of France.

*Louise de La Vallière and Children*

Louise's left hand was directed towards two books on a chair, one on top of the other, entitled "Imitation of Jesus Christ" and "Order of Saint Theresa," foreshadowing what was to come. The back of her hand notably showed disregard for the playing cards, the guitar, and the mask lying on the floor, alluding to gambling, music, and masquerades—all favorite court pastimes that would soon come to pass.

On the same plane with her mother and to the left, Marie-Anne, wearing a flowered dress with ruffled sleeves, leaned her left elbow on the table to touch a vase of flowers. With her right hand, she pointed to several rose leaves that had fallen. She faced the artist half-turned with a mischievous gaze and a flirtatious smile as she arranged flowers in a vase. Known to be precocious, the beautiful Marie-Anne showed no sign of sadness. She was either not aware of her mother's nearing departure or she could not have cared less; after all, she was the king's favorite daughter and a twinkle in every man's eye at court.

Elizabeth noticed that Louis was enthralled with his own image in the middle of the painting. He sat on a cushion at his mother's feet in a black velvet cloak and silk stockings. He held a compass in one hand and rested his other hand on a nautical chart.

"A wonderful likeness of you, *junger* Louis." But she fell silent as she noticed Louis' eyes in the portrait. His gaze was oblique and the only one that completely avoided the viewers' eyes—as if he were unworthy of their attention.

Françoise approached the portrait to read the lines on a sheet of music in the bottom right-hand corner.

*The world displays its pomp and attractions in vain.*
*I hear its voice calling me,*
*But it's the one I easily disdain to enjoy eternal glory.*
*The one that passes in a moment,*
*The one that passes in a moment.*

Elizabeth knew the court would someday understand the meaning of these verses but for the time being, she had to tend to her new charge, a young boy who would eventually need to understand his mother's sacrifice.

~ ~ ~

The summer days at Saint-Cloud were vibrant, and Louis slowly became accustomed to the château's busy social calendar. It was interrupted on one occasion, however, when Elizabeth took Louis to visit his mother in the convent. Her intentions were good.

Elizabeth's magnificent coach was lined with purple velvet, and all the trimmings were covered in gold leaf. Her tufted cushions were embroidered in silver thread and perfumed with lavender and rosemary. On the route to the convent, every time the royal carriage hit a bump on the rutty road, Elizabeth's big, round belly bounced so wildly up and down that Louis giggled until tears welled in his eyes. She, too, started to laugh. Although she was the second wife of Louis' uncle, they had quickly formed a special bond with each other. Today, he was going to pay his mother a visit, and she was pleased to see him so joyful. Still, for some reason, she had long dreaded this trip.

As the carriage neared the convent, Louis put his hand to his ear. "Aunt Liselotte, I can hear the bells

She bent an ear to the sweet plaintive melody that pealed through the blossoming trees of the boulevard. When the coach turned to the old avenue leading to the convent, however, the trees disappeared, revealing the somber edifice of the Gothic nunnery, with its tall spires and bleak façade. The floral scents of the boulevard were replaced by those of dust and aging stone.

*Carmélites Convent of the Faubourg Saint-Jacques*

When the carriage pulled alongside the gate of the foreboding entrance, lackeys jumped down and scurried to assist Elizabeth and Louis from the carriage. Two bodyguards on horseback behind the carriage dismounted and escorted them through the gate and down a narrow path bordered with neatly trimmed shrubbery. Elizabeth's dress with ropes of pearls and Louis' crimson cloak and white stockings drew a small but noisy crowd at the gate. The clamor gradually diminished, however, as they reached the main entrance, where a cool stone arch over the thick wooden door was decorated with sculptured busts and entwined with peaceful green ivy.

When the door slowly opened, a woman in a long black robe appeared to greet the visitors. She invited them inside but made it very clear that the guards were not welcome. Elizabeth motioned for them to remain outside. As soon as Elizabeth and Louis were inside, the solemn woman led them through a large, vaulted space. Only a few worm-eaten chairs and tables populated the centuries-old stone floor. The few windows that pierced the high walls resembled those of a medieval prison. When they arrived at a table at the end of the hall where incense was burning, the woman asked them to wait for a moment. She then slipped out of sight down a dark, dismal hallway.

Elizabeth watched Louis as he gazed at an oil painting on the wall. He turned to her with a puzzled look on his face.

"That's Archangel Saint Michael slaying the demon," she said softly.

Louis pointed to another painting. "And that one?" he said. "Is that the Virgin Mary?"

"No, that's Mary Magdalene."

His eyes begged to know more, but a scuffling of sandals was heard coming down the hallway.

She leaned over and whispered, "I'll tell you more about Mary Magdalene later."

Louis' mother then appeared almost ghostlike in the subdued rays of light from above. Louis walked forward to embrace her, but she held out her hands for him to keep his distance.

"Duchess," said Elizabeth with a nod.

"No, madame, I am no longer the duchess here," she said.

Elizabeth tried not to stare at Louise's cape of rough-textured cloth, her heavy linen stockings, and the black scarf around her head. But

Elizabeth was taken aback, however, by the two small blonde curls dangling from underneath her scarf. Louise noticed the direction of her gaze.

"I am permitted some leniency, madame, owing to my previous status at court," Louise said. "In all other matters, however, I am treated no differently than the others."

"Are you as comfortable here as they say?"

"No," she said. "I am not comfortable, but I am content."

Louise set her gaze on Louis. "Monsieur count, you comfort my heart."

"What do you mean, Belle Maman?"

"I heard you recently attended one of His Majesty's balls with your sister," she said. "And I was told that the court had nothing but praise for your charming manners."

Louis smiled. "Aunt Liselotte made sure I wore my best vest and breeches," he said. "Cousin Prince de la Roche showed me the gardens. We chased and teased the girls who—"

"You are only eight years old," she interrupted. "You must attend to your lessons and stay true to our religion."

Louis looked to the cold, stone floor. "Yes, Belle Maman."

"My child, I'm no longer in charge of your future. You must put aside all petty diversions, listen to your mentors, and follow your conscience to make a better life for yourself."

Louis' lips trembled, and he took a step forward, but Louise nodded to Elizabeth, who pulled him back into her arms, his head resting on her bosom. He noticed that familiar but strange sinking feeling in his stomach again. A feeling of painful emptiness.

"Wipe your tears now," said Louise. "I must turn away from you all…in order to turn to Him above."

Louise noticed the perplexed, almost menacing look on Elizabeth's face.

"Madame Elizabeth, I love Louis and his sister dearly. They are my children. But they are also the fruit of my sins with His Majesty when I was his mistress. I can no longer allow myself any maternal affection—nor can I express too much of it."

Louise gestured with a nod that the visit was over. She turned and only the scuffling of sandals could be heard as she disappeared down the murky hallway. Louis, still in Elizabeth's arms, wanted to follow her, but Elizabeth held him back.

She took his hand in hers. "Come, Louis, we need to leave now."

Although not easily moved, Elizabeth couldn't keep the tears from running down her cheeks. *He will remember this day for the rest of his life,* she thought, but she would speak to Abbé Claude Fleury, Louis' new mentor. *Louis will need kindness and understanding.*

~ ~ ~

Louis always enjoyed reciting the classics and, after speaking with Elizabeth, Abbé Fleury chose excerpts from *The Adventures of Telemachus* for Louis' first lesson. Louis' chambers were just large enough to accommodate his bed and bedside table, a small writing desk, and an armoire. The walls were papered in pale green and white, which reflected the morning rays from his window. Louis sat at his desk.

"Count Louis," said the abbé, tall and imposing in his black woolen robe, "when Telemachus was distressed after losing his flock one morning, he threw himself on the ground near a cave, expecting death to deliver him from a calamity that he could no longer sustain."

The abbé pointed to the excerpt and Louis read it aloud.

> *"But, just in the moment of despair, I perceived the mountain tremble; the oaks and pines seemed to bow from the summit, the breeze itself was hushed, and a deep voice, which seemed to issue from the cave, pronounced these words: "Son of the wise Ulysses! Thou must, like him, become great by patience. Princes who have not known adversity are unworthy of happiness; they are enervated by luxury and intoxicated with pride."*

The abbé took the book from his hands. "Louis, let these words inspire you. Do you understand why they are important?"

"Yes, monseigneur," he said. "I may not live at Versailles, but my life is still good."

"Indeed, and if you are patient?"

"If I am patient, I will be happier."

"And greater," added the abbé, smiling at Louis with his large blue eyes. "Remember that a man's happiness and greatness exist only in proportion to his restraint."

CHAPTER FIVE

# Morpheus: Master of Dreams

*Cascade of Saint-Cloud*

"Beauty awakens the soul to act."

— Dante Alighieri, *Inferno*

## Château of Saint-Cloud, August 1674

Courtiers roamed lazily about the château the morning after Madame Elizabeth gave birth to her second son. It had been a long night, but the plump, double-chinned Duchess d'Orléans chatted merrily with her ladies-in-waiting as she recuperated.

"Shh," she said, "I hear a commotion in the hallway. It must be the new nursemaid."

But when the double doors of her chambers opened, Monsieur Philippe entered in his extravagant silk breeches and a vest embellished with jewels and ribbons. His effeminate male mignons followed close behind, chatting noisily and making a fuss about each other's attire.

"So, you have found time to visit your son," said Elizabeth loudly in her thick German accent, hoping to drown out the mignons' ranting.

Monsieur shirked off the comment, motioned the mignons to quieten, and looked in the cradle. "So, you've named him Philippe II?"

"Yes, you have a son, a boy," she said as she eyed the mignons. "Well, at least for now."

Monsieur smirked, not appreciating his wife's sense of humor. He then spent a moment gazing at himself in a mirror.

"You dress more luxuriously than your wife." She grinned. "And those high heels. Why, you look like you're on stilts!"

Monsieur clicked his heels, and the mignons mimicked him with laughter.

"Doesn't His Majesty object to such outlandishness?" she said.

"If it exasperates my royal brother, madame, then I am the happier."

Elizabeth straightened up in her bed, and a lady-in-waiting scurried to arrange some cushions behind her.

Frowning, she held a handkerchief to her nose. "Mein Got! Could you and your followers be any more perfumed?"

Monsieur pulled a scarf from his sleeve and took a big sniff. "A subject, madame, about which you know very little."

The mignons snickered.

"Husband," she said. "I would like a word with you … in private."

She dismissed her lady-in-waiting. When she glared at the mignons, they jolted and scurried out of the room.

"We now have two sons," she said.

Monsieur pulled a chair up to her bedside. "Yes, an heir and a spare," he said.

"Well, I've fulfilled my marital duties," she said. "Now I would like to take up the veil."

"You jest, madame. Have we gotten along so badly?"

"Monsieur, I must sleep on the edge of the bed. So close to the edge that I often fall to the floor in my sleep."

"Madame is prone to exaggeration," he said.

"But Monsieur knows he doesn't enjoy being touched."

Monsieur wrinkled his brow.

"Whenever my foot brushes against yours," she continued, "you wake up and reproach me."

Monsieur's face reddened as he looked away.

"But I forgive you," she said. "I know I'm uglier and ruder than the first duchess."

"Princess Henriette was as flirtatious as you are lacking in vanity," he said with a smile.

"I was born German. I preferred guns to dolls. Hunting to society. If I didn't have a good heart, no one could ever put up with me at court."

"Yes, you have always been the first to laugh at your own shortcomings."

"And very successfully too," she added.

Monsieur leaned forward to place his hand on hers.

"We were but lambs sacrificed for the king's alliances, madame," he said with a sigh. "Arranged marriages for royals can be so insufferable."

She drew her hand away. "No, Monsieur, you have never once suffered."

"Madame?"

"You've yearned for nothing but eating, drinking, and wallowing in debauchery."

Monsieur smirked. "Like most men at court, madame."

"But most men do not pursue virile young men or remain the slave of a certain chevalier."

Monsieur jumped to his feet. "More the reason for you to remain by my side. Just think of the rumors!" He paced back and forth. "And forget not, madame, that I've given you two sons who will need your care and guidance."

"Yet nothing is too expensive for your pleasures. While our children lack what they need. What I need."

"But you are well fed, madame."

Elizabeth chuckled. "The courtiers say I would be as tasty as a roasted suckling pig!" she said, her smile quickly disappearing. "But that is not what I need, Monsieur. I've endured your male favorites and their obscenities for way too long."

"Well," he said, "an heir is secured. Perhaps it is time to have our own households."

"I would certainly not be doleful...if we no longer shared the same bed."

"And I would have my freedom," he said with a grin, "from that wretched aroma of sauerkraut and sausage."

"And no more vultures flying in circles above our bed," she said, trying not to laugh.

Monsieur rose from the chair, peeked at his newborn son, and bowed to take his leave. "Good night, madame."

"Monsieur, another matter if I may."

He stopped in his tracks.

"There are rumors that your Chevalier de Lorraine aims to corrupt your nephew, the Count of Vermandois, to spite the king. The chevalier has never forgiven the king for sending him to prison and banishing him from court for several months."

"Madame" —he turns toward her— "from whom do you hear such tales."

"I have many ears in the corridors of Saint-Cloud," she said. "Do I need to remind you that *junger* Louis is still His Majesty's son."

"His Majesty's bastard, madame," he said. "He contaminates the royal bloodline, and he could threaten our own son's right to the throne."

"I abhor the thought of kings having children out of wedlock, but the *junger* Louis is a bright lad. When he was abandoned by his mother, the king trusted us with his upbringing."

Monsieur threw his hands in the air. "Madame," he said. "I will speak to the chevalier. Adieu."

"And tell your mignons to mind their own sheep too!"

Monsieur left her chambers, shaking his head. "Imperious *frau*."

"I have ears too!" she snapped.

~ ~ ~

Giving birth to a prince didn't keep Elizabeth from supervising her household and enjoying her daily routines at Saint-Cloud. If she wasn't in her study writing letters to family in Germany, she was taking her well-talked-about rugged walks in the nearby wooded park, riding horseback, or joining the king for the royal hunt. She also kept an eye on Louis, receiving periodic reports from Abbé Fleury. Having heard that Louis was prone to laziness, she sent her maid-of-honor, Duchess de Ventadour, whom she affectionately called *la belle Doudou*, to summon Louis to her chambers.

Half an hour later, Louis arrived to find Elizabeth sitting in her armchair. "Why the delay, *junger* Louis?" she asked.

"He was still in his bed, madame," Doudou answered for him as he wiped the sleep from his eyes.

"At this time of day?" she snapped. "I've had the most disturbing news. Abbé Fleury tells me that you are passionate about music and dance, but lack any interest in languages, the musket, or equestrian skills. That is going to change immediately! Are you not the Admiral of France?"

"Yes, Aunt Liselotte, but..." He hesitated.

"But what, Louis?"

"If I am the Admiral of France, why don't I live at Versailles? Like my brother, the dauphin?"

Elizabeth motioned Louis to sit with her. "Doudou," she said, "bring us some chocolate."

The thought of chocolate didn't change the sober look on his face.

"Louis, there is a reason why you don't live at Versailles. Your mother was the king's first official mistress. You and your sister were the first living illegitimate children of the king."

"Illegitimate?"

"Children born to parents out of wedlock are called illegitimate," she said, "or sometimes called bastards."

Louis frowned.

"Your mother and the king were never married like the king and queen. Or like Monsieur Philippe and me. So, you and Marie-Anne are not full-blooded royals. Do you understand?"

When he nodded, she added: "That is why the dauphin remains at court."

"And my sister?"

"Marie-Anne officially lives in Paris, but she spends much time at Versailles. She has a role to play at court."

Louis frowned. "I don't understand."

"She helps the king entertain his guests at court," said Elizabeth, happy that Doudou arrived with the chocolate and hoping it would change the subject.

"And why did my mother leave Versailles?" he asked.

"She was ashamed, Louis. Before you were born, you had two brothers who died very young. By the time you were born, the king was interested in another mistress, Madame de Montespan. Her children, like you, cannot live at court. It is too painful for the queen."

Louis stared at the floor.

"But your *belle maman* still loves you very much. And *belle* indeed. She was a beautiful young maiden who charmed the king. She was the envy of all the grand dames at court. I was not here but your mother was Madame Henriette's first maid of honor."

"Madame Henriette?" asked Louis.

"Your uncle's first wife, who died from... well, some say she was poisoned. Anyway, your mother was kept very busy as the king's mistress. When you and your sister were born, the king asked Madame and Monsieur Colbert to care for you and keep your identity secret far from the court. Years later, to reward Louise for her fidelity, the king legitimized you and Marie-Anne."

"Legitimized?"

"Yes, he publicly acknowledged that you and your sister were his children, giving you some rights at court," she said, motioning for him to fix his collar. "You were also even given the title of Admiral of France, so you cannot be so idle with your studies."

Elizabeth got up, walked to the windows, and opened them. "And enjoy nature, Louis. Courtiers may frown but I'm happiest when walking in the gardens, exploring the woods, or wading in the river. You have everything here at Saint-Cloud. Take advantage of the freedom that your brother, the dauphin, does not have at Versailles."

Just as Louis took his leave, there was a knock on the door and Elizabeth's doorman announced the arrival of Monsieur, who entered with two of his mignons—all dressed in women's gowns.

"Madame, need I remind you that the king will visit Saint-Cloud tomorrow?" said Monsieur.

"Not at all. He is very interested in seeing the progress of the work in the château."

"Ha! It is more likely that he wants to visit one of your ladies-in-waiting, the pretty Mademoiselle Fontanges."

Elizabeth grinned. "She is as pretty as an angel, but still such a stupid little animal."

"It is said, madame, that you only pick the loveliest of ladies-in-waiting in order to attract the king to Saint-Cloud."

"Unfortunately, Monsieur, you are no help in such a matter," she said, glancing at his mignons. "My favorites attract kings; your favorites attract flies."

Dismissing Elizabeth's sarcasm and her boisterous laugh, Monsieur and his entourage left the room.

~ ~ ~

The next afternoon, the coaches of the king, the queen, and the dauphin arrived in the courtyard of Saint-Cloud. Just inside the entrance of the main hall, Monsieur, Madame Elizabeth, Count Louis, and members of the court, including the chevalier and the mignons, waited patiently. When the king and his entourage entered the hall, Monsieur greeted his guests and personally escorted them to the most elaborate wing of the château, beginning with the corridor lined with allegorical statues.

"Eloquence… Music… Youth… Beauty… Dance… Fortune… Peace… Virtue," said Monsieur as he passed by each gracefully carved white marble sculpture. He then led his guests up the steps to the second floor to visit the newly decorated Mars salon.

The king must have noticed the difference between his Versailles and Monsieur's Saint-Cloud. Where Versailles's decor was solemn and academically mythological, Saint-Cloud's was lyrical, elegant, and Italian. Monsieur pointed out the smallest details of the redecoration to his guests, and the king was attentive to his every word.

After the tour of the Apollo salon, Elizabeth raised her eyebrows as if to ask the king for his opinion of the work.

"I hope you find my sculptures and portraits at Versailles as beautiful as these here," said the king. He then looked at Louis. "What do you think, Count Louis?"

Having been ignored by his father since his arrival, Louis was caught off guard by his father's sudden remark. "It is difficult to say, Father," he said. "They are all beautiful."

The king nodded but did not appear too pleased with Louis' answer.

Elizabeth noticed the puzzled look on Louis' face. "Count Louis, why don't you have refreshments in the garden," Elizabeth said and then turned to the king. "We are expected at the gaming tables, sire."

When the king took Elizabeth's arm to enter the next salon, Louis bowed and left for the garden terrace which had just been embellished with iron railings and trellises intertwined with vines and blooming morning glories. Louis had never noticed how the splendor and order of the garden complemented the rest of the magnificent residence. But, not knowing many of the courtiers on the terrace, he felt alone until he noticed the chevalier and several mignons who were approaching him.

"It's a big occasion when His Majesty visits Saint-Cloud, Count Louis," said the Chevalier de Lorraine.

"Yes, but he seems very busy," Louis mumbled.

"Well, he'll be here for two days," said the chevalier, motioning one of the mignons to step forward. "Count Louis, this is the Marquis de Châtillon."

"The sun is quite hot this afternoon," said the marquis, pulling a kerchief from his vest to wipe his brow.

Louis admired the clothing of both chevaliers, especially their embroidered justaucorps with the wide turned-back cuffs of lace.

There was a time when the Marquis de Châtillon didn't have a single coin in his pocket. He earned small coins for watching nobles' clothing while they bathed in the river. Until, however, Monsieur was taken by his handsome traits and his gentle manner and took him under his wing, lavishing expensive gifts on him. Moreover, Monsieur made him the captain of his guards with a generous pension.

The chevalier looked at the marquis, prompting him to continue. "What a perfect time for a walk through the shaded woods to the river."

Louis smiled, hoping he would be invited.

"By all means," said the chevalier. "I cannot join you, but I'm certain that Count Louis would like to join you."

Louis nodded. "Yes, please."

"Very well, gentlemen," said the chevalier. "Please escort the count and make sure he returns safely before the banquet."

Louis had had very little contact with Monsieur's mignons, but he enjoyed the camaraderie as he walked to the river with them. The small talk was friendly and comforting in comparison to the short, terse exchanges with his father. Once on the bank of the river, the mignons began removing their vests and breeches. Louis's face reddened and he turned his gaze away when the young men were all naked.

"Count Louis," said the Marquis de Châtillon, "are you going to join us for a quick swim?"

Louis hesitated.

"Come now," said the marquis. "We are all boys."

"And don't worry, there are no maidens to be seen here," another mignon said.

Louis looked around, removed his vest, his nightshirt, and then his breeches and silk stockings. Covering his private parts with his hands, he watched the mignons run into the water. He followed, wading slowly with the chilly water taking his breath with every step. After minutes of splashing, yelling, and frolics, the water felt warmer but there was a sudden bang in the wooded area nearby.

"What was that? Gunshot?" cried out one of the mignons with fear in his voice.

The marquis stood still for a moment and said, "Rogues in the forest." His eyebrows raised and he then motioned everyone out of the water. "We need to return to the château. Make haste and get dressed."

They all scurried to the bank and began dressing—all except Louis. He searched everywhere for his clothes, but they were nowhere to be found. When another shot was heard, the mignons ran, disappearing into the woods.

"Wait!" said Louis. "Wait on me. My clothes are gone!"

He looked around the bushes and along the sandy bank. The chevalier and mignons were nowhere to be seen, but Louis had no idea that they were peeking from behind some trees and holding their hands over their mouths to keep from laughing out loud. They quickly retreated to the château.

When the sun began to set, Louis realized the mignons were not returning, so he made his way back to Saint-Cloud, arriving at the north side of the château near the servants' entrances and the kitchens. He had broken off a limb of an oak tree to hold in front of his exposed private parts. He slowly made his way to an entrance, hiding behind a cart and then some wine barrels before finally darting for the door.

"Halt!" yelled one of the king's guards, who were posted around the château for added security during the king's visit. Another guard grabbed Louis by the arm, making him drop his camouflage.

"I live here. Monsieur is my uncle," Louis screamed, frantically trying to escape from the guard.

"A prince?" The guard shook his head in disbelief.

"And a dirty one at that… with no clothes," said the other guard as he took Louis' other arm.

"Let go of me," Louis cried. "My father is the king."

When one of Monsieur's valets in the servant's entrance noticed Louis struggling with the guards, he quickly chastised them. "Gentlemen, that is Count Louis. He's *truly* Monsieur's nephew. You must release him."

The guards' jaws dropped as the valet removed his cloak and wrapped it around Louis' bare shoulders.

"Leave us now and there will be no mention of this misunderstanding."

The guards bowed as the valet discreetly escorted Louis into the château through the servant entrance. Unbeknownst to Louis, the chevalier and mignons had observed the entire brouhaha from a second-floor window.

"Well done, comrades," said the Chevalier de Lorraine in a conniving manner. "We almost got the impersonator a night in the dungeon."

"You will never forgive the king, will you?" said the Marquis de Châtillon.

"Never," said the chevalier. "This boy will be a shameful mark on the king's legacy. He's not even the king's real son."

The marquis' brow wrinkled. "Did you perchance start that rumor?" he asked.

The chevalier sported a proud grin. "The court can be so dull at times."

~ ~ ~

The next morning, Elizabeth heard the rumor circulating the court about the trick the mignons had played on Louis.

"Doudou," she said, "it is time that Louis learned his lesson. He should know better than to associate with such creatures. Inform the stable master that I should like to see him."

"Yes, madame," said Doudou. "I'll go now."

~ ~ ~

Doudou returned with the stable master, a short man with thinning grey hair and a pale face covered with red blotches. His small black eyes could scare the bravest of men. He bowed in Elizabeth's presence. "Guillaume Joubert, madame duchess, at your service," he said.

"Monsieur Joubert," said Elizabeth, "I need a whipping boy to be punished for the *junger* Louis de Bourbon's transgressions—in his presence, of course. Being His Majesty's son, he cannot be punished. His royal status far exceeds that of anyone at court."

"And you would like me to provide you with a whipping boy, madame?"

"Yes, I understand you have been the stable master for many years and can perhaps provide us with someone."

"Madame, as Monsieur Philippe's stable master for many years, I am known for being vigilante, careful, and inflexible with the rules. It is necessary to maintain my authority over a troop of unruly stable boys. I grant none of them any favor, but I believe my foster son, Marcel Joubert, would be a good choice."

"Monsieur, stable boys come and go, but I need someone reliable who can also keep an eye out for *junger* Louis and keep me informed of his wiles."

"Madame, Marcel would be reliable. He has his own lodging in the stable for better security of the horses...but it also deters boys from seeking employment elsewhere."

"Very well, kind sir. Please let him know that I will visit the stables at two o'clock this afternoon to speak with him. If he is satisfactory, you will be well compensated. It could also be his first step in the ladder of preferment."

~ ~ ~

Not expecting him to be on time when the clock chimed twice at the stables, Elizabeth leisurely paced back and forth outside the carriage room. Stable boys can be so unreliable, she thought. But to her surprise a young lad arrived precisely at two o'clock. He dismounted and bowed.

"With your permission, madame duchess," he said, "just a second to give him some oats before I brush him."

"Of course, *junger Mann*." Elizabeth remembered him from the hunt with Louis at Versailles. She wondered if he was really a stable boy. He was well-groomed, and his linen vest and breeches were unsoiled.

*Something is not quite right*, she thought.

She entered and looked around the well-swept, orderly stable. The boy's muddy boots were neatly placed by the door, and all the stable's tools were hanging on the wall—even the stable broom and pitchfork. From the loft came a fresh breeze through an open door with the sweet aroma of sun-soaked grasses.

The boy hung his empty bucket on a rusty hook, brushed the chaff off his vest, and bowed again. "Madame, my name is Marcel Joubert. I would be honored if I could be Count Louis' whipping boy."

*Stable Stalls*

"No, Monsieur Joubert." Elizabeth shook her head. "No, I presume the honor will be ours."

Minutes later, Abbé Fleury arrived with Louis by his side.

"*Junger* Louis," said Elizabeth. "This is Marcel, your whipping boy. Abbé Fleury will punish him for your shameful escapade last evening."

Louis turned pale. The same boy that joined him hunting at Versailles was about to be whipped for his own mistakes. When Abbé Fleury snapped his thin leather strap and approached Marcel, Louis fell, swooning to his knees with a gasp.

"Have mercy, Aunt Liselotte!" Louis cried, clasping his hands together as if praying. "Forgive me. Please don't punish him. I am very sorry. It wasn't his fault. I am the only one to blame."

Elizabeth looked at Abbé Fleury, biting her lip to keep from laughing. "What do you think, Abbé Fleury? Do you think *junger* Louis has learned his lesson?"

When Abbé Fleury nodded, doing his best to hold back a smile, she turned back to Louis. "Now, off with you both," she said. "The next time, I promise you will not be so fortunate."

~ ~ ~

During Louis' first year at Saint-Cloud, there was no next time. In fact, he and Marcel befriended each other, walking and exploring the willow-curtained riverbank of the Seine. But it wasn't easy becoming fast friends.

After running down a small grassy knoll one day, they fell to the ground and lay on their backs. Louis closed his eyes and inhaled deeply, savoring the pungency of the fresh-cut straw from a nearby field. He could tell that passing clouds were intermittently blocking the sun, because his skin tingled from the slight chills that came and went.

"It would be fun to go wading," said Louis.

"Don't you need to get ready for dinner?"

When Louis hesitated, Marcel stood up. "I'm not ready yet for a taste of the abbé's strap."

Louis acquiesced with a grin and got up. Marcel was right. He was expected to be on time for dinner today. His Aunt Liselotte and Monsieur had attended a ceremony at his mother's convent, where Louis' mother finally pronounced her vows as a Carmelite nun.

Louis and Marcel returned to the château, fantasizing about being Perceval and Galahad. They chatted about crusades they would go on and the damsel in distress they would rescue along the way, but their discussion was cut short when a stable boy on horseback approached the boys from behind. Marcel raised his hand for the rider to stop and he took the reins, patting the horse's neck.

"Come, Marcel," said the boy, "ride back to the stables with me on the new stallion."

Marcel nodded and mounted the horse behind the boy.

"Marcel, don't go," said Louis.

But to no avail. Marcel held onto his friend as the horse galloped away. And, on the way back to the château, Louis experienced a sinking feeling in his stomach.

~ ~ ~

The dinner table, as usual, was dominated by Elizabeth's boisterous voice. "The whole court, *junger* Louis, was amazed at the tranquility and joy of the occasion today," she said. "And your mother, the angelic Sister Miséricorde, with her radiant face… I shall always remember it."

Louis' eyes begged to know more.

"When she took the veil, Abbé Bossuet spoke beautifully about the weak and tormented woman who had been unhappy for such a long, long time."

"Was my father there?"

"No," interrupted Monsieur, "that would not have been proper for such a ceremony. Children were not permitted either."

"But Queen Marie-Thérèse did attend," said Elizabeth. "She was so sympathetic. She wasn't there to forgive or to humiliate an old rival but to honor Louise's penitence."

"In fact," added Monsieur, "Louise received the veil from the hands of the queen."

"And then?" asked Louis.

"The abbé's words to your mother were memorable: 'And you, my sister,' he said, 'who have begun to taste the chaste delights of divine love, come to the altar, and complete your sacrifice. The fire is lit, the incense is ready, and the sword is drawn. By wrapping yourself in this veil, you will live hidden from yourself, escape from yourself, and take such noble flight, that you will find rest only in the Father, of the Son, and of the Holy Spirit.'"

"That was beautiful," said Louis, hoping that the story would soon end.

"Yes, so beautiful that the congregation trembled," said Monsieur. "All foreheads bowed down and everyone was afraid when he said, "Go down to the altar to complete your sacrifice, the fire is lit, the incense is ready, the sword is drawn."

"Your mother became all white and all pale, but stronger than any of those who were there," said Elizabeth. "She walked valiantly to the sacrifice. The archbishop took a few steps to meet her, and she knelt, kissed the earth, and received the consecrated veil. When she spread it like a shroud over her body, you could hear the most mournful cries."

"But Sister Louise of Mercy did not cry, Louis," said Monsieur.

"No," said Elizabeth. "When the archbishop asked her what she was asking for when she prayed, she said. 'The mercy of God, the poverty of the order, and the company of the sisters.'"

Louis continued listening, but his mind was elsewhere.

"She then raised her eyes to the sky," continued Elizabeth. "'It is there,' she said, 'that I must fix my gaze! My soul detaches itself from it in this life, to enjoy its divine nature and its immortality.'"

Monsieur stood up. "She then crossed the space that had separated her from God." He then patted Louis on the shoulder and left the room.

Louis was exhausted after hearing about his mother's ordeal.

"Are you not proud of your mother, Louis," said Elizabeth. "She's truly a saint."

"Yes, Aunt Liselotte," he mumbled.

"What is wrong, *junger* Louis?"

"It's Marcel. He would rather spend time with other boys in the stable."

"I know your cousins at Saint-Cloud are too young to be companions, but you enjoy your time with Marcel, don't you?"

"Yes, Aunt Liselotte."

"Well, it's just a little jealousy. I call her Mademoiselle Leech because she lives off our self-esteem."

Louis flashed a smile. "Mademoiselle Leech?"

"Yes, but we are better than her. We must not let her steal our self-confidence," she said, rising to her feet. "We are too valuable for that, *junger* Louis."

Elizabeth embraced him before he returned to his chambers. After changing into his nightshirt, he climbed into bed. He felt that strange, sinking feeling begin to overtake him again, but his thoughts then drifted back to the willow trees by the river, and he imagined himself resting under one of them. He shut his eyes and almost fell asleep until he heard some splashing in the stream not far from him. He stood and peeked from behind the tree trunk. It was Marcel making waves as he bathed. Louis couldn't stop watching and he wanted to see more, but the wrinkled waters quickly lulled him into a dreamy, deep sleep.

# CHAPTER SIX

# A Day in the Life

*Academic Fencing*

"Then I uprose, showing myself provided
Better with breath than I did feel myself,
And said: 'Go on, for I am strong and bold."

— Dante Alighieri, *Inferno*

## Château of Saint-Cloud, September 1675

While Louis' valets were dressing him, Abbé Fleury perused the books on Louis' desk, as he did every morning before planning the day's lessons. When Doudou entered with a small tray of rolls and chocolate, the abbé bowed.

"Duchess," he said, "good morning."

She nodded with a big smile. "Good morning, Abbé Fleury," she said as she placed the tray on Louis' desk and turned to Louis. "Madame Elizabeth asked me to inform you that you will have a remarkably busy day today. We are expecting many visitors."

The abbé cocked his head.

"Abbé Choisy," she said, "will join us after dinner."

When the abbé rolled his eyes as if that were all, she added, "And Jean Renard, Sieur de Préville."

"Oh, marvelous!" said the abbé with sarcasm.

"Who is the Sieur de Préville, Doudou?" said Louis.

The abbé spoke up. "You will meet him, Count Louis, in due time." He turned back to Doudou. "Madame, I understand the Duke de Ventadour is also visiting today."

"Yes, abbé," she said, shaking her head in dismay. "My husband must have a reason for such an unexpected visit."

"We all hope it is only good tidings, duchess," he said with a bow as she left the room. He then picked up a book from Louis' desk and said, "Let us begin with Latin today."

Louis frowned. He had hoped to read selections of his favorite works from Rabelais and Perrault or any knightly adventures. Impatient for the moral of the story or just lazy, he abhorred reading books in other languages. After they spent most of the first hour conjugating verbs in Latin, the abbé wrote a sentence on parchment and read it aloud. "*Scio praecipuum officium Principis christiani esse colere Deum et pietatem esse fundamentum omnium uirtutum regiarum.*"

He handed the parchment to Louis. "Let us finish our lesson today, Count Louis, with very important vocabulary. *Praecipuum*—principal, *officium*—duty, *Principis*—prince, *christiani*—Christian, *colere*—serve, *fundamentum*—foundation, *omnium*—all, *uirtutum*—virtues, *and regiarum*—royal."

The abbé prompted Louis to read the sentence in Latin and then he translated it. "I know that the main duty… of a Christian Prince is to serve God and that… piety is the foundation of all… royal virtues."

"Well done, Count Louis," came a voice from the doorway. "Your father would have been elated to hear you speak so eloquently."

"Monsieur Lully," said the abbé, as he gathered up his materials. "I'm certain that Count Louis is happy to see you… and your…"

"My page, Lefarge," said Lully. "He will assist me today."

Lefarge clicked his castanets.

Louis closed his Latin reader and jumped up from the table. "Yes, I am ready, Monsieur Lully!"

"I will see you when the clock strikes eleven, gentlemen," the abbé said as he exited the chambers.

"Count Louis," said Lully, as he prepared his violin. "I told Monsieur Colbert how well you are doing in your dance lessons. He asked me to give you his warmest wishes."

"Thank you, Monsieur Lully," said Louis, proud that his praise was being shared with others.

"I've been very happy with your steps and especially your *pas d'expression*. Today, Lafarge will accompany me with the castanets for rhythm to help with stylizing your arm movements and upper torso. We need to focus on your wrists, as well, and the placement of your fingers."

Louis loved dancing. He not only felt socially at ease, but he enjoyed the attention. When he took a few minutes to catch his breath, he looked in the mirror and admired the muscles in his upper legs.

"Dancing, Count Louis," said Lully, watching him, "is one of the most excellent and most important disciplines for training the legs."

Louis thought of Marcel and remembered his muscles outlined under his threadbare nightshirt. Louis pointed to his torso and his arms. "And here too?"

"No, it is not becoming of young nobles to become too muscular. Only peasants who work the land get such muscles. You do not want courtiers to think you perform such tasks beneath your rank, do you?"

"No, Monsieur Lully," said Louis, slightly disappointed.

"Do not worry, Count Louis, you will have a hint of muscles from your dancing and riding," said Lully as he tapped his protruding belly. "This is more fashionable, coming from fine foods and wines."

Louis giggled when Lefarge felt his belly and, not noting any perturbance, frowned. Lully tapped his cane on the floor. "Enough, let us return to our dancing lesson."

When the clock struck eleven, the abbé, like clockwork, was at the door, prompting Lully and Lefarge to gather up their equipment and take their leave. The abbé handed Louis a towel to dry off. "Come, Count Louis, we are expected at the stables."

The abbé escorted Louis into a large room adjacent to the stables. Light from windows cast rays on the unfinished dirt floor. The only furniture in the space was a chair, a wooden horse, and an iron stand with foils.

To Louis' surprise, Monsieur arrived with a sword in his hand, and a prominent-looking noble by his side.

The abbé bowed. "Monsieur, I believe Count Louis is ready," he said with a big smile.

"Abbé, I would like to present the count's new fencing instructor, Sieur de Préville," said Monsieur as he stepped forward to present Louis with a sword. "This is a gift from the king, Count Louis, but just having a sword is not enough; it is even more important that you know how to handle it masterfully."

Louis held the sword with wide eyes. He had never received a gift from the king.

"For that reason," he continued, "I've invited one of our most honored fencing instructors to join us. He was ennobled by the king for his fencing skills."

Sieur Préville approached Louis and took the sword from his hand. "We will begin slowly, Count Louis," he said. "It is necessary that we proceed from the simple to the complex, because I must adapt to the temperament, disposition, and intelligence of my students."

Louis could not take his eyes off the silver gilt sword adorned with a portrait of the king on the guard. No, it was a portrait of his own father.

"And the study of the rules of honor too, Sieur Préville," said Monsieur. "There are rules that must be followed during fights and battles. After all, fencing has always been an art for those with honor and dignity."

Sieur Préville nodded in agreement and turned to Louis. "Your first lesson today, Count Louis, will be the manner of holding the sword." He took Louis' hand.

"Put the handle in your right hand with the thumb extended above and your other four fingers together underneath."

Louis followed his instructions and looked up for approval.

"That's correct," said Sieur Préville. "Now hold the sword with the thumb and index finger only. Let your other fingers push constantly on the handle. Only squeeze the handle when you are ready to deflect or block an incoming attack."

Monsieur adjusted the sword in Louis' hand. "Just push with your fingers. If you squeeze the sword constantly, you will be forced to execute with the wrist and not the fingers."

"Listen closely to your uncle, Count Louis," said Sieur Préville. "He has mastered the sword in many battles."

After an hour of learning different stances and the importance of footing, Louis was sweating through his tunic. Although he had enjoyed his dance and fencing lessons immensely, he was exhausted and hardly had enough time to wash his face and change his clothes before dinner. And afterwards. Doudou escorted him into the salon, which was busier than usual today and where her husband awaited her.

"Count Louis, I present my husband, the Duke de Ventadour and Governor of Limousin."

When the duke greeted him, Louis was lost for words. The man was physically deformed, and Louis had no idea that his complexion had been ruined by bouts of venereal disease due to his numerous sexual escapades. The difference between him and Doudou was startling. Hopefully, he thought, the privilege of being a duchess compensated for the unfortunate match.

The duke turned away from Louis and frowned at his wife. "I've heard the most disturbing gossip at court, duchess," he said. "It appears that when Monsieur rises in the morning with his favorites, they speak about nothing but their escapades with young cadets of the guard... like a gaggle of infatuated girls."

"Duke, when the rumor reached the king's ears, those cadets were immediately reprimanded and sent away from court," she said, her face reddening. "And I beg of you, please, in the presence of Count Louis, do not speak of such matters."

"Of what matters, madame duchess," said Monsieur as he passed by with an elegantly dressed woman.

Doudou curtseyed. "Oh, petty matters, Monsieur."

Monsieur nodded. "May I present an old friend, a writer, a priest, and a diplomat?" he asked. "This is François-Timoléon de Choisy, Abbé Choisy." He turned to the abbé. "I'm so happy you accepted our invitation to come to Saint-Cloud."

"Oh, but the pleasure is mine," said the abbé, noticing Louis admiring his white dress with gold flowers, his rose-colored ribbons, and his sparkling diamond necklace.

"Abbé Choisy, this is Count Louis of Vermandois, Admiral of France," said Doudou.

"Finally, we meet, but please don't look so surprised," said the abbé. "Monsieur has asked that I come dressed *en femme*."

The duke shook his head in disbelief. "*En femme*?"

Monsieur jumped in. "Because I wore earrings, blush, beauty spots, ribbons and even wigs as a child, the abbé's mother chose to dress him as a girl and introduce him to the court. That's how we met."

"Yes, indeed," said the abbé." In fact, my mother pierced my ears and accustomed me to women's clothes."

"And when his mother died, he inherited her wardrobe and jewelry," added Monsieur.

"The desire to be beautiful seized me with fury. I had magnificent clothes made and I put on beautiful earrings," he said, adjusting one of his diamond earrings. "The coquettish airs, the little faces, nothing was forgotten. I thought I was lovable, and I wanted to be loved."

"We both dressed lavishly whenever we visited each other," said Monsieur. "But I must admit that your couture always caused me to be somewhat jealous."

"Oh, I was jealous too," laughed the abbé. "I always wanted to be as beautiful as the Duke d'Orléans."

"We were both rivals when it came to coquetry," said Monsieur.

"We still are. Look at our skin, it's still as pale as new cheese."

"Fortunately, we wore masks or had parasols whenever outside… so fearful of getting tanned skin," said Monsieur. "To this day, I still avoid the hunt."

"But why, Uncle Philippe?" said Louis, still enthralled by the abbé's elegance.

"It is not just a standard of beauty, Count Louis, but it concerns rank and wealth."

"Indeed," added the abbé. "Pale skin, untouched by the sun, is equivalent to the luxury of not having to move a finger." He glanced at the duke's complexion. "Tanned skin is very peasant."

The duke snapped back, "Trust me, abbé, I'm only outside when riding and hunting."

Monsieur winked at the abbé and excused himself, promising to return before the music started.

"Ah, life is delicious," said the abbé. "Do you not agree, monsieur duke?"

"I must admit, sir or madame—I have no idea how to call you—that you are beautiful. But truly, are you not ashamed to wear such clothing to look like a woman, especially at court and in front of the young count? You do not appear to be in the least embarrassed?"

Doudou's face reddened.

"You should leave the salon, monseigneur Abbé," the duke continued. "I am certain that Count Louis finds you quite appalling."

"That is not true!" said Louis, his eyebrows pulled down. "And very impolite! Forgive me, I find her as lovely as an angel."

The abbé's eyes shined when hearing the compliment, which only exasperated the duke even further.

The duke said, "Au revoir," and turned abruptly to march to the other side of the salon to speak with Elizabeth.

Louis quickly realized from the duke's gestures that he was relaying what had just transpired. Elizabeth's jovial demeanor changed. Minutes later, she and the duke joined Doudou, Louis, and the abbé. When the abbé curtseyed, Louis giggled.

"*Junger* Louis!" snapped Elizabeth.

"Oh, no need to chastise him, Madame Elizabeth," said the abbé. "He is a lovely child." He then turned to Louis. "I knew your mother before I traveled to Italy, and I can see her angelic features in your face."

"But you will apologize to the Duke de Ventadour, *junger* Louis," said Elizabeth. "You must always show the utmost respect for our nobles."

Louis lowered his head. "Monsieur duke, I am sorry."

The duke did not reply, causing Elizabeth to break the ice-cold silence. "We are happy to see you at court, monsieur duke. You must have business in Paris, I presume?"

"No, madame, I am taking Doudou back to our estate in the country."

"Monsieur?" she said, looking at the pained look on Doudou's face.

"My decision is made," he said, bowing to take his leave from the salon.

Louis watched Elizabeth play cards. The gathering was festive and boisterous—until everyone spotted Monsieur returning to the salon. Escorted by the Chevalier de Lorraine, Monsieur was now dressed in a luxurious gown, high-heeled shoes, and a black wig with long wavy curls.

Louis didn't recognize his uncle at first but when he did, he couldn't believe his eyes.

"Ach, mein God," said Elizabeth under her breath when her husband approached her.

"Madame," said Monsieur, "I do not mean to disturb your game, but the chevalier and I are going to dance the minuet. I hope you will enjoy it!" He then took the chevalier's arm and nodded for the small orchestra to play.

"My dear Doudou, please show Count Louis to his chambers," said Elizabeth. "I believe he has seen enough today."

"Yes, madame," said Doudou, with a smile that didn't quite reach her ears.

"And please know I will do all in my power to keep you here at Saint-Cloud."

Doudou curtseyed, took Louis' hand, and escorted him out of the salon.

Louis noticed Doudou wiping tears from her cheeks as they made their way through the busy salons, so he was not surprised that they first stopped in her chambers for a dry kerchief. She looked in the mirror and, noticing the need to powder, she sat down at her dressing table.

Louis stood next to her, looking at her in the mirror. "I will speak with my aunt Liselotte," he said. "She will not let him take you away."

She took his hand. "No, it's not necessary, Count Louis," she said. "You will one day learn the extent of men's power over the fairer sex."

At that moment, her husband entered. "A moment in the antechamber, madame," he commanded. She quickly obeyed.

When the door closed behind them, Louis gazed into the mirror and admired his pale skin. Seeing the pot of powder on Doudou's dressing table, he picked up a powder puff, dipped in it the powder and brushed his face lightly. Pleased with the effect, he dipped his finger in her pot of rouge and dabbed some on his cheeks, rubbing it in circles and then painting his lips with the remainder on his fingertips.

When he heard a commotion in the antechamber, he darted out of the room for his own chambers. Once there, he shut the door, removed his clothes, and wrapped a bed cover around him like a Greek goddess. Just like those he'd admired in his history books.

In the mirror, he saw a pretty girl. Prettier, he thought, than his sister, his uncle, and even the grand dame, the Abbé de Choisy. He wondered, too, what Marcel would think. He then pulled off his toga, scrubbed his face to remove all the evidence of any rouge and powder, and climbed into his bed. A montage of the day swam through his mind. They exhausted him, and he sank into a deep sleep.

# PART TWO

# HUNTING FOR PREY

# CHAPTER SEVEN

# The Leader of the Pack

*Chevalier de Lorraine*

> "O human race, born to fly upward, wherefore
> at a little wind dost thou so fall?"
>
> — Dante Alighieri, *Inferno*

## Château of Saint-Cloud, March 1676

Louis grew accustomed to his daily routines, and he showed great interest in his morning history lessons. Sitting in his chambers, he listened quietly but attentively to Abbé Fleury's lectures about the lives of his royal ancestors. His was known to be pensive but because he was detached from his mother, his sister, the Colbert family, and his father, the abbé might have wondered if Louis was immersing himself in the stories to escape his solitary world.

"Emperor Charlemagne's son, Louis the Pious, was also called Louis the Debonair," said the abbé.

"You mean he was charming, monseigneur?" asked Louis.

"Yes, but not in a way befitting a true prince. He was born with Christian virtues, yet he neglected his duties as a sovereign. He destroyed all the work his father had invested in him."

"How so?"

"The prince was weak of character, indecisive, and too concerned with minutiae and trifles. Due to his personal failings, his father's empire disintegrated into independent territories and lordships."

"Then why was he called the Debonair?"

"The name Debonair suited him. He was esteemed and loved by his people."

"Like my father?"

"Yes, but unlike your father, Louis the Debonair was a weak prince."

"So, what makes a great prince," asked Louis.

"Personal virtues of generosity, mercy, humanity, and piety."

"Even at war?"

"Even at war," said the abbé. "That's where a prince can display his virtues and win glory."

"So, my father must be a great prince."

"Yes, and your uncle, too."

"But my uncle is—" Louis stopped, not knowing how to say what was on his mind. He thought of his uncle helping Aunt Liselotte with her toilet, arranging the jewels on her dresses and choosing her accessories—just as he did for himself.

"Your uncle is a very capable military commander," said the abbé. "Despite appearances, Count Louis, he has served in the French Army as the king's second in command in many campaigns."

Louis was baffled how his uncle could be an honored soldier and still dress in women's gowns. He wanted to ask the abbé, but something deep inside told him that some things are best not discussed.

At the end of the lesson, the abbé gathered up his books. "I believe you will join your cousins, Prince de Conti and Prince de la Roche-sur-Yon, at the king's levée tomorrow morning," he said. "And afterwards, we will play a new game that the king has acquired."

"Do you know my cousins?" he asked, blinking as if waking from a dream.

"Yes, when their father died, the king engaged me as their tutor at court."

"So, they live at court like Dauphin Louis, my brother?"

"Yes, they are orphans. Their mother died soon after their father, both at an early age."

Louis' heart sank. Distant cousins live at Versailles, but not him—a natural son of the Sun King.

~ ~ ~

Later in the afternoon, when Madame Elizabeth returned from a short visit to Fontainebleau, she discovered that her eldest son, Duke Alexandre of Valois, was suffering from diarrhea and a dangerously high fever. Despite the court physicians' care and relentless bloodletting, the prince died just before his third birthday.

Louis joined the family in Elizabeth's chambers with Monsieur's two daughters from his previous marriage to Henriette. Groomed as political pawns for diplomatic marriages, the princesses had their own residence, household, and governesses. Louis seldom associated with them. Even though Elizabeth was their stepmother, he could tell that they loved her very much. They held her hand with tears in their eyes as they listened to her and watched her wring her hands.

"I don't think one can die from excessive sadness," she said, "otherwise I would certainly die. What I feel inside is impossible to describe."

Louis' eyes filled with tears too. Not because he mourned his cousin's death, but because he had never seen his Aunt Liselotte so heartbroken. In fact, he'd never seen any woman so distraught—not even his own mother when she left for the convent.

Monsieur stepped forward and kissed Elizabeth on the forehead. "Please do not torment yourself, madame. You must take particular care. You are with child."

"That is my sole consolation, along with our son, Philippe, who can now take his late brother's title of Duke of Valois."

"Absolutely not," snapped Monsieur. "The title carries an evil omen. Philippe will become the Duke of Chartres."

Louis could not understand the coldness in Monsieur's demeanor on such a grievous day. After all, Alexandre was his firstborn son, one of the two heirs to his legacy and the House of Orléans.

Elizabeth's face reddened and she stood up. "That is fine, husband, but I've just been informed that you are to return to war with the king. Is that true?"

"Yes, madame," he said. "As lieutenant general, I will lead the king's forces in the siege of Flanders."

Elizabeth returned to her chair. "I do not find any comfort in your returning to war so soon after our loss. Do you not need time to grieve?"

"Grieve? How can I grieve?" he said. "His Majesty, my own brother, refuses to maintain our deceased son's pension of over 150,000 livres a year."

Elizabeth motioned for the room to empty. "Leave me to my sorrows," she said.

~ ~ ~

Louis seldom visited the Palace of Versailles, except when the king invited him for the morning levée or Mass in the chapel on special occasions. So, he was excited to meet Abbé Fleury after Mass, who quickly escorted him to a salon in a newly constructed wing of the palace. His cousins, Louis-Armand and François, and Jules-Armand Colbert were already gathered around a large round table, admiring the board game that had just been assembled.

They all bowed to greet Louis and he returned the courtesy. "I'm happy to see you again," he said with a big smile.

"The pleasure is ours," said the older cousin, Louis-Armand, who had just turned fifteen. The handsome prince with shoulder-length black hair, a round face, and a gentle demeanor was whispering with Jules-Armand.

François, the twelve-year-old Prince de la Roche-sur-Yon, motioned for Louis to join him opposite the table from his brother. Louis immediately noticed François' dark, if not mischievous, eyes. Unlike his brother, François wore a justaucorps accented with an abundance of lace and ribbons. He resembled his uncle, Monsieur Philippe, Louis thought.

Abbé Fleury joined them. "Good, we are all here," said the abbé. "Let us begin." However, when Jules-Armand and François continued whispering to each other, he raised his voice. "Gentlemen!"

Silenced, the two turned their attention to the board game, secret smiles lifting the corners of their mouths. Louis couldn't help but notice their sly glances in his direction, as if they were jesting at his expense.

"Today, we are foregoing playing the game in Latin," he said "I would prefer that you also develop a polished proficiency in French. Remember that your education should be a practical apprenticeship of your life."

When the abbé saw François still grinning and staring at Louis, he turned to him. "But first, you must learn to be gentlemen." As soon as François' grin disappeared, the abbé continued, "You need to be capable of exercising the profession you choose." And, motioning toward the board game, he added, "And whether you choose the military or politics, a solid knowledge of the history of our kingdom is paramount."

The abbé then selected markers for his students and handed them each a stack of colorful cards, "This game honors our kings, their memorable accomplishments, the lengths of their reigns, and even the places of their burials," he said, as he showed how the game was to be played by throwing the dice and moving the markers accordingly. And, in no time, he was pleased with the enthusiasm of the players. That is, until Louis landed on the square, *King Childeric II*, causing him to lose a turn.

"Why?" he asked, pouting his lips.

"Because he was one of the do-nothing-kings," said the abbé, causing the players to chuckle.

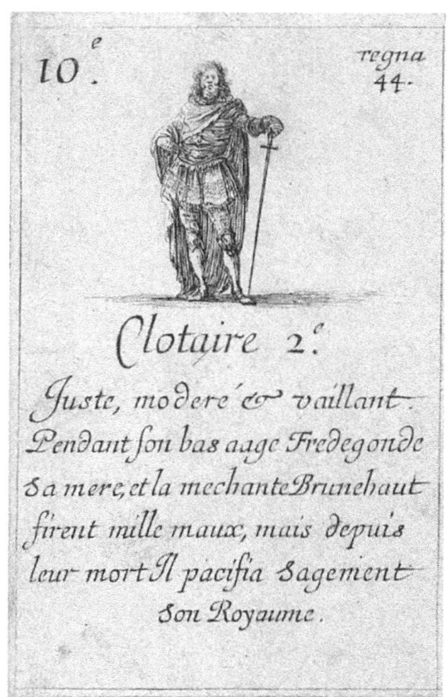


*Board Game*

When Jules-Armand landed on the square, *Saint Louis*, he was told to retreat two squares.

"*Merde alors*," he said amidst the laughter of the players. "But why?"

"Because you have to keep him company in the Sarasin prison," said the abbé. "He was captured by the Muslims on his crusade."

"Cursed," said Jules-Armand, delighting the other players with his outburst.

"And you must also pay a fine to contribute to his crusading expenses."

"Cursed," he said again, with everyone laughing that he was such a poor loser.

The joviality ended abruptly with the announcement of the king and the Grand Prince de Condé at the door. Everyone in the room came to attention and bowed. The boys were wide-eyed.

"Monseigneur Fleury," said the king, "I see your students are benefitting from the game of royal history."

"Yes, sire," he said. "And enjoying the lessons immensely… from the time of Pharamond to Your Majesty's invincible reign."

The king nodded, acknowledging the tribute, and said, "When you have declared a winner, you will join my cousin, the Great Condé, in my apartments for more games."

The king departed, leaving the boys wide-eyed.

"What an unexpected honor, students, to receive the Great Condé," said the abbé. "Such a renowned general."

~ ~ ~

Once Louis-Armand was declared the winner, to the other players' moans, Abbé Fleury escorted his students to the king's apartments where green velvet-covered game tables were set up from the salons leading to the grand gallery all the way to the chapel gallery.

Louis followed a bit behind the others, but he could hear Jules-Armand and François whispering. Suspecting that it was about him, he moved in a little closer.

"Manualization?" François asked with a mischievous grin. "What's that?"

Jules-Armand answered with a quick jiggling gesture of his hand, in front of his private parts, adding, "And his little soldier stood right up to attention. Straight up."

Louis' face reddened, but he didn't know why he was embarrassed. He cast his mind back to Jules-Armand's visits to his room at Sceaux, but he didn't know why he was embarrassed. At the time, he thought nothing about what had occurred, although he wasn't comfortable having someone's hand in his breeches. Now, he wondered why anyone would be interested in talking about it.

As the group entered the first of the game rooms, Louis' thoughts turned to the excitement at the tables, the train of servants serving wine and hors d'oeuvres, and the overpowering scent of perfumed wigs. Jules-Armand soon disappeared, leaving Louis alone with his two cousins until his sister, Marie-Anne, appeared out of nowhere. Dressed in a light cream satin gown embroidered with silver and jewels, she wore pale blue ribbons in her hair.

Louis seldom saw his sister, who spent her days either at the Colbert's small estate in Paris or at Versailles, and he was surprised to see her so elegant. Everyone at court was enchanted by her charm, so she was at His Majesty's beck and call for most social occasions. The princes bowed and Marie-Anne curtseyed, her eyes fixed on Louis-Armand, who took her arm and escorted her to the next room, leaving Louis and François together.

Although François was close to Louis' age, he looked far more mature. He had high shoulders and a way of tilting his head a little to the side, as if he were sharing a private joke with you. The ladies of the court were enamored with him, and, regarding him now, Louis could see why. He had flowing curly hair, knightly features, and large green eyes. But Louis noticed that it wasn't just the women who gazed upon François but the men, too. He was the darling of the court.

"Come, Count Louis, let's sneak some spirits," said François with his slight lisp. Louis nodded animatedly, excited to be in François's company, and they entered another salon where they found a table with rows of glasses of wine—ready for the taking. After a few sips of wine, François pointed out a young demoiselle.

Louis giggled. "Is she a boy or a girl?" he said. "She has a moustache."

François laughed so hard that the players at the game tables nearby looked up. But their frowns disappeared when they realized that it was François making the racket. That is, except the somewhat hunchbacked and graying Great Condé, who marched toward the young boys, a ferocious glare in his cold eyes.

"Prince de la Roche-sur-Yon, such noisy behavior from you is expected. But you, Count Louis, your father is the great Sun King!"

The boys bowed stiffly, the Great Condé's remarks wiping the smiles from their faces. Louis replied, "Your Highness, I would consider myself very happy if I made as much noise as you made by so many victories."

The Great Condé nodded, somewhat taken aback by the comment. When he left, however, the boys began to snicker. Louis was about to take another sip of wine when the Chevalier de Lorraine snatched the goblet from his hand.

"I heard what you said, Count Louis," he hissed. "What would the king think if he discovered his young son, Admiral of France, was drinking in excess and mocking the young demoiselles of His Majesty's court?"

The chevalier turned to François and handed him the goblet with a wink. "And you, Prince François, I see you've inherited the vices as well as the virtues of your ancestors." He leaned in and added, "But take special care when leading the king's son astray. You will need my assistance in that area."

François nodded with a grin and turned to Louis. "Come, cousin, let's find my brother and your sister," he said. "From the looks in their eyes, I'm sure they plan to unite our families."

They bowed and took their leave.

The Chevalier de Lorraine joined Monsieur at a game table.

"Careful, chevalier," said Monsieur as he watched the princes meander through the crowd to the next salon. "You're playing with fire with those two."

"You exaggerate, my prince," he said, drawing his eyebrows together.

"No, I know your type. You're like a wild beast, always ready to leap and devour your prey."

"As you well know," he said, taking Monsieur's arm. "Come, I see you've lost enough gold coins for the day. Let us hunt prey in Paris."

"Palais Royal?" he asked. "Yes, why not!" he said with a broad smile as he dragged his winnings off the table and dropped them into the chevalier's hands. "After all, we're departing for battle tomorrow."

~ ~ ~

When the king entered the salon and joined Madame Elizabeth, who was sampling the canapés at a lavishly decorated table, the Great Condé approached, looking self-important.

"Sire, I was forced to chastise the young Count of Vermandois for his brash disturbances in front of the court."

Elizabeth wrinkled her brow. "That is not like his character, Your Majesty."

"Oh, madame," he said. "I was quite taken aback by his response, too. He told me, 'Your Highness, I would consider myself very happy if I made as much noise as you made... by so many beautiful campaigns and by so many glorious victories.'"

The king laughed. "Ah, we may well make something of the boy, after all."

"Yes, certainly, sire," said Elizabeth. "He is a bright young man who, according to Monseigneur Fleury, shows great promise."

"Here comes the gentleman who is partly responsible for Count Louis' upbringing," said the king with a gleam in his eye.

Monsieur Colbert arrived and approached the king. "A private matter, sire," he said, handing the king a sealed parchment. The king moved aside to open it.

*Your Majesty, it has been some time now since I've been admitted to this pious society of chaste companions. They are young and I must respect their decency. For this reason, I can no longer see our children nor allow any correspondence with them. You can understand that the joy in seeing them only reminds me that they are the fruit of a criminal weakness—for which I still must atone. Signed, Sister Louise de la Miséricorde.*

The king folded the letter, returned it to his minister, and lifted his chin in an attempt to look confident. "Please inform Sister Miséricorde that I do not command but ask as a favor that she abandon such designs. The children's happiness, in this world and after her death, depends on her advice and moral guidance."

"Yes, sire."

"And arrange for the children to visit their mother."

"Shall I ask Madame Colbert to escort them, sire?"

"No, your good wife has been too generous in the care of the children," he said. "Madame Elizabeth shall escort them to the convent."

Monsieur Colbert bowed and left the salon.

~ ~ ~

Several weeks later, Elizabeth received a visit from Monsieur Colbert to discuss the children's visit with their mother.

"Thank you for your message from His Majesty, Monsieur Colbert, but the trip to see Sister Miséricorde does distress the poor children. She is no longer of this world, which is difficult for them to comprehend."

Monsieur Colbert stared off into space with a vacant look. "Yes, I understand, but—"

"Yes, I understand; I cannot refuse the king's request," she said. "I'll make arrangements for a coach to fetch Louis' sister tomorrow morning on our way to the convent."

~ ~ ~

Elizabeth spoke little to the king's children in her carriage. When they arrived and entered the convent gate, she produced an order from the king and the grate at the front door opened with a slow creak of the hinges. She and the children were then conducted to their mother's cell and asked to wait for Sister Louise, who was praying in the chapel.

Louis was struck by the humble and gloomy appearance of his mother's cell. Only a crucifix, a wooden chair, and a hard and narrow cot adorned the room.

"Heavens," cried Marie-Anne. "This is where Mother now spends her days?"

"Yes, mademoiselle, and we must respect your mother's decision," said Elizabeth.

Louis heard steps in the corridor. "She's coming," he said, and although he'd raised his eyes to the door in anticipation, he was still started when he saw her. Thinking she would have withered away by such harsh surroundings, he was surprised to find his *belle maman* even lovelier than ever. Her coarse robe and black veil contrasted with the fairness of her complexion and her angelic face; her piety and serenity brought a brightness to the cell.

Sister Louise approached her visitors and addressed them one at a time. "Madame Elizabeth, Monsieur Count Louis, and Mademoiselle de Blois, let us be seated." She sat on the wooden chair, motioning her visitors to be seated on the cot. Elizabeth remained standing. The few moments of silence were only broken by the sound of Elizabeth's knees cracking until she spoke up.

"You look very at ease, sister. How well you seem to get along here in this beautiful convent."

Sister Louise simply nodded and stared into the distance.

"What are you thinking about, sister?" Elizabeth asked.

She looked at Elizabeth. "What you say, madame, only reminds me of my past weakness. Had I lived in innocence… I would never have entertained the thought of coming here. Because I was powerless, I could only throw myself into the arms of God… whom I so much offended."

Elizabeth took a deep breath. "The children are doing very well. You are in their prayers."

Sister Louise glanced at them and noticed that Marie-Anne was looking at her flat and unwieldy sandals, which had cut her feet. Her ankles were bruised, and her toes were scratched red and raw.

"My daughter," she said, to divert Marie-Anne's attention, "I understand your father is selecting a future husband for you."

Marie-Anne smiled for the first time since they'd arrived at the convent. "I hope it is the person I have in mind," she said with a beaming smile.

"No matter whom His Majesty chooses," Sister Louise said sternly, "you must obey willingly."

"Yes, Belle Maman," Marie-Anne answered, her smile disappearing.

Louis sat solemnly, looking down at his hands with his shoulders drooping. "Don't you like it when we come to visit you, Belle Maman?" he muttered.

"Please understand, monsieur, that visits from the court are tedious. I long to be more severed from the memories of my past," she said. "You are minding your studies?"

"Yes," said Louis, "and I play games with my cousins, the Princes of Conti. I think my sister likes one of them."

Marie-Anne nudged him to hold his tongue, but he continued. "And François and I tease the girls at court. One has a moustache, she—"

"Louis, you must spend your time making the king proud of you," said Sister Louise, interrupting him harshly. "Such play is not befitting of a young man of your rank."

Louis' face reddened at being chastised, but he knew in his heart that his mother was right. When he nodded humbly, she got up and walked to the cell door.

Elizabeth spoke up. "Sister, is there anything you would like me to tell my brother-in-law?"

Sister Louise turned around. "No, I only speak of him to my God," she said, and she made her way down the long hallway to the chapel.

~ ~ ~

Louis sadly leaned his head against the window as the coach left the convent gates, gently rocking as it slowly made its way through the streets of Paris. Madame Elizabeth smiled at him, shut her eyes, and within minutes snored like the organ at Sceaux when it was being tuned, causing Marie-Anne to softly giggle. Louis had never known such a big-boned and awkward woman, yet he knew if he wanted to talk to her, she would answer any of his questions. But he was almost a man now. He wore breeches and he could control his emotions. Biting his lip to keep it from trembling, he refused to cry.

As the coach left the city proper, groves of graceful trees lined the road and Louis caught glimpses of the Seine and its shimmering riverbank that peeked through them. Along the way, there were also sleepy hamlets, bereft of life except for some plumes of chimney smoke and clucking chickens. Each time the royal coach passed through one, however, local boys appeared out of nowhere, whooping and hollering as they chased after it. Although they never caught up, Louis rooted for the scrappy lads with cheeks like pairs of Pippin apples. If only he could share in their jovial comradeship.

The coach soon wandered close to the river's banks as it approached Saint-Cloud. Shrubs and waving shafts of grain replaced the groves of trees and shone in the late afternoon sun. Perched on a hill and surrounded by rows of vines and shrubbery, the château's terrace overlooked the Seine with a cluster of fountains and cascades of water gushing into the air. It wasn't Versailles. But it was a little Versailles.

# CHAPTER EIGHT

# The River's Flow

*Apollo and Hyakinthus*

"And ready are they to pass o'er the river,
Because celestial Justice spurs them on,
So that their fear is turned to desire."

— Dante Alighieri, *Inferno*

## Château of Saint-Cloud, May 1677

Louis had not seen Marcel in some days, so he decided to visit the stables. When he arrived, he found him brushing a horse's mane with long, sweeping strokes.

"Good morning, Marcel. Are you always brushing your horses?"

Marcel stopped and turned to Louis. "Almost always, your highness," he said as he adjusted his sagging breeches. "It makes them happy. My father said it builds trust, too."

"Is your father here?"

"No," he said and continued brushing.

"Well, you are working. Maybe we could walk to the river another time."

"No, I'm not working today; it's the Sabbath," he said and led the horse to its stall. "I discovered a new path to the river through the woods, too."

Louis nodded, and the two left the stable. They walked to the edge of the château grounds in a silence broken by the odd rustle of leaves beneath their feet. At the entrance to the woods, Marcel looked sideways at Louis, frowning. "You are very quiet today, your highness. Are you well?"

Louis looked at the ground. "I visited my mother today."

"Where is she?"

"In a convent."

Marcel glanced at Louis with his head tilted.

"She wanted to be closer to God," said Louis. "And your parents?"

"Oh, my parents are with God. They died when I was very young."

"But your father—"

"He was killed at the Siege of Lille," said Marcel.

"But you said—"

"The stable master, who I call my father, and his wife took me in. They taught me everything I know about horses. They're good people and they don't ask me to work on Sunday."

"Your parents might be in a better place now," he said, not knowing if he should say anything at all.

As they entered the forest, the cool and quiet air reminded Louis of the musty convent with its towering damp walls. The subdued light in the woods resembled the violet rays that filtered through a convent's narrow windowpanes.

When they reached the riverbank, several village boys were nearby, getting dressed after a swim. One saw Louis and yelled, "Look, a little noble."

The others joined in, jeering and whistling until Marcel approached them with raised fists.

"If you insult him, you insult me," he said with so much vigor that the boys looked at one another, shrugged, and walked away. Louis was impressed by Marcel's gallantry, but he knew if the boys had risen to the challenge, Marcel might have gotten thrashed.

"I'm sorry," said Louis with a long face. "I should have worn my riding clothes."

When Louis turned to head back to the château, Marcel snapped. "What? So, we're not going swimming?"

Louis glanced at him and when Marcel smiled, they removed everything—but without looking at each other. Once in the water, however, Louis noticed Marcel's strong shoulders as if manhood were budding within him. Feeling close enough to Marcel to be playful, he began splashing at him. A moment later, the splashing intensified as they tried to dunk each other. Exhausted and breathless after several minutes of roughhousing in the water, they waded to the shore and walked to the grassy knoll where their clothes were scattered.

As Marcel put on his vest and pulled up his breeches, Louis stole a peek at his body, noticing muscles underneath his tanned skin. He had never seen another boy so unclothed, and he was somewhat relieved to discover another boy was also growing hair in new places.

They sat in the grass and ran their fingers through their hair to help it dry. Louis felt some color coming to his cheeks when he heard fish flapping their tails in the water nearby. It reminded him of roughhousing with Marcel in the water—the water that bound them, blessed them, and made them feel safe. Now out of the water, however, a silence numbed Louis' soul with awkward anticipation. As he dried off, the watery bond disappeared and the physical distance between them pressed on his mind. How close was too close? How far away was too far?

"Want to sleep a little in the sun?" asked Marcel.

"No," he replied quickly, before adding, "there will be news today about Monsieur's return from the war." But that wasn't the true reason for not staying at the river any longer. Louis' heart was pounding. And it pounded all the way back to the château as he struggled to answer Marcel's questions about the campaign in Flanders.

~ ~ ~

That evening in the grand salon at Saint-Cloud, Louis was all eyes and ears as he listened to the lively conversation about the war and the defining battle of Cassel.

"Let us drink to Monsieur's victory against William of Orange and the Spanish-Dutch army," said the Chevalier de Lorraine.

"You were wounded, chevalier?" said Madame Elizabeth, observing the small bandage on his temple.

"Just a scratch, madame," he said. "Monsieur's armor was hit, but he, too, was not injured. His horse, however, was killed under him."

"I am so happy that he will return tomorrow from battle," she said.

"Yes, of course," said the chevalier. "And the new addition to the court of Saint-Cloud, madame?"

Elizabeth smiled, "Her Royal Highness? She is well, thank you, and now styled as Mademoiselle de Chartres."

The chevalier leaned in. "His Majesty may not be too enthusiastic about your husband's victorious return from battle tomorrow."

"I don't expect my husband will be leading the charge of any of the king's battles in the near future."

The chevalier nodded. "Monsieur's victory certainly stole some of the king's glory."

Louis looked up at the two mignons standing next to the chevalier. He recognized the Marquis de Châtillon. "Were you on the battlefield too?" he said, eager to hear more stories.

"Yes, we all fought alongside your uncle and the chevalier, monsieur count," said the marquis, looking at Louis with a stiff demeanor.

"Please tell me more," said Louis, raising up on his tiptoes.

The marquis looked at Elizabeth for permission. She nodded.

"Well," he said, "William of Orange was leading thirty thousand Dutch troops to Saint-Omer, but he was delayed en route to Mont Cassel by a small river running through a nearby village. While not a great obstacle, the Dutch never knew about its existence and had to abandon their surprise attack. This gave Monsieur time to reorganize the lines."

When the marquis took a drink of his wine, the other mignon continued. "The next morning," he said, "William of Orange marched south to the city of Cambrai, coming face to face with Monsieur's troops. Although Monsieur was told to avoid any engagement with the Dutch, he ignored the orders and lead a heroic calvary charge. The Dutch army was routed and had to retreat. It was a heavy defeat for the Dutch."

"But your uncle," said the marquis, "followed standards of princely gallantry and sent aid and food to the survivors of William's armies. You must be very proud of him."

Louis smiled from ear to ear.

"We all are," said Elizabeth, turning to Louis. "Now, off to your chambers, *junger* Louis. Monsieur returns tomorrow and we must join the festivities in Paris with the king."

Louis could barely sleep from all the excitement.

~ ~ ~

A Mass celebrated at Notre Dame was part of the ceremony for Monsieur's entry into Paris the next afternoon. Followed by family, decorated officers and a crowd of jubilant subjects, Monsieur reached Notre Dame, dismounted, and entered the church, preceded by the clergy chanting a *Te Deum*. Troops, carrying the captured flags of Flanders with black dragons on yellow backgrounds, followed behind as the bells of Notre Dame rang out.

Louis's eyes sparkled and his face beamed when he heard the joyous cries of the people who had gathered inside the cathedral to commemorate the victory. And he couldn't take his eyes off his new heroes: his uncle, the Chevalier de Lorraine, and the mignons. They were so dignified and dashing in military regalia. The Archbishop of Paris, wearing his miter, then addressed Monsieur.

"I hasten to receive Your Royal Highness at the portal of this august cathedral, which resounds this day with the glory of France. Let our solemn thanksgivings ascend to God for the brilliant success with which He has crowned our armies. So much heroism will soon receive its recompense."

Monsieur responded humbly.

"I come here, monseigneur, to thank heaven for the triumph it has granted to our armies, for I must acknowledge that, despite the skill of our generals and the courage of our soldiers, nothing can succeed without the protection of Providence."

As Monsieur and his entourage departed, loud cries of "Victoire pour la France" greeted them from all sides.

That evening, the king and the court attended a celebratory banquet at Saint-Cloud which was followed by a magnificent display of fireworks. When Louis finally climbed into his bed, he couldn't wait to tell Marcel about the heroic warriors. He and Marcel would celebrate too. They would go to the river. They would swim again.

~ ~ ~

The next morning, when Louis' valet arrived to help him get ready for the day, Louis remained under his covers, refusing to rise.

The valet notified Doudou, who scurried to his bedside and felt his forehead for a fever. "Are you ill, Count Louis?"

When he nodded timidly, she immediately summoned the palace doctor, who arrived within minutes. He pulled the covers down to examine Louis and noticed a wet area on the front of Louis' nightshirt. He smiled with a short sigh and motioned for the valet and Doudou to leave the room.

"Count Louis, your ailment is of no concern," he said with a smile. "This is completely normal at your age. You're becoming a man when you have your first nocturnal pollution." He offered Louis his hand. "Come, rise, and get dressed. Think no more about it."

But Louis did think more about it, even trying to recreate that magical moment at the river in his mind at night before falling asleep. As a result, the mysterious explosion happened again. Twice.

# CHAPTER NINE

# Cusp of the Age of Reason

*Apartment at Versailles*

"They yearn for what they fear for."

— Dante Alighieri, *Inferno*

## Château of Saint-Cloud, October 1677

For months, Louis would toss and turn all night, dreaming of the battle of Cassell and the gallant tales he heard from the returning heroes. It was no surprise that he was groggy one special morning when Doudou tried to wake him.

"Come, Count Louis," she said. "Madame Elizabeth and Monsieur would like to see you."

"Oh, no," he mumbled.

When he didn't move, Doudou added, "Don't fret. They have a gift for you."

Within minutes, he was dressed and ready to be presented at Elizabeth's door.

As soon as he entered, a cocker spaniel puppy ran to him, jumping up and down. Louis picked up the small white ball of fur; it had a black mark around its eyes that resembled a mask.

"*Junger* Louis, Monsieur and I are giving you this new companion to celebrate your birthday."

"And our victory at Cassell," added Monsieur.

Struggling to find words, Louis let the puppy lick his face.

"You must take good care of him," Monsieur continued. "The chef has been instructed to prepare his meals."

"I will, Uncle Philippe. I promise," said Louis, his voice cracking. He touched his throat and cleared it. "I'm very sorry."

"What is wrong? Are you ill?" said Elizabeth.

Monsieur glanced at the chevalier, who responded, "Just the change, madame."

"Oh, yes, the autumn air," she said.

"No, madame," said Monsieur. "It's one of life's changes." He turned to Louis. "Don't be embarrassed, Count Louis. You're becoming a man. Your boy's voice is turning into that of a man."

"Nocturnal pollution and voice changing," said the chevalier, moving closer to Louis for a better look, "and some hair on your chin."

A flush visible in his cheeks, Louis folded his arms across his chest, wishing an end to this discussion.

"Oh, but don't worry," continued the chevalier. "It's normal. Your grandfather's first nocturnal pollution left a stain on his sheets. The shape of a pentagon. In fact, the doctors said it was a premonition of the shape of France to come."

"That is ridiculous hearsay, chevalier," said Elizabeth.

"Perhaps, but your Louis is becoming a young man," he said. "It is maybe time for him to experience the magic of the opposite sex."

"At your age, Count Louis," said Monsieur, "my brother had his first lessons from Madame de Beauvais."

"Husband, please," said Elizabeth, her neck jerking back. "Not that hunchbacked, old wench."

Louis stopped petting his puppy. His face and ears were burning.

"That old wench," said Monsieur, "earned a handsome pension and a manor in Paris for the rest of her days."

"In any event," said the chevalier, rubbing his chin, "the count here has shown no sign of attachment to any of the young ladies at court. Someone like Madame de Beauvais might open his eyes to their charms."

Elizabeth cast a glaring frown at the men and turned to Louis and the puppy. "What will you name him, *junger* Louis?"

Louis drew in a deep breath through the nose, relieved that the conversation took a turn. "He looks like a highway robber, like a little bandit," he said as he outlined the mask on the puppy's eyes with his finger. "That's it. His name is Bandit."

~ ~ ~

After his morning rolls and broth, Louis had a history lesson with Abbé Fleury. When the abbé was preparing to leave, Louis spoke up. "Monseigneur, what was the Siege of Lille?"

"A battle in Flanders in 1667, Count Louis," he replied. "Your father personally led the advance to invade the Spanish Netherlands."

"But why?"

The abbé, somewhat perplexed by the question, replied, "Because Spain had not paid him Queen Maria Theresa's dowry. So, the king felt he had the right to expand the French borders to the north."

"Was he victorious?"

"Yes, his men fought with valor."

"And the men who died in battle, what about their families?"

"War is costly, Count Louis," he said and left the room.

~ ~ ~

Louis hurried to the stables with Bandit at his side, working up a sweat in the hot autumn sun. When he arrived, Marcel had just hung a horse's harness on the wall and was grabbing a halter. When he saw the puppy, he dropped to his knees, clapping his hands. "Come here! Come here!" he said. He looked up at Louis, letting out a gasp. "What's his name?"

"Bandit."

"I can see why," he said, teary-eyed, holding Bandit up to let him lick his face.

"Aunt Liselotte and Uncle Philippe gave him to me," said Louis. "I knew you would like him."

"Are you finished with your lessons today?"

Louis nodded. "I only had a history lesson," he said, then collecting his thoughts, he added, "I asked the abbé about the Siege of Lille."

Marcel put Bandit down and stood up, his eyes narrowed.

"Your father was a hero, you know," said Louis.

"That hasn't done me any good," said Marcel with a bitter tone. "I never got to know him."

"But he died honorably, and his countrymen are in debt to him. Doesn't his reputation make you proud, Marcel?"

"Yes, I suppose."

When Marcel took the pitchfork, Louis took the hint that Marcel had to get back to work, but he hesitated and rubbed the nape of his neck. "Do you know any girls?" he asked.

Marcel's brow furrowed. "No, why?"

"The Chevalier de Lorraine says I need to meet a girl."

"Do *you* know any girls?"

Louis blushed. "Not really," he said. "Well, there's a girl at court… but she has a moustache."

"Maybe she's not a girl," said Marcel, causing the boys to chuckle.

Louis picked Bandit up. "But the chevalier said it was time for me to experience the… magic of the other sex."

"I wouldn't trust that man. The other boys at the stable don't like him."

"Why?"

Marcel, ignoring the question, leaned in and petted Bandit. "Au revoir, Bandit, I have to fetch some hay now."

"We'll come back later, Bandit," said Louis, feeling the warmth of Marcel's sweet breath on his face. "When Marcel's not too busy."

~ ~ ~

On the way to the château, Louis crossed paths with the Chevalier de Lorraine and the Marquis de Châtillon. When the marquis reached over to pat Bandit on the head, the puppy growled and nipped at his hand.

"You have a protector, I see," said the marquis, checking his hand for any marks.

"You were at the stables?" asked the chevalier.

"Yes, I like to visit the horses," Louis said. When he glanced back at the stables, he noticed Marcel watching him, before shaking his head and returning to his work. *Why doesn't he like the chevalier*? Louis wondered.

"We'll accompany you to the château, Count Louis," said the chevalier.

Louis put Bandit down and he sprang forward, chasing after a wood pigeon on the path ahead. Its wings flapping frantically, the pigeon took flight. The marquis chuckled beside Louis as they continued. "You must join us one evening at the Palais Royal in Paris, Count Louis," he said.

"Indeed," added the chevalier. "You might enjoy the baths."

Louis stopped and looked at the chevalier inquisitively. "The baths?"

"Yes, there is nothing more healthy or relaxing than lowering oneself into a steaming batch of mineral water. Great warriors have visited the baths for centuries," he replied.

Louis thought about the knights of King Arthur's court. "Even Perceval?" he asked.

"Most certainly," replied the marquis. "If I remember correctly, a most qualified man of the best manners taught Perceval about proper behavior at court, including taking a bath and getting massaged to give his bruised body some relief."

The chevalier winked at the marquis. "After a long fight or a day's ride on horseback," continued the chevalier, "it is imperative to take good care of your body."

Louis continued walking silently with Bandit at his side until they reached the château. "I would like to join you at the Palais Royal one evening," he said.

"Good," said the marquis. "We'll make all the arrangements."

~ ~ ~

Several days later, the chevalier and the marquis awaited Louis at the edge of the forest with a saddled horse. When he arrived, he shook his head. "I'm not going to ride a horse," he said. "I prefer a carriage."

The chevalier took the reins of his horse and said, "I'll hold the reins and lead you."

Louis then reluctantly mounted his ride, and the three disappeared into the dark forest. The smell of musty moss was overwhelming, increasing the apprehension of his secret excursion to Paris. He had not mentioned it to anyone. When they arrived at the Palais Royal, valets took their horses by the reins and led them away. Louis was all eyes in the midst of black-whiskered soldiers, abbés, and women of fashion. After a short walk down the Rue de Valois, the crowds diminished, and they entered a well-guarded entrance.

Once inside the simple but elegantly furnished salon with Turkish emblems on the walls, the concierge of the establishment appeared. "Good evening, messieurs."

"Good evening," said the chevalier. "A bath for the young man, followed by a massage."

"At your service," he said. "Will the water be perfumed?"

The chevalier glanced at Louis before answering, "Yes, of course, and bring us some wine."

The concierge escorted the men into a steamy room where a curly-haired *baigneur* dressed in revealing tight trousers and a short frock coat was preparing the water.

"Not too hot for the young man," the concierge said to the baigneur.

"Yes," said the chevalier. "It's his first time."

When the baigneur held up a small flask of perfumed oil with a questioning look, the concierge nodded for him to add some to the water and the aroma of honeysuckle filled the room. The baigneur then began to undress Louis, taking his vest and pulling his nightshirt over his head. When he started to undo his breeches, Louis resisted, pulling the baigneur's hands away. He had never undressed in front of strangers.

"Let him do his job," said the marquis and Louis relinquished, holding his hands over his private parts.

The baigneur motioned for Louis to sit on a settee so he could remove his stockings, and then took his arm to help him into the steaming bath. Louis grimaced as he slowly slipped into the hot water.

The marquis filled up Louis' goblet with wine. "Drink up," he said. "You'll be more at ease."

Sitting in the tub as motionless as a statue, the baigneur began scrubbing him with a sponge and soap, moving from his shoulders to his chest, to his feet, and to his legs. The chevalier and the marquis looked on, grinning at each other when the baigneur reached Louis' upper thighs. Red-faced, Louis tried to keep his private parts covered, but to no avail. The baigneur shoved his hands aside and continued.

When Louis started shivering, the chevalier refilled Louis' goblet and asked the baigneur to fetch some more hot water. But Louis fidgeted when he noticed the chevalier and marquis glaring at his body. He stood up.

"More water's not necessary," he said, stepping out of the bath with his back to the others. He quickly put on his stockings and pulled up his breeches.

"But Louis," said the marquis, "you're not finished."

"Yes, I am," he said, and he looked at the chevalier. "I would like to go home."

"But your massage?" said the marquis, glancing at the chevalier.

"That's fine, Count Louis," said the chevalier. "The first time can be overwhelming, and you look tired. We'll return to Saint-Cloud. As you desire."

Louis allowed the baigneur to help with his nightshirt and vest. After his hair was patted dry, Louis ran his fingers through it and nodded that he was ready to depart. Before leaving the baths, the chevalier said a few words to the concierge and handed him a small pouch jingling with coins.

~ ~ ~

Louis heard the church bells chime at half past three o'clock as he mounted his horse, but only after the chevalier took the reins. Although still the dead of night, the streets of Paris were beginning to come alive with merchants, who were too busy setting up their stalls to notice the three nobles. The chevalier and marquis never spoke a word on the ride to Saint-Cloud. That was fine with Louis. He was exhausted from the adventure and worried about how he would sneak into the château unseen.

Louis dismounted at the gates of the château and bid adieu to the chevalier and marquis who, after tipping their hats, turned down a narrow lane. When Louis approached the stable door, he noticed Marcel watching. He sighed heavily and thoughts scrambled through his mind, only aggravating his pounding temples more—a sudden reminder of the wine he'd drunk. *But what do I have to feel guilty about?* he thought.

Marcel was a about year older than Louis and like most stable boys at Versailles, he wore patched woolen breeches and clogs. Whenever Louis visited the stables, Marcel always pulled a vest over his sculpted shoulders, tinted by the summer sun and grime.

"I'll get a thrashing if madame finds out about your excursion," said Marcel, running his fingers through his scraggly hair.

To avoid Marcel's beady eyes, Louis flashed a quick glance at the pebbled floor. He was lost for words.

Marcel opened the gate to a stall holding a donkey and led it out.

"What are you doing?"

"It's not a good idea to have both a horse and a jackass in the same stall."

Louis removed the halter from his horse and hung it on a latch. "Why?"

Marcel tilted his head back. "A restless jackass always wreaks havoc in the stable."

"Nonsense," said Louis.

"The constitution of a good horse is like that of a man. He needs good air, good water, good food, and especially good company. Men are measured by the company they keep, *n'est-ce pas*?"

Louis rolled his eyes, knowing that Marcel was talking about the chevalier and the marquis. "A horse needs freedom," he said. "He needs to gallop... canter through the meadows..."

"Maybe, but he won't be true to himself... not without his basic needs," said Marcel, grabbing a pitchfork leaning against the wall to scoop up some hay. "Each horse must stick to his own," he continued, "and not mingle with the filth and stench of jackasses."

"You're a philosopher now?" said Louis.

"No, just a stable boy," he said sarcastically, with an upward glance.

Louis opened his mouth to retort but couldn't think of anything witty to say. "You—you're still my whipping boy."

Marcel looked at the sun rising out the stable door with an ornery grin. "It's going to be a scorcher," he said. "Shame you don't have the energy this morning for that spot on the river."

Louis motioned Marcel to help pull off his riding boots, his blood rushing in his ears. *Maybe for now*, he thought, *no answer might be the best answer*.

~ ~ ~

When Louis arrived at the front entrance of the château, Abbé Fleury was conversing with a lackey, rocking slowly back and forth with his hands behind his back. Louis took a deep breath.

"You are shirking your responsibilities, monsieur count. Madame was terribly upset this morning when she summoned me. What do you have to say for yourself?"

Louis looked to the ground.

"Come," the abbé said, "we shall all go to the stables."

Louis shuddered when he saw the birch rod in the lackey's hand. When they reached the stables, Marcel stopped unloading a cart and walked toward them. Louis couldn't bear to look into his eyes.

"Monsieur Marcel, Louis will be punished with five lashes this morning."

Louis looked at the abbé with wide eyes. "No, monseigneur, that is too harsh!" he said.

*Whipping Boy*

The abbé turned to the lackey. "At once," he said and then turned to Louis. "Or shall we make it ten?"

Louis was silent while Marcel stepped forward boldly.

"Lower your breeches and bend over," said the lackey.

Marcel didn't flinch once and as soon as the thrashing was over, he returned to the stables without a word. Struggling to hold back the tears, Louis followed the abbé back to the château with the strange sinking feeling in his stomach that cursed him at times.

When they were alone, the abbé offered Louis his handkerchief. "I'm sorry," he said. "Punishing your friend is necessary to deter you from the repetition of your faults. You understand, don't you?"

Louis wiped the tears from his cheeks and returned the handkerchief. "Yes, monseigneur."

"Very well. In the future, please remember to behave in a princely manner. Honor your rank… and give what is expected of you."

~ ~ ~

Louis had barely washed his face and changed his vest, when Doudou arrived. "Madame Elizabeth awaits you in her chambers, Count Louis."

"Is she angry?"

Doudou moved closer to him, offering a small smile. "A little, but I told her you're a fine young man. A few indiscretions can be expected."

"How did she find out?"

"Not from me. I didn't even tell her that you had not slept in your bed, because it was still made this morning."

*How could Marcel do this to me?* he thought.

When Louis entered Elizabeth's chambers, he bowed and waited to be addressed.

"*Junger* Louis, did you learn your lesson?"

"Yes, Aunt Liselotte," he said as he approached her. "I imagine that fat fish, Marcel, told on me."

"Fat fish?" she said with a grin that quickly disappeared. "It doesn't matter how I discovered your escapade. You are His Majesty's son, and you must learn to conduct yourself as such."

Louis stared down at his feet.

"And even if it was Marcel, he is not only your whipping boy, *junger Louis*, he is still your friend."

Louis didn't react.

"I'm sure the boy has not had an easy life," she said. "Speak with him and all of this unfortunate trouble will be most likely be amicably amended."

"Yes, Aunt Liselotte, I will speak with him," he said.

"And remember," she said, her tone softening. "You should never a hold a grudge against someone for doing, or seeming to do, what they cannot help… no matter who they are."

Louis bowed reverently and left for the stables, his mind whirling with conflicting thoughts of remorse, of blame, and of uncertainty. His aunt had spoken like a true Christian, but he worried that he would not be able to control the anger building up with his every step.

He entered the stable to the sound of chewing noises and tails swishing. "Did you tell Aunt Liselotte on me?" he blurted out.

Marcel squinted and replied with the heavy thump of a horse blanket being shaken.

"Why would you tell on me?" Louis said.

"I didn't. I swear I didn't." When Louis continued to look unconvinced, Marcel said, "What do I have to do to prove it to you?"

Louis was lost for words as he looked around the stable. When he saw an insect on the wall, he pointed to it. "Eat that bug."

In one fell swoop, Marcel grabbed it and swallowed it. When Louis' jaw dropped, they broke out laughing.

When they caught their breath, Louis said, "The river?"

"Why not? Just give me a minute to get some hay for the stall."

Marcel leaned a ladder against the wall and climbed to the fodder loft. Through the attic hatch, he threw down two bales of hay. As he descended the ladder, Louis noticed the red welts on the backs of his legs. A wave of guilt overcame him, and he thought back to Marcel's words about the chevalier. *But the chevalier didn't mean any harm*, he thought. *Did he?*

Marcel prepared some fresh bedding for the horses by untying the bales and spreading the straw in the stalls.

"Finished," he said. "Come to my room."

Louis had never been in Marcel's room. He expected to find dirty clothes scattered on the floor or items shoved under the bed, but the room was tidy, tidier than his own. Once inside, someone called for Marcel.

"It's the stable master," Marcel said. "I'll be right back."

Louis looked around the room and noticed a piece of yellowed parchment pinned to the wall above his friend's bed. He leaned over to read the handwritten note.

*August 1665*

*Please have mercy on this poor child. His father died in battle, and I am too sick to care for him. He is baptized, his name is Marcel, and he is ten days old. I pray that he ends up in the hands of good people who will teach him to pray and keep the Sabbath. God will reward them.*

Marcel returned, and Louis looked up at him, struggling for words.

"My mother died when I was born," said Marcel. "Just a month after my father was killed." He glanced at the note on the wall and continued. "Could you read it for me? I've forgotten exactly what it said."

Louis squinted for a moment, surprised at Marcel's request. Then he read the note.

"Thank you," said Marcel. "I only know that after I was nursed by a nursemaid who was appointed by the church, she took me to the Hospital of Found Children. But days later, she returned with her husband, Monsieur Joubert. They had decided to keep me and promised to give me an apprenticeship."

"You are very fortunate," said Louis.

"Well, they are not nobles."

"You're fortunate that they're not."

Marcel's brow wrinkled. "But Monsieur and Madame Elizabeth are good to you," he said.

Louis nodded. "Aunt Liselotte is a good person. She makes me laugh when she curses like a sailor. And she farts like one too."

When they stopped chuckling, Marcel asked, "And Monsieur?"

"He is timid, always suspicious, and easily fooled by his closest companions, his favorites who he supports and keeps at court. They hate him and treat him roughly too, so he's always in hot water with them."

"Why?"

"Because of their horrible jealousies. Even though they owe him for everything, they are always in want of new clothing, jewels, and grand carriages."

"The unkind wretches."

"And if he cannot please them, they spread the most malicious rumors about him at court."

"Ready to go?" said Marcel, removing his vest.

Louis tugged on his collar. "It's very warm in this jacket."

"You can leave it here."

When Louis took it off and handed it to Marcel, he noticed that Marcel's eyes were fixed on the medallion on his lapel. "My father gave me the title of Admiral of France when I was two or three years old."

Marcel rubbed his fingers over the shiny surface. "Gold?"

"Yes."

Marcel put the jacket on his bed and turned to Louis. "Admiral," he said, "have you been to the sea?"

"No. I'd rather be a soldier, anyway. Knighted. Like Perceval."

"Perceval?"

"A boy who met King Arthur's knights one day in the forest, in a forest like ours," said Louis, "and he decided then and there that he would become a knight too."

"Tell me more," said Marcel.

"Perceval went to King Arthur's court and, when he arrived, said, 'Beloved King Arthur, I would very much like to be one of your valiant knights.' But looking like a country dolt in shepherd's clothing, all the knights laughed at him."

Marcel was all ears.

"At that very moment," Louis continued, "the wicked Red Knight burst in, knocked all the gold plates and goblets off the table, insulted King Arthur's queen, and challenged any knight to fight him."

Marcel bumped Louis on the shoulder. "What happened then?" he asked, his face beaming.

"All the knights put on their swords and helmets. They swore they would strip the armor from the Red Night."

"And Perceval?"

"He was already outside facing the Red Knight on his donkey, screaming, 'I must have your armor!' But the Red Knight thought King Arthur had sent the court jester to insult him, so he charged Perceval and knocked him off his donkey."

"And then?"

"Perceval bounced to his feet and hurled his lance, plunging it into the visor of the red helmet. The wicked knight was dead."

"And he became one of Arthur's knights?"

"Yes. And he was given a seat at the Round Table."

Louis became silent. *Will I ever learn my place at the court of Versailles,* he thought as he left the room.

Marcel closed the door behind him. "Oh, I forgot. The stablemaster asked me to put up some tack," he said.

"Can I help?"

"No, it will only take a minute," he said, as he hung the equipment next to a stack of hay. Louis noticed that Marcel's disheveled hair seemed to disappear like blades of cut grass in front of the hay, except for several strands that were wet from the sweat on his forehead.

"To the river!" he said when he had finished.

Marcel led the way, always a few paces ahead of Louis during the twenty-minute walk. Louis didn't mind. He noticed how Marcel removed his nightshirt and stuck it in the waistband of his trousers as soon as he was far enough from the château. Louis didn't mind following Marcel, and he secretly admired how the summer sun had bronzed Marcel's rounded shoulders and statuesque back.

Louis knew they were becoming friends. But, still, Louis felt their bond had a strain of competitiveness. Not only was Marcel faster on foot, but he was also an expert rider and physically stronger. Louis was proud, however, that he excelled Marcel in fencing and dance. Louis had noticed, too, that his body was changing when he looked in the mirror. He was not as muscular as his friend, but he felt more comfortable around him; he didn't worry any more about removing his shirt in front of him.

When they arrived at the riverbank, Marcel pointed out the grassy knoll that had become their favorite spot. Once there, Marcel kicked off his clogs and stretched out on his back. The limbs of a weeping willow created a dance of shadows on his stomach that reminded Louis of a kaleidoscope. When Louis sat next to him and pulled off his boots, he noticed Marcel eyeing him. *Is he looking at my skin?* he thought. It wasn't as tanned as his, but it was soft, covered with fuzz. Like that of a fresh peach.

Marcel shut his eyes with a slight smile, as if to invite Louis to stretch out alongside him. Louis complied. This was a world without the prying eyes of the court, the servants, or even other stable boys. Louis glanced at Marcel, whose cheeks were red from the brisk walk, and his peculiar odor reminded Louis of summer fruit. His long-lashed eyes were closed, and he breathed deeply but peacefully. Louis wanted to tickle him with a blade of grass. To wake him. To make him feel what he was feeling—even though he couldn't explain why.

Then, as if Marcel could read Louis' mind, he jumped up, grabbed Louis' arm, and pulled him up. "To the water!"

They ran, laughing uncontrollably. The water refreshed their bodies. They were reborn. Soon exhausted from swimming, they retired to the knoll. While drifting in and out of their nap in the grass, time seemed to stop and only the sound of flying ducks finally woke them. They looked at each other, got up, and put on their shoes.

"It's getting late," said Louis, rubbing the sleep from his eyes.

"Race! Race back to the stables!" Marcel shouted.

They raced as if a kingdom depended on the outcome. At first, Louis was at least ten feet ahead. When he turned to laugh at Marcel, his foot caught in a tuft of grass and he fell. He was up in a moment, but Marcel had made up the difference and took the lead. Although Louis almost made up the difference, Marcel beat him to the stable door.

"You did well," Marcel said, out of breath and grinning from ear to ear.

"I was winning easily," said Louis, holding his stomach, "until I was—"

"Grassed!" said Marcel laughing.

"All the better for you," said Louis, trying not to laugh.

The sun was setting, and it was getting dark in the stable. Marcel fetched Louis' coat. "I'll light the lanterns. Do you need to wash up?" he asked.

"Better not. Doudou will be looking for me," said Louis, putting his coat under his arm. "I don't want to get into trouble again."

Marcel grinned, rubbing the back of his trousers. "Yes, please don't."

They both laughed.

Louis looked to the ground, scuffing his feet against the ground. He didn't want to leave. But he did, and after walking a piece, he turned to see Marcel, who still had an eye on him. When he waved, Marcel waved back, returning inside with a big smile on his face.

Louis' smile, however, disappeared when he caught a glimpse of the Chevalier de Lorraine and the marquis from afar. *Were they spying on him*?

~ ~ ~

For the next year and a half, Louis' daily activities were rather routine, other than occasional worries about the king's health, secret but innocent excursions to Paris with the Chevalier de Lorraine, and exploring the woods and dales near Saint-Cloud with Marcel.

The routine was disrupted one morning, however, when Louis was unexpectedly summoned to Versailles. After he entered the king's chambers, he noticed that the prudish Madame de Maintenon was standing next to his father. He bowed with reverence to both, knowing that the elderly woman was his father's new mistress. He noticed she was not as beautiful as the last mistress, her black eyes contrasting with the whiteness of her skin—like crows in the snow.

"Count Louis, my son, there are rumors about your journeys to Paris with the Chevalier de Lorraine. Unacceptable behavior for the son of a king."

"But father—"

Madame de Maintenon raised an eyebrow. "You need better surveillance, Count Louis," she said eloquently. "It is better that you remain at Versailles for the time being. You will have Monsieur Saveur as your tutor; he teaches the Princes of Conti and my charge, the Duke de Maine."

Ignoring the king's new love interest, Louis turned to the king. "But father—"

"Count Louis, the decision has been made. Madame de Maintenon has your best interests at heart. To avoid any more gossip at court, you are officially at Versailles to assist with your sister's upcoming wedding."

"But father—"

"I understand that the demoiselles of the court are rather smitten by your charms," he said, casting a glance at Madame de Montespan. When she nodded, he continued, "So, in the meantime, you will be instructed as to the behavior of a young man at court with respect to them." He smiled at Madame de Maintenon, who motioned for the valets to open the doors.

"You will be directed to your temporary quarters, Count Louis," she said.

Louis opened his mouth to speak but was lost for words. Instead, he lowered his head, bowed, and left the room.

~ ~ ~

Louis spent the next few days brooding in his small apartment when he was not attending his father's monotonous levée and coucher. He did, however, enjoy strolling in the palace gardens or attending Monsieur Saveur's lessons with the Princes of Conti and Jules-Armand Colbert. In fact, he was so curiously fascinated by geometry that his new tutor presented him with a silver compass in a red velvet-lined case.

One morning, Monsieur Saveur asked Louis, François, and Louis-Armand to remain behind after his lesson. "His Majesty asked me to speak to you about an important subject today," he said, and then he looked at Louis-Armand. "Especially for you, Monsieur Prince de Conti. You will soon have conjugal duties to observe when you wed Mademoiselle de Blois…"

Louis and his cousins' eyes widened as Monsieur Saveur picked up a book and leafed through it. "You need to learn, at least theoretically, how to multiply the species," he continued, with beads of perspiration appearing on his brow. He then read a passage from the book.

> *"The male and the female can produce their resemblance only by an intimate union of their sexified differences. It is for this reason that nature has made one with protuberant parts, and the other of a form suitable to receive them, so that they can unite closely and fit exactly into each other."*

"That is how babies are made?" asked Louis-Armand, raising his eyebrows.

"Yes, well, there are two theories," Monsieur Saveur said as he leafed through the book's pages again. "Aha, here it is."

> *"The first group of scholars says a seed is formed in the womb by the mixture of male and female fluids. The second group says that the seed is not only fully formed, but already very much alive in the father, who introduces it into the womb. The mother, like the earth, only gives lodging and food to those who are predestined to life."*

Louis' expression remained blank as he tried to understand the lesson, while Louis-Armand asked, "Which theory is true?"

"Well," said Monsieur Saveur, "I agree with the first group. The second appears to give man a natural superiority over woman."

"And what is the male fluid?" asked François.

Monsieur Saveur's face blushed all the way to the roots of his hair. "The Liqueur of Hermes," he said. "It is the effusion of this liqueur that causes pleasure in males."

Louis's mouth opened in wonder. He now knew what the liqueur was. He had experienced the effusion.

"Any more questions about this subject?" asked Monsieur Saveur. When his students said nothing, he added, "Fine. You are dismissed."

Leaving the room and walking down the corridor, Louis-Armand boasted, "You may be too young to understand the master's words, but I heard you've already experienced the nocturnal pollution."

When Louis frowned, François continued, "Don't worry, most of us have by your age. If you ever need any advice, just ask me."

Louis was uncomfortable speaking about the subject in such a banal manner. He would rather guard his secret sensation, thinking his cousins wouldn't understand what caused it… or who caused it.

"I'm the expert on the Liqueur of Hermes," said Louis-Armand. "No, I'm a goliath." When his companions snickered, he continued, "You laugh, but I can make a such a big pond on my belly that you could sail a boat on it."

Louis was finally relieved when they went their separate ways. When he arrived in his small apartment, his eyes lit up when he saw Marcel with Bandit wriggling with excitement in his arms.

Louis ran to get Bandit. "Thank you for bringing him to me," he said.

Marcel was all smiles. He pointed to a small packet on Louis' bed. "Madame Elizabeth also sent some bonbons."

"Let's have some!" Louis said.

"I'm sorry," Marcel said with a sad smile. "I have orders to return immediately."

At that moment, an elegant woman entered Louis' chambers, causing Bandit to bark. Louis nodded to Marcel, who left the room after a quick bow to the mysterious woman.

"I am Madame d'Or," she said with a short curtsey. "And you are Count Louis of Vermandois?"

"Yes, madame."

"I am here on the part of His Majesty," she said, closing the door behind her. She then removed her chemise to reveal her pale, white bosom and approached Louis. When he backed up to the foot of his bed, she stepped closer. "Don't be afraid, young man. I'm here to help."

Louis cringed at the smell of her breath, which reminded him of a fetid marsh near Saint-Cloud. When she took his hand and placed it on her breast, he pulled it away. She then grabbed hold of Louis' vest to pull him closer, but he jerked away and dashed out of his room and down the corridor—leaving his vest behind in her hands.

Louis meandered in the garden for most of the afternoon, wondering how other young men his age would have handled such a bizarre situation. He would certainly never reveal the incident to anyone.

The next morning, after the king's levée, he was summoned to the king's chambers where he found his father talking to the same well-dressed woman who had visited his chambers the day before. His mouth dropped.

"I understand, Count Louis, that Madame d'Or visited you in your apartment yesterday."

"Yes, Father," he said, his face turning pale.

The king turned to Madame d'Or. "And your report, madame?"

"The count performed his task to my satisfaction, sire," she said with a discreet wink to Louis.

The king, pleased with the answer, motioned that the audience was over for Louis, and the valets opened the doors for him to exit. His heart was pounding in his throat as he left.

~ ~ ~

For the next few weeks, Louis was fortunate not to cross paths with Madame d'Or, except for one morning after the king's levée in the salon. When he saw her, he also spotted Marie-Anne near the windows and quickly approached her to avoid any contact with the elderly matron. His sister ignored him, however, and continued her conversation with the dauphin as they gazed at the young Duke de Maine at the far side of the room.

"Why would the king be angry with me?" she said to the dauphin.

"You said that the little Duke de Maine was horribly lame," he said.

"Not so loudly, monsieur," said Louis, spotting Madame de Montespan in the doorway. "His mother is coming this way."

"Do you forget, mademoiselle, that the king cherishes the Duke de Maine?" asked the dauphin. "After all, he is your brother."

"My brother?" exclaimed the princess with impetuous haughtiness. "That is not true, monseigneur dauphin. I have only one brother and he is the Count of Vermandois." She glanced at Louis and raised her voice. "Louis, stop fidgeting with the ruffles of your chemise."

"Mademoiselle," said the dauphin, "I'm sorry to disagree, but the king is the Duke de Maine's father, just as he is yours."

"But the Marquise de Montespan is his mother. Unlike mine, she is married. Her children with the king cannot be legitimized like the Count of Vermandois and me."

"Beware, mademoiselle," he said. "The king can do anything he pleases."

~ ~ ~

After an early morning walk in the gardens with Bandit the next day, Louis returned to the palace to attend the king's levée. Two royal soldiers guarding the entrance opened the front doors for him at the same time the dauphin was exiting with two well-dressed pages. Seeing Louis, he held up his hand.

"Weren't you instructed to use the servants' entrance?" the dauphin asked, taking a wide stance. His pages snickered behind him.

Louis turned red in the face. "Is this how a future king acts, Monsieur?" he said with a shaky voice. He was at his wits' end with living at Versailles.

"Crazy boy," replied the dauphin, "do you forget that we are brothers?"

"Brothers! So, you admit that I'm the king's son too?" asked Louis.

"But my mother is Queen Maria Theresa of France." The dauphin moved forward and flipped Louis' ear with his forefinger. "Your mother was just one of the king's whores."

Louis' lips tightened. "Insolent! I'll show you," he said, stepping forward and punching the dauphin in the face. He gasped for air when he understood the gravity of his actions.

The dauphin, dazed, lost his balance. When his pages leaped forward, he motioned them back and addressed Louis. "You may do what you like, monsieur count, but I will never fight you. If I were to kill you, I would only be known as your murderer. If I were killed, you would go to the scaffold."

Louis felt the beads of sweat on his lips and forehead.

"Guards, arrest this dolt!" said the dauphin.

Louis struggled as the guards took him away. Chuckling, the dauphin and his pages went about their day—but not without stomping their feet and yelling obscenities to scare and chase Bandit into the gardens.

~ ~ ~

The sun's rays streamed through the windows onto the marble floor of the Apollo Salon. The king and his somber queen sat silently on their thrones. Followed by two jailers, Louis entered the salon and approached Their Majesties, stopping but a few paces in front of the dais. Looking down, Louis fidgeted with the hem of his jacket.

"Closer," said the king. When Louis didn't react, the king nodded for his guards to nudge him.

The queen was tapping her fingers on the arm of her chair but paused when the dauphin arrived and took his place a few paces from Louis.

The king rose. "Count Louis, the punishment for striking a Prince of the Blood is—"

"Death by hanging," the dauphin interrupted.

Louis looked up at his father. "He called my mother a whore," he said, his voice quivering.

"Striking the dauphin was a grave offense, Count Louis, an inexpiable crime," said the king.

"Inexpiable?" said Louis, squinting.

"A crime that cannot be forgiven," replied the king. "Court sentiment forced me to summon my ministers. They were unanimous that the law is imperative, calling for you to be condemned to death."

Louis' heart sank. His lips and chin trembled.

"But you *are* my son," said the king, causing the queen to sigh and look away. The king, his brow furrowed, turned to her and said, "Unlike a king, madame, a father must always find it in his heart to show mercy."

Louis bowed with humility, noticing that it softened the king's dire look.

"My son," said the king, "the dauphin is not only your brother, but he is also next in line to the Bourbon dynasty. You must treat him with the respect he is entitled to receive."

"Yes, Father," said Louis.

The queen's face reddened. "You really must make a severe example of him," she said.

"Yes," said the dauphin, "it would be a scandal not to do so."

"An example? A scandal?" cried the king. "Mon Dieu, if I were to make an example of all the scandalous things that go on here, I would spend the rest of my days signing arrest warrants for the Bastille!"

Looking away, the dauphin grunted, "Hmm."

"Heaven knows I have signed enough of them as it is," said the king as he stood up. "Now, embrace each other as brothers and let us hear of no further grievances."

Louis embraced the dauphin but pulled away when the dauphin did not return the sentiment. They both then bowed low to the king and queen, leaving the salon through different doorways.

Louis walked numbly through the salons, past courtiers playing cards at velvet-covered tables, past servants hustling from salon to salon, and past giggling demoiselles. He walked, looking straight ahead and wishing he could walk all the way to Saint-Cloud. When he arrived at his apartment, he was surprised to find Bandit lying in front of the door. He was wet, muddy, and trembling with a bone tied to his tail. Louis picked him up to untie the bone and held him close, kissing him on the ear.

"Let's get you cleaned up, little fellow," he said, unable to hold back the tears. "We don't belong here."

~ ~ ~

Braving his fears on horseback with Bandit in his arms, Louis found himself traveling at a slow pace on the road to Saint-Cloud. He knew he would have to answer for his impromptu and secret departure from court, but he hoped Aunt Liselotte would understand. He couldn't turn back.

Just east of the heavily wooded village of Marnes-la-Coquette, about halfway to the château, Louis noticed what appeared to be a gentleman approaching him on the road. When the man brought his horse to a stop, Louis pulled on his reins.

"My god! Count Louis?" said the Chevalier de Lorraine. "Is it really you on the road to Saint-Cloud? And alone? You're not an experienced rider."

Astonished to come face to face with the Chevalier de Lorraine, Louis was lost for words.

"Shouldn't you be at Versailles?" asked the chevalier.

"No, I am fine, monsieur," Louis said. "Don't worry. You can go about your business."

"I have no more business, Count Louis, since I have the good fortune to be in your company."

"But I must take your leave and continue my journey to Saint-Cloud."

"If I were in your place, Count Louis—"

"You would do what I am doing," said Louis in a melancholic tone. "You would leave your cares behind you."

"I'm sorry to hear this," said the chevalier with an understanding nod. "You will at least allow me the honor of escorting you to Saint-Cloud. The sun is setting, and Marnes-la-Coquette is unsafe at night, especially for lone travelers."

"Yes," he said, finding some comfort in the chevalier's company, yet they never spoke a word during the journey. Arriving at the stables, they dismounted.

"You can retire to your chambers, Count Louis," said the chevalier as he took the reins of Louis' mount. "I shall care for the horses."

"Thank you," said Louis, rubbing his sleepy eyes. "Adieu."

~ ~ ~

Finding Louis in his old chambers later in the morning, Doudou woke him, saying. "Count Louis! You must come with me to Madame Elizabeth. Come now, since you are still clothed!"

Half asleep, Louis followed Doudou to his aunt's chambers.

"*Junger* Louis!" said Elizabeth. "We received word this morning from Versailles that you left without any notice. His Majesty has been worried about you… as were we. Why did you leave the court?"

"Aunt Liselotte, I couldn't bear the humiliation any longer. The entire court tormented me," said Louis. "Especially the dauphin. He even pestered poor Bandit."

When tears ran down Louis' cheeks, Elizabeth motioned him to her and embraced him. Looking at Doudou, she saw her tearing up. "Oh, Doudou, wipe your eyes," she said, biting her lip to keep from laughing. "And send a message to His Majesty that Louis is safe and sound at Saint-Cloud. Also, inform him that I request an audience tomorrow to speak with him."

~ ~ ~

The following day, when Elizabeth entered the king's chambers and curtseyed, the Grand Prince de Condé and Monsieur Colbert were present.

"Ah, my good sister," said the king. "The Grand Prince de Condé is here to sign his son's marriage contract with Mademoiselle de Blois."

"My congratulations, Your Highness," she said to the prince.

After the prince signed the contract, the king added his signature and gave the contract to Monsieur Colbert, who bowed and left the room.

"I presume you are here to speak about my son, Count Louis, madame?" said the king. When she glanced at the Prince of Condé, the king continued, "Please, you may speak freely in front of my cousin."

"Sire, *junger* Louis was very unhappy at court. I beg you to let the count remain at Saint-Cloud. I will pay special attention to his education and keep better surveillance over him."

"Madame, I accept your proposal. The young count met much resistance at court. In fact, there is even a rumor floating around the palace that his father is actually the Duke de Lauzun."

"Sire, impossible. He not only resembles his lovely mother, but he has the king's noble features." When the king did not reply, she added, "But I am happy that you are making an allowance for the count."

"If I may, sire," said the Prince of Condé. "Count Louis is a fine young man. I have a story to tell you about him."

"Please continue, cousin," said the king.

"When I visited the Count of Vermandois to congratulate him on his sister's wedding to my nephew, the young count invited me to sit. But instead of taking an armchair, he showed me extraordinary respect by taking a folding chair, allowing me to sit in the armchair. At first, I dared not accept it due to his rank, but the young count insisted."

"I am pleased, cousin, that the count showed you the recognition that you deserve," the king said with a warm smile. "Moreover, I am happy that you show all of my natural children the consideration they are due. I am grateful that you are permitting your son to marry my daughter."

"Sister," the king said to Elizabeth, "when we celebrate Mademoiselle de Blois' happy occasion, we will also recognize Count Louis' thirteenth year."

"Yes," said the Prince of Condé. "A fitting occasion to welcome him to the age of manhood."

~ ~ ~

Louis wasted no time in summoning Marcel to visit him in his chambers at Saint-Cloud. Marcel was all smiles, especially when Louis showed him the silver compass that Monsieur Saveur had given him. But Louis wondered if it was the compass that thrilled Marcel or the fact that he'd returned to Saint-Cloud.

"When are you expected back at Versailles?" asked Marcel.

"I'm not," he said with a smile. "Aunt Liselotte has arranged for me to stay here at Saint-Cloud."

"But Versailles, it's so amazing," said Marcel, frowning with narrowed eyes.

Louis picked Bandit up and scratched him behind the ears. "We didn't like it that much, did we, fella?"

"You'll come to the stables tomorrow?" Marcel asked.

When Louis nodded, Marcel patted Bandit on the head and mumbled, "I'm glad you're back."

~ ~ ~

After the initial relief at being back at Saint-Cloud and seeing the abbé again, Louis' lessons began to become interminable as he daydreamed of dashing to the stables to spend his afternoons with Marcel. Over time, they became inseparable. Every day was an adventure, but Louis couldn't put their mystical friendship to words. They spoke of traveling together on exotic excursions to Africa, of escaping pirates and sword-bearing sheiks, and of building their own retreat... far from the pretentious courts of Saint-Cloud and Versailles. The secret dreams concocted on every long walk only brought them closer together. So close that Louis sometimes wondered if they would one day be together, closing that gap of incertitude about their relationship. He thought about it but never brought it up. Was he too shy? Or was he too proud to risk rejection?

One afternoon during their walk, Louis grabbed Marcel's cap.

"Give it back," cried Marcel.

"Never," said Louis and he took off running.

Marcel followed closely behind and almost caught him until Louis jumped a small ravine. Marcel jumped after him but slipped, scuffing up his knee, but he continued chasing Louis until Louis could go no further. Stopped in his tracks by a tree and heavy thicket, Louis turned to face Marcel, holding the cap behind him. Marcel reached for his cap with both hands, getting so close to Louis that he could feel Marcel breathing against his chest. For a moment, they didn't move, even after Louis let the cap fall to the ground.

"You're lucky," said Marcel, out of breath, picking up the cap and backing up.

Louis grinned. "Why?"

"I would have caught you if I hadn't slipped," he said, wiping some blood off his knee with his kerchief and tossing it aside.

"Sorry about that," Louis said. "Maybe we should head back."

"Race!" cried Marcel as he took off running.

Louis followed, but only after picking up the handkerchief and stuffing it in his vest pocket. He'd find a hiding place for it that night.

~ ~ ~

The day of Marie-Anne's wedding arrived, along with the recognition of Louis' age of majority—whether he was ready to be considered a man or not. Louis' chambers buzzed with excitement as his valet brushed his velvet jacket and Doudou finished combing his hair.

"I can't find my gold medallion, Doudou," he said.

Exasperated, her eyes looked heavenward. "I haven't seen it, Count Louis," she said, shaking her head in disappointment.

"My father will be upset if I don't wear it today."

"Here," she said, handing him a cloak. "This will cover your lapel. We'll keep looking, but please learn to take better care of your valuables."

Louis looked at the small table beside his bed, where he'd last seen his silver compass. It had gone missing too.

# CHAPTER TEN

# A New Household

"For pride and avarice and envy are the three
fierce sparks that set all hearts ablaze."

— Dante Alighieri, *Inferno*

## Palace of Versailles, December 1679

The Princes of Conti, Marie-Anne, and Count Louis stood erect in the council chamber. They bowed in tandem when the king entered and joined Monsieur Colbert in standing behind the ornate oak table. The king nodded for his minister to proceed with the formalities.

"Louis-Armand of Bourbon, Prince of Conti," said Monsieur Colbert, "the king and queen, being your godfather and godmother, grant you 50,000 livres and a pension of 25,000 livres per annum to honor your marriage to Marie-Anne de Bourbon, Mademoiselle de Blois."

Louis' eyes widened, and he took a deep breath.

Monsieur Colbert turned to Louis-Armand's brother. "François Louis, Prince de la Roche-sur-Yon, you will receive a pension of 20,000 livres."

The two princes bowed reverently. "We are very honored to accept such generous gifts," said Louis-Armand.

Monsieur Colbert then turned with a warm smile to Marie-Anne. "And Mademoiselle de Blois, His Majesty gives you one million livres and an annual pension of 100,000 livres." He picked up a small wooden case and opened it to reveal a collection of glimmering gems amid gold and silver jewelry. "He also presents you with this token of his affection to celebrate this grand occasion."

The king cleared his throat.

"Oh, yes," said Monsieur Colbert, "you will also receive the Duchy of Vaujours. It previously belonged to your mother, Duchess de La Vallière."

Marie-Anne curtseyed with that special sparkle in her eyes, meant only for her father.

Monsieur Colbert turned to Louis. "His Majesty also congratulates you, Count Louis of Vermandois, on reaching the age of majority. He is confident that you will learn from your past mistakes and prove yourself worthy of your rank."

Louis blushed with embarrassment when his sister and cousins glanced at him. *Isn't the brother of Mademoiselle de Blois worthy of even the smallest of gifts?*

The king walked past the four young royals, recognizing them one at a time with a gracious nod. When he approached Louis, last in line, he raised his head and looked down upon Louis' lapel.

"Count Louis, I do not see your medallion," said the king. "Are you not the honorable Admiral of France?"

Louis, tongue-tied, faintly remembered the last time he saw it. "Yes, Father, I am the Admiral of France," he said. "But please forgive me. In all the excitement, I forgot to wear my medallion today."

~ ~ ~

The following day, the court gathered in anticipation of the wedding. Louis, Monsieur Philippe, and Elizabeth entered the grand salon, where everyone's attention was focused on the Princes of Conti.

Abbé Fleury joined them. "I see your cousins, Count Louis, are the center of attention," he said.

"They please everyone," said Monsieur Philippe, "from the shoemaker and the lackey to the ministers of state and the army generals. My brother has always been partial to them, too, since their father's death."

"Especially, Prince Louis-Armand," Elizabeth said. "The king takes pleasure in seeing one of his princes so amorous."

"In love he is," said the abbé with a sparkle in his eyes. "This morning, he didn't know whether he was coming or going. He even made his way to Mademoiselle's chambers, ignored Madame Colbert's pleas, and forced the doors open to throw himself at his fiancée's feet and kiss her hands."

Louis giggled as he listened, not taking his eyes off the nervous prince who was either fingering the diamonds on his vest or arranging his frizzy, powdered wig.[1] *This was Goliath?* he thought. *And why is he wearing a wig? His hair is what makes him one of the most handsome young*

[1] The prince's governess, Madame de Longeron, created the straw-colored velvet vest embroidered with diamonds and black lace. When the color of the velvet was deemed a disaster at court, Madame de Longeron was so embarrassed and humiliated that she took her own life.

*men at court.* On the other hand, his brother François was showering Marie-Anne with attention. Louis had no idea that his cousins were both so infatuated with his sister.

~ ~ ~

The marriage took place with great solemnity, but it was followed by a grand feast with music by Lully and dancers from the Opéra. The grand salon resembled a theater built by fairies with orange trees laden with flowers and fruits. Marie-Anne strolled through the glittering crowd with her bridal bouquet adorned with pearls and sparking jewels. Madame Elizabeth entered the salon with Monsieur and the Chevalier de Lorraine, leading her favorite spaniel on a leash. Louis followed closely behind.

Everyone and anyone important at court dared not miss the special occasion. Awaiting the arrival of His Majesty, courtiers whispered behind a flock of flittering fans while servants meandered through the crowd with trays of glasses filled with wine.

*Princess Marie-Anne de Conti*

*Prince Louis-Armand de Conti*

"Quite the uproar at Versailles this day, husband," said Elizabeth.

"About?"

"Two items," she said. "First, about Marie-Anne's signing the marriage contract. Unlike the daughters of Marquise de Montespan, Marie-Anne has an advantage over her half sisters."

"Why does she have an advantage, Aunt Liselotte?" asked Louis with a squint.

"Your mother, then Duchess de la Vallière, was not married and could be named on Marie-Anne's baptismal certificate. The Montespan was not named on her daughters' certificates, however, because she was married. It would have caused a great scandal."

Louis frowned.

"She would have been admitting to royal double adultery," she said. "She and the king were both married."

"What about my sister signing the marriage contract?" he asked, still squinting.

"Bastard daughters can only sign their *first* name on their marriage contracts," she said. "But your sister added the words 'legitimated by France,' after her name. That clearly marks her difference from her half sisters."

"How so, Aunt Liselotte? Louis asked.

"Well, her half sisters would not write 'legitimated by France,' because it would only accentuate their bastardy."

Monsieur grinned. "Princess Marie-Anne must have written it then to humiliate her half sisters," he said and yawned. "And the second item, madame?"

"People are whispering that the king forever dishonors members of the younger branches of the royal family by marrying his bastard daughter to a Prince of the Blood," she said. "I'm just pleased that she wasn't promised to our son."

Monsieur Philippe put his hand on Louis' shoulder. "Madame, you forget that Count Louis here is Princess Marie-Anne's brother."

Louis had felt a heaviness in his chest to hear his aunt speak about his sister in such a manner. His gaze was downcast, and Elizabeth pulled him close beside her.

"*Junger* Louis, you know my feelings about the king's misborn children," she said. "It is not an affront to you or your sister. It's just a matter of royal lineage and heredity."

"Yes, Aunt Liselotte," Louis said with a tearful voice.

"Of all the legitimized children, *junger* Louis, I have only been partial to you and your sister. You both look like your mother, a dear and loving friend. When I first arrived from Germany, she made it her duty to welcome me and teach me the ways of the court."[2]

Louis looked up at her.

"Unlike the despicable Marquise de Montespan, who shunned me. Her children are not welcome at Saint-Cloud. They are bastards of double adultery, the children of the worst woman that the earth can bear. She has been abandoned by her husband and now the king. And *mein Gott,* her only link with the court is her son, the Duke de Maine."

"The Duke de Maine?" asked Louis.

"Her firstborn. The king is fond of him… even though he limps. You haven't seen him at court because Widow Scarron cares for him at her own residence. But beware, *junger* Louis, both the Montespan and the Widow Scarron blemish your name when in the king's presence… to the Duke de Maine's advantage."

"Madame Scarron?" asked Monsieur Philippe. "You mean Madame de Maintenon, the king's new love interest."

"No, she will always be the widow of that disgusting, pox-ridden poet, Scarron," she said. "She only married him to rise in Parisian society."

Madame de Maintenon walked past, stopping for a quick curtsey.

"Bonjour, madame," said Elizabeth gleefully. When Madame de Maintenon smiled and continued her stroll, Louis looked up at Elizabeth with a questioning grin.

"I am only cordial to her… and to Montespan… because court requires it," she said in her gruffest German accent.

---

[2] Poor Madame Elizabeth! She was far from foreseeing that one day she would have for a daughter-in-law one of those same adulterous bastards she dearly hated.

Marie-Anne walked past, recognizing Elizabeth and her husband with a quick curtsey, but ignoring her brother with an insolent air. Louis rolled his eyes. "She is—"

"The Princess de Conti, *junger* Louis," said Elizabeth. "She is now a Princess of the Blood."

Louis mumbled, "I wish she were just my sister."

The salon buzzed with excitement when Louis-Armand and François arrived with the Chevalier de Lorraine.

"Congratulations on this festive occasion, Your Highness," Elizabeth said to Louis-Armand, who bowed and then cast a glance at Marie-Anne on the dance floor.

François looked at Louis and said, "Truly, your sister is a girl who knows how to dance very well. Mon Dieu, just look at her!"

Louis-Armand sucked in a quick breath. "You forget about whom you are talking, my brother."

The chevalier grimaced and excused himself. Elizabeth, however, broke the silence and addressed the two princes. "You must bring the Princess de Conti to Saint-Cloud for a few days, Your Highnesses. Your cousin Louis and I would enjoy your visit."

~ ~ ~

Days later, François and Marie-Anne arrived at Saint-Cloud, welcomed by Elizabeth, Louis, and the Chevalier de Lorraine in the grand salon.

Louis greeted his sister. "Where is Louis-Armand?" he asked.

Ignoring him, she turned to Elizabeth. "Thank you very much for the invitation, Aunt Elizabeth."

Elizabeth nodded graciously and said, "Would you like to be directed to your chambers, Your Highness?"

"First, I should like to explore the garden," she said and glanced at François with a coquettish smile. "It's such a beautiful day."

When Marie-Ann had left, Louis asked François, "Where is Louis-Armand? They are married, aren't they?"

"Well," François said in a low voice conspiratorially, "they're not as happy as they were on their wedding day."

Elizabeth sighed. "It's not their fault," she said. "They are both very ignorant of the world… and of themselves. The Princess de Conti is only fourteen years old. He's barely nineteen."

The chevalier smirked. "Rumor has it that the princess declared her husband was not, I would say, well-equipped."

Elizabeth drew her head back quickly, casting a vicious glance at the chevalier.

"Oh, the goliath!" François said, causing Louis to giggle.

"The goliath?" asked the chevalier. "What about goliath?"

When François didn't respond, the chevalier continued, "I just wonder how a girl of her age could have ever learned how men *should* be equipped."

"Chevalier, you are being impudent," said Elizabeth, her face reddening.

"Well, she has quite a few reasons to complain about her husband," he said.

"I will tell my husband of such reckless impertinence."

"You may do so, madame, but I'm sure Monsieur Philippe already knows."

Louis wrinkled his nose. "I don't understand."

"Never mind, *junger* Louis," Elizabeth said, casting a frown at the chevalier.

"Anyway, how could she have fallen in love with that awkward Louis-Armand when she had before her eyes the handsome Prince François de la Roche-sur-Yon?" the chevalier said, directing attention to François with a slight nod.

François blushed but did not object to the compliment.

"Remember, you were the one who most enjoyed her dancing on their wedding day."

"Well, she *was* dizzyingly light on her feet; so beautiful and so graceful," said François, watching her in the garden as she ran and sprang into the air like a hummingbird. "Oh, if only I had been the eldest."

Louis elbowed him and said, "Let's join her." They bowed and quickly left the room.

"I believe," said the chevalier, "that Prince de la Roche-sur-Yon is jealous of his brother. He is certainly in love with the princess."

Elizabeth looked around to see if anyone could overhear and then turned to the chevalier, "I would be careful about making such assertions, monsieur."

~ ~ ~

A week later, Louis was visiting Versailles for his father's levée, when he encountered his cousin, Louis-Armand, sitting on a bench in the gardens.

"Count Louis," said Louis-Armand, standing up, "Finally, a friendly face."

"What's wrong?" said Louis.

"My wedding was a disaster."

"I don't understand," said Louis with a frown. "I thought it was a wonderful feast."

"It's what happened later that is the talk of the court. It's said that I was a brute to my new princess. That I frightened her when I reacted to her *strawberry season*."

Louis squinted. "Strawberry season?"

"Never mind," he said. "Do you see the Chevalier de Lorraine by the fountain? He's speaking with the Marquise de Montespan?" When Louis nodded, he continued, "Fetch him please. Tell him that I *must* speak with him."

When Louis returned with the chevalier, Louis-Armand's nostrils flared. "Rumor has it, Monsieur Chevalier, that you said my brother, Prince de la Roche-sur-Yon, is in love with my wife." When the chevalier did not reply, Louis-Armand stood with clenched fists and continued, "You have offended me, Monsieur Chevalier, with your reckless chatter. You must do me the honor of a duel."

When Louis laughed at his cousin's whim, Louis-Armand snapped, "Count Louis, you do not understand the gravity of the situation. I must defend my honor, that of my wife and especially that of my brother. The chevalier has accused him of being my rival."

"You would risk your life for the sake of your honor?" asked Louis.

"Yes," he said, turning back to the chevalier. "For my second, I will take Monsieur Jules-Armand Colbert."

"And I shall take the Marquis de Châtillon," said the chevalier. "Hopefully, the two noblemen will resolve this with terms acceptable to both of us."

"Agreed," said Louis-Armand before taking his leave.

Louis looked at the chevalier, perplexed by his cool demeanor after such a confrontation. He was indeed the most gallant man he'd ever known, and he couldn't take his eyes off the silk scarf he wore around his neck.

The chevalier removed the scarf and handed it to Louis. "This would actually compliment you more than me, Count Louis. It's Italian."

"Thank you, monsieur chevalier, I've never seen anything like it," Louis said as he wrapped the scarf around his neck. "May I ask you a question?"

The chevalier nodded.

"Why didn't you refuse my cousin's request to fight?"

"If I were to refuse on the spot, rather than consent, the prince would've been angry. He would most certainly have spread rumors at court… that I am a spineless man."

Louis couldn't believe that anyone could believe the chevalier a coward. He was a war hero, wounded in battle. Louis excused himself. He needed to speak with his sister.

~ ~ ~

"A duel? With the Chevalier de Lorraine?" Marie-Anne said, her eyes lighting up. "Did he offend my husband?"

"Yes, Prince Louis-Armand said the chevalier offended you and his brother, too, with stupid remarks."

After Louis had explained what had happened, she frowned. "You shouldn't be involved in my personal matters." When Louis looked pained by her words, her frown softened. "But we should inform the king before there is any silly chatter at the palace. Come, I'm sure our father will forbid such a duel to take place."

~ ~ ~

"Children," said the king. "Thank you for bringing me this information. I will speak to the Prince of Conti. His behavior may be warranted, but he would be no match against the chevalier. Trust me, there will be no duel."

Smiling warmly, he motioned that they were dismissed, but Marie-Anne spoke up, "Father, a word?"

"Yes, of course," he said, and she approached him while Louis left the chambers.

"I beg you to not be too harsh with the Prince de Conti," she said. "He was only thinking of my honor."

"He must learn that his actions have consequences, my daughter," the king said. "But do not worry. I will be firm but considerate."

She curtseyed. "You have been too kind to my husband and I, Father."

"Then why the long face? It does not suit you, my angel."

"It's my brother."

~ ~ ~

Louis returned to Saint-Cloud and went directly to the stables. He knew Marcel was there because the stable door was wide open. He had second thoughts about entering. He was in a bad mood.

"Good day," said Marcel, as he finished brushing a horse and patted it on the neck. "Did you enjoy your days at Versailles?"

"They were chaotic," he said, fidgeting with a lock of hair.

"Is there something on your mind?" said Marcel, his eyes narrowing.

Louis paused a moment, then said, "I'm curious if you might have seen my gold medallion?"

"Did you lose it? When was the last time you saw it?"

"When you were admiring it. In your quarters here."

"I haven't seen it," said Marcel. But when Louis remained silent, he added, "You can check my room if you like."

Louis looked him straight in the eyes. "And my silver compass?"

Marcel cringed. "Why in heavens would I want those silly things?"

Louis shrugged and looked down. "I should go check on Bandit."

~ ~ ~

When Louis returned to the château, Doudou was waiting on him. "Count Louis, I am to escort you to madame's chambers."

"What have I done now, Doudou?"

"Just come with me."

In Elizabeth's chambers, Louis stood erect, feeling like a prisoner on a firing line. Bandit sat up straight behind him without making a sound, even though Elizabeth's spaniels growled a little at him.

"Hush," Elizabeth said to her dogs and then looked at Louis. "I must commend you, *junger* Louis. Your Bandit is very well-behaved."

Louis loosened up; Elizabeth was in a good mood.

"I have wonderful news for you," she said.

"Oh?" he said.

"You are going to get your own residence in Versailles... not far from the palace," she said, causing Louis' eyes to widen. "And I am going to help you set up your household."

"Oh, Aunt Liselotte, tell me more."

"The king purchased the Hôtel de Bellefonds very close to the Grand Stables. It will be all yours."

"How is that possible?" he said, still in shock.

"I believe your sister spoke to your father about it."

"Marie-Anne? Why would she..."

"Perhaps she feels a bit guilty; the king showers her with so much attention at court."

Louis nodded, thinking she'd received much more than just attention.

"You must promise me to be responsible, junger Louis," Elizabeth continued. "Doudou and I will not be able to care for you as we have. And, alas, Marcel will no longer be your whipping boy, so—"

"Oh, that's fine," he said, looking to the floor. "I don't think I can trust him anymore."

"*Junger* Louis, he is your friend," she said, her smile disappearing. "What happened?"

"I think he took something of mine."

Elizabeth was speechless for a moment. "That's a shame," she said. "I thought about Marcel managing your small stable at Bellefonds… and keep an eye on you."

~ ~ ~

Doudou was busy helping the valets pack Louis' things in his chambers. She folded his clothes meticulously and withheld some items that had become too small. As the valets were packing away his books, toy soldiers and ships, and everything else from his writing table, Bandit ran to the armoire, scratching and growling at something underneath it. One of the valets went to see why Bandit was troubled. When he looked under the armoire, he pulled out a gold medallion, a silver compass, and a silk stocking.

"Count Louis, I believe these are yours," he said, showing him the objects.

"Bandit, shame on you!" said Louis, his gaze fixed on the medallion and compass. His heart sank. *How could I have ever mistrusted Marcel?*

Doudou stopped packing. "Oh, I'm so happy you found them," she said, taking them from him and placing them in his trunk. "Madame Elizabeth will be pleased."

Louis wanted to run to the stables to say goodbye to Marcel, but Doudou told him there was no time.

~ ~ ~

Louis' eyes sparkled when his coach passed through the intricately designed iron gates into the courtyard of the Hôtel de Bellefonds. When the coach reached the end of the courtyard, Louis noticed members of his new staff at the top of a large, stone staircase.

A stern-faced gentleman walked forward and bowed to welcome Louis. "Count Louis, I am Monsieur de Monchevreuil. The honorable Abbé Fleury appointed me your governor at Bellefonds," he said.

When the door to the main gallery was opened, Louis entered the elegant but bare room—except for a table covered with a green velvet tapestry bordered in gold edging. Louis scanned the array of papers, cards, and gifts from Elizabeth, the king, and other members of the court that adorned the table. A gift from the Chevalier de Lorraine, however, outshone the others—a leather bound tome etched with a deeply engraved title in Greek.

"Plutarch," he said to himself.

Overcome with emotion, Louis scanned the grand gallery. It isn't the Palace of Versailles, but it's not far away, he thought.

He was surprised, however, when the Chevalier de Lorraine appeared out of nowhere. "Welcome to Bellefonds, Count Louis." Surprised, Louis' gaze went distant, but the chevalier continued, "I wanted to give you a tour of your new residence."

"Welcome to my new residence, monsieur chevalier," he said, tilting his head to the side, "but why do you want to give me a tour?"

"Well, it belonged to me. I purchased it from Marquis de Bellefonds several years ago. When the Grand Stables were built, the marquis decided they spoiled his view of the palace. So, he sold the château to me. Now, the king has bought it for you… paying me 100,000 livres for it. A price I couldn't refuse. Come, we'll walk to the chapel."

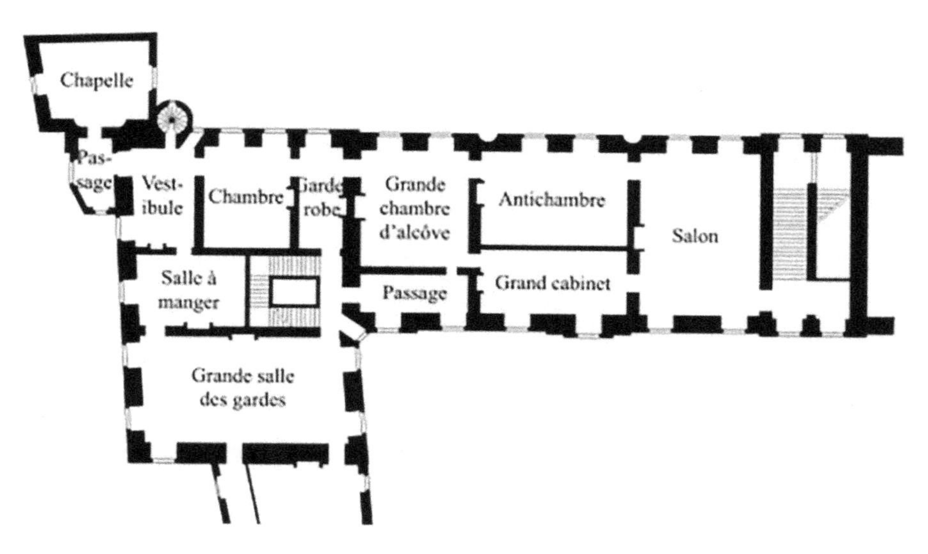


*Floor Plan: The Hôtel de Bellefonds*

They walked through several sunlit chambers to the chapel, where the rays of the afternoon sun were filtered through two small stained-glassed windows, giving the chapel a peaceful, serene air. The chevalier stood close to Louis, so close that Louis could feel his breath on his forehead.

"I will miss our little conversations, Count Louis, now that you are no longer at Saint-Cloud," said the chevalier. He was just reaching his arms out to him when they heard footsteps approaching the chapel doorway.

"There you are, Louis," said Marie-Anne, her smile disappearing when she saw the chevalier.

"I was just giving Count Louis a small tour of his new home, Your Highness," said the chevalier.

"Why?" she asked, her eyes narrowing.

"Because it used to be mine… before I sold it to His Majesty."

Marie-Anne's brow wrinkled, as if her question wasn't really answered.

The chevalier bowed. "Good day, Your Highnesses, I have important matters at Versailles," he said with a bow. "It appears that the king has heard of my encounter with the Prince de Conti."

As soon as the chevalier left the room, Marie-Anne chastised Louis. "You should not be seen in that man's presence."

"Why?" he asked.

"He's Aunt Liselotte's most dangerous enemy. She says he's a wicked, insinuating villain with the most poisonous fabrications."

"I am surprised he visited me," he said. "After warning our Father that he accepted a duel, I thought he might be angry with us?"

"Certainly not with me," she said. "*You* were the only one present when he accepted the duel with my husband."

"And Father was not angry with your husband?"

"Madame de Montespan said he talked to Louis-Armand for over two hours with more gayety than anger." When Louis cast a confused glance, she continued, "But with a tone of authority, which must certainly have caused him to repent. In any event, never trust the chevalier. He's unprincipled and given to every sort of debauchery."

Louis was shocked to hear his sister speak in such a manner.

"Do not keep his company," she said. "Better yet, you must truly consider marrying soon. Did you know that the dauphin has a fiancée now?"

"Who will he marry?"

"The Duchess Maria Anna of Bavaria."

"Have you seen her?"

"Yes, this morning in her chambers. She's as ugly asleep as when she's awake," she said, causing them both to chuckle.

Louis was surprised. Was this the first time they'd laughed like this together?

After catching her breath, Marie-Anne looked around the chapel. "Do you like the Hôtel de Bellefonds?"

"Yes, very much; it's amazing," he said. "Thank you for speaking to our Father about it."

"Oh, I didn't do it for you," she scoffed. "I did it because François de Conti has a small manor nearby. I will let everyone think I'm visiting you when I go to him."

~ ~ ~

Later in the afternoon, Monsieur Philippe, Madame Elizabeth, and the Chevalier de Lorraine arrived at Bellefonds together.

"We are on our way to dine with the king and queen this evening, *junger* Louis, but we wanted to see that you are well situated in your new residence.

"Yes, I am," he said. "Thank you, Aunt Liselotte."

"The walls are a bit bare though," said Monsieur to the chevalier. "Did you ever stay here for any length of time?"

"Only on several occasions late in the evening, when I was in no condition to return to Saint-Cloud," he said with an ornery wink.

Elizabeth looked around the grand salon. "I will make sure you have some fine fittings... especially paintings above the doors and the fireplace, *junger* Louis," she said and pointed to a bare wall. "A tapestry would be lovely here and I'm certain that Monsieur would not object to having a work commissioned by Monsieur Mignard to adorn the chapel."

Monsieur nodded graciously before taking the chevalier's arm and leading him to a table with refreshments. When Elizabeth rolled her eyes at Louis, he giggled.

"And *junger* Louis, to be sure that you have the best of care, I'm providing you with a small allowance, in addition to your father's, and your own personal valet."

Overwhelmed by Elizabeth's generosity, Louis teared up. "I don't know how to thank you, Aunt Liselotte."

"Well, first, you can promise to listen more closely to Abbé Fleury, to pay attention to your lessons, and to beware of the likes of those two," she said, tilting her head toward her husband and the chevalier.

"I promise, Aunt Elizabeth," he said, his grin disappearing when he noticed the serious look in her eyes.

~ ~ ~

The following morning, Louis awoke to Bandit barking excitedly. He raised his head from his pillow to see the back of a well-dressed young man opening his armoire door.

"Stop," he cried out. "Identify yourself, Monsieur!"

When the stranger turned around, Louis jumped up. "Mon dieu! Marcel?"

"Monsieur Marcel, if you please," he said. "I'm your new valet. I'm also in charge of your small stable."

"A remarkable rise in status," Louis said with an incredulous stare.

"Yes, Madame Elizabeth is quite generous."

Still in his bed shirt, Louis got out of bed and pulled up his breeches. After a short silence, he said, "I am sorry for ever thinking that—"

"Don't worry," Marcel said, looking down at Bandit, who was jumping up and down. He picked him up and shook him affectionately. "You're worse than a highway robber, aren't you?"

Louis leaned in to embrace Marcel, but Marcel, seeing someone in the doorway, backed off.

"Forgive my interruption, messieurs," said the Chevalier de Lorraine. "It appears I am always finding myself in the most embarrassing situations."

Louis was startled. "Oh, no, monsieur, we—"

"Adieu, messieurs," said the chevalier, and disappeared.

When Marcel grimaced, Louis said, "He was the previous owner of Bellefonds."

"Oh, that's why he was chatting with the servants in the kitchen. Rather gleefully actually."

When Marcel began to arrange the armoire, Louis said, "Time for a walk in the woods nearby? Maybe explore a little."

"You're the master," Marcel said with a wide grin, closing the armoire door.

~ ~ ~

After wandering half an hour through the woods, Louis and Marcel reached a small, misty clearing with a pond. They tasted some berries from a bush laden with raspberries in the secluded spot, where only the trilling of birds and the music of crickets broke the silence.

Louis eyes turned to Marcel's new valet breeches and vest. "Very handsome," he said with a shaky voice, but Marcel answered with a humble look. Although Marcel was a little older than him, he was not much taller. When Louis gazed into his eyes, the blood seemed to leave his body; he was chilled and feverish at the same time. The idyllic scene became a mysterious world with no past and where nothing else existed.

Louis wanted to give Marcel a hug but, at that moment, a flutter of crying water hens announced someone was approaching. From their clothing, they appeared to be two stable boys.

"Look at the buggers… in velvet and ruffles," cried one of the boys.

"Like the court mignons," said the other.

When Louis froze, Marcel moved in front of him. "It's not what you think," he said.

"*Quelle horreur*!" said the first boy. "These monsters think they can own us… or buy us."

"Like Monsieur always trying to seduce us," said the other. "Let's give 'em a good beating."

Marcel took a step toward the boys. "You can be flogged and sent to the dungeon for assaulting the king's son," he said.

"The king's son?" said the first boy, running his hand through his hair.

"Yes, the Count of Vermandois. I'm his valet and I will protect him with my life," he said, raising his fists.

The ruffians looked at each other and darted back into the woods. Louis looked as if he wanted to thank Marcel, but Marcel returned the look with disdain, simply saying, "Let's go."

Returning home, no one spoke a word.

~ ~ ~

The next morning, when Marcel woke Louis to ready him for the king's levée and Mass, he was standoffish.

Louis wondered if Marcel could think of him as a coward.

Later, when his carriage left the stable, he turned to see Marcel laughing with one of the young gardeners as they watched him depart. He pulled his hat down low, thinking they were laughing at him. Having known Marcel for some time, he couldn't believe that Marcel would betray him in such a manner.

~ ~ ~

After the levée, Louis strolled through the long corridors behind Monsieur, Elizabeth, and the chevalier to the chapel. He noticed how well the chevalier was dressed. Although much older than Marcel, the man was just as fit physically with his well-defined calves and arms. Louis couldn't stop gazing at the chevalier, even though he was just minutes from confession—where he couldn't reveal his innermost thoughts. *Am I cheating by not confessing them? If I did confess, would the king find out?*

During Mass, Louis was struck by the verse of a psalm: "Blessed is the man who does not follow the advice of the wicked or take the path of sinners or join a group of mockers." Torn by his strange bodily urges and the readings of the "Sacred Band," was his life spiraling downward? Was he condemned to perdition?

The chevalier, on his way to Saint-Cloud after Mass, accompanied Louis to Bellefonds. When they arrived at the front gate, Louis noticed Marcel watching from the stable. For a reason unknown to him, Louis pretended to be enjoying the chevalier's conversation and company in Marcel's sight.

The chevalier responded to Louis' congeniality. "Count Louis," he said, "will you join us tomorrow afternoon for a coach ride to Paris?"

After a quick glance toward the stable, he said, "Why not? Thank you, monsieur."

~ ~ ~

Louis watched the crowds of Parisian gawk at the chevalier's splendid carriage studded with silver and gold. The chevalier, the Marquis de Châtillon, and another mignon chatted among themselves until Louis spoke up. "Where are we going?"

"First to Notre Dame," said the chevalier.

"Quite the brouhaha this afternoon in Paris," said the marquis.

"Finally, an end to the Leroux-Mercier affaire," said the chevalier.

Louis frowned. "Leroux-Mercier?"

"Two scoundrels who assaulted and violated a seventeen-year-old lackey," said the chevalier. "They were known at court to solicit young ruffians on behalf of nobles."

"Like Antoine Morel de Volonne," quipped the marquis.

Louis was lost for words and the more he understood the conversation, the more his face reddened. He knew of Antoine Morel de Volonne, the steward of his aunt's household, and wondered why he wasn't condemned as well. At Notre Dame, the regal coach rolled slowly past the forecourt, and he saw two men in nightshirts with ropes around their necks and kneeling in front of a priest.

When Louis wrinkled his forehead, the marquis said, "Leroux and Mercier are making amends."

The chevalier leaned out the window and addressed the driver, "Place de la Grève."

He then turned to Louis. "It's nearby. Where the men will pay for their crimes."

"But their tongues are chopped off first," said the mignon nonchalantly.

"Why," asked Louis.

"To keep them from embarrassing the court in any manner."

When the coach came to a halt at the Place de la Grève, Louis shuddered. The prisoners were being shoved up a ladder to the scaffold and chained to a post. The chevalier and marquis snickered when they saw the look on Louis' face as the executioner set the fire beneath the men and quickly engulfed them. Louis could see the men screaming, but he couldn't hear them over the cries of the surging crowd: "Burn them! The buggers!"

Louis turned his head to the side with the eyes tightly closed, but he could almost taste the smoke. After the bodies were burned alive and reduced to ashes, the ashes were thrown to the wind. Then the chevalier motioned for the carriage driver to depart.

Louis remained silent as the carriage returned to Saint-Cloud. He thought of the two men, Leroux and Mercier. The initials of the two men were L and M, the same as those of Louis and Marcel.

At Bellefonds, he bid his hosts adieu. Exhausted by the ordeal, he went to his chambers and, as soon as he climbed into his bed, he quickly fell asleep.

~ ~ ~

When Louis woke the next morning, he was surprised to find his governor, Monsieur de Monchevreuil, laying out his clothes for the morning rituals at Versailles.

"Where is Monsieur Joubert?" he asked, rubbing his eyes.

"He left you a note, Count Louis," he said, pointing to Louis' night table. Louis unfolded the parchment.

*Master, I must go to Saint-Cloud. I received news that my foster father died yesterday. With your permission, I wish to remain at Saint-Cloud and resume my duties in the stables. Signed, Marcel Joubert.*

Louis stared out the window with Bandit half-asleep at his feet. He would journey to Saint-Cloud as soon as possible.

~ ~ ~

When Louis entered the salon after Mass at Versailles, he found Liselotte in a heated argument with the Chevalier de Lorraine. It ended when Louis approached them, and the chevalier took his leave with a short bow. Marie-Anne joined them.

"Aunt Liselotte," she said, "Was the chevalier annoying you?"

"No more than usual," she said. "How are the count and princess today?"

Louis forced a smile. "Fine, thank you."

"Not me," Marie-Anne jumped in. "And it's all Madame de Maintenon's fault."

"Princess?" said Elizabeth, raising her eyebrows.

"Thanks to her, Mass is now required, plays are banned during Lent, and I am obliged to go out for long drives with her. So boring."

"I am so sorry, princess, but I cannot help you. Perhaps you can speak to your husband?"

"That dolt?"

Louis tilted his head. "Why are you calling him names?" he asked. "He is a gentleman."

"Are you so sure?" she said. "We attended the theater last month with the king, the queen, and the dauphin. The play was so bad that we were already laughing by the end of the first scene. But the laughter was uncontrollable when my husband, laughing so hard, fell below to the orchestra pit."

Louis chuckled when he thought about his cousin, the goliath.

"I'm not finished," she said, cocking her head and shaking it. "He tried to save himself by the curtain cord, but, instead, he pulled the curtain down over the lamps and set fire to it. The flames were immediately extinguished and the actors, perfectly unaware of my husband's escapades or afraid to acknowledge them, continued with the play."

"Such a spoiled boy, the prince," said Elizabeth, shaking her head in disapproval. "I would have preferred that you marry a valet or a lowly servant, my dear. Someone who would appreciate such a charming wife as you… and not make it his ambition to embarrass you."

Louis stopped giggling. Surprised by Elizabeth's sincerity, he thought of Marcel.

When Marie-Anne frowned, Elizabeth added, "Surely, you are aware of his debauched lifestyle and infidelities with certain ladies at court."

Louis was overwhelmed with a pang of the heart when he observed the hurt look on his sister's face. Making his excuses, he bowed and set out for Saint-Cloud.

~ ~ ~

Riding through the woods, Louis rehearsed what he would say to Marcel. As he approached the stable at Saint-Cloud, his anxiety amplified. He dismounted and entered the stable to find Marcel in his quarters, dressed in black.

"Forgive me," he said, struggling to hold back his tears. He took a deep breath and continued, "I am very sorry to hear about your father."

Marcel nodded. "Thank you."

"Is there anything I can do?"

Marcel shook his head. "No."

Louis' breathing turned shallow. "There is something I need to say."

Marcel's forehead wrinkled.

"You are more than my valet. You are my friend."

Marcel looked to the floor.

"Why did you leave? Do I embarrass you?"

"Embarrass me?" asked Marcel, drawing his eyebrows together.

"In front of that gardener, you—."

"Him? That silly fish?" Marcel interrupted with a smile. "He's always playing the fool."

"Then why did you come back to Saint-Cloud?" asked Louis.

Marcel's lower lip trembled. "I don't know. Maybe I don't belong in Versailles," he said. "And you are too kind to me."

"That's all?"

"Well, I feel a little out of place when I'm with you," he said, looking down.

"You shouldn't if I don't," Louis said with the most reassuring look he could muster.

"But I'm just a servant."

"You are more than that," said Louis. "Come back with me."

"Well, I suppose I could," said Marcel teasingly, with a tear falling down his cheek. Then he grinned and quipped, "But only if you promise to change your nightshirt a little more often."

"Stable boy, valet, and now the court jester," Louis said, giggling when he saw Marcel roll his eyes.

CHAPTER ELEVEN

# Warriors of Thebes

"Wisdom is earned, not given."

—Dante Alighieri, *Inferno*

## Hôtel de Bellefonds, June 1680

Louis groaned when Marcel opened the shutters with a clatter, letting the morning rays fill his chambers. "Why so early?" he grumbled.

"Fencing lessons."

Abbé Fleury entered the room. "Still in bed, Count Louis?" he said. "I see your habits have not changed since leaving Saint-Cloud."

"Good morning, monseigneur," Louis said, yawning and stretching, as Marcel handed him his vest and breeches.

"Good morning," he said. "Madame Elizabeth asked me to pay you a visit and report back to her about your well-being. I do, however, apologize for not coming earlier to see your new residence."

"I am doing fine, monseigneur," he said with a warm smile. "And I am happy to see you. I know how busy you are."

The abbé noticed a book on the night table and picked it up. "What are you reading?" he said, frowning when he noticed the title and leafed through it. "Who gave you permission to read this?"

The abbé's tone was so severe that Marcel stepped back a few paces. Louis' face reddened. "It was a gift from—"

"Never mind, I know who it was from," he said, holding the book up. "This tome, *The Life of Pelipodas,* recounts the tales of the Sacred Band of Thebes, a troop of select soldiers who formed a victorious Theban army; however, the troop consisted of male… male couples." He hesitated before continuing. "Such writings are odious. I pray that you will not confuse Eros with Philia. Or with Agape."

"Monseigneur?" Louis said as he sat on the edge of his bed, knowing he was about to receive a lecture.

"Eros," the abbé said, "is more than the Greek god of love. Eros is the god of carnal desire and attraction."

Marcel's eyes widened when the abbé glanced at him and continued, "Phila, on the other hand, represents the bond among friends. It's the care, respect, and compassion we Christians have for one another in the Bible."

"And Agape?" said Louis, listening attentively.

"It's the immeasurable love of God for mankind. It's unconditional," said the abbé, glancing at both of them. "It's the love to which you must commit yourselves."

The abbé bowed and left the room, leaving Louis and Marcel speechless.

~ ~ ~

"Stop," said the Sieur de Préville in the makeshift fencing-room at the stables. "Stand perfectly upright. You must look at your adversary with your right side towards him." He then bent over to move Louis' right heel to the hollow of his left foot. "Now, follow me."

Louis mimicked his instructor's movements, raising his right arm with the point of the foil directly in front of him until the hilt was as high as his head. Then he turned his thumb down and made a diagonal sweep of the blade in front of him.

"Well executed, Count Louis," the Sieur de Préville said as he removed his fencing mask. He then collected his equipment, readying to depart. "Just remember to keep your shoulders back. Posture is the sign of good swordsmanship."

Louis removed his mask. "Thank you, monsieur."

As the instructor was leaving, Marcel entered the room and hastened to help Louis pull his vest down over his nightshirt. Perspiration was dripping off the ends of Louis' long hair. "You're sweating like a nettle bush on a dewy morning," Marcel said.

Louis squinted, unfamiliar with the saying. "Fencing brings all of your limbs and torso into exercise. That's how you develop muscular power."

Marcel laughed. "I think it is more recreation than exercise," he said. "What dancing is for girls, fencing and stick fighting are for boys."

Louis scowled. "A gentleman must have the means to defend himself."

Marcel picked up a foil, brandishing it back and forth. "I could defend myself."

"Says the jester," said Louis with a wide grin.

"Oh, those are dueling words, my count," Marcel said, pointing his sword at Louis.

Louis picked up his foil. "We'll see if you're right," he said, tossing Marcel a mask. Marcel removed his vest and nightshirt. Louis' heart skipped a beat when he saw hair below Marcel's navel, running down to a small patch of dark curls just above where his breeches had drooped. Louis removed his own nightshirt in turn.

They took their places opposite each other, their foils glittering in their hands from the sparse rays filtering through the windows. When Louis cried out, "*Allez-y*," they began sparring with sabers plunging to and thro as they jumped about right and left. Although the points of the blades were treated so they could barely penetrate the skin, Louis carelessly miscalculated Marcel's lunge and, when the point of Marcel's foil scratched his chest, Louis cursed, "*Sacré bleu*!"

When Marcel noticed the blood he'd drawn, he dropped his foil and removed his mask. His face flushed, he cried out, "I'll summon a doctor."

Louis inspected the cut and chuckled. "It's just a scratch," he said, "but where did you learn those maneuvers?"

"From watching you and your teacher." When Louis squinted, he added, "Through the stable windows at Saint-Cloud."

~ ~ ~

Louis and Marcel returned to Louis' chambers, where Louis removed his bloodstained nightshirt. Marcel poured water into a ceramic bowl and wetted a sponge to dab the blood from Louis' chest. He stood so closely that Louis could smell the sweet earthy smell of Marcel's body. Louis' heart began to beat rapidly and, afraid that Marcel would notice his breath deepening, he took the sponge, finished wiping the last traces of blood, and handed it back to Marcel.

While Marcel was cleaning the sponge in the bowl, he noticed the book that had aggravated the abbé. He pointd to it and asked, "What is the title of your book?"

"*Η ζωή του Πελοπίδα*, Life of Pelopidas," he said, hoping to impress Marcel with his knowledge of Greek. "Would you like to hear a little?"

"Yes," he said, his smile reaching his eyes. "Please."

Louis took the book, sat on his bed, and leafed through several pages until he found one of his favorite passages from *Life of Pelopidas* to translate for Marcel, who took a seat at Louis' desk. He often sat there and, having dipped a quill in an ink well, he started scribbling lightly on some parchment. Then Louis cleared his voice to get Marcel's attention and began translating the text.

> "The sacred band, we are told, was first formed by Gorgidas… who camped in the citadel. For that reason, too, they were called the city band; for citadels in those days were properly called cities. But… some say that this band was composed of lovers and their beloved."

Louis glanced at Marcel. When he noticed no reaction, he continued:

> "Citadel soldiers take little care of their clansmen in times of danger; whereas a band that is held together by the friendship… between lovers is indissoluble and not to be broken. Because the lovers are… ashamed to play the coward before their beloved, and vice versa, they both stand firm in danger to protect each other. This is no wonder…. since men have more regard for their lovers than for others who are present. It was natural, then, that the band should also be called sacred, because… even Plato calls the lover a friend 'inspired of God.'"

When Louis paused, letting Marcel know he was finished, Marcel spoke up. "They were never defeated?"

Louis leafed through a few more pages and continued. "It is said that the band was never beaten until the battle of Chaeronea."

Louis closed the book, rose from his bed, and returned the book to his desk, where Marcel was sketching soldiers in armor, copying them from one of the history books that lay open on the desk.

"You're an artist too?" Louis asked.

"No, but I'd like to learn how to draw horses," Marcel said with a blush, immediately folding the parchment and sticking it in his vest pocket. "Thank you for reading to me about the Greek warriors. Were there many of them?"

"I think three hundred. One hundred and fifty pairs. They reminded me of Monsieur, the chevalier, and the minions returning from the Battle of Cassel. They were victorious, you know. Real heroes."

"In the eyes of the king, too?"

"Especially in his eyes," Louis said, putting his hand on Marcel's shoulder. "Maybe we could train together and go to war. We would be heroes, too." When Marcel didn't move, he continued. "I could make my father proud. Like my brother, Dauphin Louis."

Marcel turned to see Louis' face. "That would make you happy?"

Louis nodded.

"Then we should train together," said Marcel. When Louis put his other hand on Marcel's other shoulder, Marcel stood up. "With your permission," he said with a wavering voice, "I need to go to the stable."

Louis nodded and Marcel left the room. Louis' stomach fluttered. Had he made Marcel feel uncomfortable?

~ ~ ~

The next morning, Marcel joined Louis in his fencing class in a room adjacent to the stables. When Louis asked the Sieur de Préville for advice on strengthening their bodies, the instructor suggested having a stout rope, knotted at the end, in the room where they practiced. When a rope was hung from the rafters, he then instructed them, "You need to grasp the rope with both hands, raise yourselves up, and then remain in that position for as long as possible… without touching the ground."

Louis went first and lasted at least a minute before letting go of the rope and wringing the discomfort from his hands. Marcel jumped and grabbed the rope. He held on for several minutes until Louis tugged on Marcel's vest. "That suffices," he said with a chuckle. "You have made your point."

~ ~ ~

Training went well for several months until it was interrupted, however, by the festivities celebrating the dauphin's marriage to the unattractive but charming Duchess Maria Anna of Bavaria. The king and his court gathered to watch the long-awaited carrousel at the Château Saint-Germain-en-Laye. The race, composed of two quadrilles of seven riders, featured Dauphin Louis at the head of one and Prince François de la Roche-sur-Yon at the head of the other. Riders raced in a circle but also had to pierce a ring with their lances. This time in form of ring races. Consisting of the most agile riders, the prince's quadrille won by far. The prince himself even beat the dauphin by a head at the crossing line. Yet no winner was proclaimed.

François' pouted when he joined Louis and Marie-Anne, who threw her hands in the air. "But you won," she said. "Why in heavens weren't you declared the winner?"

François shrugged. "Court etiquette, I imagine."

"You are the better horseman, cousin," said Louis.

Marie-Anne took François by the arm. "We can still go celebrate?"

"No, I'm going to Bellefonds to practice for the dance tomorrow," he said, causing Marie-Anne to grunt.

"We have two dances, one as zephyrs and one as young beloved, in Lully's new opera," said Louis proudly.

Marie-Anne shook her head and marched away.

François turned to Louis. "I'd rather celebrate with you anyway," he said with a chuckle.

~ ~ ~

When Marcel entered Louis' chambers later in the afternoon, Louis and François stopped dancing. Louis wiped his forehead with his sleeve. "My sister is probably upset with you for coming here," he said to François.

"Well, I like you as much as I like your sister," he said with a big wink.

Feeling embarrassed by his cousin's remark, Louis glanced to see Marcel's reaction. "Marcel, will you excuse us?" he said. "We need to continue practicing."

Early the next morning, Marcel entered Louis' chambers again to find François and Louis dressing for their dance. Louis had nothing on as he stepped into his tights, François standing behind him. "I can't believe they're letting my sister and the dauphin's wife dance today," Louis said.

"The first time ever that ladies have danced in an opera," said François, pulling Louis' silk tights up above his waist and then slapping him on the derrière.

When Louis giggled, Marcel left the room.

~ ~ ~

The opera hall buzzed with anticipation as the king and his courtiers took their seats, but the theater quieted when Lully tapped the floor with his long hardwood cane and began conducting the orchestra for his *Le Triomphe de l'Amour*. Minutes later, after the introductory scenes, Louis arrived on the stage with a torch in his hand. As one of the group of dancers called the Young Loves, he was asked to sing a short verse:

*"This Young Love, from love itself,*
*And from the hands of the Graces born,*
*Prepares his army for war and is not forlorn.*
*And, prouder than he is handsome,*
*Not content to just shine on the earth's lea,*
*He will carry his torch to the center of the sea."*

Zephyr of *Le Triomphe de l'Amour*

In later dances, Monsieur Philippe, the dauphin, the dauphine, Marie-Anne, and François appeared in various roles. Toward the end of the opera, Louis appeared again with his cousin, François, as two of the group of Zephyrs. François sang first, facing Louis.

*"Zephyr, go as you please,*
*But I lament those who will follow*
*To find only hearts and bones to mend.*
*I will not allow anyone to see me,*
*Like these other Zephyrs,*
*Spend my blood for such a fruitless end."*

Louis then stepped forward, drawing the marked attention of Madame Elizabeth. She listened carefully to his every word, because his voice, although melodic, was much softer when compared to his cousin's bravura.

*"This tender Zephyr only lives and breathes*
*To flourish in this Empire divine.*
*He only curls the surface of the ocean's swell,*
*While the majestic land is at peace.*
*But let it be known to the deepest seas,*
*He threatens foes with the fury of hell."*

Louis had scarcely ended his verse when he was recognized by the entire audience with joyful applause.

During the pause before the next scene, Elizabeth leaned into the king's ear. "The Count of Vermandois is very talented," she whispered. When the king proudly nodded, she added, "But I am surprised, sire, that you do not object to the royal family showing themselves publicly on stage."

"Having danced myself when younger, madame, I have no objection. I do not think it beneath their dignity to act at court entertainments."

"And ladies on stage, sire? Even princesses?"

"There has always been a shortage of dancers of the gentler sex. I hope now this will change, because I find young boys pressed into donning ladies' clothing not to my taste any longer."

A row behind the royal onlookers, the Marquis de Châtillon turned to the Chevalier de Lorraine, sitting closely next to him. "The Count of Vermandois—is he a child or a man?" he said with a broad, but half-sinister smile. "Under that sumptuous costume you could see his broad shoulders, the narrow hips, those arched loins—"

"He is as attractive as he is accomplished," said the chevalier.

"He certainly captured everyone's attention," said the marquis. "Especially the king's eye."

"Yes," said the chevalier with a contemptuous frown, "but the king does not know of one of his son's peculiar relationships."

"Perhaps some blackmail is in order?"

"No," said the chevalier. "I have other ideas in mind."

~ ~ ~

Louis' costume was damp from the proudly earned sweat when he arrived in his chambers at Bellefonds. He threw his props, the sword and shield, on the bed and kicked off his shoes. He removed his tunic and, after pulling his tights down to his ankles, he sat on the bed to remove them, letting them drop to the floor. He had enjoyed performing in Lully's opera, but he was relieved to rid himself of the costume. Then he walked to his armoire to select a clean nightshirt and when he closed the armoire door, he noticed himself in the upright mirror.

He didn't immediately recognize himself. It was as if he saw a stranger in the reflection. His big round shoulders contrasted with his slim abdomen and signs of muscles rippling across it. He ran his hand over his chest, that had become more defined. He then turned one of his legs to see the silhouette of the muscles of his thigh and calf. He smiled. When he rotated to see his derrière, he was convinced that the training was producing admiral effects—although Marcel's derrière was more defined.

He then approached the mirror to look at his face more closely. The hairs on his chin and jawline were sprouting sparsely, giving him the impression that he was no longer a boy.

Louis' face reddened when Marcel arrived and noticed him admiring himself in the mirror. "Will you help me with my nightshirt," he asked.

Marcel complied, pulling the nightshirt over his head and tugging it down to his waist. "And the opera?" he asked.

"The audience applauded… and my father congratulated me too," Louis said. Even though he enjoyed the attention on the stage and was proud of his performance, he felt a surge of joy at being home, especially with Marcel at his side. He moved toward Marcel and, with spontaneity that surprised him, embraced him.

Marcel froze, backed up, and then turned to pick up some clothing lying on the floor.

As Marcel left the room, Louis mumbled, "I'm sorry."

Whether Marcel heard him or not, he didn't reply.

~ ~ ~

"Good morning," Marcel said the next morning as he walked to the windows to open the shutters. When Louis mumbled, he continued, "We need to start training."

After stretching his arms and yawning, Louis pulled off the blanket and sat on the side of the bed. The first thing he remembered from the night before was Marcel resisting his innocent embrace. "I'll be training alone from now on," he said.

Marcel's smile disappeared. When he went to the armoire to fetch Louis's clothing, Louis stood up. "I can manage this morning on my own."

When Marcel bowed, shut the armoire door, and left the room, Louis wondered why he was behaving in such a manner.

~ ~ ~

Ever since Louis had been installed at Bellefonds, he noticed how frequently the Chevalier de Lorraine visited, not only calling on him but also conversing with many of Louis' servants and gardeners. Whether they were his spies or not, the chevalier had access to Louis' whereabouts at all times of the day and night, and Louis was becoming curious about the chevalier's interest in Bellefonds—other than his previous ownership of the hôtel.

At times Louis sensed that the chevalier might be following him as he walked through the lush gardens of Versailles on his way, when invited, to the king's levée and Mass. On this day in particular, Louis wandered through the groves and was mysteriously drawn into the labyrinth, an infinity of little intermingled passageways of gravel. Louis felt confined being fenced in by the high hedges, all trimmed with geometrical exactness. When he heard the scuffling of gravel somewhere in the labyrinth, his heart began pounding rapidly. He wondered why anyone else would be in the maze at this early hour in the morning.

His gate quickened until he came to a clearing with a statuesque fountain and a stone bench. Confused, he sat down to keep from making any noise and to hear the slow approaching steps, so slow that they reminded him of a predator stalking its prey. His heart still pounding, he couldn't put the exhilaration he felt to words.

When Louis felt a presence behind him, he glanced over his shoulder. The chevalier, with his piercing black eyes, stared down at him. Frightened, Louis' breath caught in his throat. "I need to leave," he said, making to stand up.

"Not yet," the chevalier said calmly, placing his hands on Louis' shoulders and pushing him back down.

A coldness in his spine, Louis told himself to move, but he couldn't. He shut his eyes as the chevalier lifted up his nightshirt with his right hand to feel his nipples. Unaccustomed to anyone touching him, Louis' body tensed. He wanted to tell him to stop, but the words died in his mouth when the chevalier stroked his stomach and slipped his hand into his breeches. Louis realized that the chevalier was using the same tactics Jules-Armand Colbert had tried at Sceaux. The chevalier was undeterred, however, and even continued when Louis whispered, "Stop."

But it was too late. Louis' entire body shook, his shoulders shivering and his toes curling. The chevalier offered Louis his handkerchief and, before taking his leave, said, "Before going to the levée, be sure to wipe off the nectar."

Louis complied after the chevalier disappeared, wiping his stomach and tossing the handkerchief into some shrubbery. He then left the idyllic clearing with his head bowed. The sound of gravel below his feet sent a coldness throughout his body. The exotic, mesmerizing labyrinth suddenly seemed dull to him.

~ ~ ~

After Mass, the Chevalier de Lorraine joined Monsieur and Madame Elizabeth in the salon, awaiting the arrival of the king.

"A very busy occasion when the dauphin marries," said the chevalier. "Now for some respite from the balls, carrousels, and operas."

"It has been chaotic," said Elizabeth, "but I've enjoyed every minute of it."

"Especially the opera," said Monsieur. "The princes and princesses were exceptionally talented."

"They practiced their parts meticulously," said Elizabeth. "Especially the Count of Vermandois."

"I don't see how kissing one's valet on the mouth constitutes practice," said the chevalier and, seeing Elizabeth's face redden, quickly disappeared into the crowd.

Louis entered the salon minutes later and quietly joined his aunt and uncle, avoiding any eye contact, even though he doubted if they had any idea about what had just happened in the labyrinth.

Monsieur tapped his foot nervously, uncomfortable with the silence. "Madame, you fell asleep in Mass today… again," he said, winking at Louis. "I even think you snored."

Louis giggled, hoping he was acting naturally. Fortunately, Elizabeth smiled too. "Going to church is a great trial for me," she said. "The sermons most invariably put me to sleep. But no one has ever reprimanded me for it, so I have grown accustomed to it."

Monsieur shook his head. "Tsk, tsk."

"Husband, to listen a whole hour to a fellow shouting to himself, whom one may not contradict, is not pleasant," she said. "But don't worry, I read verses every day from the German Bible."

"Madame's religious ideas are extremely simple," said Monsieur. "Now, my brother—"

"Your brother," said Elizabeth, swinging around to face her husband, "believes everything that the priests tell him… as if it comes from God himself."

She turned her gaze to Louis. "And all the while, the court surrenders itself to the sway of lust and debauchery."

Louis could feel the warmth in his cheeks. He wanted to leave but his Aunt Liselotte continued, "If only everyone was as scrupulous in their attendance at Mass as they are behind the palace tapestries on in the garden's shadows."

She straightened Louis' collar behind his neck. "*Junger* Louis," she said, "what is important is to live well in a Christlike manner and be merciful and diligent in virtue."

When he nodded, she smiled and said, "Now run along. It looks like I've burdened you enough."

He bowed and walked away, his mind in a dizzying flurry. He was worried that Elizabeth's words had been directed at him. There was something weighing heavily on his heart, but he couldn't quite name it.

# PART THREE

# FALL FROM GRACE

## CHAPTER TWELVE

# A Wolf in Lamb's Clothing

*Chevalier de Lorraine as Ganymede*

"One ought to be afraid of nothing other than things possessed of power to do us harm."

— Dante Alighieri, *Inferno*

## Hôtel de Bellefonds, June 1681

With Bandit by his side, Louis paused a moment before knocking on the door to Marcel's chambers. It was located beneath the main staircase in the salon. When Marcel opened, Bandit jumped up and down, wanting Marcel to pick him up.

"Sit," said Louis, and when he obeyed, Louis handed Marcel a scarf. "I thought you might like this," he said. "It's silk from Milan. Everyone is wearing them at court."

Marcel's brow furrowed. "It looks like a scarf the chevalier would wear," Marcel said, but Louis didn't hear him due to Bandit's barking. After Louis quieted Bandit down, Marcel continued, "Thank you."

Louis nodded. "I need to be on my way. Thanks to Madame de Maintenon, everyone must attend Mass during Lent," he said. He left with a smile, wondering if he should have asked to see Marcel's chamber or at least have asked if it was comfortable enough.

~ ~ ~

Louis squirmed in his designated place as he listened to Père Bourdaloue, who was called to deliver the Lenten course of sermons. The tall, corpulent priest spoke with superiority but with a simplicity that discomforted Louis, especially when the priest appealed to the king to purge the court of certain sinners.

> *Scripture forbids me to name them, but it is sufficient that Your Majesty knows and detests them… They will not withstand your disfavor nor the weight of your indignation, and when you will it, these vices, shameful to the name of Christianity, will cease to outrage God and to scandalize men. It is for that, Sire, that heaven has placed you on the throne.*

The mention of "these vices" caused some whispering in the chapel and when the Chevalier de Lorraine snickered, Madame Elizabeth cast him a menacing glance.

After Mass, Louis joined Jules-Armand and his cousin, François, in the salon. Jules-Armand grinned. "So, the Italian vice is now the topic of sermons?"

Louis' face reddened. He had some idea about what they were talking but he didn't dare say a word.

François then held his belly and protruded it, mimicking the priest. "Gluttony should surely have been the topic of the sermon today."

Jules-Armand laughed, but Louis squinted, unable to believe his cousin could ridicule the priest. "Did you hear," François continued, "that Père Bourdaloue, on his way to Carcassonne one evening, asked a peasant, 'Do you think I shall be able to enter the gate?' He meant, of course, whether it was likely to enter the town before the closing of the gates. But the peasant, eyeing his round belly, said, 'To be sure, père. If a cartload of hay can get through, why couldn't you?'"

Louis couldn't help but laugh at the jest, and the three laughed so hard that they were shushed by frowning courtiers nearby. Jules-Armand spoke up, "I don't think our presence is appreciated here. Shall we go to Bellefonds? Perhaps drink some wine?"

When everyone glanced at Louis, he nodded. He was excited to host his friends, but he was still uneasy being around them. He was shy but, fortunately, François would join them. He was naturally talkative.

~ ~ ~

The noise in the courtyard at Bellefonds piqued everyone's curiosity as the young nobles stepped down from their coaches. Even the gardener stopped raking. The hôtel had always been a peaceful abode, but François and Jules-Armand had also invited their valets to join them, and they had already drunk from the flasks of brandy they brought along in their coaches. The servants inside gawked at the young men as they invaded the residence.

Louis called on the chamberlain, a very reserved gentleman, to offer his guests wine in the garden and to have the kitchen prepare a tray of light fare, usually a collection of small frangipane, apple, and pear tarts. A few minutes later, Louis' governor, Monsieur de Monchevreuil, returned with the chamberlain.

"Count Louis, I believe your impromptu fête is ill-advised," said his governor.

"Ill-advised, monsieur?" said Louis with a frown. "Do you forget that I am the son of His Majesty Louis XIV?"

The governor's complexion paled as he nodded for the chamberlain to proceed with Louis' request, and they returned inside. Louis invited François and Jules-Armand to have a seat on some benches while their valets mingled with each other near the small fountain in the middle of the garden.

"The church should not meddle in such affairs," said François, continuing the conversation they had earlier at the palace.

Jules-Armand took a glass of wine from a tray the chamberlain held in front of him. "I heard that after a Capuchin father preached in their church on the Rue Saint-Honoré and gave the blessing, another religious took the floor and said that everything the preacher had just said was fine and good, but it did not address the large number of sodomites and magicians in the congregation."

"What happened?" asked François.

"Someone covered the man's mouth to prevent him from speaking. Then, the preacher went back up to the pulpit, begging everyone to excuse the lunatic."

The more the valets drank, the louder they chatted among themselves. The governor was seen observing from a window from time to time, and Marcel came and went, but did not associate with Louis or any of his guests. On one occasion, when Jules-Armand noticed him, he elbowed François and turned to Louis. "Where did you find that one?" he asked with an ornery grin.

Louis, afraid that Marcel might hear him, was lost for words.

"Have you enjoyed him?" asked François?

Louis squinted, his lazy left eye a little lazier than usual.

Jules-Armand jumped in. "Have you at least manualized it?"

"Manualized what?" Louis asked.

"His soldier... his crossbow... his spear," said Jules-Armand.

The ensuing laughter made Louis blush, but François continued, "His scepter, his dagger?"

Louis shook his head. "No, I would never—"

"I know a verse," interrupted Jules-Armand, standing up and flipping his glass with his finger to get everyone's attention, including the valets by the fountain.

*If, when your valet is given to drink, we look at his beauty,*
*You become angry and your mood is bad.*
*Isn't it disgraceful to treat us that way?*
*Does nature forbid us to admire such a handsome lad?*
*Believe me, be wiser from now on*
*And when you drink the wines you adore,*
*If you can't bear to have your page seen*
*Then give him dinner at the Twenty-Four.*

Everyone laughed except Louis. "What is the Twenty-Four?" he asked. "A restaurant?"

His guests doubled over in laughter. "It's a hospital for the blind," said Jules-Armand. "You're so naïve."

Louis, feeling the effects of the wine, didn't react, and François jumped in. "My count, you probably haven't heard about the new fraternity either," he said as he stood up and turned to Jules-Armand. "We should tell him about it."

"Yes, we should... but not here," said Jules-Armand, looking around to see if anyone overheard him. "Let's go to that magnificent residence on the Rue aux Ours."

"Yes," said François. He then turned to the valets and shouted, "To the bordello."

Everyone bellowed with joy. Everyone but Louis. When he saw Marcel watching from the doorway, he said, "I can't." And a moment later he ran behind some of the sculptured shrubs—where he gagged and vomited.

"True, I believe he is indisposed at the moment," said Jules-Armand, chuckling. "Come, let's leave the count in peace."

As soon as the crowd left, Marcel hurried to Louis's side, taking him by the arm and pulling him up.

"I'm fine," said Louis, pulling away from Marcel. He started for the door but staggered enough that Marcel had to help him. With an arm around his waist, he managed to get Louis to his chambers and on his bed.

Half asleep, Louis mumbled as Marcel removed his boots, "My only friend… if you only knew…"

~ ~ ~

Without opening his eyes, Louis could tell the sun was rising. He had no idea what time it was, but he hoped he wasn't going to hear Marcel open the windows any time soon—but to no avail.

"Good morning," said Marcel with the clang of the long iron window frames.

Louis didn't answer. His mind was still numb from the night before and he had faint memories of Marcel helping him to his chambers. Marcel was just too good to him, and he was embarrassed that he had neglected him lately.

A few hours later, in what seemed to Louis a few minutes, Marcel touched him on his shoulder. "The chevalier is here. He wishes an audience."

Louis nodded. "I'll see him in the garden as soon as I am presentable," he said with a raspy voice. He rose to find his breeches and vest neatly folded at the foot of his bed. Marcel returned minutes later with broth and rolls and quickly departed.

~ ~ ~

The Chevalier was pacing back and forth when Louis arrived. When the chamberlain arrived, he bowed and said, "It's good to see you again, Monsieur Chevalier."

The chevalier nodded. "Please bring us some wine." When he saw the pained look on Louis' face, he added, "It is the only cure, my count, to remedy the aftermath of such an evening escapade."

"You know about last evening?" Louis asked, trying to open his eyes wider.

"The entire court knows about it," he said. "Your band of young friends visited a bordello and caused quite a raucous. When they were asked to leave, they ran onto the streets, pulling down lanterns. One of them even tore down a crucifix on the Petit Bridge of Paris and set it afire."

"Mon Dieu," said Louis, making the cross across his chest and causing the chevalier to chuckle.

"Oh, I am certain it was an enjoyable night," he said. "I remember rampaging Paris when I was their age." When he saw Louis yawning, he added, "Well, I won't keep you any longer from your busy schedule. I must be on my way to Frémont."

"Frémont?" asked Louis, his eye a little lazier than usual.

"I have a hunting manor in Frémont, about five leagues from Paris… on the route to Fontainebleau. Quite delightful. I am meeting there with the Prince de Turenne, the Marquis de Créqui, and my brother, Count de Marsan." He emptied his glass of wine and grinned. "The buggers."

"Buggers?"

"You know," said the chevalier with a wink. "Someone who hits your target… who dips in your well of love… who picks from your orchard." But Louis was still squinting. "Mon Dieu, Count Louis, taking it in your derrière."

"Oh," said Louis, finally realizing what the word meant, the blood rushing to his cheeks.

"The meeting might interest you, but that will have to wait for another time. For now, my count, adieu."

~ ~ ~

Louis had barely recovered from his first encounter of overindulging in wine and spirits, when he received word that François and Jules-Armand were planning another visit. He would've preferred a quiet evening reading, but he couldn't decline their request. He had no friends and Marcel had become so distant.

No sooner had Louis changed his clothing than he heard his guests' noisy entrance, arriving in the main hall. And the group had grown in number with more valets and lackeys, all well-dressed and well-groomed. Louis noticed that his governor no longer arrived to chaperone him. In the garden, the chamberlain acquiesced to everyone's requests and as the wine flowed, the brash chatter intensified.

"I have another verse," said Jules-Armand, his lips now tinted purple.

"No, enough, let's just enjoy the wine," said François. "You only talk about rhymes and needless poetry."

"What's that, my prince?" said Jules-Armand.

"Let's sing! Let's go! Let's sing the music of drunkenness!"

"Yes, why not!" said Louis, holding up his glass. "I'll have a little more!"

François began to sing off tune. "I like the wine that falls singing into our glasses. I like the champagne that bathes our lips in the sparkling foam of its kisses." He then held up his empty glass. "Come on, monsieur chamberlain, do me right." He then took another glass of wine from the garnished tray and toasted Louis. "I drink to you, Admiral Louis of France."

"Me, I drink to fortune," said Jules-Armand, "the only mistress who has ever remained faithful to me."

"I drink to love," said François. "And to beauty… and to youth… and to life!"

They all looked at Louis, who slurred, "Me... I drink to forget who I am. Better yet, to freedom!"

The entire crowd cheered, causing Louis to giggle. "Wine makes the heart happy."

"You should be happy, my count," said Jules-Armand. "You are certainly the most handsome young gentleman at court."

"Indeed, after me, undeniably," said François, making everyone hoot and hiss jovially. "But you still need to watch out for all the buggers at court."

"Like that Count Zinzendorff," said Jules-Armand.

"The count who?" said François.

"Zinzendorff," he said. "He's visiting from Austria. A strange nobleman. When he visited the Grand Stables, Monsieur Philippe summoned twenty pages expert in horseback acrobatics to perform for him—but only in their nightshirts. When Count Zinzendorff saw the spectacle, he couldn't eat for days."

"He was ill?" asked Louis.

"Ill with desire," chuckled Jules-Armand. "He started the fashion of soliciting pages at the Small Stables by whistling. That was told to Count Morel, who couldn't believe it. So, he went to the stables alone, started to whistle, and immediately pages ran up to him from nowhere." As soon as the laughter lessened, Jules-Armand continued. "And that's not all; amongst them was one of his own pages."

The chamberlain returned with more wine, but Louis declined. "I don't think I should drink anymore," he said to his guests. "Look at you; wine doesn't even raise your eyebrows. You all have stomachs of iron... and heads of marble."

"I drink wine to wake up in the morning and I do just fine," said François with a proud smile. "Surely, you can have another glass with us."

"No, no more wine," said Jules-Armand. "Wine is good for demoiselles, but men drink brandy. A good *eau-de-vie* burns like the flames of hell."

"And that's why you are my dear friend," said François, patting Jules-Armand on the back, "but, alas, we brought no brandy with us."

"Madame Alexandra has brandy," said Jules-Armand slyly.

"To the Rue aux Ours!" cried François.

The crowd, instantly invigorated, finished off their glasses of wine. But when Louis glanced at Marcel standing in the doorway, he saw disapproval written all over his face.

"I don't know," said Louis, "I am not sure I should join you. Aunt Liselotte says it's not safe at night in Paris." He was lying, but he wanted an excuse to stay at Bellefonds.

"Au contraire, my count," said Jules-Armand. "All the streets and all the roads have been paved and lanterns put up in the streets and the courtyards. When were you last in Paris?"

Louis shrugged and finished the last few drops of wine in his glass. "To Paris!" he cried out.

~ ~ ~

The happy band of young men arrived at the corner of Rue aux Ours, just a few steps from a tall house with a gloomy façade. Jules-Armand knocked to announce their arrival, and the door opened. Once inside, the décor surprisingly changed as they entered a large salon with giant mirrors, intricately carved furniture with red velvet upholstery, and a small gathering of ladies and gentlemen half-dressed. Louis stood behind François and Jules-Armand, who was arguing with Madame Alexandra, a stout, good-looking woman in a beautiful corset that resembled the shiny décor of the bordello. Louis saw her frown change to a smile when François handed her a small bag of coins.

As they entered the next room, the valets followed and soon disappeared among the scantily clad ladies flirting on sofas, servants arriving from the kitchen with trays of canapés, and couples dancing and laughing as a naked young woman played the harpsichord.

François and Jules-Armand led Louis past an antechamber where a feast was underway. Louis' eyes widened at the sight of nude bodies glistening with sweat in the candlelight as they whimpered and moaned in an erotic ritual. In another antechamber were men dressed like pirates and women dressed like Greek goddesses.

Suddenly, a dainty lady in a satin corset with long blonde curls, pulled on Louis' arm, inviting him into the room to indulge the flesh like the others in every imaginable way. Another lady joined her, and they danced around him, teasing and caressing him.

Louis looked for François and Jules-Armand, but they had disappeared. Disgusted by the ladies' vulgar advances, he pulled away and staggered to the front door. The doorman, aware that Louis was getting sick, quickly opened the door, shoved him outside, and slammed the door behind him. In a cold sweat, he shook his head and looked about him. Seeing some empty wine barrels in the dark street, he took a few faltering steps towards them and dropped to his knees, gagging and heaving with tears rolling down his cheeks.

He waited several minutes before trying to get up but, when he heard footsteps in the dark shadows behind him, he froze. And when a hand grabbed him by the arm, he wanted to shout, but his entire body went taut.

"Come, get up," said the stranger.

When Louis was helped to his feet, he turned cautiously, not knowing if he would be robbed, beaten, or murdered. When he thought he saw a familiar figure in front of him, he blinked his eyes to see more clearly.

"Come, Count Louis," said Marcel. "We need to get you back to Bellefonds."

Taking Louis' arm, he led him to his mount. After swinging himself into the saddle, Marcel then held his hand out to Louis. "Are you able to ride? We can share the saddle if you stay close," he said, patting the swath of suede stuffed with padding. When Louis hesitated with a frown, Marcel held up his arms hands added, "Or shall we walk to Versailles?"

Louis glanced back at the house of ill repute as if he should wait on his friends, but then took Marcel's hand and mounted the horse behind him. Without a word, Marcel clicked his tongue and tugged on the reins.

~ ~ ~

After leaving the gates of Paris, the road led them through thickly wooded hills. Louis watched the vertical shadows marching in and around the tall trees, reminding him of the tales of Perceval. The solemn stillness of the sultry woods was only interrupted by the shallow clip-clop of the horse's hooves and an occasional cry of a night owl.

With no breeze in the air, Louis could feel the warmth of his breath reflected from the back of Marcel's neck. He held his arms around him but tried not to lean too heavily against his back. He no longer detected the earthy scent of the stables on his valet. He didn't detect any perfume either, unlike his friends or their valets. The scent seemed natural to him. A sugary odor of boy's sweat with a hint of lye soap.

Suddenly, the horse spooked. Marcel grabbed the reins to pull the horse's head down. "Whoa!" he said, holding the reins tight until the horse slowed down enough to keep from throwing them out of the saddle.

Louis grasped Marcel's waist tighter—not knowing whether it was acceptable or not. As he leaned on Marcel's muscled back and shoulders, his pulse began to race. He thought of the ladies who hounded him earlier and he felt nothing but disgust. Now he was accosting Marcel through no fault of his own, rubbing against him with every sway of the horse. It was far from disgusting, but he wondered if Marcel felt the same way. He didn't want to think any more about it, but he never thought of the ladies like others do. The more he thought about it, the more his thoughts were muddied.

"Look!" said Marcel, pointing to a wolf standing twenty yards away.

"The dauphin must have missed one," said Louis, feeling Marcel chuckle.

The wine was still playing havoc on Louis's mind. He was perturbed that Marcel had again stepped in as the Good Samaritan and, at the same time, he felt guilty and ashamed for getting into such predicaments. But the prospect of being so close to Marcel took him back to better times, like promenading in the woods and splashing in the river. Joyful times.

Louis was so absorbed in his thoughts that he didn't know Marcel had pulled on the reins, stopping at the steps of the hôtel. The chamberlain opened the door when Louis dismounted, and Marcel took the horse to the stables without a word.

Louis climbed into his bed, wriggling around until he found his favorite position on his side with his hands under his cushion, but his mind was turning over and over. Tomorrow would be another day. He would speak with Marcel in the morning. He tossed restlessly most of the night, trying to think what he would say. He was humiliated, but he told himself that everything would be fine. They could go for a walk in the woods. But his mind again went in circles, deciding exactly what he would say and how he would say it. Why couldn't he just turn his mind off like an oil lamp?

~ ~ ~

Marcel shook Louis' shoulder lightly. "Count Louis," he said in a calm voice.

Louis looked up and squinted as the sunlight flooded the room when Marcel opened the louvers.

"You have visitors," said Marcel.

Louis grumbled and pulled the cover over his head. "What fools would visit so early in the morning?"

"The Chevalier de Lorraine and the Marquis de Châtillon."

Louis sat up, rubbed his eyes, and watched Marcel as he poured water into the ceramic basin and laid out fresh soap. He wanted to talk to Marcel, but he left before he could find any of the words he'd practiced all night long.

When Louis joined the chevalier and marquis in the salon, they bowed and he returned the courtesy.

The chevalier approached him. "Do you know what happened at the bordel last night?"

Louis had to think for a moment. "No, I cannot remember too much. I know I made it home safe and sound." He looked at Marcel, who was holding open the door so the guests could gather in the garden. "Thanks to my valet," he said with a slight smile.

"You were with Prince François and Jules-Armand Colbert and their louts, were you not?"

"Yes, how did you know?"

"It's all the court is talking about today. Rumors are flying that after an orgy, you and your drunken young friends rambled through the streets until you came across a waffle boy. You found him so attractive that you pulled him into an alley. You pinned him against the wall of a building and stripped his breeches off."

Louis, frowning, shook his head in denial. "I was not involved," he said. "Ask my valet."

They looked at Marcel, who also shook his head. "No, he was not," he said. "He left earlier than the others."

"Good," said the marquis. "Apparently, the waffle boy fought back with his fists, unwilling to let the boys bugger him."

The chevalier jumped in. "And when he fought back, he angered one of your friends, who pulled out his sword and cut off the boy's…well, one of his virile parts."

"*Mon Dieu,*" said Louis in disbelief.

"That's not all," said the marquis. "They left the boy lying in his blood, ignoring his cries for help."

"Did he die?" said Louis.

"We have no news," said the chevalier, "but the king has been informed of the tragic event. It appears that one of the valets committed the crime."

The marquis scoffed, "But he won't be treated harshly."

Louis was flushed. "Why not? The poor lad might have died."

"Esteemed families are involved," said the chevalier. "If the valet had been attached to a family of lesser rank, he would've been condemned to burn at the Place de la Grève."

Louis, still feeling the effects of the late-night tryst, sat down on one of the garden benches.

The chevalier sat next to him and put his hand on his shoulder. "Count Louis, you should be more circumspect as to whom you invite into your inner circle."

Louis nodded, his head hung low.

"You were very fortunate last evening that you were not involved," added the chevalier.

The chamberlain, arriving with a letter on a silver tray, said, "Monsieur count, a message from Madame Elizabeth."

Louis opened it, read it, and stood up. "I apologize, messieurs, but my presence at Saint Cloud is requested this afternoon."

The chevalier stood and motioned for the marquis to depart. "Perhaps you will join us tomorrow evening. Monsieur Charpentier is presenting *David and Jonathan* at the Opéra in Paris. I have heard that it could not receive any greater ovation."

"All of his works, Count Louis," added the marquis, "have enjoyed great success."

Louis nodded. "Adieu, then. Until tomorrow."

~ ~ ~

The chatter of mignons gathering in small circles, the faint smell of cabbage, and the yapping of dogs told Louis he had arrived at Saint-Cloud. When Elizabeth's doorman escorted Louis into her library, he found her putting a seal on a letter she had just written.

"Come, *junger* Louis," she said, "take a seat."

Louis' heart skipped a beat and his smile disappeared. He knew that tone of her voice very well. Was he about to get a scolding?

She waved her letter in the air for her doorman to dispatch it and turned to Louis. "Do you know why I've asked you here today?"

Louis had an idea, but he shook his head. "No, Aunt Liselotte."

"You went to Paris last evening with the Prince of Roche-sur-Yon and Monsieur Colbert's son. Am I correct?"

"Yes, Aunt Liselotte, but I wasn't—"

"I know you were not involved in that horrific incident," she said. "I've already summoned your valet, Marcel, this morning, but that's not why I asked to see you."

Louis took a deep breath, feeling he was somewhat out of the woods.

"*Junger* Louis, your heart is full of excellent and noble qualities, but you are still impetuous and petulant. Since you have lived at Bellefonds, you have known naught but unruly behavior and pleasure... with the most debauched individuals. Moreover, your governor, Monsieur de Monchevreuil, is a man of weak constitution, giving you too much rein at the hôtel."

Louis' cheeks burned with embarrassment at hearing his aunt speak to him in such a manner.

She stood, walked around her desk, and stroked Louis' hair. "Please know, however, that I myself feel responsible."

Louis tilted his head to look up at her with a squint.

"Responsible, because I brought you to my husband's most devious court."

"But I had nowhere to go, Aunt Liselotte," said Louis, affected by his aunt's feelings of guilt written all over her face.

"I understand, but I also brought you here to repay your mother for her unconditional kindness toward me," she said and returned to her seat.

Tears welled in Louis' eyes. He had overlooked his aunt's kindness to him and to his mother.

"And I do not regret it, *junger* Louis, but Saint-Cloud—like Versailles— is overrun by atheists and sodomites." When Louis' forehead wrinkled, she added, "You know the word. Buggers."

Louis opened his eyes wide, surprised to hear his aunt use the word.

"Oh, I know who they are," she said, staring off into the distance. "Take our chief steward, Antoine Morel, who is in charge of the household. You've seen him before. He's one of Monsieur and the chevalier's favorites."

Louis nodded, but he wasn't sure.

"He has the spirit of the devil. He's lawless and has no soul. He used to recruit boys and sell them like horses, going to the pit at the orchestra to conduct his depraved deals. Now, he provides a steady flow of young boys to engage with Monsieur, making sure that he himself is not replaced as favourite by any of them. One of the boys, a valet named Bolgar from Lyon, must be more loyal than the others because Monsieur presented him with a sword adorned with diamonds… at a time when my children and I are in need."

"Monsieur Morel, he's an atheist too?" asked Louis, fascinated by the subject.

"Yes, he's as faithless as he is unscrupulous," she said. "He's as clever as the Devil and he told me himself that he had no beliefs. He steals. He lies. And he blasphemes."

Louis looked at his aunt. She was not beautiful. Her voice was gruff, almost manlike. But she was so charming, even when she was angry, that it didn't matter to him.

"And there's Colbert's son too," she continued. "He, the Duke de la Ferté, and the Count of Bérain were all dead drunk one evening and sent out for ice creams. When they discovered that the vendor was a handsome lad, they wanted nothing better than to *use* him. When he struggled to defend himself, the dolts struck him with the flat of the swords."

Louis listened with wide eyes. He had no idea that Jules-Armand could have behaved in such a manner.

"And the Chevalier de Lorraine is cut from the same cloth, *junger* Louis. Granted, he is beautiful as one paints an angel, but he is vain, overbearing, and contemptuous. You would be wise never to take his counsel."

"Yes, Aunt Liselotte," he said, unable to meet her eyes, knowing that he would join the chevalier at the Opéra the very next day.

Louis was relieved when the overwhelming visit was finally over, but he had forgotten how happy he felt whenever she hugged him farewell.

"*Auf wiedersehen, junger* Louis," she bellowed with a strong German accent.

~ ~ ~

Louis sat between the Chevalier de Lorraine and the Marquis de Châtillon, admiring the rich decorations and scenery as the curtain rose. Although Louis was well aware of the story of David, the young shepherd and harpist David who killed Goliath and became King Saul's favorite, he didn't know the opera would be so captivating. He sat on the edge of his seat when the muted strings of the orchestra colored the supernatural atmosphere of the prologue and Saul's horrifying desperation—especially when a witch foresaw that King Saul would lose everything: his children, his friends, and even his crown.

At the beginning of Act I, the joyous explosions of the trumpets and melodic flutes, along with the opulent costumes, bewildered Louis' senses. This was so far unlike any of the operas he'd ever seen. From his Bible studies with Abbé Fleury, Louis knew that King Saul had felt threatened by David's fame and his claim to the throne, but he didn't remember that David and Jonathan, King Saul's son, were so close. After all, they were from rival families.

In Act II, Louis was mesmerized by the voice of the boy soprano, who sang the part of Jonathan. And his heart skipped a beat when Jonathan made a covenant with David, saying he loved him as he loved himself.

In Act III, when King Saul was told how David was plotting his downfall, he accused David of treason and forced him into exile. Louis now understood why the jealous king banished David; the king had to take drastic measures to ensure his son's place as the ruler of Israel.

However, King Saul went a step further in Act IV, deciding to fight the Philistines and destroy David. Louis' eyes welled with tears when David reluctantly parted from Jonathan, lamenting, "I am distressed for you, my brother Jonathan. You have been very pleasant to me. Your love to me was more wonderful than the love of women."

In the majestic Act V, the wind players of the orchestra took up the more funeral sounding flutes. Jonathan, mortally wounded, lay lifeless in David's arms. Louis couldn't hold back the tears. If only he could commit David and Jonathan's words to memory.

David

Save Jonathan… get help, quick, run! Ah, but to no avail. I can see his blood flowing. Jonathan lives no more!

Jonathan

What sad voice calls me back?

David

What, I haven't lost you?

Jonathan

This last light that I see—without so faithful a friend by my side—would be nothing but night for me.

David

Ah, you must live!

Jonathan

I cannot.

David

It is me, David, who gives himself up to utter agony.

Jonathan

Despite the harshness of my fate, at least I can still tell you that I love you.

Tears streamed down Louis' cheeks, but he was too engrossed in the final scene to wipe them away.

David

Heaven! Heaven! He is dead! Did ever so faithful and tender a love suffer a more miserable fate? He was fairest of all to me, but all my efforts could not protect him from such a cruel death. Heaven alone could have forged bonds of such beauty. Alas! Does heaven now take him back and leave me here? Ah, can I stay here any longer? I have lost the one I love.

The final chorus praised David, the new king of Israel, but it was little consolation in David's grief for Jonathan. The crowd stood with an abounding ovation when the curtain fell. As Louis, the chevalier, and the marquis left the opera, the marquis offered Louis his handkerchief.

"I believe you enjoyed the opera, Count Louis," he said.

With a smile and sniffle, Louis said, "Yes, most certainly."

"I am pleased you enjoyed it," said the chevalier, as he hailed his coach.

Louis dreamt of the opera on the trip back to Versailles. When the coach arrived at Bellefonds, Louis stepped down from the coach. "Thank you for a captivating performance," he said.

The chevalier nodded with a broad smile. "I am traveling to Frémont, my manor in the countryside for a fortnight, he said. "I've asked several good friends to dine with me the day after tomorrow. You are welcome to join us."

"Thank you, monsieur chevalier. I accept your invitation."

"Good, I will send a coach to fetch you," he said. "I think you will enjoy the short respite and you will have the opportunity to meet new friends. Adieu."

~ ~ ~

Minutes later, Louis entered the hôtel and Marcel took his cloak, following him to his chambers. As Louis undressed for bed, he watched Marcel pour water into his basin. "The opera was incredible," he said. "It was about David and Jonathan from the Bible."

Marcel glanced at Louis. His eyes widened because Louis rarely spoke of his nightly adventures.

"I would like to hear about it," said Marcel.

"I'm very tired now, but I promise to tell you all about it tomorrow, if you like."

Marcel nodded with a smile as he laid out soap and a towel for Louis.

Preparing for his trip to Frémont, however, Louis never found the time to continue his conversation with Marcel.

# CHAPTER THIRTEEN

# The Darkest Days

*Justice Triumphant*

"The language of our sense and memory
lacks the vocabulary of such pain."

— Dante Alighieri, *Inferno*

## Hôtel de Bellefonds, April 1682

Louis joined the Marquis de Châtillon in the coach that awaited him in the courtyard. He was happy to have company for the trip to Frémont, especially with a young man who was as witty as he was handsome with his large eyes and long black hair. He was dignified, but there was a touch of feminity about him—something that Louis was accustomed to at the court of Saint-Cloud.

"We shall have an enjoyable ride today, Count Louis," said the marquis, his eyes taking on a silver glow as he gazed out the window. "And a delightful dinner at Frémont, I am sure."

"Yes, Monsieur," Louis said as he admired the marquis' gold-embroidered justaucorps and lacey cravat.

"Do you know who will be dining with us tonight?" asked the marquis.

"No," said Louis.

"I believe the Duke de Gramont, Prince de Turenne, Marquis de Manicamp, Chevalier de Tilladet, and Count de Marsan will honor us with their presence at the Chevalier de Lorraine's table."

"I've only met the chevalier's brother, the Count de Marsan," said Louis.

"Well, Prince de Turenne, the cousin of Minister Louvois, was *maréchal de camp* in the wars in Germany and is now colonel of the Royal Dragoons. Chevalier de Tilladet is captain of the king's Swiss Guard, and the Count de Gramont, before becoming a duke, had distinguished himself honorably in the king's campaign against Holland."

"And the Marquis de Manicamp?" said Louis.

"Oh, yes," he said. "Monsieur de Longueval. He was one of the king's pages and a captain of the cavalry before he was given the title, Marquis de Manicamp."

Louis took in the scenery as the coach rode past wooded areas and patches of open fields before arriving at the Chevalier de Lorraine's small château. The smell of flowering weeds permeated the coach and Louis reminisced about his walks with Marcel in the countryside until the coach arrived at Frémont. It was tucked away behind waist-high stone walls, and not far from it stood the remains of an old, ruined castle.

The chevalier greeted his guests when they stepped down from their coach. "Welcome," he said affably. "It gives me great pleasure to see you here."

*Le Petit Château de Frémont*

Once Louis entered the manor, he glanced around the manor's luxurious furnishings with an incredulous stare. "It is a small paradise, Monsieur Chevalier," he said.

"Even the king finds it pleasing to the eye. He occasionally lodges here after hunting near Fontainebleau," said the chevalier, directing valets to open double doors to the dining room. "My guests are awaiting your arrival."

~ ~ ~

Everyone at the long oak table all stood and bowed when Louis entered with the chevalier and the marquis. "Gentlemen, this is Louis de Bourbon, Count of Vermandois and Admiral of France," the chevalier said and then turned to Louis. "Count Louis, I introduce you to the Duke de Gramont, Chevalier de Tilladet, Count de Marsan, Prince de Turenne, and Marquis de Manicamp." Each of the guests nodded reverently as their names were called.

Louis noticed that the chevalier had spared no expense for the table's feast. Besides the pigeon pies, mutton, and roasted duck, there were fresh oysters and langoustines that had to be delivered to Frémont specifically for this occasion. Wine flowed in all directions as well as the conversation—until the chevalier tapped his goblet with a spoon.

"Count Louis," he said. "You may wonder why you've been invited to join us this afternoon. We are creating a new fraternal order. It is modeled on the Order of Saint Lazare."

The Chevalier de Lorraine clapped his hands, summoning a valet who arrived with a leather case. The chevalier opened it and removed a cross. "Messieurs, we will all wear this cross between our shirts and waistcoats. You will see that it resembles the cross of Saint-Michael, but instead of the saint trampling a dragon, here we have a man trampling a woman under foot."

When the chevalier handed it to Louis, he examined it closely before passing it along to the others. "It will be a society only for men?" Louis asked with his trademark squint.

"Well, if women were included or aware of the order, they would surely reveal their mysteries to other curious ladies, making it most likely that the king would soon learn about it," said Prince de Turenne.

"Yes," the Duke de Gramont said with an ugly twist of the mouth. "Ladies of the court have been so wayward and so corrupt that their charms are simply disgraceful."

"Our fellow courtiers are painting their faces now," added Prince de Turenne. "They have to cover the signs of God's wrath for the ladies' wicked ways."

Everyone nodded in agreement, except Louis. He was uncertain what the prince meant by the ladies' wicked ways.

"Yes, that terrible affliction," said the Marquis de Manicamp. "It is no wonder that men must drink wine and seek to pass their time with each other."

"Fortunately, I find it just as pleasurable," said the Duke de Gramont.

"But I don't think His Majesty would approve of the order," Louis said, getting everyone's attention.

"No, not at all," said the Chevalier de Lorraine. "That is why the order must remain secret. The king has shown an inconceivable horror for these sorts of pleasures, but he is easily disobeyed incognito."

"And disobeyed by certain people of quality, I might add," said the Count de Marsan.

Louis was silent. He understood the count was alluding to Monsieur, his uncle.

"That is why our members will need to take an oath of secrecy to renounce women," said the Duke de Gramont, unrolling a parchment. "We have drafted the rules of the order... and I am happy to read them to you... with your permission, of course."

When the Chevalier de Lorraine nodded, the duke cleared his voice and began to read.

*Article 1. That henceforth people will not be received into the Society who have not been visited by the Grand Master, to ensure that all their body parts are healthy... so they are able to bear any austerities.*

*Article 2. That they will take a vow of obedience and chastity with regard to women, and that if any contravened it, he will be expelled from the Order without being able to return to it under any pretext whatsoever.*

*Article 3. That everyone will be admitted indifferently into the Order, without distinction of quality, which will not prevent one from submitting to the rigors of the novitiate... which will last until the beard has grown on his chin.*

*Article 4. That if any of the brothers should marry, he will need to declare that it is only for the good of his business, or because his parents oblige him to do so, or because he must provide an heir. That he will swear at the same time never to love his wife and only sleep with her until he has an heir, and then only with permission, which can only be granted to him for one day of the week.*

*Article 5. That the brothers will be divided into four classes, so that each grand prior would have as many mentees as the other. And that, with regard to those who will present themselves to enter the Order, four grand priors will each have the new mentees in turn, so that jealousy will not harm their coalition.*

*Article 6. That, with regard to uninvolved persons, it will not be permitted to reveal the Order's mysteries to them, and that whoever does so will be deprived of membership for eight days, or even longer, if the grand master so desires.*

*Article 7. That, nevertheless, one can open up to those whom one hopes to attract into the Order, but that it must be revealed with so much discretion that one is sure of success before taking such a step.*

The Duke de Gramont looked up when he had finished reading. "Are there any questions?"

"Who is the grand master?" Louis asked, wondering if the wine had given him the courage to speak up.

"That needs to be decided this evening," said the duke.

"I believe I should have that honor," said the Marquis de Manicamp. "I have more experience when it comes to the art of manipulating young men."

"But I've been a peer. I am far from lacking in such skills," said the duke.

"Whatever advantages any of you may have," said the Chevalier de Tilladet, "please remember that I was head of the Order of Malta. An essential prerequisite of that order was to be perfectly debauched, and none of you can surpass my experience in this regard." He turned to the Marquis de Manicamp. "And you, Monsieur Marquis, I have never witnessed the vigor about which you are boasting."

The conversation at the table turned chaotic, with everyone trying to speak at once. The Chevalier de Lorraine tapped his goblet to get everyone's attention. "One at a time, gentlemen."

"Moreover," said the Chevalier de Tilladet, "the Duke de Gramont should be excluded from taking the role. He loves his wife too much."

"Yes," said the Marquis de Manicamp. "That is surely incompatible with our oath."

The Duke de Gramont laughed. "Oh, gentlemen, I assure you that the fine chevalier speaks the truth, but that was a long time ago… and no longer the case. I renounced the love of the fairer sex when my wife's valet became her love interest."

"We thank you, monsieur duke, for your humility," said the Chevalier de Lorraine with a wide grin. "Perhaps the Order is going to be too renowned to have just a single master. I suggest that all three of you, Marquis de Manicamp, Chevalier de Tilladet, and Duke de Gramont are worthy of the office. And, since we need four priors, why not add the Count de Marsan and all the priors will be masters." He looked around the table and when he saw everyone shaking their heads in agreement, he continued, "So be it."

As the wine flowed, the discussion turned to the relationships between valiant warriors and their mentees. Louis was all ears.

"Yes, heroes were like that," said Prince de Turenne. "Hercules, Theseus, Alexander, Caesar, all of them were like that. They all had their favorites too."

"And don't forget the tastes of William of Orange," said the Count de Marsan. "What they say about that brilliant military commander is all but true."

When the valets began lighting the lamps in the dining room, the Chevalier de Lorraine requested that the Marquis de Châtillon escort Louis back to Paris. He turned to Louis. "It is getting late, my count, and I want you to return safely to Bellefonds," he said.

Everyone at the table rose to bid Louis adieu. Outside, Louis thanked the chevalier for an enjoyable afternoon and entered his coach. Returning to Bellefonds with the Marquis de Châtillon, his mind was clouded by the wine, but he felt at ease as he relished the trip through the countryside. More important, there were important men at his father's court who shared his innermost longings. He was not alone, but he pondered why he wasn't invited to join the new order.

~ ~ ~

The next morning, Louis was awake when Marcel arrived in his chambers. After Marcel placed a tray with broth and rolls on the side table, he opened the shutters. "You slept well?" he asked Louis.

"Yes, thank you," he said bright faced, sitting up to take a roll. "It was an interesting journey yesterday."

Marcel's eyes widened. "Did you go to Paris?"

"No, I dined at Frémont."

"Frémont?"

"The Chevalier de Lorraine's retreat in the country," Louis said, standing to pull up his breeches that Marcel handed him. "I met the members of a *secret* society."

"Why is it secret?" asked Marcel.

Louis was silent for a moment and then said, "Well, I can trust you. It is a secret order and it requires total avoidance of women."

Marcel's jaw dropped. "Why do they want to stay away from women?"

"For many reasons," said Louis, as Marcel helped him pull a fresh nightshirt over his head. "Maybe we should go for walk to the river and I can tell you all about it."

Marcel nodded as he helped Louis with his vest.

At that moment, the chamberlain arrived at the door, clearing his throat. "Count Louis, the Chevalier de Lorraine arrived and wishes to speak to you."

Louis cast a frown at Marcel. "Another time?" he asked.

"Yes, of course, I understand," said Marcel, his voice going quiet as he left the room.

Minutes later, Louis greeted the chevalier in the grand salon. "Good morning, Monsieur Chevalier."

"Good morning, Count Louis," he said. "I would not have come unannounced this morning, but I wanted to speak with you about an urgent matter."

Louis led the chevalier to a pair of armchairs. As soon as they sat down, the chamberlain arrived to see if they needed anything. The chevalier motioned that nothing was required.

"I have news that there are many requests to join the order, including those from the Princes of Conti, Jules-Armand Colbert, now Chevalier Colbert, and several of Monsieur's favorites," he said, pulling a parchment from his waistcoat. "Here are the finalized ordinances. They are the same that you heard last evening with two additional ones for more clarity."

Louis took the articles and turned to the chevalier with an inquisitive look.

"We would like you to join, Count Louis," he said. "It would be an honor for the order to have someone of your standing."

"Thank you, Monsieur Chevalier," he said. "I am happy to become a member."

"Feel free to enlist others as you please... according to the rules, of course," said the chevalier. "Do you have anyone in mind?"

"There are distinguished men of the court in the order, so perhaps the dauphin might accompany me," said Louis. "It would be an opportunity for us to overcome our differences."

The chevalier stood up. "I am happy to hear you will join us, Count Louis, but it is not wise to involve the dauphin. He would be able to spy on you—and the proceedings—only to report his findings to His Majesty. You may not be aware of certain developments at court, but Madame de Montespan has contrived to turn the dauphin—and your father—against you."

Louis looked to his feet and nodded in agreement.

"I must take my leave, Count Louis," said the chevalier. "I will soon have information about your initiation ceremony."

"At Frémont?"

"No, in Paris," he said. "Adieu."

~ ~ ~

Several weeks later, Louis received word when the initiation would take place. On the said evening, he waited impatiently for the Chevalier de Lorraine to arrive. When the chevalier was announced, Louis welcomed the chevalier in the grand salon but was interrupted by his governor, Monsieur de Monchevreuil.

"Monsieur Chevalier," said Louis' governor, "I have received a message from Madame Elizabeth. Count Louis must not leave the residence in the evenings without a chaperon."

The chevalier turned to Louis with a harsh glance. "This is absurd," he said and turned to Louis' governor. "Are you going to escort the count?"

"No, Monsieur," he said. "Madame suggested the count's valet, Monsieur Joubert." He looked at Louis with a pained look.

"That is fine, Monsieur de Monchevreuil," Louis said. "Madame Elizabeth means well."

"But your *valet*?" asked the chevalier.

Louis shrugged his shoulders. "He is most trustworthy," he said and addressed his governor. "Will you please inform Monsieur Joubert to prepare a mount. He will join us this evening."

Within minutes, Marcel joined Louis and the chevalier in the courtyard. They departed just as the sun was setting and entered Paris just as the lamps were being lit along the quays. As they passed the Pont-Neuf bridge, Louis had second thoughts about riding the horse, but knew they would be traveling at a slow pace. He had second thoughts, too, about joining the order, wondering what Marcel would think.

When they reached the Rue des Marais, they had to ride in single file; two horses could not pass at the same time in the narrow lane—until it opened to a square with several glorious-in-their day residences. Stopping at the front of the gate of one of houses, the chevalier dismounted and knocked twice, using the door knocker in the shape of a goat's head. Once Louis and Marcel had dismounted, they were all introduced to a courtyard with walls covered in nettles and thistles. Louis was taken aback by the mysterious venue and unable to speak a word as they walked along a broad path of moss-eaten stones. Age-worn, chipped statues and nymphs were scattered about the garden amidst sycamores with rough bark and stunted branches.

Two servants in long white woolen robes appeared and took the horses to the stable. Two more servants in white arrived and led the chevalier and his guests into a cellar-like banquet hall—except for Marcel, who was asked to wait in the garden.

When Louis looked back at Marcel, the chevalier said, "Do not worry. Your valet will be comfortable there."

As soon as the chevalier and Louis appeared in the hall, the masked guests seated at a long oak table greeted the newcomers with cries of "welcome." But when the crowd recognized Louis, they respectfully rose from their seats and several rushed to greet him personally.

Louis took a step backwards and shuddered. "I'm being ambushed," he whispered in the chevalier's ear. "Who are these people? You expect a prince to eat at their table? I should leave."

The chevalier moved to Louis' side to refrain him from leaving the room. "Do not be vexed, my count," said the chevalier in a muffled voice, smiling warmly. "These are all men of quality. You will be treated here like a king among his feudal lords."

"Well, I will not stay long," he said. "My valet is waiting outside."

"He'll be fine," said the chevalier, leading Louis to the head of the table. He addressed the members once they were all seated. "My brothers, I present to you His Highness Louis de Bourbon, Count of Vermandois… who honors us by accepting our invitation to join the order."

"Your Highness," said one of the members, slurring his words, "I am the Duke de Gramont, and I claim the right to sit to your right. My ancestors have always held the favor of kings."

Louis squinted, looking at the chevalier.

"Brothers, I regret that we have little time for conversation. His Highness needs to return to his residence at a proper hour."

"So, we will not breakfast?" asked another prince with a scowl, his voice reminding Louis of that belonging to Prince de Turenne.

"We have no time to waste then," said the Duke de Gramont. He turned to the servants in white robes and commanded, "Wine and do not let the glasses rest empty! Not for a second!"

Louis took his place between the Chevalier de Lorraine and the Duke de Gramont. The chevalier motioned for one of the members to begin the proceedings. At least six feet tall with broad shoulders and a plump waist, the member raised his glass and said, "Brothers, may our hearts come together tonight like our glasses." Louis immediately recognized the voice of the Count de Marsan.

Prince de Turenne stood. "Yes, we are all equal here in the temple of Bacchus. We will love one another, help one another, and drink this wine together to our heart's content."

"Amen!" they all cried, drinking to each other's health. Toast after toast, the servants kept the wine flowing.

Louis's eyes were as wide as silver coins and glistened from the wine. Although he enjoyed its numbing effects, he wished he were home at Bellefonds. There was something amiss about the members' behavior. The Count de Marsan refilled his goblet every time he emptied it.

When Louis asked one of the servants for some water, the Duke de Gramont scolded him. "Your Highness, only a brother can serve the son of a king," he said. "Please do not dishonor us by cutting your wine with water. It would be an affront to us."

Servants in white robes then opened the side doors to a dank, dark chamber lit only by candlesticks on an altar. The chevalier led Louis to the altar and waited for all the members to find their places. He nodded at Prince de Turenne, who began reading the names of all those present, and they removed their masks as their names were called: "Gramont, Manicamp, Tilladet, Turenne, Châtillon, Colbert, Conti…"

Louis did not pay any attention to the remaining names called out. His face reddened when he saw Jules-Armand Colbert and his cousin, François, in the crowd. The marquis continued by reading the articles of the order's charter. When finished, the marquis nodded to the chevalier to begin the initiation, handing him a parchment.

"Count Louis of Vermandois," the chevalier said, "by signing this declaration of obedience to the Order, you swear to uphold the articles you've just been read?"

Louis's body trembled but he nodded. "Yes, Monsieur Chevalier," he said, taking the parchment. "Please bring me some ink and a quill."

The chevalier grinned when he heard the tittering in the audience. "No ink," he said.

"Will you have me sign it with blood then?" said Louis, his voice quivering.

"No, my count, with Liqueur de Hermes," said the chevalier. "Whom do you choose to manualize you?"

Louis facial muscles went slack as he turned to the chevalier with a flat glaze.

"My count, you must choose someone," said the chevalier.

Louis's face burned red as he scanned the audience. He could not choose one of his closest friends. That would be too embarrassing. He saw the Marquis de Châtillon, who had always been kind to him, and he nodded to him.

The Marquis de Châtillon joined Louis and the chevalier at the altar. He removed Louis's cape and handed it to the chevalier. Then he placed Louis' palms on the altar and pulled his breeches down. From behind, the marquis busied himself with his task. Louis, knowing he was hidden from view by the marquis and the chevalier, allowed himself to be pleasured while the chevalier held the parchment in front of Louis' waist. His body stiffened and then slumped against the altar, causing the crowd to murmur in delight when the chevalier held up the parchment for the members to see.

The marquis pulled up Louis' breeches, and the chevalier placed the Order's medallion around his neck. "You will wear this secretly under your waistcoat," the chevalier said. "And because you are the most valued member of the order, you will not be obligated to allow the four priors to satisfy themselves with you—as they do with other new members.

The Duke de Gramont and Prince de Turenne growled. "That is a shame," mumbled the duke, and the prince nodded in agreement.

"I want to leave," said Louis, holding back the tears. When the chevalier did not respond, Louis glared at him. "Now."

The chevalier turned to those gathered. "Please continue with the other initiations. Our guest of honor bids you adieu." He then addressed the Marquis de Châtillon. "Please escort Count Louis to Bellefonds."

When Louis and the marquis joined Marcel in the courtyard, the white-robed servants promptly brought the horses. Louis did not look at Marcel or speak to him until they arrived at Bellefonds. After saying farewell to the marquis, Louis and Marcel dismounted and Marcel took the horses' reins to lead them to the stable.

Louis said, "Good night," before retiring to his chambers. He was too ashamed to say anything more, wondering if Marcel had any idea about what had happened at the altar.

~ ~ ~

Louis' summer activities were routine, but busy. He regularly attended the king's levée and Mass and frequently attended court functions and special events like the king's illuminated soirées. Although Marcel still fulfilled his duties as valet, he spent increasingly more time in the stable. Louis noticed that their relationship had become more strained with little time for promenades in the forest or swimming in the river.

The Chevalier de Lorraine visited Louis at Bellefonds several times a week to report on the activities of the secret order. At the end of July, he invited Louis to attend a special fête, commemorating the death of Adonis.

"Why?" asked Louis.

"He was a youth of remarkable beauty in Greek mythology," said the chevalier.

"I accept your invitation," said Louis. "I will inform Monsieur Joubert to prepare my coach."

"If he swears secrecy like other members' servants," said the chevalier, "he can come along, wait in the grand hall, and observe the festivities... but in no way participate in them."

Louis tilted his head and squinted.

"Do not worry," added the chevalier. "There will be no initiations."

~ ~ ~

The grand hall buzzed with excitement as the members played cards at the tables. When Louis and Marcel entered, Marcel was shown to a row of benches in the back of the hall, where other servants sat quietly and avoided eye contact with the newcomer. Louis was shown to a table in the center of the hall, where Prince de Turenne, the Marquis de Châtillon, the Count de Marsan, and the Chevaliers Colbert and de Lorraine were seated.

"Good evening," said Louis. He glanced at Jules-Armand. "Is my cousin François attending this evening?"

"No, I am sorry," he said. "He has social obligations at court."

Prince de Turenne shuffled the deck of cards and turned to Louis. "Do you prefer Faro or Hoc Mazarin, my count?" he asked with a grin.

"I've watched Madame Elizabeth play Hoc at Saint-Cloud," Louis said.

"Hoc it is," said the prince, pulling a velvet pouch of coins from his waistcoat. "Let us open the bidding with ten coins, shall we?"

"But I have no coins," said Louis. "I've never gambled."

"That is no problem at all," said the chevalier. "We honor your word and will keep track of your winnings."

After the first hand, Louis was asked if he wanted to declare, raise, or pass. "I raise," he said, "by thirty coins."

"I'm sorry, my count, but the maximum is twenty coins," said the Count de Marsan.

"Let it be twenty then," said Louis, with a straight face.

"You must have learned the art of bluffing from madame," said the prince. "I've seen her leave many a table with her purse full of coins."

Louis, the only player left at the end of the hand, pulled in his winnings. "This is going to be an enjoyable evening, messieurs," he said boisterously. Everyone nodded in agreement, praising Louis for his card-playing skills.

The order's white-robed servants kept the players' goblets filled with wine. Louis, unaware of the discreet sprinkling of powders in his goblet, occasionally slurred his words while playing. After finishing a goblet of wine, he would refuse another until he was told that the wine was from one of France's most renown vineyards. He didn't notice, however, that he was losing games—one after another.

He turned to the chevalier. "I should return to Bellefonds."

"Yes, of course, after the next hand of cards," said the chevalier. "Wouldn't you like to recuperate some of your losses?"

Louis acquiesced and played another game but lost. "Fill up my goblet," he said, laughing. "I'm sure I will win the next game."

When he lost again, Marcel approached him timidly and whispered in his ear, "Master, it is two o'clock in the morning. Governor de Monchevreuil will have been alerted."

The players frowned when they realized that Marcel had spoken to Louis, breaking game etiquette. When Louis tried to get up, the Chevalier de Lorraine held him back by the arm.

"Please relax, Count Louis. You are enjoying yourself, aren't you?" he said, motioning for Marcel to return to his bench.

"Count Louis, please," said Jules-Armand." Just a few more games."

Louis took a big gulp of wine. "Yes, but then I must be on my way."

Playing. Drinking. Laughing. Louis forgot about the time until Marcel whispered in his ear. "Master, it is after six o'clock. The sun is rising."

"Where is my coach?" asked Louis.

"It is ready, master," said Marcel.

Louis struggled to get up, causing Marcel to take his arm.

"But wait, Count Louis," said the Count de Marsan. "We must propose a toast to our Admiral of France."

Louis, unable to respond, ignored the comment and left the grand hall with Marcel still holding onto his arm.

"Farewell," the Chevalier de Lorraine cried out. "We will feast again soon."

Louis didn't reply.

~ ~ ~

Louis removed his clothes and sat on his bed, unable to remember how he returned to Bellefonds. He laid back but the room started to spin, causing him to get up and walk around the room. When he looked in the mirror, his sight was a bit blurry, but he noticed how his body was changing. It was certainly for the better, because he didn't lack any admirers. In fact, he had reached those high points of pleasure with several of them. But they didn't satisfy him. An unlikely stable-boy turned valet did, however, even though his hair was often unruly and his demeanor sometimes distant. But they were made for each other, so why not tell him?

Louis tiptoed to the salon and knocked lightly on Marcel's door. When Marcel opened the door enough to see who was getting him out of bed, his face reddened when he saw Louis completely bare.

When Louis stumbled for words, Marcel asked, "Do you need something?"

"I want..."

"You want to ask me something?" asked Marcel.

"I want..."

"What do you want?" Marcel said, tilting his head trying to understand.

"I want to be with you," said Louis, wondering if the wine was talking for him now.

"You are handsome," Marcel, said, but not letting his eyes stray. "No one could dream of anyone so handsome."

"But?"

"But you don't need anyone," Marcel continued. "You have many acquaintances and all those gentlemen from your society."

Louis looked to his feet. Was he being chastised?

"You should go to your chambers before someone sees you," Marcel said, trying not to grin.

"Pardon me," he said and when Marcel nodded that his apology was accepted, Louis returned to his bed. He would make it up to Marcel. He had learned his lesson.

~ ~ ~

Marcel tried to wake Louis the next morning, but to no avail. It was not until Louis was summoned to Saint-Cloud in the afternoon that Marcel managed to get him dressed and on his way.

When Louis entered Elizabeth's chambers, the look on her face made his heart skip a beat. The whites of her eyes were showing.

"Good day, Aunt Liselotte," he said.

She didn't reply, casting a quick gesture at the armchair in front of her desk. Once he took his seat, she said, "I am very, very disappointed, *junger* Louis."

"Aunt Liselotte?" he said, squinting with beads of sweat forming above his lips.

"I paid the Chevalier over four hundred gold coins today," she said, her eyes protruding. "You drink, you gamble, and you stay out all night long in Paris. What if your dear mother knew of your affairs?"

"I am ashamed, Aunt Liselotte," he said, crumpling under her scrutiny and his temples throbbing from the effects of the prior evening's wine. "I wish you had not paid him."

"I had no choice," she snapped. "He threatened to go to His Majesty. It appears he is urgently in need of funds… some new scandal, I presume."

When a tear rolled down Louis' cheek, he wiped it with his sleeve.

"I never want to hear a word about that dreadful secret society you joined," she continued.

"I promise, Aunt Liselotte."

"And *junger* Louis, you will never associate with the chevalier or any of his associates again."

"Never."

"Nor any members of that society," she said. "You will swear to me or I shall never see you again."

"I swear, Aunt Liselotte," he said.

"Return to Bellefonds now," she said. "Governor de Monchevreuil is ordered to report to me should you not keep your word."

"Yes, Aunt Liselotte," he said as he rose from his chair.

Before he left the room, Elizabeth stood. "And I will ask Abbé Fleury to visit you more often," she said, her voice softening.

Louis stopped and turned around. "I would like that, Aunt Liselotte."

# CHAPTER FOURTEEN

# New Beginning

*Louis de Bourbon, Count of Vermandois (1682)*

"Soon you will be where your own eyes will see the source and cause, giving you their own answer to the mystery."

— Dante Alighieri, *Inferno*

## Hôtel de Bellefonds, October 1682

Louis woke early the next day. Stillness still reigned in the stately manor, only making the grandiose thoughts in his head even louder. He could fix what was broken and start a new life. He had dreams. He had dreams about having a son like the dauphin's newborn, the Duke of Burgundy. He had dreams about being honored as a Bourbon prince at his father's court. Without waiting on Marcel, he rose, opened the shutters, and dressed himself before sitting at his cluttered desk. He took a piece of parchment, inked a quill, and began writing, "Saturday, October 17, 1682…" But at that moment, Marcel arrived with his tray and made a place on the desk for a ceramic plate of rolls and a cup of broth.

"You rose early today," Marcel said as he looked around the room. Seeing a blue waistcoat lying on the floor, he picked it up and brushed it off with his hand before taking it to the armoire.

Louis put his quill down. "Shall we go for a walk this afternoon? To the river?"

"Yes," said Marcel, looking out the window. "A great day for a walk."

There was a knock at the door and Louis motioned for Marcel to open it.

"Monsieur de Monchevreuil," Marcel announced. When Louis nodded, Marcel let the governor pass as he left the room.

"A word, monsieur count?" said his governor.

"Yes, of course," said Louis, looking up at the tall and thin servant. Louis was struck by his stern features. Even though his posture was upright, he had a craggy, slightly crumpled look.

"Madame Elizabeth was not happy with my service in your household, monsieur count, but I begged her to allow me to remain in service here at Bellefonds," he said without making eye contact. "She agreed but instructed that I must keep a better watch over the… the household."

Louis had never noticed that his governor's hair was graying and thinning. "Monsieur de Monchevreuil," he said, "I am happy to have you at Bellefonds."

The governor bowed and left the room.

~ ~ ~

As Louis and Marcel walked through the forest, Louis gazed about the pristine surroundings but was surprised to see how suddenly nature had changed. Breaths of autumn breeze stirred the gold and brown leaves rustling in the branches. Louis had forgotten how much he enjoyed these walks with Marcel. They had seen less of each other lately and sometimes he had trouble remembering Marcel's face when they weren't together. Walking through the forest, Louis occasionally stole a glance at him out the corner of his eye. Today, Marcel's peaceful features meshed with the warm hues of the forest trees and the melody of distant bluebirds.

Marcel caught Louis looking at him. "You must be feeling well today," he said with a grin.

"Why do you say that?" asked Louis.

"You were out of your bed before daybreak," Marcel said. "Was it that miserable rooster crowing?"

Louis couldn't help but smile. "No, I couldn't sleep thinking about my visit with Aunt Liselotte yesterday." When Marcel's grin disappeared, Louis added, "I doubt if you will ever see the Chevalier de Lorraine or my cousins at Bellefonds again."

Marcel raised an eyebrow. "Did something—"

"My debt. Aunt Liselotte had to pay the chevalier for my gambling losses. Now she forbids me to associate with him… or any of the others."

"And the secret order in Paris?" asked Marcel.

"I am no longer a member," said Louis, looking at Marcel to see his reaction.

"Perhaps it's not a bad idea, considering the drinking and gambling there."

"Yes, I agree," said Louis, not wanting to speak any more about the order, especially about what transpired during his initiation. He saw a tree nearby with apples hanging from the bough. He picked two and tossed one of them to Marcel, who rubbed it on his vest and then took a big bite.

When they reached the space that opened up to the river, Louis recognized a spot where they'd slept before on sunnier afternoons. "It's cool and shady there," he said, hinting to stop and rest.

Marcel nodded in agreement. "We could relax for a moment," he said, taking another bite of his apple.

The grass was no longer green on the knoll. It was straw-brown but still comfortable to sit on the tufted dead grass. Not far away were the remains of an old stone structure. Marcel pointed to it. "I don't remember seeing that ruin over there," he said. "Do you?"

"No, I wonder what it was," Louis said with a dreamlike squint. "Maybe a hunting cottage."

"It would have been wonderful, living in nature like that," said Marcel.

"Surely," added Louis. "With animals, and horses, and with someone who… enjoys a simple life far from court."

They sat for a while without talking. When the sun hid behind the gray autumn clouds, Marcel rubbed his arms to warm them. "Shall we return?" he asked.

"Yes," he said, looking at the sky, "it might rain."

Marcel rose first and held out his hand to help Louis to his feet.

"Thank you," he said, still holding Marcel's hand. "And for the company, too." Then he leaned over and gave Marcel a kiss on the cheek. The smell of lye soap was at the same time acrid and sweet when mixed with Marcel's own scent.

"Why did you do that?" Marcel asked.

Louis shrugged, glancing at Marcel to see the reaction on his face, but there was none. As they returned, silence prevailed except for the rustling of the leaves underfoot. Louis remembered how they used to race back like frightened foxes, but now they walked. They were becoming young men with worldly thoughts pressing on their minds. Or maybe it was just the unexpected kiss.

When Louis retired to his room, he couldn't bring himself to look at Marcel directly. "Would you like to explore that ruin by the river tomorrow?" he asked, looking at his feet.

When Louis looked up, Marcel said, "Yes," with a big smile and went to his room.

~ ~ ~

Louis was fast asleep when Marcel arrived the next morning, reminding Louis that he was expected at the king's levée and Mass. After fulfilling his duties, Louis joined the courtiers in the salons, where he noticed Jules-Armand and his cousin, François. When they motioned for him to join them, he did so. But reluctantly.

"I am no longer a member of your order," he said before they could greet him. "If you will excuse me."

François and Jules-Armand cast a puzzled glance at each other as Louis walked away. Louis, not knowing where to go, spotted the girl who he had once mocked with his cousin. Approaching her, he was surprised to discover that she didn't have a moustache after all. She did have, however, bold and coquettish eyes.

"Count Louis of Vermandois," Louis said with a forced smile.

She curtsied. "It is a pleasure to meet Your Highness. I am Jeanne d'Orbay. My uncle is Monsieur François d'Orbay, assistant to Le Vau."

"Le Vau?"

"The king's architect," she replied, inspecting Louis from head to toe.

"Oh, yes, of course," said Louis. "The pleasure is mine, mademoiselle.

Jeanne's parents arrived. "Jeanne, I hope you are not bothering His Highness?" her mother said before turning to Louis with a curtsey. "Madame d'Orbay and my husband."

Louis nodded respectfully when Monsieur d'Orbay bowed.

"Our Jeanne loves to talk," she continued jovially. When Jeanne's smile showed she didn't object to the comment, her mother added, "Just yesterday she heard a little swallow perched in the tree, chirping incessantly. Our Jeanne was sure the little bird would be tired when it returned to its nest."

"Mother, please," said Jeanne, blushing.

"But I told her," said her father, "that I have a little swallow, too, that is never silent, but never seems tired at all when she goes to sleep."

Jeanne laughed and turned to her father. "His Highness must dine with us. Isn't that true, Father."

"Yes, of course," he said, turning to Louis. "Tomorrow evening perhaps?"

"Please accept my apologies, but I cannot join you tomorrow evening," said Louis.

"Well, tomorrow afternoon I could visit the Hôtel Bellefonds," said Jeanne. "I've heard the gardens are beautiful."

"Mademoiselle, I am very sorry," said Louis, "but I have a very busy day tomorrow. Court affairs." He then nodded at Jeanne's parents to take his leave. "I've enjoyed meeting you," he said. "Adieu."

Leaving quickly, he encountered the Chevalier de Lorraine before leaving the salon.

"Good day, monsieur count," said the chevalier.

Louis's face reddened. "You dare go to my Aunt Liselotte for my debts… without my permission?"

"No reason to be upset," said the chevalier. "I would never impose upon her, but I am having particular difficulties at the moment. And how are you doing?"

When the chevalier reached forward to put his arm on Louis' shoulder, Louis stepped back and said, "Monsieur Chevalier, in the future, please request an audience should you ever wish to visit Bellefonds again."

Louis departed, leaving the chevalier standing with his mouth agape.

~ ~ ~

The next afternoon, Louis and Marcel left the hôtel early to have plenty of time to explore the deserted stone cottage near the river. After a brisk walk and jumping over a small ditch, they arrived at the structure covered with ivy growing from the cracks between the stones. There was so much ivy that the cottage seemed to be caught in a trap.

Louis looked back at the ditch. "That might have been a moat," he said with a big smile and then walked to the entrance. "I wonder who used this?"

"It smells of suffering and death," said Marcel, glancing at the river in the distance. "Maybe courageous soldiers used it to defend Paris from invasion by pirates sailing up the Seine."

"Or it was used to store grain," said Louis in such a serious tone that they both broke out laughing before plopping down on a fallen tree trunk.

"My brother has an heir now," said Louis, picking some dead bark off the tree and flipping it into the brush. "Louis, Duke of Burgundy… another Louis."

"Congratulations," said Marcel, smiling until he saw a frown on Louis' face.

"If I were considered an heir to the throne, that would make me third in line now after the Grand Dauphin and the Petit Dauphin. Maybe I should start my own dynasty like my uncle, the Duke d'Orléans."

"Do you want to have children?" asked Marcel.

"I've thought about it, but to be a father like the king?" he countered. "Committing adultery? Setting aside laws of marriage to legitimize children? Hiding indecencies with a cloak of court etiquette?"

Louis kicked the dirt with his feet, not expecting any reply from Marcel about such matters. He, too, was surprised that he'd spoken so candidly.

"Did I ever tell you about the demoiselle with the moustache?" he asked, feeling the need to lighten up the conversation.

"Yes," said Marcel with a grin, "but is there more?"

"To escape members of the secret order at court yesterday," Louis said, "I greeted her. What a mistake."

"Why?"

"She could not stop wagging her tongue," he said. "And then I was accosted."

"Accosted?"

"By her family."

Marcel wrinkled his nose. "I'm sure she was flirting with you."

"Not only did she flirt with me, but she had the imprudence to write me a note this morning, inviting me to join her family for a walk in the palace gardens."

"Maybe she's attracted to you," said Marcel. "Or maybe she thought you were trying to seduce her."

Louis gasped. "Trust me, she awakened no singular feeling in me," he said. "And the onslaught of conversation with her and her family was so torturous that I had to excuse myself quite impolitely."

As they returned to the hôtel, Louis thought about Marcel's interest in Mademoiselle d'Orbay. Perhaps he was jealous, he thought. He then grabbed Marcel's hat and took off running. Marcel chased after him until they approached the hôtel and noticed a coach in the courtyard.

Louis, chuckling, tossed Marcel's hat back to him and walked toward the unexpected coach just as the lackey opened the door to help a young lady step down.

"Mademoiselle d'Orbay?" said Louis with a squint. "What brings you to Bellefonds?"

"I didn't receive a reply to my letter, so I thought I would pay you a visit. I hope you are not too unhappy with my unannounced visit," she said, looking curiously at Marcel, who quickly entered the hôtel. "Is he a relative? I didn't know you had a brother."

Louis was lost for words. "No, Marcel Joubert is my valet. I only have a sister."

"Yes, the lovely Princess de Conti," she said. "So, have you considered my invitation?"

"I will check with my governor and reply to your letter with haste," he said, motioning the lackey to open the coach door. "But I must leave you for now—with your permission, of course."

"As you wish, Your Highness," she said with a slight scowl. "Adieu."

When Louis entered his chambers, Marcel was closing the shutters and lighting the oil lamps. "The silly damsel thought you were my brother," Louis said, laughing. He then picked up a book from his desk. "Shall I read to you about David and Jonathan?"

Marcel nodded and took a seat at Louis' desk. Louis jumped up on his bed and began reading.

*Jonathan gave his weapons to the boy and said, "Go, carry them back to town." After the boy had gone, David got up from the south side of the stone and bowed down before Jonathan three times, with his face to the ground. Then they kissed each other and wept together—but David wept the most.*

"Look," said Louis, "here's a drawing of them." When he motioned Marcel to join him, Marcel sat on the side of the bed and leaned over to see the illustration. Louis continued reading.

*Jonathan said to David, "Go in peace, for we have sworn friendship with each other in the name of the Lord, saying, 'The Lord is witness between you and me, and between your descendants and my descendants forever.'" Then David left, and Jonathan went back to the town.*

By the time Louis had read the verse describing Jonathan's death, he and Marcel were both in tears.

*Jonathan, my brother, I miss you! I enjoyed your friendship so much. Your love for me was wonderful, stronger than the love of women.*

~ ~ ~

Just before daybreak the next morning, Monsieur de Monchevreuil knocked on Louis's door and opened it to find Louis and Marcel lying next to each other asleep on the bed. Marcel woke and rose, shaking Louis' shoulder to wake him.

Louis sat up and rubbed his eyes to focus on Marcel quickly leaving the room and his governor entering and approaching him. "Monsieur count," he said. "You have a visitor, your sister. She awaits you in the salon."

Louis, still dressed from the night before, brushed off his vest and followed the chamberlain to the salon.

"Is there anything wrong, Marie-Anne?" asked Louis with a furrowed brow.

Marie-Anne paced back and forth with her jaw clenched.

"Marie-Anne," he said. "What is it?"

She stopped and put her hands on her hip. "I am taken by the court to be the most foolish of princesses."

"Please come and sit," Louis he as he took a seat. When she began to pace again, he snapped, "Marie-Anne!"

She reluctantly took a settee opposite him. "My wedding night was a catastrophe. Louis-Armand knew nothing about the correct behavior of a husband."

Louis' face reddened, having never heard his sister speak so informally.

"And it has been rumored that I am enamored with my brother-in-law."

"François?" said Louis. He looked to the floor as thoughts of his cousin at the secret order ran through his mind.

"And now, rumors are flying about the palace that my husband takes refuge in the debauchery of the court with courtesans, causing scandal after scandal. He surrounds himself with the most fashionable women and even…"

Louis looked at her with a squint.

"Never mind," she said. "I just fear that ugly disease."

Still squinting, he said, "Ugly disease?"

She rolled her eyes. "No matter."

"Perhaps you should speak to our father," he said.

"That would be most embarrassing, considering I begged him to let me marry Louis-Armand in the first place… especially after the Emperor of Morocco had asked for my hand."

"You were to marry the Emperor of Morocco?"

Marie-Anne stood and started pacing again. "The Moroccan ambassador had my portrait painted for the emperor and told him of my admirable modesty and charming manners. My image was so engraved in the emperor's mind that he wrote our father asking for permission to marry me."

"That is incredible, sister," said Louis, now completely awake.

"The emperor would take me as his wife according to the law of God and his prophet Muhammad, but he assured our father that I would keep my religion and my ordinary way of life," she said before sitting down again."

"I had no idea," he said.

"Fortunately, the emperor's request was denied," she said. "Our father was worried about his daughter not marrying in the Christian faith, but the courtiers enjoyed the story... even writing verses about it."

Louis' eyes widened. "Oh, tell me one," he said. "Please?"

She looked off into the distance for a moment and then recited one.

*Why do you refuse the glorious tribute*
*Of an emperor who awaits you, and your beauty will discover?*
*Since the land of thyme is calling you,*
*Leave, for it may be where you will be kept a faithful lover.*

For some reason, Louis didn't feel sorry at all for his sister, knowing that she loved being the center of attention at court and that she was also his father's favorite child.

Marie-Anne sighed. "Oh, well, at least our father is happy about your behavior at court."

"Sister?" he said, his head slightly tilted.

"He has heard rumors of your attention to Le Vau's niece, Mademoiselle d'Orbay."

Tidings of his father's pleasure in such matters made Louis smile, even though he had no interest in the young lady at all. "I am happy," he said, "that at least he finds something pleasing about me."

"He would be even more pleased, I am certain, if you should marry her."

"She is not a princess," he said. "Why can you marry a prince and I not a princess?"

"Well, according to the Grand Dauphin, you are not even the king's son," she said. "Apparently, the Duke de Lauzun, is your father."

"That dolt! That is absurd!" Louis snapped, jumping to his feet and his cheeks turning fire red.

"Yes, it is. But you know how courtiers love to flap their tongues," she said and then stood. "I must go. I need to speak with François. He's been too distant these days."

Louis didn't dare to mention why François was ignoring her. At that moment, Marcel entered the salon. When Louis noticed his sister casting a curious glance at Marcel, he said, "My valet," he said. "Monsieur Joubert."

She frowned and said, "Adieu, brother." She promptly left.

Louis took a deep breath, somewhat shocked at the impromptu visit and the most unusual conversation. "My sister, Princess de Conti," he said to Marcel.

"I thought so," Marcel said. "I could see the resemblance."

"Any resemblance to the king?" When Marcel's brow wrinkled, he added, "No matter. We should go for a walk."

"I've been thinking," said Marcel. "Why not saddle the horses and go riding for a change?" When Louis wavered, he added, "With some practice you could soon overcome any—."

"Fear?" he said, biting his lip. "You are right, and it is a great day for a… a short journey."

"Wonderful," said Marcel, "we have a new horse, too, from Saint-Cloud, a gift from your uncle."

"Why would he give us a horse?"

"Probably because it's Italian," Marcel said with a giggle.

"What?"

"Well, the breeding of Italian horses has really been neglected and their standard of excellence is not what it used to be," Marcel said. "But they are good carriage horses."

~ ~ ~

As Marcel and Louis rode at a calm pace along the well-trod path to the north, Louis broke the silence. "What are the best horses, then?"

"Belgian horses are known for their great size and beautiful form, but I find them a bit slow. The heavy horses can draw heavy loads. Alas, for stable boys, they require more feeding and exercise to keep them strong."

Louis' eyes widened as he heard Marcel speak. "And French horses?" he asked, as if to test Marcel.

"Some say they are equal to English ones, but that's not true," he said. "French horses are not as powerful, as fast, or as beautiful. But there are some good breeds raised in France, especially from Limousin. I think they're the best hunting and saddle horses I've ever seen."

Louis was proud to hear Marcel speak with such candor. "You've been riding since you were a child?" Louis asked.

"Yes, but it was difficult at first," he said. "It was really a long time before I could master the reins. I couldn't keep my trousers from falling to my knees... until I was given straps to hold them up." When Louis stopped laughing, Marcel continued. "But little by little, I was allowed to ride with Papa Joubert in the countryside until I was able to go alone. Later, I joined him buying new mounts and, soon afterwards, he allowed me to buy mounts on my own."

"You procured mounts for the stable."

"Yes," Marcel answered. "The first time, though, I was afraid I would disappoint Papa Joubert."

When Marcel didn't continue his story, Louis pulled on his reins and motioned Marcel to pause riding. "Well, tell me about it!"

Marcel was all smiles. "Well, there was a horse dealer, Lenoir. I thought he was respectable, so I told him the type of horse I wanted. He just looked at me, winked, and said, 'I have exactly what you want.' Then he nudged me in the ribs with his elbow and put a finger to his nose. I didn't really know what all that meant. I thought it was just the way that people do horse transactions. Then Lenoir said, 'Don't worry. Once he takes off, no one will ever see who you are or what you are riding.'

"I told him that it didn't matter, because I was never ashamed for people to see what I was riding. He then went into the stable and after some brushing, led the horse out. It had a white face and legs, but I noticed it had a roving eye too. After watching it trot with its head and tail high in the air, I agreed to pay fifty coins... not too large a sum.

"The next morning the horse arrived, and Papa Joubert and several stable boys praised the horse's tapering legs and his wide nostrils. He was still saddled, so I thought it would be a great time to show everyone my riding skills. I mounted him with a bit of difficulty, but I was able to gently urge the horse to move forward.

"After riding a short distance, I turned him back and gently shook the reins for greater speed. When he broke into a trot to the joy of the small crowd, I decided to call him 'Treasure.' However, his behavior suddenly changed. He tossed his head, snorted, and moved at an uneven pace. I could hardly keep my seat on him.

"At the end of the path were some gardens between a ditch and a high hedge. As we approached the end of the path, he cocked his ears and quickened his pace. I was worried about the danger ahead, so I pulled on the reins. But the result was not what I expected. As the hedge rose high before my eyes, we were upon it. I closed my eyes and I felt like we were flying through the air until we landed on the other side of the hedge. Still wrapped around Treasure's neck, I opened my eyes. We had safely landed in the gardens.

"An old woman was working in one of them and shouted, 'Oh, you villain, I'll have your hide.' But I was too overcome with joy to worry about her garden. I directed Treasure to the road nearby, which led through the gardens back to the stable gate.

"Once through the gate, I saw the crowd. I'm sure everyone wondered how I managed, considering the hedge was too high for them to see what happened on the other side. When they finally saw me, they shouted 'Bravo! Bravo!' They thought the jump was intentional on my part."

Louis struggled to keep from laughing, but Marcel continued. "They loved the jump," he said, "but I'm glad they couldn't see me hanging desperately onto Treasure's neck on the other side of the hedge."

"And no problems with Treasure after that?" Louis asked.

"No," he said, "but feeding him myself must have made me his special friend."

"Why is that?" asked Louis.

"One day, another stable boy fed him and when he bent over to rub his legs, he got an agonizing nip on that part of his body that was up in the air. The pain must have been serious, because he cried out and fell on his face in the straw. When he saw me watching from the stable door, he said, 'Marcel, this horse is not safe; he just tried to eat me."

The boys laughed as they turned their horses to return to Bellefonds. As they entered the village of Versailles, a *chaise à porteurs* approached.

Louis pulled on his reins and dismounted in front of it, causing it to come to a halt. He then ran to the side of it and cried out to the person inside, "Is it the sword or the cudgel you want, you wretched fish?"

To Louis' surprise, the Duke de Lauzun jumped out of the chaise. "Oh, pardon me, monsieur," said Louis. "I thought I was speaking to the Grand Dauphin."

The duke returned to his chaise, mumbling obscenities. As it departed, Louis remounted and turned to Marcel. "I apologize for my behavior," he said. "I am fortunate that it was not the dauphin. My father would have been terribly upset with me... again."

*Chaise à Porteurs*

Marcel only nodded, and they resumed their ride home. When they reached the Avenue de Paris, they passed a coach, from which a gentleman waved wildly with his cane and yelled to his coachman, "Stop! Hold! For mercy, hold!"

Louis and Marcel brought their mounts to a stop, turned, and approached the coach as two gentlemen stepped down from it.

"Monsieur count," said the first, dressed in a blue coat and a vest trimmed in gold lace. "What a pleasant surprise to see you."

Louis smiled when he recognized him. "Monsieur Lully, the pleasure is mine to see you again. It has been some time since my dancing lessons at Saint-Cloud."

"I present you with my... well... my protégé, Brunet," Lully said with a wink and then looked admiringly at Marcel. "I assume this handsome young man is yours?"

Louis blushed. "No, he is just my valet," he said. Worried that he might have hurt Marcel's feelings, he cast a quick glance at him but detected no reaction.

"You both must join us," Monsieur Lully said. "We are on our way to a jovial tavern."

Dark-haired Brunet was dressed in a black velvet coat and breeches with black silk stockings. "Yes, you both must join us," he said, admiring Marcel. "We will sing and abuse the wine until we lose our voices."

Louis looked at Marcel, whose demeanor had not changed, and said, "I am sorry, but we are expected at Bellefonds."

"Very well," said Lully. He bowed and motioned Brunet back into the coach.

"Adieu, Messieurs," said Louis as he and Marcel resumed their ride. They were still several minutes away from the hôtel, but they didn't speak until Louis broke the silence.

"You are more than a valet, Marcel. You are an accomplished horseman, a—"

"I understand," Marcel said dryly. "There's no need to explain."

Louis felt like he would forever be sorry for his thoughtless words. He realized that nothing was ever gained when he acted so impulsively.

~ ~ ~

The next morning at daybreak, Monsieur de Monchevreuil arrived with a tray and placed it on Louis' desk. When he opened the shutters, the noise woke Louis.

"Oh, please tell me that my sister is not here again."

"No, monsieur count, it is more serious."

Louis sat up and pulled the covers down. "What is it?"

"Monsieur Joubert was taken away in the middle of the night," he said, with a pained look on his face. "By the police."

"And you did not wake me?"

"I am sorry, but he asked me to let you sleep. He said you had to attend the levée this morning."

Louis put his hand on his forehead. As he watched his governor fetch his vest and waistcoat, he wondered if the old man had told anyone about Marcel sleeping in the same bed with him.

Monsieur de Monchevreuil helped Louis with his waistcoat. "Can I do anything more for you, monsieur count?" he asked.

"No, I think you've done enough, monsieur."

~ ~ ~

After the levée, Louis hurried to visit Abbé Fleury who was speaking with fellow ecclesiastics near the chapel. When the abbé saw Louis, he excused himself and approached him.

"Count Louis, you are flushed. Are you well?" he asked.

"Yes, I am, monseigneur," he said. "But my valet, Macel Joubert, was arrested this morning."

"For what reason?" asked the abbé. "What did he do?"

"I have no idea," said Louis, "but perhaps you can..."

"I'm sorry, Count Louis," he said, shaking his head. "I cannot help you with such matters." When tears swelled up in Louis' eyes, he lowered his voice. "However, I do know Lieutenant General de la Reynie very well. I will speak with him. In the meantime, however, make your way to Saint-Cloud this afternoon and wait for me there."

"Saint-Cloud?"

"Yes, I have no influence in secular matters, but your aunt... she has the king's ear."

Louis fidgeted with the hem of his waistcoat in the carriage en route to Saint-Cloud. He wondered how Aunt Liselotte would react to the news of Marcel's arrest—especially if his sleeping in the same bed with him was the cause. He remembered how viciously she lashed out about the debauchery and the *vice italienne* at court. He was so light-headed from worry that when he stepped down from the coach, he almost lost his balance.

He was directed to Elizabeth's chambers, only to find his aunt as big and jolly as ever. "Come, *junger* Louis, embrace me," she said.

Minutes later, Abbé Fleury arrived with Lieutenant de la Reynie, bowing respectfully. The lieutenant, a tall man in his fifties and dressed in a coat and breeches of woven black wool, removed his hat.

"I received your message, Abbé Fleury," said Elizabeth, "requesting an audience to speak of an urgent matter. Pray tell."

"Madame duchess," he said, "Count Louis' valet has been arrested. I've taken the liberty to invite Lieutenant General de la Reynie to join us."

She stood up. "Why in heavens was Monsieur Joubert arrested?"

The abbé deferred to the lieutenant for an answer. "Madame duchess, it appears the count's valet made particular advances on a noble's daughter," he said.

"That's absurd!" cried Louis.

"Please, *junger* Louis, let the lieutenant speak," Elizabeth said, turning to the lieutenant. "Who is this young lady who makes such a claim?"

"Mademoiselle Jeanne d'Orbay, madame."

"Her?" cried Louis. "She's never even met Marcel."

Fleury hushed him and turned to the lieutenant. "What actually transpired, Monsieur de la Reynie?"

The lieutenant pulled a parchment from his pouch and took a quick glance at it. "It appears," he said, "that Mademoiselle d'Orbay received a note, asking her to join Monsieur Joubert for a rendezvous in the gardens. She received it from a lackey, claiming to be his friend. It was signed Marcel Joubert."

Louis stood frozen with his mouth agape.

"*Junger* Louis," said Elizabeth, "I am deeply sorry to hear this. I know your valet was a valuable member of your household, but do not worry. We will find you a new one."

"But she is lying," said Louis. "She is jealous of Marcel."

The abbé shushed him, putting his finger to his lips.

"But monseigneur, Marcel couldn't write a note," Louis cried. "He has never learned to read or write."

Elizabeth looked at the abbé. "Is that true, monseigneur?" When the abbé nodded, she addressed the lieutenant. "Monsieur Lieutenant, the young gentleman must be released immediately!"

"Yes, of course, madame duchess, I will return to Paris at once," he said with a bow. "I hope it is not too late, because Monsieur Joubert was sentenced to be flogged."

"Please make haste, Monsieur Lieutenant," she said. "You will be rewarded for your prompt assistance."

~ ~ ~

Louis returned to Bellefonds and waited all day to hear news of Marcel's fate, only to fall asleep at his desk. The next morning, someone shook his shoulder to wake him up.

Louis jumped up. "Marcel," he cried and embraced him. "Please tell me you were untouched by the whip."

"Yes, I'm fine," he said, pulling back and covering his nose with a grin. "Come, you need to bathe and change for the levée this morning."

His face glowing, Louis couldn't stop smiling during the levée and Mass. Instead of visiting the salon afterwards, he planned to hurry back to Bellefonds, but Monsieur Colbert told him he was expected to dine with the king and attend various activities at court before returning home.

Later in the evening, Marcel knocked on Louis' door and entered the room. "Thank you for the writing table that was delivered this afternoon."

Louis put his book down on the desk and stood, taking a small package from his desk and handing it to Marcel.

"What's this?" Marcel asked, wrinkling his brow.

"Just open it," Louis said.

Marcel slowly untied the string and unwrapped the paper to find a box with ink and quills. "Thank you!" he said. "Are you going to teach me to read and write?"

"No," said Louis. "You have a tutor now."

"Hmm," Marcel said, trying not to grin. "Now I can really write letters to all of your demoiselles at court."

Louis motioned jokingly for Marcel to give the box back, but he resisted. Then, looking at his hair, Louis handed Marcel a comb.

"What's this," Marcel asked.

"A gift," Louis said, biting his lip to keep from laughing. "It looks like a battlefield." They burst into laughter.

The rest of the evening they teased each other, giggling and roughhousing throughout the hôtel. Bandit enjoyed it too, running in circles around them from room to room.

~ ~ ~

The next morning, Marcel woke to a noise in the courtyard. It was daylight, and he had overslept. When he realized he was in Louis' bed, he slid quietly out from under the covers, slipped on his breeches, and made his way down the corridor to his own chambers. On the way, however, he encountered Monsieur de Monchevreuil with the king's Swiss Guards.

Monsieur de Monchevreuil shook his head with dismay and said, "I am sorry, Monsieur Joubert, but you must—"

"Please, monsieur," he said. "Please let me get my coat. It gets so cold in the—"

"No," said Monsieur de Monchevreuil. "The guards are not here for you; they are here for Count Louis. The king requested an audience this morning. Please ready him."

# CHAPTER FIFTEEN

# The King's Wrath

"These dwell among the blackest souls, loaded down deep
by sins of differing types. If you sink far enough,
you'll see them all."

— Dante Alighieri, *Inferno*

## Hôtel de Bellefonds, October 1682

Louis tried to shake off the autumn morning chill in the carriage. He had no idea why he was being summoned to the palace. When he arrived, the royal guards escorted him to the Apollo salon, where the king sat upon his throne decorated ornately with silver plaques and sculptures. The room's intimidating grand arches with images of Greek antiquity towered over Louis, reminding him of the king's God-given power.

The king's endless stare made Louis so uncomfortable that he began wringing his cold and clammy hands. His throat was so dry he could hardly swallow. Suddenly, he dropped to his knees, his heart hammering as beads of sweat dripped down his spine. He thought the king *knew*.

"Father, joining that secret order was the biggest mistake of my life," he said, his voice quivering. "Please forgive me."

"Secret order? You weren't summoned here to speak of any secret order, Count Louis," the king told him dryly. "I only wished to inquire if you were aware of any scandals involving the Chevalier de Lorraine at Saint-Cloud."

Louis, still on his knees, looked up and wiped the tears from his cheeks with his ruffled sleeve.

The king narrowed his eyes. "Of what order are you speaking?" he asked, but Louis looked down to avoid his eyes. "Speak up!" thundered the king.

"It is a private fraternity, Father," he said, but the king's eyes demanded to hear more. "The Chevalier de Lorraine's order," he added more quietly.

"The Chevalier de Lorraine?" The king started tapping his fingers on the arm of his throne and then halted. "You? You've sinned against human nature? Against the Almighty? You? The descendant of Bourbon kings?"

Louis' face tingled with heat. He felt like he was suffocating and he struggled to breathe.

"You're accused of sacrilege!" cried the king.

"But Father, I—"

Louis shuddered when the king jumped to his feet. "Your uncle has publicly and without shame established himself in such vice... in vice of the worst kind. I will not tolerate the same from my son," he said, his face contorted with rage. He turned to his guards. "Take him to the dungeon. Justice demands he be flogged tomorrow... after Mass... in public."

The guards lifted Louis to his feet and escorted him out of the throne room. He couldn't bring himself to look at the king.

~ ~ ~

The next day, in the cold, marble-tiled courtyard, Count Louis' hands were tightly tied above his head on a wooden ladder. Humiliated, he was bent over, his bare back and buttocks facing the king, who sat on a tufted red velvet armchair, wearing a smug smile. Not that Count Louis could see this. But he could feel the eyes of the nobles and courtiers of Versailles on his naked backside as they stood silently behind him like a brigade of soldiers awaiting orders to strike. The crisp, clear air tingled Louis' bare thighs. His legs quivered from the strain of holding his body up on tiptoes and he wondered, not for the first time, how he'd landed himself in this situation.

The executioner approached the king to present a bundle of freshly cut birch twigs and the king nodded with approval, causing the crowd to gasp. Then the courtyard became silent, and the executioner took a deep breath before delivering the first of three lashes. Louis crumpled as the ferocious pain spread across his backside like a forked flash of lightning, but he refused to make a sound. He wondered how a father could be so cold-hearted. He'd done nothing wrong.

The executioner delivered the second blow, but this time Louis didn't flinch. The crushing pain only made him grit his teeth and stand straighter. As he looked to the right and then to the left at the onlookers, he promised himself that he would show every one of them. Although he didn't see a boy with blonde, unruly hair and red blotchy cheeks in the crowd, he could feel Marcel's presence. He knew Marcel's eyes would be glistening with tears.

Louis collapsed after the final blow that stung the most, his body dangling on the ladder's frame. When the crowd gasped, the king raised his hand to end the spectacle and he rose from his armchair. Before he departed, he motioned for his son's lifeless frame to be carried away.

Hours later, in a dungeon cell reeking of rat urine, Louis woke up on a cot with vermin-infested straw prickling his bare stomach. Curled up like a wounded animal, he was delirious from the pain and hovering on the edge of unconsciousness. Despite the sounds of vicious dogs growling and drunken jailers cursing in the corridors, his mind wandered back to his youth. He wondered where he took the wrong path, ending up in a dark, dank prison. He lost all hope of ever being worthy of his namesake, Louis XIV, the Sun King.

Not knowing day from night, Louis had lost track of time. He'd been imprisoned for three days when he heard a commotion in the corridor. Louis' weak body jolted at the clanking of the massive cell door's lock. Three brutish jailers entered and poked him with their muskets, motioning for him to get up.

A common, unadorned coach awaited him outside. He had no belongings except for his soiled trousers and a damp, bloodied nightshirt that stuck to his backside like needles in a pincushion.

When Louis stepped into the coach, his heart skipped a beat. "Abbé Fleury?" he said.

The abbé nodded. "I received orders last evening to escort you to Bellefonds."

When Louis saw the disappointed look on the abbé's face, he silently took his seat. No matter how hard he squeezed his eyes shut, tears still ran down his cheeks. The abbé noticed the glimmer on Louis' cheeks but said nothing.

The stern appearance of the abbé, with his short-cropped grey hair and neatly pressed black robe, filled Louis with despair, but his mentor was still a welcome sight. He had been responsible for Louis' education for over eight years—ever since Louis' mother, Louise de La Vallière, took up the veil to make amends for her adultery with the king. Now that his father had banished him from court, Louis prayed the abbé would not abandon him too.

"What is going to happen to me, monseigneur?" Louis asked.

"We will gather some belongings at the hôtel, and you can say your farewells," the abbé said dryly. "Then you will be sent to the Château of Fontainebleau until further arrangements can be made."

"So far away?" Louis asked.

"Yes, but I will join you at Fontainebleau, Count Louis," the abbé said and he when cast a forgiving smile, Louis took advantage of the abbé's generosity.

"How could the king do this to his own son? In front of the entire court?" he said, looking out the window to hide his trembling lower lip. "I suppose all the others involved can still roam about the palace."

"Yes," said the abbé softly, "I am afraid so."

"Even the Chevalier de Lorraine?"

"Yes," said the abbé. "He is still the favorite of the king's brother."

"How is that fair?"

"Well, he can attend court...but never in the king's presence," said the abbé, hoping Louis would find solace in the Chevalier being shunned. The abbé then took a mouchoir from his pocket and handed it to his student.

Louis wiped his eyes. "I am sorry for everything, monseigneur."

"What is done is done, Louis. You must be a man and bear it. If you are weak, it will only crush you."

"But I may never see anyone again," Louis said.

"At least now you will have time to understand the true meaning of friendship."

Louis clenched his jaw, unwilling to sit through a dressing-down, but the abbé continued regardless of Louis' obstinance.

"Your friends cultivated a peculiar passion for the physical body," said the abbé, "when divine love or heroic glory should be one's ultimate goal."

"But monseigneur, it's no secret that my grandfather, Louis XIII, had a particular affection for men," said Louis, unable to look the abbé in his eyes.

"From whom did you hear such slander?" snapped the abbé.

"The Chevalier de—"

"I know who," the abbé interrupted and paused for a moment. "I think it is time for you to read Plato, Louis. You will learn that morals are like chameleons. They change shape at various times in history and in different situations."

When the coach arrived in the courtyard at Bellefonds, Louis found himself needing help to get up.

Fleury flashed a warm smile and took his arm. "These pains will soon heal too."

~ ~ ~

Monsieur de Monchevreuil met Louis and Abbé Fleury as they stepped down from the coach. He bowed reverently. "Monseigneur," he said to the abbé. "Per your orders the household, except for myself and a lackey, has been sent to Saint-Cloud."

Louis frowned. "And Monsieur Joubert? Is he not here?"

Monsieur de Monchevreuil deferred to the abbé, who said, "No, Count Louis, he is resuming his post in the stables at Saint-Cloud."

Louis looked around the courtyard. "And Bandit? Where is Bandit?"

"Monsieur Joubert took Bandit with him," said Monsieur de Monchevreuil. "We were instructed that no personal items could be taken to Fontainebleau."

"And my books?" he asked.

"No, I am sorry," said the abbé. "There is a trunk in your chambers for your clothes. Your governor will help you pack it."

Louis replied with a sad nod.

"The abbé bowed and said, "I will return tomorrow morning, Count Louis. I still have some final matters which need attention at the palace."

"Monseigneur, may I please write a letter to Madame Elizabeth?" asked Louis.

"Yes, of course," he said and turned to Monsieur de Monchevreuil. "I am certain that your governor will ensure a prompt delivery of any correspondence."

When Monsieur de Monchevreuil nodded, the abbé left and Louis retired to his chambers. He sat at his desk for at least half an hour, deciding what to write. Finally, he inked his quill and carefully wrote the letter, paying special attention to his handwriting because his hand was trembling.

*Hôtel Bellefonds, November 22*

*My dearest Aunt Liselotte,*

*May I please have permission to visit you? I am no longer a boy, but you have been like the birth mother that I never had. I am ashamed of my mistakes, mistakes that are unpardonable at any age. I look into the future, but a black curtain hangs before my eyes. Please allow me to have an audience, my dear aunt, because I am so miserable.*

*Your nephew,*
*Louis de Bourbon*

Monsieur de Monchevreuil immediately arranged for the letter to be delivered to Saint-Cloud and after Louis had supped, a courier arrived with a reply. Louis was euphoric that his aunt was so prompt, promising a favorable reply.

*Saint-Cloud, November 22*

*Junger Louis,*

*When I discovered the story of your debauchery, I was extremely angry with you. I warned you about keeping company with men like the Chevalier de L*** and his band of rogues. And I told you that if you behaved in such a manner, I would cease to love you.*

*I am sorry, but I am too upset to receive any visitors at the moment.*

*Aunt Liselotte*

Louis returned to his desk and laid his head on his arms until Monsieur de Monchevreuil arrived, patting him on the shoulder.

"Count Louis," he said, "let us remove your clothing."

After removing his soiled clothing, Monsieur de Monchevreuil led him to the basin with water and softly sponged his backside. After his governor patted him dry, Louis climbed into his bed, but he had trouble falling asleep. The hôtel, practically empty, was as quiet as an empty chapel. He tossed and turned. He missed Marcel and worried about Bandit, but he knew Marcel would take exceptionally good care of their favorite companion. Drifting in and out of sleep, he finally rose at the first sign of the sun's rays in the room. He went straight to his desk to write another letter.

*Hôtel Bellefonds, November 23*

*Dear Aunt Liselotte,*

*It is just hours since I received your letter, but how heavy is my heart. Please allow me to come to Saint-Cloud and beg your forgiveness. All my good resolves have been scattered to the four winds. I should never have allowed myself to be influenced in such dreadful ways by such dreadful men. I must journey to Fontainebleau today, but just a single positive word from you would make the agony of my departure much easier to bear.*

*Your nephew,*
*Louis de Bourbon*

After Monsieur de Monchevreuil dispatched the letter, he returned with rolls and broth for Louis' morning meal and he laid out clean attire: stockings, breeches, a nightshirt, and a vest. While Louis dressed himself, the governor carefully folded clothes and packed them in the trunk that was sitting in the middle of the floor.

"What will happen to my books and maps?" he asked as he rubbed his gold medallion between his fingers.

"Everything will be taken to Saint-Cloud and kept there for you, Count Louis," said Monsieur de Monchevreuil in a soothing voice. "Until you return, of course."

Not knowing that his governor was watching him, he walked to the window, cracked it open, and tossed his medallion to the ground below. Then he noticed a coach arriving in the courtyard.

"*Mon Dieu*," he said and turned to his governor. "My sister. It might be best if I meet her in the salon."

Monsieur de Monchevreuil scanned the cluttered room. "Yes, that would be best," he said and scurried to the main entrance.

Louis arrived in the salon minutes later, finding his sister standing erect with her arms folded in front of her.

"Good day, Marie-Anne," said Louis.

She approached him, her arms falling to her sides. "It is *not* a good day," she said. "You, my own brother, have been banished from court, and François has been sent to Chantilly."

"It is shameful to be exiled, sister," he said.

"No, what is shameful is the stain on my prominence at court," she said, her eyebrows furrowed. "The dauphine, that ugly fish. I'm certain she is already wagging her tongue with the most noble ladies at court."

Louis tilted his head. "Our father would be very unhappy with her if he knew," he said. "You must inform him."

"I don't dare. I am overcome with shame and confusion," she said, dabbing her eyes with her kerchief. "Any discussion of the debauchery in your circle causes me such torment. It maddens me."

When Abbé Fleury arrived with his lackey, he bowed and greeted Marie-Anne. "Hello, Princess de Conti," he said.

"No, it is farewell, monseigneur," she snapped and departed.

Louis shook his head when the abbé looked at him. "I apologize for her behavior. She is terribly upset."

The abbé nodded understandingly and motioned for the lackey to take Louis' trunk. He put his hand on Louis' shoulder. "Shall we, Count Louis?" he asked. "It is time."

"Yes, monseigneur," Louis said and when he entered the courtyard, he saw Monsieur de Monchevreuil helping the lackey load the trunk on the abbé's coach. When it was tied down, his governor approached him.

"I hope you will one day soon return to Bellefonds, monsieur count," he said with a reverent bow. "Both you *and* Monsieur Joubert," he added with a warm smile.

"You have been very kind, Monsieur de Monchevreuil," he said. "Adieu."

Louis then walked to his coach but was distracted by another coach entering the courtyard. He looked at the abbé and cried out, "I am expecting a letter from Aunt Liselotte!"

Louis' smile disappeared when he discovered the coach belonged to none other than Mademoiselle d'Orbay. Monsieur de Monchevreuil approached the coach as she leaned her head out of the window.

"I am here to speak with His Highness," she said.

Monsieur de Monchevreuil looked at Louis, who shook his head and rolled his eyes.

"I must insist that you leave at once, mademoiselle," said Monsieur de Monchevreuil. "You will likely never see the count again."

Her eyes widened. "*Sacré coeur*! What has happened?" she asked.

Monsieur de Monchevreuil knocked on the side of the coach and yelled to the driver, "Depart!"

When the coach left with a creak and a jolt, Monsieur de Monchevreuil winked at Louis and said, "And good riddance."

~ ~ ~

As soon as the coach left Versailles, it wound its way through the nearby woods and thicket down to the riverside. Louis' heart ached, thinking of the walks he took for granted with Marcel. Although the banks of the river were now barren, he visualized the two of them splashing in the water and dropping breathlessly on the grassy knolls. The ruins they once explored brought back the memory of the earthy smell of ivy clinging to carved stones. It was as if his life was passing before his eyes as the coach rambled along the dirt road.

The memories of roughhousing with Marcel to Bandit's delight quickly disappeared as the coach passed Frémont, the Chevalier de Lorraine's country estate. The picturesque surroundings would be the perfect subject for an artist to paint, thought Louis, as long as the painter knew nothing of what transpired behind the welcoming façade.

"Count Louis," said the abbé, interrupting Louis' thoughts, "you are not the only one to be exiled from court."

Louis' gaze begged the abbé to continue.

"Monsieur Colbert had his son Jules-Armand Colbert locked up at Sceaux and beaten," said the abbé. "He is to be married to Mademoiselle de Tonnay-Charente."

"My cousin, François?" asked Louis.

"Prince François de la Roche-sur-Yon has been sent to Chantilly with Prince de Turenne," the abbé continued. "The Chevalier de Tilladet requested a reprieve to mend his ways, but the king refused him, and he was sent away."

Louis squinted. "And the Chevalier de Lorraine?"

"As I told you before, the chevalier was not exiled, but he *was* ordered to never appear at cour," said the abbé. "He continues to show himself everywhere at Versailles, however, but he takes great care to avoid being seen by the king."

"And the Count de Marsan?" asked Louis.

"The Count de Marsan was also implicated," said the abbé. "Although the king has always held him in high esteem, he could no longer look at him without horror. In the king's eyes, the count was a monster for his role in leading you down the wrong path."

Louis turned to stare out the window. He was silent for the rest of the journey to Fontainebleau.

~ ~ ~

Madame Elizabeth, having received another letter from Louis, requested an audience with the king. She left Saint-Cloud as soon as her wish was granted, and the king was thrilled to see her.

"It has been some time since we've hunted, sister," said the king. "Perhaps you are with child?"

"No, sire, that is yet another story circulated at court by the Chevalier de Lorraine."

"Of course, I should have known better," he said. "What brings you to the palace on this cold and dreary day?"

"First, I wanted to visit His Majesty's new grandson, the Petit Dauphin," she said. "My warmest congratulations. He is as healthy and as plump as a German dumpling."

"Thank you, sister," the king said with laughter. "As the Duke of Burgundy, I hope he will not be as dull or lazy as his father." When Elizabeth's smile disappeared, he continued, "Now, what do I really owe for your visit? I can see you are preoccupied with another matter."

"I am hoping that Your Majesty will not refuse me a very small, humble prayer," she said.

The king flashed a warm smile. "It has always been difficult to refuse my dear sister any request," he said.

"Sire, I'm asking for the grace of the poor Count of Vermandois."

The king scoffed. "I know you are a good friend, but the Count of Vermandois has not been punished enough for his crime."

"Yes, I am a good friend. My own children could not be more attached to me than he, but the poor lad is repentant of his misdeeds," she said. "His letters to me are covered with tears, begging forgiveness."

"I do not feel disposed to see him… or pardon him at this time," said the king with a firm resolve. "I am still too angry with him."

Madame Elizabeth nodded as if she understood the king's pain. She curtseyed and took her leave.

# PART FOUR

# THE SPOILS OF WAR

# CHAPTER SIXTEEN

# Exile

*Château of Fontainebleau*

"But the stars that marked our starting fall away."

— Dante Alighieri, *Inferno*

## Château of Fontainebleau, November 1682

Louis's eyes widened as the coach approached the colossal Château of Fontainebleau and entered the front gates to the immense courtyard. Abbé Fleury pointed to the imposing fountain graced by a statue of Ulysses in white marble.

"The fountain was constructed by King François I," said Abbé Fleury, "and it has four jets of water… when the king is in residence."

Louis admired the fountain's peaceful reflection in the limpid waters of its vast pond, whose edges were shaded by garden shrubbery. When the coach arrived at the entrance, the doormen helped Louis and the abbé down from the coach and escorted them into the main gallery, which was as solemn as it was magnificent.

Louis looked up to the long, narrow ceiling, paneled in walnut and covered with sculptured salamanders. He turned to the abbé, "Salamanders? Crowned salamanders?"

"Yes," said the abbé with a smile, "the emblem chosen by François I… just like the sun is the emblem chosen by your father. The salamander was associated with both fire and poison; it was greatly feared."

As Louis and the abbé walked along the well-lit corridors to Louis' chambers, they passed first through the Salon de François I. "Your grandfather, Louis XIII," said the abbé, "was born in this very room in 1601."

Louis gazed at the large portraits on the wall, recalling the finest period of Italian art. "This must be the most elegant salon I have ever seen," he said before entering the next salon, where he was shown the entrance to his chambers. Entering, he found his room to be just as elegant as any salon with a view of the gardens opposite the courtyard. A statue of Diana rose from the middle of the basin.

Louis soon found life at Fontainebleau remarkably simple with only a small household of maids, valets, cooks, and an occasional courier from Versailles—who, to Louis' mind, was most likely an informant for the king. Life was so simple that, after several weeks, Abbé Fleury announced he would begin tutoring Louis to help pass the time—using maxims from his current work, *Treatise on the Choice and Methods of Studies*.[3] On the first morning of lessons, Louis was wide awake at the long table in his chambers. Light and heat poured from the wood burning fire on the marble hearth, the perfect touch for another cold autumn day.

"Why are we studying classic warfare of the ancients, monseigneur?" Louis asked. "My father has won many heroic battles. Why not learn about them?"

"Knowing the stories of the great Greek and Roman captains is imperative," he replied. "We need to understand, in as much detail possible, the military discipline and the art of war that has placed them ahead of all other commanders."

Louis nodded, satisfied with the answer.

"But do not worry, we will discuss modern warfare," the abbé said. "And we will have geography lessons in the afternoons, too."

"Geography, monseigneur?" Louis asked with a downward gaze. "We studied that when I was younger," he mumbled.

"Geography, Count Louis, is most necessary," he said sternly. "Leaders cannot know enough about the country where they make war nor the exact topography where they will engage in battle. His Majesty's success campaigns depended on him and his generals having such knowledge."

When Louis perked up, the abbé added, "There is another subject we shall address, one that many men of the sword ignore—the jurisprudence of war." When Louis's brow wrinkled, he continued. "There should be legitimate causes for war, certain courtesies exercised, and well-defined rules followed for the conduct of our troops."

"What kind of rules?" Louis asked.

"The king's army has specific rules for discipline," he said. "For example, we will discuss how to handle desertion and other military crimes."

The abbé then handed Louis a book. "This is the first tome of my maxims for war, Count Louis."

Louis reverently leafed through it. "Thank you, monseigneur," he said.

---

[3] *Traité du choix et de la méthode des Études, 1674.*

"But before we begin today, Count Louis, you should understand that the most essential lessons about warfare cannot be learned in books or in lectures. They depend on physical exercise of the body, conversations with military leaders, and the utmost devotion of anyone desiring to serve their king."

~ ~ ~

After his lessons in the afternoons, Abbé Fleury allowed Louis plenty of time to walk in the grounds surrounding the château and, unknowing to anyone, provided him with more books on what was becoming his favorite subject—military history. Louis showed so much promise that the abbé sent a message to the king on his behalf:

> *Sire, Count Louis is devoting much time to his studies. Also, the poor boy regrets his past mistakes and asks for forgiveness. Please find it in Your Majesty's heart to show him mercy. Pardon him, I beg of you.*

A few days later, the abbé received the king's reply:

> *Honorable Abbé Fleury, I appreciate your concern for the Count of Vermandois, but you must understand that he has offended me very grievously. He cannot be forgiven and receive my blessing until he repents all his sins and asks the blessing of God. He must banish from his bosom the demon that possesses him. Only when he repents and is lifted out of that mire of iniquity shall I be able to pardon him.*

The abbé never spoke to Louis about the need to repent. He must have known that repentance alone could never earn the king's good graces. Instead, the abbé turned to lecturing about the Greek classics to inspire him.

"Why Plato, monseigneur?" asked Louis, impatient with the plethora of maxims.

"From Plato, you can learn to distinguish between those subjects that are merely necessary and those that make men worthy," the abbé said. "You must begin with your thoughts, Count Louis. Organize them, express them precisely, and then make beneficial use of them."

Although Louis, like most young royals, had studied how to maintain regiments, establish camps, and deploy an army on the battlefield, he lacked specialized training in ballistics and riding. To complete Louis' training, the abbé first secured an instructor in ballistics and general military training. As the training progressed, the abbé soon realized that Louis was on the right path to winning back the king's favor when he said, "Monseigneur, I will make amends to my father on the battlefield. Through glory in His Majesty's army is my only opportunity."

Abbé Fleury looked directly into Louis' eyes. "In the past months, Count Louis, I believe you have learned a good lesson," he said. "A wise man must venture to take the first step before he can ever see where his path will lead him."

The abbé then pulled a book from his leather satchel and handed it to Louis.

"What is this?"

"A gift to celebrate Christmas," he said. "It was written by your mother's uncle, Jean-François de la Baume le Blanc, Chevalier de La Vallière."

"Practicalities of War," said Louis, reading the title and smiling from ear to ear. "He was a soldier?"

"Renowned," said the abbé. "He was Lieutenant Captain of the Dauphin's Regiment of Light Horses and with his writings, we will deliberate on the duties of all army officers… from orders to march, camp, attack, fight, surprise, and defend positions."

Louis looked up at the abbé with gleaming eyes. "Can we begin today?"

~ ~ ~

Louis was forbidden from having any visitors while in exile but, unbeknownst to him, the abbé had secured permission from the king's brother at Saint-Cloud for someone to assist Louis with his horsemanship. One early spring morning, the abbé discreetly escorted a scruffy blonde boy through the courtyard where Louis was training. The boy's eyes widened when he spied on Louis carrying out his drills with a musket—a heavy, six-foot-long weapon with a bayonet—on his arm, practicing with unfaltering zeal.

After the abbé showed the boy his accommodations, they then waited in Louis' chambers for him to finish his exercises. Minutes later, Louis arrived.

"Marcel!" he said with a wrinkled forehead. "What are you doing here?"

Marcel glanced at the abbé, his eyes begging him to answer Louis' question.

The abbé put his hand on Marcel's shoulder. "I have summoned your valet to join us, Count Louis. He will be most valuable in helping you perfect your riding skills."

The abbé then left the room, but not because he was uncomfortable with the pressing silence of the boys' averted glances. On the contrary, it seemed like an excellent opportunity for the boys to rekindle their relationship.

"You saw the flogging?" said Louis, his voice wavering.

Marcel nodded as he looked about Louis' chambers, smelling the musty parchment of maps and books strewn across the long table. Louis had always been fascinated by warfare, so Marcel was not surprised to see a miniature fortification with formations of soldiers on his desk.

"So, you know I am banished from court?" said Louis.

Marcel, still avoiding Louis' eyes, said, "Abbé Fleury told me you offended the king."

"To say the least," said Louis, his eyes tearing up. "And you would still come so far to help me?"

"What?" he says, finally turning to look at Louis. "You know I would."

A faint smile appears on Louis' face. "I am truly happy you are here."

"*Mon Dieu*," Marcel said with a grin. "I am just happy I'm no longer your whipping boy."

When the laughing succumbed, Louis spent the rest of the day showing Marcel around the château and the grounds before the abbé showed Marcel to his own chambers and visited Louis with a letter in his hand.

You have received a letter from Prince de la Roche-sur-Yon," he said, handing the letter to Louis, who carefully opened it and read it to himself.

*Château of Chantilly*

*Dear Count Louis,*

*It has been six months since being exiled here at Chantilly, but my uncle, the Grand Condé, has obtained permission from His Majesty for my return to court. Little by little, others are also quietly returning. I feel partially responsible for your despairs, cousin, and I hope you will pardon me and soon be able to join us at Versailles.*

Louis showed the letter to Abbé Fleury, who read it. "There is hope," said the abbé with a warm smile.

"Until then, I am very happy that Marcel is here," said Louis.

Worried about any rumors in the past about his peculiarly close friendship with Marcel, Louis was curious if the abbé feared any retribution from the king for reuniting them. He felt somewhat assured, however, when the abbé added, "No one deserves to be isolated like a monk in a monastery, especially at such a young age."

~ ~ ~

Abbé Fleury must have been especially pleased with the progress in Louis' military training, because he overlooked the young men's unusually long rides in the forest.

After exploring the small streams snaking through the woods near the château, Louis and Marcel often found a secluded spot for a swim. On one day, Marcel's silence spoke more than words as they dried off in the warm afternoon sun. Louis thought that it was time to explain what happened on that last peaceful day at Bellefonds. He found a place on a grassy knoll overlooking the stream and motioned for Marcel to sit next to him.

"The day before the flogging, I received a message that the king wanted to see me at Versailles," Louis says. "I remember when I arrived in his chambers that my palms were sweating and my throat was so dry that I could hardly swallow."

"Why?"

"I thought the king had heard what I had done...so I fell to my knees and begged for forgiveness."

"Forgiveness for what?" says Marcel, digging his toes into the fresh grass.

"For joining the secret fraternity."

"I'm confused," says Marcel.

"The king was confused, too. He said I wasn't called to his chambers to speak of any fraternity. He only wanted to know if I was aware of any scandals at Saint-Cloud, notably any that involved the Chevalier of Lorraine."

Marcel threw a twig into the stream. "And then?"

"He ordered me to tell him everything about the order, including the names of all those involved."

Marcel lowered his head. "You know, you never told me much about that fraternity."

"I was so confused then... I wasn't myself... I'm truly sorry, Marcel. If I only knew then what I know now..."

Marcel smiled with a small nod, as if to say the apology was accepted. "And the king?"

"He was as furious as a mad bull. 'You've sinned against nature! Against the Almighty!' he said. 'You, the son of Bourbon kings!'"

"*Mon Dieu*," Marcel murmured.

Louis continued. "Then he jumped to his feet and yelled, 'You are accused of the vilest of vices. It is sacrilege! You will be flogged tomorrow in public!' And when the guards escorted me away, the last thing I heard was a vase crashing to the floor behind me."

Marcel puts his arm around Louis' shoulder, and they watch the burning sun slowly disappear behind the drooping willow trees. Louis took several deep breaths. He felt whole again, as if his life had a purpose and as if he had found something in Marcel—something he didn't know he had never lost.

~ ~ ~

When Louis and Marcel returned from their afternoon excursion, Abbé Fleur greeted them at the door with a letter in his hand. He handed it to Louis and said, "It is from Monsieur Colbert."

Louis opened it and read it aloud.

*Château of Sceaux*

*My dear Count Louis,*

*I received His Majesty's permission to visit you at Fontainebleau to discuss my proposal, but I am not well enough to travel such a distance at this time. My correspondence concerns your marriage to Princess Anne Louise Bénédicte de Bourbon, the daughter of the Grand Prince de Condé. Although she is only eight years of age and too young to marry, I would like your blessing to make arrangements for her to be promised to you.*

*I understand that this may appear to be a premature proposal, but I believe it will be a step in the right direction for you to win back His Majesty's good graces. I will present the proposal to His Majesty if you approve. A miniature portrait of Her Highness has been painted for you. Signed Jean-Baptiste Colbert.*

Louis opened the pendant to find the likeness of a thin young lady with a very wide mouth, irregular teeth, very white skin with painted cheeks, and fair but frizzy hair.

He showed the pendant to Marcel and said, "I cannot marry this child," he said.

The abbé shook his head. "Count Louis, it is *just* a proposal and Monsieur Colbert only has your best interests at heart," he said. "You should be thrilled that he would like to present this plan to the king."

"I will thank Papa Colbert for his good intentions, but I would first like to write Aunt Liselotte for her counsel."

The abbé nodded. "I will ensure that your letter is dispatched at once."

~ ~ ~

At Saint-Cloud, Madame Elizabeth requested Monsieur' presence in her chambers. The last time he had visited her there was to observe the birth of their last child five years earlier, when they agreed to sleep in separate bedrooms.

"Madame," he said, "You must have urgent news. Are you threatening to join a convent again?"

"No, husband," she said with a grin. "Unfortunately for you, your brother has refused to grant me that wish."

"Yes, I heard he was angered by your proposal," he said. "But… better you than me."

"I certainly learned my lesson," she said, looking off into the distance.

Monsieur cleared his voice. "So, madame, for what do I owe the honor of this meeting?" he said.

"I received correspondence from *junger* Louis," she said solemnly. "It is proposed that he marry the Princess Anne Louise Bénédicte de Bourbon."

"A Princess of the Blood?" asked Monsieur.

"More like a *doll* of the Blood—with her small body and lame arms," she quipped. "She looks like a little toad."

"Madame," he said with a broad grin. "I detect a sarcastic tone. Is it because another marriage with a bastard will dilute the royal lineage even more?"

"That is not the only reason," she said. "Her father, the Grand Condé, is only motivated by personal ambition. And, my husband, the girl is unruly, with a terrible temper."

"Yes, I remember the child being very outspoken for her age… but perhaps my brother is behind this; he may not appreciate any grumbles," he said, then bowed and took his leave.

Madame Elizabeth immediately inked her quill to reply to Louis.

*Saint-Cloud, April 1683.*

*My dear junger Louis,*

*Thank you for asking my opinion regarding Monsieur Colbert's proposal to marry the Princess Anne Louise Bénédicte de Bourbon. Let us not muddy the waters since Monsieur Colbert has been kind enough to propose such an arrangement. And, after all, she is thought to be the most attractive of the Grand Condé's daughters and she would make a delightful wife. Signed Aunt Liselotte.*

~ ~ ~

Days became weeks, and weeks became months. By July, any boredom was quickly extinguished by passionate discussions of heroic deeds and laurels in battle. Besides riding lessons every day, Louis and Marcel also discovered the joy of wrestling in a secluded courtyard, where they wouldn't be disturbed. The last days of July were hot and humid, but it didn't stop them in their shirts, tights, and short boots when they slapped each other on the back for a new match. And as soon as they finished, Abbé Fleury, who coached their every move, gave them further commentary.

When Louis compared himself with Marcel, he thought Marcel had the advantage in height, but he wasn't sure about the breadth of his shoulders. He noted Marcel's symmetry, too, as the light shone through his thin shirt, showing the muscles on his shoulders as they flexed when he moved his arms. Marcel's collar was open, showing the swell of his chest muscles, laying in layers like a row of cordage from his breastbone to his armpit. Louis noticed for the first time how much their bodies had developed.

Marcel looked steadily at Louis with his bold and clear eyes—as if to intimidate him—before he made a sudden rush, but Louis stood his ground and allowed Marcel to play around him. However, Louis kept his eyes fixed upon Marcel's gaze, following and reading every look. Suddenly, Marcel caught Louis by the shoulder so handily with a grip of his left arm upon his neck and back that Louis' right arm was pinioned. As Marcel closed in, his arm upon Louis' back and neck took a firmer hold and his hand came over Louis' right shoulder from the back, locking on his neck. Louis groaned from the strain and for a moment, all the breath seemed to be squeezed out of his lungs.

Abbé Fleury moved in closer and, seeing Louis was able to breathe, pulled back. Marcel, trying as he might with his arms about Louis, could not bend Louis' neck. Backward and forward, they moved, each bringing forth all the strength they could muster, but neither of was able to make any gain. And the abbé called it a draw.

"Today, you should practice the cross-buttock," the abbé said, while Louis and Marcel stretched their backs and wiggled their arms to release the tension. "For this throw, you will turn your left side to your opponent, get your hip partially under him, then quick as a flash of lightning, cross both his legs with your left foot and lift him from the ground. You will both go down, but you opponent will be undermost." The abbé pulled Louis into position. "You go first, Count Louis," he said.

Louis attempted the throw, but it was too uncoordinated. The abbé stepped in. "Count Louis, try it again but more rapidly," he said. "Also, your arms must be kept tightly about your opponent's neck or shoulders."

Louis' second attempt produced the desired effect, and he got up and extended Marcel a hand to help him up.

"Well done," said Marcel.

"Now, our next lesson will include the hank—the most dangerous throw I've ever seen," said the abbé to the delight of his wrestlers. "Your opponent will certainly bite the sod when properly executed."

Louis and Marcel shook hands. "I hope you like the taste of sod," said Louis, causing them both to chuckle.

After wrestling, Louis splashed his face with water in the fountain while the abbé handed Marcel his vest. "I've noticed Count Louis' new vigor," he said. "It appears someone has given him the will to slay all the dragons that have haunted him night and day."

"Master Louis has always been a warrior at heart, monseigneur," said Marcel with a smile. "Must be in his blood."

"Indeed," said the abbé.

~ ~ ~

In the early morning hours of July 12, a thick layer of straw was spread on the pavement in the Rue Neuve des Petits-Champs, where Monsieur Colbert's summer residence, the Hôtel de Colbert, was located. By noon, the passage of carriages and coaches, except for those belonging to courtiers or nobles, was prohibited near his hotel. Immediately, rumors spread that Monsieur Colbert was dangerously ill, and they were confirmed when visitors found the large door at the entrance closed, indicating the minister was not receiving anyone.

By four o'clock in the afternoon, most carriages and pedestrians had abandoned the Rue Neuve des Petits-Champs, where only a few curious onlookers remained. Suddenly, there was a confused noise of horses, carriages, and cries of "The king!" When the king's procession arrived at the front gates of Colbert's hotel, they crashed open to receive him. However, he refused to allow the coach to enter the large courtyard. He stepped down from the coach, followed by several Swiss Guards and his personal valet. When the door to the hôtel opened for him, he gestured for everyone to stay there until he returned.

Once inside, the king's doctor, Guy Fagon, greeted the king with a low bow.

"How is my minister, Monsieur Fagon?" asked the king.

"Without a miracle, he will not live another day, sire," said the doctor.

"But you can cut the stone out," said the king.

"Sire, he has always refused to be cut and now the operation is impossible," said Fagon.

"I will speak with Madame Colbert first," he said.

"This is not possible, sire," said Fagon. "He has said goodbye to his family. He did not want anyone to witness the horrible tortures of his agony."

"I shall speak with him," said the king.

"Allow me, Your Majesty," said Fagon, taking a step forward to follow the king.

"No, monsieur," snapped the king. "I shall go alone."

He climbed the stairs to a large salon and walked down a silent hallway toward the apartments. Dressed in a gray wool waistcoat, an elderly valet sat crouched on a stool by the entrance, sound asleep. Then a large cry was heard in the back of the apartment.

"*Mon Dieu*. Is it the king?" cried Monsieur Colbert, who approached the king and, bowing awkwardly, almost lost his balance. He was as white as a specter.

"Is my minister ill?" asked the king. "I have come to find out about your condition."

"I do not feel any pain," said Colbert, "when I am in His Majesty's presence."

"Monsieur Fagon tells me you are very ill, but you will get better and heal soon," said the king. "Then I can rely on your good services again."

"Sire," said Colbert, "I am afraid I must resign my position at court."

"No, Monsieur Colbert, impossible—you are not yet deceased," said the king. "You are still controller of my finances, superintendent of my buildings, secretary of state, and—"

"Dying," he interrupted. "I am dying."

"Impossible, your services to me are in great need," said the king. "You cannot speak of resignation now. I have only come to urge you to recover quickly. I must now be on my way. I bid you adieu."

When the king turned to depart, Monsieur Colbert murmured, "Sire, you leave me so soon?"

"You will clearly be able to join us at the Council within four or five days," said the king. "We must discuss the war in Flanders."

"Would Your Majesty grant me one small favor?"

"My good minster, you are too inconvenienced as it is," said the king. "You have left your sick bed to receive me."

"Will Your Majesty join me in my cabinet for a moment?" asked Colbert in a gentle tone.

The king nodded and Colbert walked ahead of the king until he staggered, causing the king to take his arm to support him. When they entered the cabinet, Colbert offered the king a large, gilded armchair with a high back and a seat covered with elegant tapestry, only testifying to the minister's tastes. The king glanced at the paintings, statues, books, medals, and maps on the walls, while Colbert slowly made his way to his chair.

"Pray tell, good minister, the reason for this meeting," said the king, smiling.

"Sire," said Colbert as he opened a desk drawer and pulled out a parchment. "I have an order that Your Majesty must sign."

"But there is plenty of time to attend to such formalities," said the king, his brow furrowing.

"Not for me, sire," murmured Colbert. "I must quickly put an end to matters of this mortal world... to occupy myself with only those of my salvation."

Colbert handed him the parchment and a quill.

"I normally sign with confidence," said the king, looking over the document, "but I would prefer to know what I am signing."

"Sire, this relates to amnesty for Count Louis of Vermandois."

"My good minister, you are quite mistaken," said the king with wide eyes and shaking his head. "No, no, no, monsieur. I am in favor of your proposal of the count's marriage to Princess Anne de Bourbon, but how does Louis' amnesty involve the glory or honor of your king?"

"Sire, the justification of your son."

"Nasty subject," murmured Louis XIV, biting his lips.

"But he is innocent!" said Colbert.

"Innocent? The libertine who dishonors my name?"

"Sire, he was revoltingly led astray by others," said Colbert. "He is still young, compassionate, and worthy of repentance."

"Enough, Monsieur Colbert," said the king. "Enough about this subject."

"That was my very last request of Your Majesty," said Colbert, his gaze waning.

"You cannot die before me!" he said, getting up in a hurry. "Adieu, Monsieur Colbert. I'll send Fagon to you."

"Adieu, sire," said Colbert, struggling to get up from his seat as the king departed.

In the hallway, the king found himself in front of the sleeping valet. "Sir! Go and help Monsieur Colbert. He is dying."

The valet looked up, nodded, and went back to sleep.

~ ~ ~

During a riding lesson, Louis and Marcel brought their horses to a standstill and sat stiffly upright in their saddles. Louis' eyes narrowed. "Who is that?" he asked Marcel, the muscles of his face tensed up. "Do you know who that is?"

A heavily bearded and robust of frame man approached them, sitting on his horse with the grace of an experienced rider. Louis recognized him. "Good day, Maréchal d'Humières," he said.

"My apologies, monsieur, but have I had the pleasure?" said the maréchal.

"Count Louis of Vermandois, monsieur maréchal," Louis said.

The maréchal nodded with respect. "Yes, of course, Your Highness," he said, his smile glowing. "What brings you to the countryside of Fontainebleau?"

"Riding lessons," Louis said proudly. "I am learning to master the gait and the gallop."

"Very good, Your Highness," said the maréchal, then turning Marcel. "The gait has several degrees of elevation and is capable of great speed. Isn't that correct?"

Marcel's eyes widened. "Yes, monsieur, the horse's body, more lifted than chased, embraces less space," he said. "But the gait is very tiring for the horse; it requires a great employment of all its muscles… particularly in the column."

"A well-versed man in equitation, I see," said maréchal. "My compliments to you, Your Highness. Concern for the safety of the horse is a valuable lesson in the military. I would only caution that when one of the lateral bipeds offers its two limbs further apart than those of the opposite side which, on the contrary, has its close together, this can constitute a disunited gallop and can harm the solidity of the animal."

In awe of being in the maréchal's presence, Louis was lost for words. But the maréchal broke the silence, again looking at Marcel. "I see your student has his chest well forward, monsieur," he said. "I am curious. Why is he riding without the stirrups?"

"I strongly recommend occasional practice without the stirrups," said Marcel.

The maréchal tilted his head, wanting to hear more. "It allows the rider's position to change with the horse's gait," Marcel said. "It gives the rider more confidence, monsieur, especially before we attempt a jump."

The maréchal, looking satisfied with Marcel's answer, took his reins. "I bid you adieu, messieurs," he said with a nod and continued riding.

Louis turned to Marcel, who had a big smile on his face. "Maréchal d'Humières is one of my father's most respected officers."

Marcel's smile disappeared. "I know," he said. "My father fought under his command."

They hardly spoke as they rode back to the château. Once there, they took their horses into the stable and unharnessed them. While they were brushing them, Abbé Fleury entered.

"Count Louis," he said, "I have the most distressing news. Queen Maria Theresa has been ill for several days, but this morning her illness worsened. Our queen has died, and we are summoned to appear before the king."

Louis' mouth fell open, and he glanced at Marcel, who said, "I will prepare the carriage."

"Monseigneur," Louis said, removing his riding cap. "I will make myself presentable."

Louis fumbled as he changed his clothes in his chambers, wondering why he was summoned to appear at court. Wouldn't it be too great of a scandal for the king's bastard son to pay his respects to the queen? He only wished he could visit Versailles under different and more opportune circumstances.

# CHAPTER SEVENTEEN

# To Arms!

*Count Louis of Vermandois*

"It is necessity and not pleasure that compels us."

— Dante Alighieri, *Inferno*

## Versailles, July 1683

As the coach approached Versailles, Louis watched with wide eyes as the multitude of people swarmed the road to the palace.

"They are hailing from Paris for information," said the abbé. "They want to make sure the rumor is not just a cruel mystification."

When the guards made way for the coach to enter the palace gates, Louis pointed to the large crowd of courtiers who had already gathered in the courtyard under the king's chambers. "That is unusual," he said.

Then the king appeared on his balcony and the abbé said, "There is no longer any doubt. His Majesty's sorrow does not belong to him exclusively—he must surrender to the sight of his subjects."

As soon as Louis and the abbé stepped down from the carriage, they were quickly escorted into the palace and up the marble staircase to the Hercules Salon. Its colored marble and a monumental fireplace with gilded inlays were muted by the black chiffon draping.

Madame Elizabeth was tasting fresh berries at the dessert table with Monsieur. "I wonder with great sadness who caused this outrage, snatching from us such a gentle and exemplary queen," she said, picking a berry seed from between her teeth. "Doctor Fagon voiced his opposition about a bleeding of the foot, but the other doctors prevailed, especially that wretched Doctor D'Aquin. And what is certain, husband, is that a few moments after the bleeding, the queen's condition became desperate. So, we should not be surprised about the promptness of the queen's death."

"Yes, madame," said Monsieur, who was busy tasting new wines with the Marquis de Châtillon and admiring the new addition to the salon, a statue of Cupid.

"One of Bouchardon's best works," said the marquis. "The plaster casts were made from live bodies."

"I can see that," said Monsieur.

Louis, on the way to the king's chambers, couldn't help but notice Monsieur in his black velvet attire that only highlighted the diamonds that embellished it—even though court etiquette disdained such trimmings during times of mourning. Next to Monsieur stood Madame

Elizabeth in an unadorned black cloak with a long train, and Louis made his way through the crowd to greet her with the abbé following closely behind.

"Aunt Liselotte," he cried out, and she opened her arms to embrace him.

With tears rolling down her cheek, she squeezed him and whispered in his ear, "I am certain, *junger* Louis, that you will one day return to court." When she saw Abbé Fleury put his hand on Louis' shoulder to lead him away, she added, "Go now and be strong, *mein Liebchen*."

When they departed, Elizabeth wiped her cheeks with her sleeve and turned to Monsieur. "Everyone is weeping… about the queen," she said. "The pain of Madame de Maintenon seems to me sincere, founded on esteem and gratitude. But I cannot say the same, husband, for the Montespan. She is crying a lot, but surely only from fear of being sent away from court."

"Yes, madame," said Monsieur, filling up his goblet and returning his gaze to the intricate white marble statue.

~ ~ ~

The king received Louis and Abbé Fleury in his armchair. Louis' legs trembled when he leaned over to bow.

"Sire," said the abbé, "we regret the sad news of Her Majesty."

"This is the first chagrin which she has ever given me," he said, staring blankly into the distance.

"Yes, Father," continued Louis, "please accept my sincerest condolences."

"Thank you," said the king, then turning to the abbé. "As you can understand, Monseigneur Fleury, the pain I have just felt can only be relieved by the grace of God."

"Yes, sire," said the abbé, "and it is our firm hope that the Almighty wanted to crown—and to crown early—the high virtue and piety which accompanied all the actions of Her Majesty's life."

The king nodded graciously and then glanced at Louis, examining him from head to toe. "My son, I must compliment you on your well-being. The good abbé has informed me of your dedication to physical exercise and military training."

"Yes, Father," he said with a wavering voice. "I am persistent in improving."

"And for that reason, I am permitting you to return to Bellefonds."

Louis fell to his knees. "Oh, Father, I will make you very proud."

The king motioned for the abbé to help Louis up. "You are indeed no longer in exile, Count Louis, but I have *not* forgiven you for your errors. For that, you will need to prove yourself in your service to France."

"Yes, Father," he said. "I understand."

"I have asked Marquis Henri de Mornay to continue with your military training. He has served as a distinguished *aide-de-camp* in many of my campaigns. You will *not* be allowed to leave the Hôtel Bellefonds, however, without his advance permission," said the king dryly. "If, and only if, the Marquis de Mornay recommends you, you will leave for Flanders in mid-September to join Maréchal d'Humières forces."

Louis nodded reverently.

The king turned to the abbé. "Monseigneur, your devotion to Count Louis has been commendable, but now I have other young princes in need of your guidance."

"I am at Your Majesty's service," said the abbé, nodding respectfully.

The king looked at Louis for a moment, as if to collect his thoughts. "My son, this may be your only chance to please the throne," he said. "I want nothing more than to welcome you back to court," the king said and then motioned they were dismissed.

Louis and the abbé bowed and left the room. "Why the long face, Count Louis?" asked the abbé.

"I did not know you would be leaving, monseigneur," said Louis.

"Having Monsieur de Mornay's guidance in the coming weeks is truly a step in the right direction for you," said the abbé.

"Yes," said Louis. "That is true, but…"

"Say no more," the abbé said, patting Louis on the back. "My door will always be open to you."

~ ~ ~

As the carriage entered the gates and onto the sunny courtyard of Bellefonds, Louis' eyes brimmed with happy tears when he saw all the smiling servants assembled to receive him—quite a contrast to the teary-eyed farewell months earlier when he was sent to Fontainebleau. The chamberlain opened the coach door when it came to a stop, and Monsieur de Monchevreuil stepped forward to assist Louis' descent from the coach.

Louis' heart swelled when his governor said, "Welcome home, monsieur count. Your chambers are ready for you."

Marcel then stepped down from the coach with Bandit. Ecstatic to see the staff, the dog ran from one servant to another for a pat on its back, but he showed one of them more attention than the others—the chef, who just happened to have a morsel in his pocket. The staff curtsied and bowed as Louis entered the hôtel and made his way to his room, where several trunks had been placed in the middle of the floor. When he cast his eyes on his desk, he saw several letters. He opened one hastily and read it.

"The Marquis de Mornay will visit tomorrow," Louis said to Marcel, who was opening the window's louvers.

Louis felt the warm afternoon breeze, and he took a deep breath. "We are young and healthy," he said with a dreamy expression. "Life has painted a new landscape for us… with all our tomorrows stretched before us like the waves of the sea."

"All I can see is waves of baggage," said Marcel, giggling as he unpacked clothing to hang in the armoire.

"You will see even more waves of baggage," Louis said, glancing at Marcel to see his reaction, "when you are my personal *aide-de-camp*."

When Marcel's eyes widened, Louis grinned and walked to the open window, listening to the hôtel hum with excitement. Servants were dusting furniture, cooks were rattling pots and pans in the kitchen, and gardeners were raking in the courtyard. He was home again.

~ ~ ~

The next morning, the chamberlain knocked on Louis' open door. "Marquis Henri de Mornay has arrived," he said.

"I will receive him in the salon," Louis said, checking his appearance in the mirror before leaving his chambers.

When Louis approached the marquis, he greeted him with a warm smile. "I am happy to meet you, Monsieur Marquis," he said graciously. "I was honored when my father suggested I profit from your guidance in the coming weeks."

"No, the honor was mine, monsieur count," the marquis replied coldly. "But I can understand that you may not have been too pleased."

"Not at all, Monsieur Mornay," said Louis, his brow furrowing. "I am pleased you were asked to replace the revered Abbé Fleury, who has other duties."

"I only wish I could make myself worthy of this request, monsieur count."

"I am confused, sir," said Louis, his head tilted. "What do you mean?"

"I mean," he said, "I must ask your permission to leave a charge too heavy for my strength and to hand it over to someone else for the instruction you need."

"But you were recommended by the king," Louis said.

"I beg you to believe, monsieur count, that my determination has nothing personal to do with you."

"Your motive then?" asked Louis.

"I have no other motive than the desire to live outside the intrigues of the court."

"If I may, where does this suddenly come from?" asked Louis.

"It's because there has suddenly been a disruption in my ideas, in my plans, in my..."

"You have your secrets, monsieur marquis, and I have no right to them," said Louis.

"I will only insist on this point," he said. "I would have been happy to devote myself to this service… if it were not for..."

"You may speak without embarrassing yourself," said Louis.

"Well, tongues wag in certain circles that your personal valet lives in this hôtel, coming and going freely."

"My valet, Monsieur Joubert, is not only an important member of my household, but he is also a faithful servant and a loyal friend."

"Yet, there are other rumors, monsieur count," said the marquis. "Like any other young and noble prince, it is not uncommon to neglect one's Christian duties."

Louis was silent for a moment, his face reddening. "Honorable marquis," he said, "I assure you that the son of a mother as pious as Sister Miséricorde does not lack religion… but the piety of a prince cannot be that of a saint either."

The marquis looked to the floor, biting his bottom lip.

"Please know that I have repented, I have made amends, and I have been forgiven," said Louis. "Abbé Fleury can attest to the progress I've made to earn back my father's esteem."

"Monsieur count, when you pronounce the name of your holy and venerated mother, I recognize that your fortitude can only be noble," said the marquis. "By speaking so wisely, I would regret separating myself from you under these circumstances."

"Thank you, monsieur marquis," said Louis. "I will dedicate myself wholly to the challenges in the days ahead. I will be forever grateful for you counsel."

"I accept the charge out of pure devotion," said the marquis. "Let us begin tomorrow."

~ ~ ~

Louis was diligent and attentive the first few weeks of the Marquis de Mornay's lectures; however, Louis noticed that the marquis' voice had an increasingly more metallic ring to it and his face had grown sterner. With his iron-gray hair, hard service and a rough diet had certainly done their work upon the marquis.

"The policy of war is intimidation," said the marquis as he paced back and forth in front of Louis at his desk. "It demands respect for might. It does not command admiration by right."

"Monsieur marquis, what about honor?" asked Louis, deep in thought. "Abbé Fleury taught me that certain courtesies in war must be exercised and rules followed for the conduct of troops."

"Strength and numbers are superior to any honor in war," said the marquis in a disdainful tone. "As for the conduct of troops, your methods of training are practically unfettered by any rules. The only thing required of you is that your company be highly disciplined and always in a state of readiness."

Louis looked down, hinting that he was not in agreement with the marquis' opinion.

The marquis stopped pacing. "No matter how we look at an army, it is an expensive machine," said the marquis, "but pray tell, monsieur count, is it profitless?"

Louis rubbed his chin with his fingers. "Not if there is victory, I presume."

"No, monsieur count," snapped the marquis. "The results of disciplined troops can be absorbed into civil life. Although it is a safeguard and a defense for the country, there are other outcomes from military training, such as the dexterity of body and the confidence in the mind... all necessary for a country's defense."

The marquis took his books from the table, signaling that the lesson was ending. "Self-preservation is the first law of nature and of nations, monsieur count," he said and departed. Before leaving the room, however, he turned around. "His Majesty informed me that you will attend the funeral cortege to Saint-Denis tomorrow."

Louis nodded. "Yes, monsieur marquis."

"I must warn you that His Majesty also gave me the strict orders that you are not to leave Bellefonds without prior consent," said the marquis. "You can join the cortege, but you must return to Bellefonds with no deviation in your journey."

"Understood," said Louis. The marquis bowed and departed. When he met Marcel just outside the door, Marcel bowed and then entered Louis' chambers.

Louis shook his head at Marcel, his left eye a little lazier than usual. "I am so disappointed with my progress."

Marcel's forehead wrinkled.

"Am I deceiving myself?" asked Louis. "I have so little skill in military strategy. I am sure to be exposed as a fraud on the battlefield."

"Who have you fooled? The Marquis de Mornay?" asked Marcel. "I don't believe so."

"If anyone is an imposter, it's me!" said Marcel with a grin. "Your aide-de-camp. I don't even know what that means!"

Only Marcel could make Louis giggle. "You will help arrange transportation, oversee the camp tent, and just be there… for me… like you are now."

~ ~ ~

On August 10, Louis joined Abbé Fleury at the Palace of Versailles to take part in the funeral cortege for the queen, whose body was being taken to its final destination at the Basilica of Saint-Denis. With all the pomp and ceremony worthy of a great queen, the cortege, drawn by a group of black horses, passed by Saint-Cloud, Boulogne, along the walls of Clichy and Saint-Ouen.

The three carriages of the king and those of the queen were followed by regiments of French and Swiss guards, the king's bodyguards, two companies of musketeers, three hundred officers of the queen's household, and her chaplains. Between and around the carriages, pages followed on horseback and valets on foot, all carrying lighted torches on the gray, overcast day.

From his coach, Louis noticed his sister Marie-Anne, his aunt Liselotte, and his uncle Philippe in the cortege. His brother-in-law, Prince Armand-Louis of Conti, was absent, currently serving in the imperial army at the siege of Vienna against the Turks. In addition to the dauphin and dauphine, the Princes and Princesses of the Blood appeared in the cortege, as well as many foreign ambassadors and delegates.

When entering Saint-Denis, Louis had only a moment to greet Elizabeth, who whispered how happy she was to hear of his return to Bellefonds. She pinched his ear and cast a warm smile. "Now, conduct yourself as the king's son."

Walking past Marie-Anne, he wanted to speak a word but when she saw him, she quickly turned away. Louis, feeling slighted, stopped for a moment until Abbé Fleury nudged him to move forward.

Seated behind the Princes and Princesses of the Blood and his sister, Louis felt out of place; only his cousin François turned to greet him with a slight nod. But his mood changed when he heard Charpentier's dramatic choral motets, which were followed by Lully's *Dies Irae*.[4] He was temporarily breathless when he heard Lully's bass solo sing the following verse:

*Among Thy sheep grant me a place,*
*And separate me from the goats,*
*Placing me at Thy right hand.*

Louis tried to concentrate as he listened to Bishop Bossuet's long sermon, but his train of thought was disrupted every time Elizabeth's head started to bob up and down. Biting his lip to keep from laughing, he prayed that she would not snore. Although Louis had a rather complex, if not abusive, relationship with the deceased queen, he needed to show his respect. "Blessed are those who mourn, for they shall be comforted," he said to himself.

[4] The Day of Wrath.

After the funeral, Louis and Abbé Fleury returned solemnly to their coach and returned to Bellefonds. The abbé rubbed his hands together. "Now, pray tell, how is your training progressing with the esteemed Marquis de Mornay?" he asked. "He is well versed in military strategy."

"He certainly demands perfection, monseigneur," said Louis, rolling his eyes.

"Perfection in training helps guarantee victory in battle, Count Louis," said the abbé. "Give him time. You still have a month before marching to Flanders."

"That is true," said Louis, looking out the window. "If he recommends me for the assignment."

~ ~ ~

For several weeks, Louis struggled with the Marquis de Mornay's military training and, especially, the cumbersome formation of battalions. Louis understood that impeding any advance depended upon adjusting proper formations like tactical columns in conjunction with the individual training of soldiers, but he worried about distinguishing between the real attack and the false attack.

Louis had also heard about the illness of Monsieur Colbert. Abbé Fleury had written to Louis that his old mentor was confined to his bed with stomach aches, causing him much distress. Because he was reduced to eating moist bread dipped in chicken broth, Louis was worried. He wanted to visit Papa Colbert.

"Monsieur marquis," Louis said, thinking his lessons for the day were finished, "I have news that Monsieur Colbert is very ill."

"And?" asked the marquis while he arranged maps on Louis' desk.

"Could I please have permission to visit him?" Louis asked kindly.

"I would prefer we not disrupt our lessons, monsieur count," he said. Then, after a sigh, he continued. "But I will send a request to Versailles for permission to leave Bellefonds."

"Thank you," said Louis, "Monsieur Colbert was—"

"I believe," interrupted the marquis, "we should turn our attention to an important subject… discipline."

Louis kept a straight face, not wanting the marquis to notice the slight he felt by the rude interruption.

The marquis began pacing. "Discipline is the all-availing, all-prevailing requirement of an army," he said. "It makes an army but lack of it reduces it to an armed mob. It is the result of drills, good habits, and the influence of your superiors. In short, it is professional training."

He stopped pacing and turned to Louis. "Why is discipline important, monsieur count?" he asked.

Louis rubbed his chin. "It will permit everybody to fight?"

The marquis put his hands on his hips, taking a staunch stance. "It is all very well to say, my count, that it allows *everybody* to fight," he said. "But *everybody* cannot fight on a battlefield which demands combined intelligence, subordination, and devotion—not just discipline. War is the mechanization of men, in which the nature of the service required by each man may be changed at any moment. Therefore, it requires a submissive readiness to fall into place and to perform the duties assigned without any hesitation, without any inquiry, without any doubt, without any reluctance."

While wiggling his feet underneath his desk, Louis couldn't think straight. He tried to tell himself that the class would soon be over.

~ ~ ~

On September 1, Louis received permission to visit Colbert, now said to be on his deathbed despite Doctor Fagon's prediction a month earlier that he only had hours to live. When Louis arrived at Colbert's hôtel, he was escorted upstairs to the minister's chambers. Louis waited while Monsieur Colbert's valet tapped on the minister's door. When there was no reply, he slowly opened it and softly announced, "His Royal Highness, the Count of Vermandois."

Monsieur Colbert opened his eyes. "Is it possible?" he asked. "Come closer!"

"Papa Colbert," said Louis, saddened by the pitiful sight of his first mentor, "you are ill—too ill for my visit. I shall come another day."

Monsieur Colbert struggled to sit up until his valet hurried to his side and arranged his pillow behind him. "Please, Your Highness, please stay," he said. "Heaven has sent you to me."

"Oh, but it would be too cruel to remain another minute, considering the state you are in."

"Do not cause me such grief," said Monsieur Colbert, seeming somewhat revived. "I am not yet dead."

"But I did not know you were in such a painful condition. I came directly from Bellefonds, after receiving permission, to speak with you about a small matter. But it can wait."

"Please, Your Highness, come sit by me," he said. "As long as I have a breath of life, I am at your service… as I was the day you were born."

Louis took his seat in a gilded armchair next to the bed. "It concerns my assignment in the king's army. It hangs in the balance; it depends on Marquis de Mornay's recommendation."

"And you think I have the king's ear?" Monsieur Colbert asked.

Louis nodded. "Yes, Papa Colbert," he said humbly.

"I have already spoken to His Majesty on your behalf," he said. "But I will dispatch a reminder of our conversation to him this very day."

"Thank you," said Louis with teary eyes.

"In the meantime, pay close attention to the Marquis de Mornay's guidance."

Louis stood to take his leave and Monsieur Colbert added, "I will inform Madame Colbert of your visit. She will be pleased."

Louis nodded and left the room quickly, fearing he might weep in front of his illustrious mentor.

~ ~ ~

One morning, minutes before the Marquis de Mornay was expected for lessons, Marcel entered Louis' chambers with a letter in his hand.

"Pardon me," said Marcel, "but I have an important message. It just arrived from the palace."

Louis took the parchment, opened it, and read it aloud.

*His Majesty sadly mourns the loss of his Minister of Finance, the honorable Jean-Baptiste Colbert, who died yesterday. He was the indispensable righthand of the King. With his eye of vigilance on everything, he was the pillar of the King's business and finances. Honoring the minister's request, his body was conveyed last night to the church of St. Eustache with no marks of honor or service.*

*Abbé Fleury.*

"I am very sorry for you," said Marcel.

"Thank you, but Monsieur Colbert had been ailing for a long time past," said Louis. "I don't believe he ever looked after himself. He was always himself with no more respect than a mere clerk."

"He was interred at night?" asked Marcel.

"He was not loved by the people of Paris… to say the least," Louis said, folding the parchment and putting it in his vest pocket. "I shall write a letter to Madame Colbert, though. She was like a mother to me when I was a little boy."

When the Marquis de Mornay arrived, he motioned for Marcel to go about his way. Marcel glanced to Louis as he departed and when Louis whispered, "The river?" Marcel nodded with a wide smile and shut the door behind him.

The marquis cleared his throat, gesturing for Louis to take his seat. "We must continue with the behavior of leaders vis-à-vis their relationships with their troops. This is our last lesson."

When Louis looked up at the marquis with a wrinkled brow, the marquis approached him. "Tomorrow is the fourteenth day of September," he said. "We have a very important audience with the king."

Louis nodded. He couldn't believe how quickly time had passed since his first lessons with the marquis.

"Monsieur count," said the marquis sternly, "today's lesson is important because I have doubts that you will be able to treat all your troops with perfect equality. Undue familiarity among officers and men should never be allowed. Do you understand?"

"Yes, monsieur marquis," said Louis, wondering why the marquis was so concerned.

"Officers in quarters or in camp should never mingle with the enlisted men."

Louis pretended to be concentrating throughout the final lesson, but he was secretly daydreaming about swimming later in the hot summer sun. With Marcel. His aide-de-camp. Hours later, Louis and Marcel said little as they rested on the knoll by the river. The slow-moving air, pungent with the drowsy aroma of the nearby forest, hugged them. Marcel laid on his back, pretending to be asleep, while Louis, sitting upright, watched the sun's rays glimmer across the surface of the water as the sun set. He felt connected to nature as he reflected on the humming sound from insects overhead and the water splashing the riverbank. And he felt connected to those he loved—even though some loved him less.

Louis would commit these connections to memory should he need to draw on them in the future. With all his inner strength, he promised himself that he would keep them intact.

~ ~ ~

Louis leaned out of his coach window for fresh air. It was cool, but it didn't help the sweat gathering on his forehead and above his lips. When he arrived at the palace, he walked along the palace corridors, patting his face dry with his ruffled sleeves. Waiting outside the king's chamber, his cousin François was sitting on a bench. When he spotted Louis, he started to get up but the doormen immediately opened the door to the king's chambers for Louis to enter.

Louis bowed when he approached the king, taking his place next to the Marquis de Mornay who, standing erect, did not acknowledge Louis' arrival.

"Count Louis, I have had a very interesting conversation with your mentor," said the king. "It appears that his pupil was at times obstinate and headstrong."

"Father?" asked Louis, not understanding how the king came to such a conclusion.

“Being headstrong can lead to outbursts in the ranks,” said the marquis.

“Yes, but the Marquis de Mornay and I have come to the conclusion that a degree of determinedness can be beneficial on the battlefield,” said the king. “You will depart tomorrow for Harlebeck to join Maréchal de Boufflers’ commanders.”

Louis’ heart fluttered. Lost for words, he bowed with the deepest respect.

“Marquis de Mornay, you will assist Maréchal de Boufflers as his aide-de-camp,” added the king.

“I am honored to serve Your Majesty again,” he said.

“Count Louis, my son, I expect to hear of your gallant leadership on the battlefield.”

“I shall not disappoint you, Father,” Louis said, looking directly into the king’s eyes.

The king then held a sealed parchment up for Louis to take. “This is a letter that I must personally deliver to you.”

Louis looked at the letter, staring at the handwriting and recognizing that of his mother.

“Thank you, Father,” he said, bowing to take his leave. He turned to the marquis, “Thank you, too, monsieur marquis. I will strive to make you proud.”

~ ~ ~

Louis held the letter tightly in his hand as he traveled to Bellefonds in his coach. As soon as he was alone in his chambers at Bellefonds, he collected himself for a moment while he gazed tenderly at the black wax seal bearing the arms of Duchess de La Vallière. He avoided breaking this seal, carefully tearing the paper around it. Tears moistened his eyes when he saw the large and beautiful handwriting, reminding him of that of his father, too.

*Carmelite Convent, Faubourg Saint-Jacques*

*Monsieur Count of Vermandois,*

*"As I hold my pen to write to you, I pray to the Almighty in Heaven that this will not be the last time. You cannot fathom the sad omens that struck my heart, when I heard that His Majesty forgave you and gave you permission to join his army in battle.*

Louis paused reading for a moment, his heart swelling with joy. This was finally his opportunity to show everyone what he was capable of on the battlefield—like all his heroes before him. He then continued to read the letter in a faint voice.

*"I should be grateful for the king, who has forgotten your mistakes—so far as to recall you to grace. But, nevertheless, my soul is overcome with sadness, and I find myself regretting that the king has forgiven you, since he is sending you to war!*

*Alas, I also fear for you a thousand pitfalls from your enemies. Those who were able to dishonor you in the eyes of His Majesty will certainly not hesitate to throw you into the abyss. I beg you, my son, to watch carefully over yourself. Do not expose yourselves recklessly to unnecessary perils and do not seek death. It is tempting Providence to want to die before the hour.*

*Nevertheless, remember what is the blood that runs in your veins and show yourself worthy of your illustrious birth, offering to all a fine example of courage and firmness. It is by this that you will rise in the spirit of the king; this is how you will erase the wrongs that are imputed to you.*

*My dear son, may God protect you! May God lead you and bring you back unharmed! I place you in His hands, I entrust you to His holy custody.*

*Sister Miséricorde*

She added the following postscript:

*"Obey Abbé Fleury, as I have transmitted to him my full powers and my authority as a mother. He is a reliable and dedicated guide. And, because*

*I want you to appear in the army with the status of a Prince of the Royal Blood, I have given orders so that you will not lack the resources. I am endowing you, without the knowledge of the king, the sum of twenty thousand louis to provide better for your troops.*

Louis stared into the distance, still absorbed in the feelings which his mother's letter had awakened in him. When Monsieur de Monchevreuil entered his chambers, Louis' eyes widened when he saw the large ebony coffer he was carrying. When it was placed on his desk, Louis ran his fingers over the silver inlays, bearing the arms of France. Then, Monsieur de Monchevreuil pulled a key from his vest pocket, handed it to Louis, and bowed to take his leave.

"Monsieur de Monchevreuil," said Louis, "will you please summon Monsieur Joubert?" The governor nodded and left the room.

Louis opened the coffer and found the twenty thousand louis that his mother had promised him. The gold coins were divided into twenty silk bags, each containing one thousand coins. In addition to the money, Louis found an envelope with an inscription written in his mother's hand:

*"This is a blessed talisman which will protect from any accident the person in whose hands it remains. Blessed Virgin Mary, Mother of God, pray for us!"*

Louis broke the seal and discovered a small needlepoint in purple velvet on a silk cord, with the monogram of Jesus Christ and the Virgin Mary, embroidered in gold filament.

When Marcel arrived, Louis showed him the talisman. "It is from my mother," he said. When he struggled to put it around his neck, Marcel stepped in and tied it securely. Louis then tucked the needlepoint under his nightshirt to hide it.

Louis turned to Marcel, who was eyeing the contents of the coffer on the desk, and said, "I don't believe I have ever praised you enough for your loyalty, Marcel." He pulled a silk bag from the coffer. "And words cannot express my satisfaction."

"My count," said Marcel, "your unfailing trust in me is more than I could ever deserve."

"Please take this, my dearest friend," said Louis, handing him a bag of a thousand louis."

"My count," said Marcel with teary eyes. "You embarrass me."

"But you will need this should I die."

"Die? Why speak of dying?" asked Marcel. "There are forests to explore, streams to swim, and…"

"And battles to be fought," said Louis, forcing Marcel to take the coins. "The Marquis de Mornay gave my father his recommendation. We leave for Flanders tomorrow."

At first, Marcel was reluctant to take the bag of coins, until Louis took his hand and put the coins in it. Marcel's smile expressed his gratitude.

"We have much to do today," said Louis. "Aunt Liselotte and Abbé Fleury are paying us a visit this evening."

Louis and Marcel were so busy packing their trunks that they had forgotten about the visit until Monsieur de Monchevreuil announced that the guests were waiting in the main salon.

When Louis arrived in the salon, Madame Elizabeth embraced him before he could say a word. "I am very proud of you, *junger* Louis," she said. "Now, muster the courage and strength to endure your duty on the battlefield."

"Yes, Aunt Liselotte," he said and then turned to the abbé. "Monseigneur, thank you for the invaluable lessons."

"Count Louis," said the abbé, "you will do fine. Remember, you have the blood of a long line of Bourbon kings."

Madame Elizabeth cleared her voice to get the abbé's attention and glanced at Marcel.

"My count," said the abbé. "I must sadly report that Monsieur Joubert may not join you in Flanders."

"But why, monseigneur?" asked Louis. "He is indispensable."

"I am sorry, but the king gave express orders… and without any reason."

Elizabeth looked at Marcel and said, "Monsieur Joubert, you will remain at Bellefonds, but you are always welcome at Saint-Cloud, especially to prepare my mount when I hunt with His Majesty." When Marcel nodded kindly, she held out her arms to embrace Louis again. "You will be in our prayers, *junger* Louis," she said with tears rolling down her cheeks.

~ ~ ~

The day had finally come. Marcel opened the windows and laid out Louis' wool uniform, consisting of blue breeches, a grey-white waistcoat with blue cuffs and at least four dozen brass buttons, and some dark gaiters to cover his lower legs. While Louis was dressing, Monsieur de Monchevreuil entered the chambers to deliver a letter.

"From whom?" asked Louis as Marcel helped him with his night-shirt.

"The Chevalier de Lorraine, my count," he said.

Louis looked at Marcel and then turned to Monsieur de Monchevreuil. "Can you read it please?" he asked. Monsieur de Monchevreuil broke the seal and unfolded the parchment.

*September 15, 1683*

*Your Royal Highness,*

*Before I congratulate you on your military promotion and your regiment in Flanders, I beg your pardon for all the pain and sorrow that I may have caused you in the past. I wish you Godspeed and a speedy return to Versailles as a hero.*

*To prove my sincerity, I have spared no expense to order a new saddle from the best saddler in Paris. It will be delivered before your first campaign.*

*M. Chevalier de Lorraine.*

Louis looked at Marcel, who shrugged. Once Louis was dressed, they made their way to the salon to exit the main entrance, where they found the staff of Bellefonds all lined up in the courtyard. The teary-eyed ladies from the kitchen had offerings of apples and cheeses.

Monsieur de Monchevreuil approached Louis and held out his hand.

"My medallion!" said Louis, and the governor proceeded to pin it on Louis' lapel.

"I knew that you would have use of it one day," he said.

Louis' smile was nothing short of pure gratitude. He then picked up Bandit. "You must stay out of trouble until I return," he said, letting Bandit lick his face before putting him down.

Deciding to ride horseback to Flanders, Louis nodded at the coach driver to proceed. Outside the gate, his troops were mounted and waiting for their new commander. He waved at his staff and then looked at Marcel. His tearful glance told more than words could ever convey.

~ ~ ~

It was going to be a long day. Not even halfway to Harlebeck, Louis was already exhausted, as well as the men in his company. Although they were all fair horsemen, exhaustion and thirst amplified the ordinary discomforts of the horse soldiers. In addition to bruises, chafing, and sore muscles, there was also a sense of panic building among the troops. They understood that Maréchal de Boufflers had been camped at Harlebeck since early September, but the surrounding countryside was still unsafe, and troops were urgently needed.

Louis had good reason to feel his troops' anxiety, too. The soon-to-be, sixteen-year-old son of the King of France was riding at the head of his own regiment for the first time. The need to prove himself to his father, his Aunt Liselotte, his sister, his mentors, and the court of Versailles was a heavy burden for such an inexperienced warrior.

By the time the troops reached Harlebeck, they were hot and dusty from carrying the axes, saws, shovels, and cordage needed to unhitch wagons and carry them over ditches and marshy areas. Louis also noticed that his men were soldiers not because of their patriotism, their loyalty to his father, or their desire to defend France against longtime enemies, but because they were escaping poverty or a disreputable past—not too unlike his own situation. But all the men yelped with joy when they got their first glimpse of the camp in the valley before them.

Louis had never seen such a picturesque sight—if only he could have shared it with Marcel. Campfires lit the area dotted with thousands of tents whitened by the sun. Soldiers roamed in all directions to the sound of bugles and the rolling of drums. Louis was amazed, too, at the speed with which his troops were installed. Apart from the officers' tents, which were erected in advance, everything was prepared before a battalion arrived at the place of its encampment, which was marked by a post.

For the troops' tents, with the blink of an eye, the beams were formed with three poles to support the top of a tent and six small pegs secured the ends to the ground. Under this elementary shelter was laid a bed of fresh straw and a supply of blankets to accommodate six men. Between the officers' tents and the kitchens which border the camp at the rear, the officers' horses were kept on picket.

Twice a day, at six o'clock in the morning, before soup, and at half-past four, after dinner, the troops received a ration of coffee but—more often than not—they preferred drinking wine or eau-de-vie brandy in their quarters. On one of the first nights at camp, two soldiers had their fill of the brandy and were quarreling in front of Louis's tent. When they came to blows, the profanity and curses roused the attention of a nearby commander, who threatened them with a fine for every oath.

Hearing the commander chastise the soldiers, Louis came out of his tent, half-dressed and rubbing his eyes. "What is the problem here?" he asked.

"Your men deserve a good thrashing," said the commander.

"Thank you, I will handle this matter," Louis said, gesturing for the two soldiers to enter his tent.

"Punishment for such behavior is severe, messieurs," he said. "Drinking and exhaustion are not a good mix, so embrace and return to your quarters."

They did so, and Louis saw the surprise on the soldiers' faces that an officer had actually given them another chance. In the days ahead, Louis quickly learned that he would need to earn the respect of his troops if he were to lead them in battle. He was fortunate that he had ample financial resources. For example, having cash at his disposal was advantageous if his soldiers' wages were ever delayed too long.

The cash was also put to clever use when he shared a drink with his men. He did not drink excessively, but he did play cards and gamble. Strangely enough, however, he never won. Rather, he discreetly guaranteed that his men, if losing, should win—knowing that many of them had nothing to their names. He would even secretly send a gold coin to one of his men whenever he heard a rumor of any hardship.

~ ~ ~

Each day, the ranks of the army swelled at the camp of Courtrai as masses of eager and patriotic soldiers arrived from Lessines, where Maréchal d'Humières was camped. On October 26, Louis was summoned to Maréchal de Boufflers' quarters. The tent, erected in the middle of the front line, was spacious and the turf was covered with a tapestry. It was divided by drapes, with his bed on one side and his table cluttered with maps on the other. Louis presumed the small bed to the side of the table was that of Marquis de Mornay, because aide-de-camps often lodged with their commander.

Also summoned were six other officers, including Louis' cousin, Prince François de la Roche-sur-Yon. They greeted each other with a nod and a proud smile—they were soldiers of His Majesty's army. Maréchal de Boufflers observed his officers, who stood at attention, with the Marquis de Mornay at his side.

"At ease, messieurs," said the marquis.

Then, the maréchal began speaking succinctly, carefully choosing his words. "Spain has declared war on France today."

The officers gasped.

"Since 1670, His Majesty has gained many strategic territories; however, many of these areas were not well-mapped. We have found that not all the lands we thought were ours have not been granted to us. We have laid claimed to many of these lands except for Luxembourg, which is held by the Empire."

François spoke up. "Monsieur maréchal, what prevented His Majesty from taking the city?" he asked.

"Because, Your Highness," he said, "The Empire was being attacked by the Ottomans at the time."

Louis tilted his head. "I don't understand, Maréchal de Boufflers."

"His Majesty refused to get involved in the conflict," he said. "Although His Majesty encouraged the Ottomans to weaken the Empire, his reputation was at stake—a Christian king could not attack a Christian city, especially when it was defending itself against a non-Christian army."

The maréchal motioned for his officers to approach his table. "However, the king has now raised forty thousand troops, demanding that Spain and the population of the Spanish Netherlands to pay *contribuere*." When the officers looked up for an explanation, the maréchal continued. "An allotment of goods and money for his troops. Unfortunately, Spain has joined forces with the Netherlands and, as I announced, has today declared war on France."

Then, the marquis pointed to the map in front of him. "You and your detachments will join Maréchal d'Humières from Lessines in four days. Marching on Courtrai will be our first maneuver."

After dismissing his officers, Maréchal de Boufflers sat at his desk to write a letter.

*Harlebeck, October 28, 1683.*

*Your Majesty,*

*In reply to your inquiry about the conduct of M. Count of Vermandois, I did not want to proceed with our mission without taking the liberty of telling you that the Count, according to the Marquis de Mornay, is much changed these weeks and to his advantage. He has earned the respect of his company and we have decided that he will leave Harlebeck on the first day of November with his troops to join Maréchal d'Humières' attack on Courtrai.*

*He is proving himself a princely soldier... in heart and soul.*

~ ~ ~

It took Louis a week of drills and exercise to feel confident about joining Maréchal d'Humières' forces. The night before marching on Courtrai, Louis had a shivering fever. His camp bed, although not straw like his troops, was just as uncomfortable. Smelling the dying embers of the camp's fires, he drifted off to sleep. He dreamt of finding a hiding place in a forest where he could lie down and stretch his limbs. The dark birch trees resembled the columns of a cathedral. The moon, strange with red hue, illuminated the tops of the columns, all half-charred from canon fire.

In a nearby clearing, an apple tree with half-roasted apples dangled from its scorched branches. Curious, he approached the tree, picked an apple, and was eating it when a drunken sailor, who was passing, rudely called out to him and seized his apple, taking a big bite and spitting out in Louis' face. The blood rose to Louis' head, and he seized the wretch by the neck. "You dare assault the Admiral of France?" he cried out.

A fight ensued and the soldier, intoxicated as he was, still dealt a powerful blow, knocking Louis down. He was delirious, but when he saw Marcel hovering above him and wiping the sweat off his brow, his body relaxed. A sense of calm serenity swept over his body, and he slept soundly until the early morning bugle woke him.

# CHAPTER EIGHTEEN

# The Agonizing Victory

*Battle Scene*

"Do not be afraid; our fate cannot
be taken from us; it is a gift."

— Dante Alighieri, *Inferno*

## Lessines, November 1683

Under the direction of Maréchal de Boufflers carrying out Maréchal d'Humières' orders, Louis would today see the application of the maxims that Abbé Fleury and the Marquis de Mornay had diligently taught him. Although he was still carrying a fever, he was in his element. He was alert, straightforward, good-natured, and his fellow officers as well as his troops praised him. As he approached his mount, he admired the new saddle that was promised by the Chevalier de Lorraine. His heart swelled. He would proudly address his men before leaving the camp at Harlebeck.

He mounted the saddle. Then, with his feet in the shiny silver stirrups, he rode to his troops at the rear of the camp. Surprised, he saw the Chevalier de Lorraine with the Marquis de Chatillon on horseback at the gate. He nodded gratefully for the saddle and continued to his men already in formation. As he turned his horse around to face them, the cinch below his horse's belly unbuckled and Louis fell to the ground on his back. His men gasped, but one rushed to help him up. Louis brushed himself off and looked to the gate, seeing the chevalier and marquis doubled over with laughter.

Louis took the reins of his horse and led it back to the gate, motioning for his soldier to bring the fallen saddle along. At the gate, he looked at the chevalier, who smirked and yelled, "Did you truly think I would ever forgive you for telling the king about my role in the society?"

Louis, refusing to acknowledge the chevalier, continued to the picket and with his soldier's help, resaddled his horse with the old saddle before returning to his men. Once there, he looked them straight in the eyes and spoke loudly and clearly.

*Soldiers of His Majesty's army! I may fall from my saddle in battle, but I will remount my horse with determination, wounded or not, to continue the fight to victory.*

The troops cheered at Louis' resolve.

> *I need not address you at any length, as we are all about to fight a common cause. Indeed, the very sight of our troops in uniform inspires more confidence than any eloquent appeals of our enemies with a weaker force behind them. Mindful, then, of the true character we bear, we will charge our adversaries gallantly.*
>
> *I am far from being one of the strongest among you, but I will share all the dangers and anxieties of the humblest of soldiers.*
>
> *Be on the watch yourselves to secure the safety and good order of our march, and let every man remember that the ground he is forced to contest, will, if he maintains it, prove to be that of his country and his fortress... for it is men, not walls, nor ships without men, that make the nation of France.*

The troops reacted to Louis' speech with a mad, rambling roar. Several of his troops' horses reared up to the delight of their riders. Turning his gaze to the gate, Louis noticed the surprised but defeated looks on the chevalier and the marquis' faces. Their obvious ruse to humiliate him in front of his men had failed.

~ ~ ~

On November 1, Maréchal d'Humières, encamped a half-day's march from Courtrai at Ronse and formulated his plans to open trenches against Courtrai for its siege, sending orders for Maréchal de Boufflers' regiments to encircle the city. Subsequently, Louis' troops crossed the Lys River en route to Courtrai, taking position there between two of its city gates to start digging trenches. When other regiments arrived, Courtrai closed all the gates to defend the city, only heightening its citizens' anxiety.

Maréchal de Boufflers' spies discovered that the Spanish garrison consisted of two battalions of infantry and a squadron of cavalry. The garrison, five hundred men in all, was confined in the citadel, leaving the inhabitants to defend their city on their own—or face a fine of three florins.

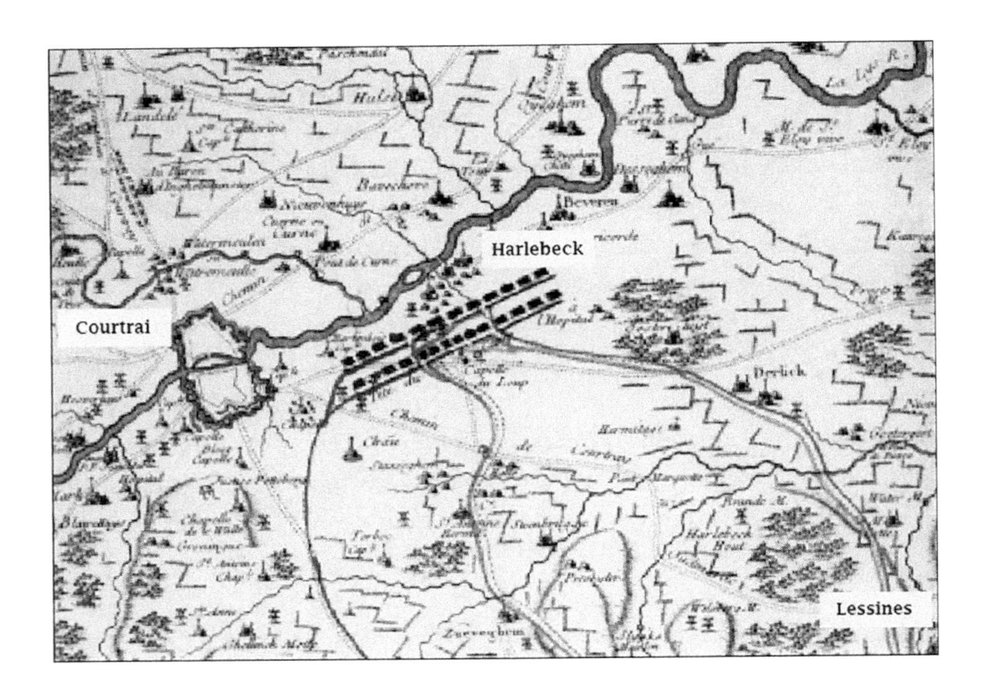


Louis' troops fared well, but he was becoming concerned about his fever, which he concealed for fear of being prevented from joining the assault on Courtrai.

~ ~ ~

By the end of the day on November 2, Courtrai had been surrounded with the entire French army taking shelter in the trenches. That night, the city bourgeois stood guard on the ramparts, firing shots randomly at French troops.

By the next morning, Spanish horsemen had left the citadel and entered the city. The citizens were distraught; they closed their doors, shut their windows, and hid everything that was precious. The bourgeois had also abandoned their guard posts on the ramparts and fled to their homes. The mayor of Courtrai sent a messenger to Maréchal de Boufflers, asking him what he wanted and why he had surrounded the city. The maréchal replied, "Your surrender."

Louis, now alarmed about his incessant fever, summoned the camp physician, Doctor d'Aquin, who was also the king's physician assigned to the siege of Courtrai.

Doctor d'Aquin examined Louis, then struggled to find the right words. "How long has Your Highness had this fever," he asked, shaking his head in disbelief.

"Several days, monsieur," Louis answered, looking to the ground.

"Your Highness should confine yourself to bed for much needed rest," he said.

"But the siege of Courtrai?" said Louis. "We are so close to taking the city."

"I beg Your Highness," he said, picking up his satchel, "please, you must promise you will take my advice."

"I promise, monsieur," Louis said.

The doctor nodded with a warm smile. "Send for me if the fever worsens," he said before leaving the tent.

Louis agreed to the doctor's orders, but he didn't obey them. Before returning to the trenches, he joined fellow officers around Maréchal de Boufflers' table in his quarters.

"We have now surrounded the city," said the maréchal, "but we are faced with fierce resistance from the besieged. At all costs, we must hold the line."

Louis leaned over the table and pointed to a spot on the maréchal's map. "Could we not storm the city between the citadel and the nearest gate?" he asked. "Otherwise, we risk prolonging the siege."

His cousin, François, tilted his head and glanced at Maréchal de Boufflers. "Such a maneuver *would* be straightforward," he said.

"We have discussed such a tactic, but please understand that it would needlessly cost the lives of many valiant soldiers," said the maréchal. "Considering the city's powerful artillery, it would not yield any less quickly."

The officers agreed and, despite the regular and sure fire of the city's defenders, they bravely fought in the trenches near the ramparts. Although they held their positions, more than one hundred and forty troops were killed, including two from Louis' company.

Louis, too, was struck by a musket ball from the rampart.

~ ~ ~

Louis lay on his back with his eyes closed. The silence was deafening. Inhaling deeply, he smelled the straw that had been littered in the trenches to make them as comfortable as possible. It reminded him of the isolated grassy knoll where he and Marcel used to collapse after swimming in the river. The passing of clouds intermittently blocked the sun, causing his skin to tingle from the slight chills that came and went. It was the same sensation he had when they rested in the shadows of the weeping willows. The low-hanging branches swayed back and forth, protecting them from the sweltering sun—hiding them too from the prying eyes of the rest of the world.

Louis' breathing intensified. He pictured himself lying close to Marcel when their hands first touched. A strange, but wondrous moment. Neither of them flinched, but they breathed in and out more deeply, almost deliberately, in sync.

Louis felt some color coming to his cheeks, hearing fish flapping their tails in the water nearby. It wasn't a far cry from the uncontrollable splashing when he and Marcel roughhoused in the joyful sunshine. The color in Louis' cheeks begins to heat up. A bittersweet pang struck Louis' heart. He and Marcel hadn't done anything more than what lackeys in the stables were known to do, yet many lads had burned at the stake for such crimes against nature. Did the fires of Hell also await those who committed such offenses--even if you were the son of a king?

Louis broke into a sweat and his body quivered. He remembered that horrific day when he shuddered before His Majesty, Louis XIV, who looked down upon him from his throne with a stern gaze. "My son," said the king, "you've soiled the body I gave you. You've tainted the blood I transmitted to you."

Louis' body weighed heavily against the trench floor. He writhed when he recalled the stinging lashes. He was stunned that his father ordered him to be flogged in public. If his mother had been the queen of France and not the king's mistress, would he have been spared such wrenching humiliation?

His heartbeat quickened. He pictured his uncle adorned like a perfumed actress with ribbons, sparkling jewelry, and a long powdered wig. Everyone at court knew that the king's only brother had affairs with men. Although his uncle jested about all his conquests and even boasted of watching such transgressors burn at the stake, he was never punished—or even chastised—by the king.

Louis' heartbeat began to pound in his throat. His hypocritical uncle! No, his hypocritical, adulterous father! And his mother! How could she desert him to take up the veil? He recalled her speaking to a lady-in-waiting. "It is necessary that my children know that I cherish them," she said, "just as much as I curse myself for ever having conceived them."

The muscles in Louis' body tightened, and he struggled to relax by focusing on the waves of the water gently lapping the sandy riverbank. It's the same hypnotic rhythm that swept Louis and Marcel's cares away. Clouds floated motionless in the sky when Marcel dared to take his hand in his for the first time. He was just a stable boy, but his cheekbones were as high as those of a Greek warrior. His bold eyes encouraged Louis to confront his fears. They fantasized about fighting side by side on the battlefield, like the amorous soldiers of the Sacred Band of Thebes.

Louis' body pressed more heavily against the ground, He remembered the helplessness of living far from court. For months he longed for forgiveness...until a weight was lifted from his body. When he returned to Bellefonds, the king summoned him. "Son," he said, "you will join my army in Flanders. Be brave, return victorious, and you will earn back my esteem."

Louis heard the waves calling him to sleep, but he wouldn't surrender. He searched for more memories. They gave meaning to his life. They mustered his strength, they healed his wounds, they summoned his dreams. He struggled. He struggled to picture Marcel's face one more time, but his body fell limper and limper--except for a slight smile on his lips that he refused to relinquish. He felt nothing more.

When he woke, Louis was still lying on his back—not on the ground but on an army cot. The stale air in the tent suffocated him as sweat dripped down his forehead from the bandages covering his head and the side of his face. He felt the body heat of a priest who hovered too closely above him, tracing the cross from his eyes to his lips and from ear to ear. He squeezed his eyes shut and journeyed back to that breezy, grassy knoll for a just a moment before opening his eyes.

His memories, so powerfully intertwined with his life, made him whole again. He smiled in his mind. He would create new memories, better memories. With Marcel.

~ ~ ~

By November 5, Courtrai had surrendered to Maréchal d'Humières' army. Only the citadel remained in Spanish hands. Doctor d'Aquin wrote to the king that Louis' condition remained stable but because his fever was still not breaking, the Marquis de Mornay wanted to move Louis to Lille for better care.

The next day, Maréchal d'Humières received a dispatch from the king.

*November 6, 1683*

*Honorable Maréchal d'Humières,*

*Since Monsieur Count of Vermandois is in no state to march with the army, I agree with the Marquis de Mornay that he be sent to Lille. I believe he will be more comfortable there.*

The fever did not subside, and Doctor d'Aquin determined that Louis should be bled. Louis rejected the doctor's advice until the Marquis de Mornay finally persuaded him to allow the doctor to proceed. Ordered to keep the king apprised of Louis' condition, the doctor wrote to the king on November 8.

*Your Majesty,*

*Monsieur Count of Vermandois' fever continues but there are no complications. His wounds are also healing. Although he had a slight repug-*

*nance to bleeding, the matter was solved, and he was bled. He is now showing signs that he is much better for it.*

*Monsieur Count of Vermandois was advised to remain in bed when I was first apprised of the fever. If he had taken my counsel, he would have avoided falling into his current state. However, if he had done so, his men would never have conferred on him the marks of courage he showed when attacking the ramparts.*

By November 10, the citadel had been delivered to Maréchal d'Humières' army and all conditions were accepted by the defeated army. The bells rang and the enemy withdrew from the ramparts, except for a few sentries who were waiting to be replaced by the victors. The gates to Courtrai were all opened, allowing the French troops to enter and occupy the city. On the same day, the king wrote to Maréchal d'Humières with further instruction about the care for Louis.

*Honorable Maréchal d'Humières,*

*I have received the letter Doctor d'Aquin wrote to me from Lille. I am very pleased with the report on the condition of my son, the Count of Vermandois. But I am not the less uneasy, because the fever has still not vanished. You have done well to take him to Lille, and he may remain there as long as needed for his health. I have nothing else to add, except that I am always very pleased with your immeasurable achievements.*

~ ~ ~

On November 13, Maréchal de Boufflers wrote to the king that Louis' mind was beginning to be affected by his illness and that bleeding him from the feet was necessary. The following day, the Marquis d'Humières arrived in Lille to find that Louis' condition had taken for the worse.

Doctor d'Aquin stood at Louis' bedside. "I am so confounded by the count's fever," he said, "that I dare not try any extreme remedies."

"I believe, however, that the need is urgent, monsieur doctor," said Maréchal d'Humières, glancing at the Marquis de Mornay."

"I agree," said the marquis.

Doctor d'Aquin nodded in agreement and prepared an emetic to give Louis, which produced all the effects desired. After the evacuations and vomiting, Louis' condition appeared to have improved.

The doctor pulled the blanket up to Louis' chin. "The fever is quite diminished," he said. "He is breathing easily too, but I find him a little drowsy and his head is not as clear as it should be. He spoke to me—but only for a moment."

"As I don't have much to do at present," said Maréchal d'Humières, "I believe the king would not object to me staying here for another day. I would welcome a good night's rest."

~ ~ ~

On November 15, Louis was occasionally agitated and delirious with beads of sweat running down his face from his bandages, but Doctor d'Aquin assured the Marquis de Mornay, Maréchal de Boufflers, and Maréchal d'Humières that there was nothing more they could do. They departed Lille to continue their campaign in the north against the Spanish. The next day, Louis was in such danger that the doctor arranged for him to receive the last communion.

~ ~ ~

King Louis XIV's chambers glowed from the light of the oil lamps. He sat at his desk to write a letter, the pale parchment absorbing his pen's ink as black as the tenebrous night.

*Sieur Bishop of Arras*

*Having learnt with very sensible sorrow, that our very dear and well-beloved son, the Count of Vermandois, Admiral of France, has lately died in the town of Courtrai in Flanders, and desiring him to be placed in the cathedral church of your town of Arras, we send word for you to receive the body of our said son, when it is brought to the Cathedral of*

*Arras, and to have it buried in the choir of the church with the ceremonies observed at the burial for persons of his rank. Given at Versailles, November 19, 1683. Signed, "LOUIS."*

The king then summoned his ministers and courtiers to the Salon de Guerre, its walls covered with portraits of the king's victorious campaigns. Everyone jostled for a place to hear the monarch.

"Yesterday, the eighteenth day of November, Louis de Bourbon, Count of Vermandois and Admiral of France, passed away gently in his sleep," he said. "The entire army is in mourning. His fellow officers and troops weep for him."

The crowd gasped and Louis' sister, Marie-Anne, shrieked and fainted. The king, unaffected by neither his son's death nor his daughter's grief, continued. "His body will be interred in the Abbey of Saint-Vaast at Arras," he said dryly and then gestured that the audience was dismissed.

Madame Elizabeth and Monsieur retreated to the Salon of Venus where a banquet had been prepared. "My deepest condolences, madame," he said. "I know how attached you were to the young count."

"Thank you, husband," she said, "I am worried, however, about the Princess de Conti. Although they were not close, she suffers greatly at the loss of her brother." She glanced at the princess and Madame Colbert at the far end of the salon. "Poor Madame Colbert is still in mourning for Monsieur Colbert."

Monsieur glanced at Madame de Montespan. "The Montespan does not seem to upset about the King's loss."

"No, not at all," said Elizabeth. "I heard that she is not sorry at all. She's very glad that her son the Duke de Maine now has no brothers in front of him… except for the dauphin."

"Our sons will certainly take precedence over those of that contemptible woman," said Monsieur.

"Contemptible, indeed," said Elizabeth. "When Bishop Bossuet spoke of the loss of *junger* Louis, placing him above the greatest of men, she told him to moderate his praises so they could be believed. She said a man of that age could never have all the qualities that are given to him."

Monsieur shook his head in disgust. "At least the Grand Prince de Condé deeply regrets Count Louis' death," he said.

"Only because *junger* Louis was betrothed to Mademoiselle de Bourbon," she snapped and then turned to depart.

"Where are you going, madame?"

"I must pay a visit to Bellefonds. They need to hear the sad news and I prefer they hear it from me."

When Elizabeth arrived at the hotel, she asked Monsieur de Monchevreuil to gather the staff. Before speaking with them in the grand salon, however, she asked to see Marcel in private.

When Marcel saw Elizabeth enter Louis' chambers, his face tightened. "Is it about Count Louis?"

"Yes, Monsieur Joubert," she said. "I am sorry, but *junger* Louis will not be returning from battle."

Marcel's lips trembled as he tried to hide his pain.

"Come to me," said Elizabeth, holding out her arms.

Marcel wept. "It is all my fault," he cried. "I should have gone with him."

"Shh, shh," whispered Elizabeth. "You *were* with him; of that I am certain."

Marcel wiped his eyes with his sleeve and looked about Louis' chambers. "I should prepare his belongings for the palace. I have much to do."

"Yes, but first I have a request for you, Monsieur Joubert."

"Yes, madame," he said. "Anything."

"I am going to gift you one of my small farms in Germany... with a pension," she said. "I would like to have Louis' body laid to rest in peace there in the serene hills of my homeland... far away from that horrific battlefield."

Marcel wipes his eyes again. "What will I do there, madame?" he asked.

"You will manage the farm for me as well as prepare Louis' resting place," she said. "The king has given us permission, but no one must know about it."

"I will honor your request with the best of my ability," he said.

"Of that I can be sure, Monsieur Joubert," she said. "Prepare to leave as soon as possible." Then, she returned to the salon to speak to the household. The entire staff sobbed upon the news of Louis' death.

Madame Elizabeth approached Monsieur de Monchevreuil. "Sir, out of your kindness to *junger* Louis, I am providing for you and your staff... until new residents are found for the Hôtel de Bellefonds. Your diligent care for the prince will not go unrewarded."

~ ~ ~

The next evening after sundown, the king's coach, flanked by the king's musketeers, arrived at the Carmelite Convent of the Faubourg Saint-Jacques in Paris. The mother superior greeted the king in the courtyard and escorted him into the convent. She excused herself to arrange for the king to discreetly meet Sister Miséricorde and, minutes later, she escorted him into a small, candle-lit cell with a crucifix on the wall. She then left, closing the iron door behind her.

In front of the king sat a small-framed nun, sitting on a meager cot and mending socks. He approached her but she didn't flinch.

Sister Louise," he said.

She looked up and asked, "Madame de Montespan retires early these days, your majesty?"

The king was not amused. "I've come to tell you that our son has died on the battlefield," he said. "In Courtrai."

She solemnly put the mending in her lap without looking up.

"But he died courageously," said the king.

She looked directly into his eyes. "I should lament the poor child's birth more grievously than his death."

The king took a moment to collect his thoughts. "The count will be interred at the Cathedral of Arras," he said. "Bishop Bossuet has already left in a royal coach to administer the ceremony. I have also arranged for a Requiem Mass to be said every day for the remainder of the year."

"It makes kings and dictators, it makes heroes, it makes widows, it makes cemeteries, it makes mothers cry," said Sister Louise, looking off into the distance.

"What, madame?"

"War."

The king pulled Louis' gold medallion from his pocket and handed it to her, but she wouldn't take it. "We gave him this heirloom when you entered the convent."

Sister Louise frowned. "I entered the convent with abhorrence of my affair with the King of France," she said, picking up and resuming her sewing. "And I'm still seeking atonement."

The king, wordless, exited the cell and walked down a dismal hallway lit by torches hanging on the wall. He took Louis' medallion from his pocket, looked at it for a moment, and then held it tight to his chest. A single tear rolled down his cheek.

Later, at the foot of the crucifix, the nun united herself completely with her Mother Mary in tears and prayer, the language of two mothers mourning the loss of their sons.

~ ~ ~

Bishop Bossuet prepared for a spectacular service for the son of Louis XIV in Arras. The people, the clergy of the different parishes, and the friars of the mendicant orders of the town assembled at the cathedral. The infantry lined the road from the entrance of the town to the cathedral, and at noon the roar of cannon and the tolling of bells announced the arrival of Count Louis of Vermandois' coach, draped with black velvet and escorted by the cavalry of the garrison.

Bishop Bossuet, clothed in his pontifical robes, advanced in procession to receive Louis' body, and masses were said without intermission until the next day in the Chapel of Saint-Vaast, where the body had been placed. The choir and the nave of the cathedral were adorned in black, upon which shone silver plaques emblazoned with the arms of Vermandois. Amid the mournful light of the candles, the sad and silent troops, and the spectators all clothed in mourning, the bishop concluded his eulogy.

*His proud bearing, the supreme distinction which he inherited from his royal father, drew attention to him even more than his high origin. To these exterior charms, to these feelings of exquisite delicacy and natural goodness, which attached to him the soldier as well as the officer, the Count of Vermandois added a prompt spirit, an unfailing courage, a strong desire to distinguish himself and to deserve by actions of brilliance the eminent dignity, in which, from the age of two, the affection and pride of His Majesty Louis XIV had raised him.*

Bishop Bossuet wrote to His Majesty, describing the ceremony and the grief of his subjects for the passing of his son. What he did not report, however, was that the same coach left the church early the next morning… and not on the route to Versailles. Sightings of the coach by others would soon lead to rumors at Versailles. Courtiers speculated that the prince was not truly interred at the Cathedral of Arras.

# CHAPTER NINETEEN

# Rumors Abound

*Country Farm*

"The poets leave hell and behold the stars again."

— Dante Alighieri, *Inferno*

## The Palace of Versailles, December 1683

Stories swarmed throughout the salons of Versailles. One tale spread by Madame de Montespan narrated Louis's death, describing how he died from drinking too much eau-de-vie, not because water was scarce, but because he participated in orgies and debauchery. Many understood, however, that she only spoke of Louis in such a manner as to elevate the status of her own bastard child, the Duke de Maine, in the eyes of the court.

Another story which was widely circulated was that Louis was the Man in the Iron Mask. Louis had supposedly been replaced with an unknown fallen soldier and then whisked away to be incarcerated for life at Pignerol, a secluded prison for those who were considered an embarrassment to the crown.[5]

The liveliest conversation at court, however, narrated the story that Louis's body had been sent to Germany. Louis' body was replaced by an unknown soldier who had fallen in battle for interment at the Cathedral of Arras. Moreover, a royal coach *did* depart from Arras on the morning after Louis' funeral, and it was not destined for France.

~ ~ ~

When the coach emerged from the Black Forest in Germany, it arrived at Marcel's secluded farm, nestled in a valley surrounded by towering, dark evergreen trees. Marcel, having made preparations to receive his master's body, approached the coach from the timbered farmhouse to welcome it. Bandit followed along cautiously. When it came to a halt, the burly driver stepped down and brushed the dust from his coat with his hat, causing Bandit to growl and bark at the stranger.

"Don't worry, messieurs," said Marcel. "He won't bite you."

---

[5] This was later disproved because it was documented in 1691 that the Man in the Iron Mask had been a prisoner for twenty years. Count Louis of Vermandois could not have been a prisoner for twenty years in 1691, having presumably died only eight years earlier in 1683.

Keeping an eye on Bandit, the driver, proceeded to open the carriage door.

Marcel watched the driver as he helped a soldier in bandages step down from the coach. When Marcel recognized the soldier was Louis, he cried with joy. "Master!"

Tears ran down Louis' cheeks. "No, Marcel," he said, "it's just Louis now."

~ ~ ~

Courtiers engaged in heated debates about whether Louis could have been given a new life in Germany. The most important question was why His Majesty would have ever exiled his son. Answers ranged from the shame he felt for Louis' debauchery, the pressure from Madame de Montespan in favor of her own son, and the illicit, personal relationship Louis had with his valet.

Another question that arose was how His Majesty arranged for the exchange of a fallen soldier with Louis. Courtiers concluded that Madame Elizabeth arranged for Louis to be replaced with a fallen soldier. She had begged the king to allow her *junger* Louis to live his days far from Versailles, avoiding the king any embarrassment and ensuring Louis a happy life for the rest of his days. The king agreed but declared that both young men would be forbidden to ever return to France—upon pain of death.

The person who could have easily managed the exchange was the king's own physician. But many believed that Madame Elizabeth had blackmailed the Chevalier de Lorraine to help arrange the exchange. She had proof that the chevalier, a veritable thorn in her side for years, was an accomplice to the murder of Henriette, the first Duchess d'Orléans. A valet-de-chambre had told her how the head of Henriette's household, Marquis d'Effiat, had conspired with the chevalier to poison Henriette's cup from which she had sipped tea that day.

Everyone was easily persuaded that the king was aware of Louis' disappearance, agreeing that he showed no emotion that doleful evening when he reported Louis's death to the court. He must have given Elizabeth his approval for the covert undertaking, allowing Louis to live with Marcel on her secluded lands.

The rumors occupied the court to such an extent that the king finally arranged for Louis' coffin to be opened at the Cathedral of Arras. He later reported to the court that there was decisive proof for those who were tempted to believe that anybody other than that of his son, Count of Vermandois, had been put to rest in the coffin. Although the proof verified the existence of "an entire and well-shaped body,"[6] the king did not reveal that the body in the casket could not be identified as Louis' remains. Nevertheless, the rumors soon subsided.

~ ~ ~

The snow on the Black Forest hilltops glistened and the chirping of the purple finches pierced the brisk winter air when Louis and Marcel walked along the shallow, gurgling brook in the early morning. Bandit followed behind, stopping occasionally for a quick drink.

Louis stopped to pick up a stone and skipped it across the water. "You know, for sixteen years I lived in the shadow of the great Sun King," he said, picking up another stone. "I wasn't a prince then, and now I've disappeared from the eyes of the court… and from its memory."

"You can shut those palace doors behind you," said Marcel, "but remember, those who cared for you know you left as a valiant warrior in His Majesty's army," Marcel said, noticing something under Louis' nightshirt.

"What is that?" asked Marcel, pulling on a silk cord hanging around Louis' neck.

"An amulet," he said. "My mother made it before I went to Flanders," he said, pulling it out from underneath his nightshirt.

[6] A *procès-verbal* was drawn up on December 16, 1686, in the presence of the Bishop of Arras, the provost of the cathedral, the head of the vestry, and the procureur-général, ordering the coffin to be open and inspected.

Marcel took the amulet in his hand to look at it more closely, "Yes, I remember you showed it to me. It's beautiful." Then, noticing a small piece of white cloth tied in a knot above it, he asked, "And this?"

Louis, lost for words, blushed.

"Tell me," said Marcel, tugging playfully on the cord.

"Do you remember chasing me in the forest at Saint-Cloud… when you slipped and cut your knee?" said Louis, his face turning red.

Marcel tilted and shook his head, letting Louis know he had no recollection.

"You wiped the blood off with your kerchief and threw it in the brush," said Louis. When Marcel rubbed his chin with his fingers, Louis added, "I fetched it when we returned to the château."

Marcel's eyes teared up. "To remember me?"

Louis grinned, "No, to remember that I won the race," he said, laughing and dashing away to avoid any repercussions. But Marcel and Bandit quickly caught up with him in a small clearing, bathed in sunlight. The air was crisp and clear, allowing the birds' hymns to carry on the cool breeze. The tall trees, their branches reaching for the sky, stood sturdy with deep roots covered with centuries of moss.

"The magic of this wood reminds me of a Psalm in the Bible," said Louis. "Let the land be joyful, and all that is on it. Then, all the trees of the woods will sing for joy."

The rays of sun filtered through the boughs covered with snow like a kaleidoscope with a symphony of colors. Louis looked at Marcel. "I wouldn't have left you alone," he said. "I promise."

"I know," said Marcel, taking Louis' hand. "Should we explore these mysterious woods? I'm sure they're filled with strange creatures and hidden wonders."

"Behind every twist and turn, danger might be lurking," said Louis, putting Marcel's hand on his heart to let him feel his strong and regular heartbeat. "But see, I'm not afraid."

"Then, I'm not either," said Marcel. "Not now."

# AUTHOR'S NOTE

## The Forgotten Prince

*Death of Sister Louise de la Miséricorde*

> "Our powers, whether of mind or tongue, cannot
> embrace that measure of understanding."
>
> — Dante Alighieri, *Inferno*

Any moment is but a moment of history, and history today will be called history tomorrow. Historically, it is confirmed that Count Louis of Vermandois was the illegitimate son of Louis XIV and Louise de

Vallière, that he participated in a secret gay society, that he was flogged and exiled from court by his father, and that he died as an officer in Flanders.

When it comes to the scandals that plagued the reign of Louis XIV, such facts are often stranger than fiction. Not only did the Sun King have a handful of mistresses, but he also fathered at least sixteen royal bastards with them. Such tainted blood was a threat to the royal lineage's purity, and no one was more aware of this than the king himself. "No issue should ever come of such species," the king once said, yet he soon found himself marrying his misborn offspring into prestigious noble and royal families. One of them, the estranged Count Louis of Vermandois, however, was the exception.

Louis never married but it must be noted that *garçons* like Louis at the court of Versailles were considered men at the age of thirteen—often married and starting families, trained for the military, and even serving in the king's campaigns abroad. The king himself was introduced to the charms of the opposite sex at the age of twelve, the rendezvous being arranged by his own mother, Queen Anne.

Historical documents also attest to the fact that Count Louis of Vermandois was sexually abused at thirteen and initiated into a secret same-sex *confrérie*, or brotherhood, the following year by his uncle's gay lover. Because Louis met his tragic death at the early age of sixteen, and to stay true to the social considerations of the period, I have decided to keep the historical timeline intact and not change Count Louis' age to accommodate modern-day Western standards and morals. Moreover, masculine sexual identity during the reign of Louis XIV was expressed through a sub-culture that tolerated same-sex relations and effeminate behavior within specific parameters at court, despite religious, social, and legal prohibitions against them.

Louis' sister, Marie-Anne, contracted smallpox a year after Louis' death. Although she survived the ordeal, her husband, Prince Louis-Armand of Conti, died after he contracted her disease. Marie-Anne then became the Dowager Princess of Conti and when her mother, Louise de la Vallière died in the convent in 1710, she received her mother's fortune as well as the title of Duchess de La Vallière.

Remaining a widow as well as one of the richest women in France until her death in 1739, Marie-Anne's life as dowager princess was encumbered by perpetual ruses over the question of rank and privilege with her half sisters and sisters-in-law. Her goal? Humiliate them at every turn.

Indeed, the quarrels were so frequent and so chaotic that the king threatened to banish the princesses from court if they couldn't settle their differences. But Marie-Anne, one of the most beautiful women at court had no reason to worry. Several foreign princes had asked for her hand in marriage, but the king declined their offers. The presence of his dazzling and musically talented daughter at court was crucial to his happiness—he could never be separated from her.

Unlike his son, Count Louis of Vermandois, the Admiral of France.

# List of Illustrations & Credits

All illustrations found in *The Bastard Prince of Versailles* originate from a variety of sources in the public domain due to their age, being in the public domain in its country of origin and other countries where the copyright term is the author's life plus 100 years or less.

**PART ONE: ABANDON**

Cover: Louis de Bourbon. *Louis de Bourbon, Comte de Vermandois*. François de Troy (c. 1679).

Count Louis of Vermandois. *Louis de Bourbon, Count of Vermandois*. Louis-Édouard Rioult (1839). Commissioned by King Louis-Philippe.

The Château of Sceaux. *Château de Sceaux*. Jacques Rigaud (1736).

The Palace of Versailles. *Château de Versailles*. Israël Silvestre (1682).

The Staircase of the Grand Monarch. *Le Grand Escalier du Château de Versailles*. Charles Le Brun (1725).

King Louis XIV and Louise de La Vallière. *The King and La Vallière*. Edmund H. Garrett (1893). In *The Vicomte de Bragelonne* by Alexandre Dumas.

Château of Saint-Cloud. *Veüe de la maison de Saint Cloud.* Israël Silvestre (c. 1670s).

Louise de La Vallière and Children. *Portrait of Louise de La Vallière, one of Louis XIV's mistresses, with her children from the king (Marie Anne and Louis, Count of Vermandois)*. M. Schmitz, after a painting by Pierre Mignard (1865).

Carmélites Convent of the Faubourg Saint-Jacques (17th century). *Le monastère des carmélites de Notre-Dame-des-Champs au milieu du XVIIè siècle* by Jean Marot.

Cascade of Saint-Cloud. *Veüe de la cascade de Saint Cloud.* Jacques Rigaud (1730).

Stable Stall. *Inside of a Stable*. John Stewart (1856). In *The Stable Book.*

Academic Fencing. *The Fencing Student*. Johann Georg Puschner (1725).

## PART TWO: HUNTING FOR PREY

Le Pot-Pourri de Loth. *The inhabitants of Sodom provoke divine wrath.* François-Rolland Elluin (1781).

Chevalier de Lorraine. *Chevalier de Lorraine.* Edmund H. Garrett (1893). In *The Vicomte de Bragelonne* by Alexandre Dumas.

Board Game. *Jeu royal et historique de la France.* Stefano della Bella (1674).

Apollo and Hyakinthus. *Apollo e Giacinto.* Jacopo Caraglio (1527).

Apartment at Versailles. *Quatrième chambre des apartemens.* Antoine Trouvain (1696).

Hôtel Bellefonds. *Hôtel Bellefonds.* Jouvin de Rochefort (1672).

Princess Marie-Anne de Conti and Prince Louis-Armand de Conti. *Marie-Anne, Légitimée de France, Princess of Conti* and *Louis Armand, Prince of Conti.* De L'Armessin (1682).

The Whipping Boy. *Edward and Whipping Boy.* Walter S. Stacey (1929).

Floor Plan: *The Hôtel de Bellefonds.* By Author (1680).

## PART THREE: FALL FROM GRACE

Phaeton. *The Fall of Phaëton.* Hendrik Goltzius (1588).

Chevalier de Lorraine as Ganymede. *Portrait du Chevalier de Lorraine dépeint en Ganymède.* Baldassare Franceschini (c. 1760).

Justice Triumphant. *Justice Triumphant.* Gleich und Anders (1730).

Louis XIII's Versailles, as constructed circa 1630—1640. *Vue du premier château de Versailles.* Comtesse-Héloïse de Gomboust (1652). Work in the public domain.

Le Petit Château de Frémont. *Veüe et perspective du chasteau de Frémont à quatre lieues de Paris sur le chemin de Fontainebleau.* Israël Silvestre (c. 1780).

Louis de Bourbon. *Louis de Bourbon, Comte de Vermandois.* François de Troy (c. 1679).

Chaise à porteurs. *Design of Sedan Chair.* Robert Adam (1675). Adulterers Whipped in Public, In: *La France et les Français à Travers les Siècles.* Augustin Challamel (1889).

## PART FOUR: THE SPOILS OF WAR

Jeton: Louis of Vermandois. *Louis de Vermandois, Amiral de France - Jeton de la Marine Royale* (1681). Author's Collection.

Château de Fontainebleau. *Veüe de la cour des Fontaines de Fontaine Beleau.* Israël Silvestre (c. 1666).

Louis of Vermandois. *Louis, Count of Vermandois.* Pierre Mignard (c. 1678).

# Glossary

| | |
|---|---|
| Abbé: | abbott, priest |
| Baigneur: | bather |
| belle: | beautiful |
| Château: | castle |
| Chere, Cherie: | dear, darling |
| Chaise percée: | commode chair |
| Confidante: | trustworthy person |
| Coucher: | sleep |
| Débauché: | excessively indulgent in sex, alcohol, or drugs |
| Eau-de-vie: | brandy |
| Ecu: | French coin |
| En femme: | as a woman |
| Faux pas: | mistake, indiscretion |
| Fête: | feast, gala, party |
| Frau: | woman |
| Femme-de-chambre: | lady-in-waiting |
| Garçon: | boy |
| Grand coucher: | formal first ceremony before retiring (sleep) |
| Grand couvert: | ritual dining in front of public |
| Grande levée: | public ceremonial or second toilet with court |
| Grandes Eaux: | Versailles fountains |
| Junger: | young |
| Justaucorp à brevet: | knee-length coat |
| Louis d'or: | gold coin |
| Maréchal: | high ranking military officer |
| Mein Gott: | my god |
| Mein Lieber: | my dear (masc.) |

| | |
|---|---|
| Mein Liebchen: | my sweetie |
| Merde alors: | dammit |
| Miséricorde: | mercy, forgiveness |
| Mon Dieu: | my god |
| Petit coucher: | informal second ceremony before retiring (sleep) |
| Petite levée: | private ceremonial of first toilet with family |
| Plats de la dessert: | dessert trays |
| Rue: | street |
| Sacre coeur: | sacred heart |
| Salon: | reception room |
| *Te Deum*: | hymn to God |
| Vice italienne: | Sexual acts among men |

# Selected Bibliography

I am referencing the sources researched when writing *The Bastard Prince of Versailles* but due to the limited amount that has been written about the Count of Vermandois, much information has been extrapolated from secondary sources as well.

Abbott, John Stevens Cabot. *Louis XIV*. New York: Harper & Brothers Publishers, 1898.

Beaumelle, M. de la. *Memoirs for the History of Madame de Maintenon and of the Last Age*. London: A. Millar and J. Nourse, 1757.

Bertrand, Louis. *La Vie amoureuse de Louis XIV*. Paris: Frédérique Patat, 1924.

Boigne, Comtesse de. *Memoirs of the Comtesse de Boigne*. London: Charles Scribner's Sons, 1907.

Bourg, Edme Thédore. *Amours et galanteries des rois de France: mémoires historiques sur les concubines, maitresses et favorites de ces princes*. Bruxelles: Louis Tencé, 1830.

Chevallier, Pierre. «Les Étranges Amours du Roi Louis XIII.» *Historama* 336, (1979): 1.

Duclos, Charles. *Mémoires secrets sur le règne de Louis XIV, la Régence et le règne de Louis XV.* Paris: Firmin-Didot Frères, 1846.

Dussieux, Louis. *Le château de Versailles: histoire et description*. Versailles: L. Bernard, 1881.

Elbée, Jean de. *Le Mystère de Louis XIII*. Lyon: H. Lardanchet, 1943.

Farmer, James Eugene. *Versailles and the Court Under Louis XIV*. Versailles: Century Company, 1905.

Hardy, Blanche Christable. *The Princesse de Lamballe: A Biography*. London: Archibald Constable and Company, 1908.

I. W. F., *The Story of Louise de La Vallière*. Norwich: Fletcher and Son, 1870.

Jacob, P. L. Memoirs of Cardinal Dubois. London: L. Smithers & Co., 1899.

Mazé, Jules. *La Cour de Louis XIV*. Paris: Hachette, 1944.

Montpensier, Mademoiselle de. *Mémoires*. Amsterdam: Jean-Frédéric Bernard, 1729.

Moret, Ernest. *Quinze ans du règne de Louis XIV.* Paris: Didier et Cie, 1859.

Orléans, Charlotte-Elisabeth. *Correspondance Complète de monsieur de d'Orléans*. Paris: Charpentier, 1891.

Patmore, Katherine Alexandra. *The Court of Louis XIII*. London: Methuen, 1909.

Prudhomme, Louis. *Les crimes des reines de France: depuis le commencement de la monarchie*. Paris: Bureau des Révolutions de Paris, 1791.

Ritchie, Leitch. *Versailles*. London: Longman, 1839.

Sourches, Marquis de. *Mémoires du Marquis de Sourches sur le Règne de Louis XIV*. Paris: Librairie Hachette, 1882.

Topin, Marius. *L'Homme au Masque de Fer*. Paris: Didier et Cie, 1870.

W. M. R. D. *Vie De Louis-Philippe-Joseph, Duc D'Orléans*. London: Palais Saint-James, 1790.

Milton Keynes UK
Ingram Content Group UK Ltd.
UKHW050230160923
428759UK00002B/25